Clare Connelly was raised in small-town Australia among a family of avid readers. She spent much of her childhood up a tree, Mills & Boon book in hand. Clare is married to her own real-life hero, and they live in a bungalow near the sea with their two children. She is frequently found staring into space—a surefire sign that she's in the world of her characters. She has a penchant for French food and ice-cold champagne, and Mills & Boon novels continue to be her favourite ever books. Writing for Mills & Boon is a long-held dream. Clare can be contacted via clareconnelly.com or her Facebook page.

Dylan Rose is a writer from New York City who is obsessed with watching romantic comedies, taking hot baths on cold nights and finding the perfect red lipstick. Her debut novel for Mills & Boon Dare is *Turn Me On*. Follow her adventures on Instagram, @DylanRoseRomance.

If you liked *The Deal* and *Turn Me On*
why not try

Naughty or Nice by Rachael Stewart
A Sinful Little Christmas by J. Margot Critch

Discover more at millsandboon.co.uk

THE DEAL

CLARE CONNELLY

TURN ME ON

DYLAN ROSE

MILLS & BOON

First Published in Great Britain 2019
by Mills & Boon, an imprint of HarperCollins*Publishers*
1 London Bridge Street, London, SE1 9GF

The Deal © 2019 Clare Connelly

Turn Me On © 2019 Dylan Rose

ISBN-13: 978-0-263-27393-9

MIX
Paper from
responsible sources
FSC™ C007454

This book is produced from independently certified FSC™ paper
to ensure responsible forest management.
For more information visit www.harpercollins.co.uk/green.

Printed and bound in Spain
by CPI, Barcelona

THE DEAL

CLARE CONNELLY

MILLS & BOON

For Sharon Villone Doucett,
who was one of the first readers to find my books,
and who has been such a champion and supporter ever since.

PROLOGUE

Five years earlier, Becksworth Hall,
Wiltshire, England

'YOU'RE A ROTHSMORE, for Christ's sake.'

My father is perhaps the only person more apoplectic than I am.

'She is aware of that.' Surprisingly, my voice comes out clear and calm, even when I feel as if I've run a marathon. I reach for the Scotch on autopilot, topping up my glass. My hand shakes a little. Shock, I suppose.

And I *am* shocked.

'This isn't like Saffron.' My mother wrings her gloved hands in front of her pale peach suit, the wedding corsage still crisp and fragrant. I reach for my own in the buttonhole of my jet-black tuxedo jacket, and dislodge it roughly, pleased when the pearl-tipped pin snags on my finger. A perfect circle of burgundy blood stains the white rose at the decoration's centre.

'How do you know, Mother?'

I don't mean to sound so derisive, but in the four hours since my cousin received a text from my bride's best friend explaining that the love of my life wasn't going to be showing up to our wedding, I've had to endure more platitudes and Saffron-defending than I can stand.

'Well, she's…' Antoinette Rothsmore struggles to describe Saffron. There are any number of words I could offer. *Suitable. Wealthy. Privileged. Appropriate. Beautiful. Cultured.* Words that describe why my parents introduced us and cheered from the sidelines as we hooked up. But the reason we got engaged is simple.

I love her. And she's left me.

'Nice,' my mother finishes, lamely.

Saffron *is* nice.

Too nice for me?

Perhaps.

I haven't seen her in three days, but when I did, she was in full preparation mode for our wedding, reminding me that the photographer from *OK!* magazine would be coming to take pictures of the party so not to let my groomsmen get too messed up on Scotch before the ceremony.

I throw back the single malt and grip the glass tightly. How many have I had? Not enough to make this feel like a distant dream.

'Nobody does this to a Rothsmore.' My father's face has turned a deep shade of puce. I'd think it's sweet that he cares so much except I don't for a second imagine he cares about the fact I just had my heart handed to me in tatters in front of five hundred of Europe's elite. Princes, dukes, CEOs—everyone.

Not that I care about the embarrassment. I care about Saffy. I care about the fact we were supposed to be married and she's sent me a 'Dear John' text via a friend and my cousin.

'What would you like to do, Father? Sue her?'

'If only,' he snaps, then shakes his head. 'Though the last thing this family wants is a scandal. Damn it, Nicholas. What did you do to her?'

I blink, his question something I haven't considered.

What did I do to her?

Is it possible I said or did something to turn her away?

No.

This isn't about me.

This is pure Saffron. Passionate, affectionate, changeable.

I grimace, rubbing a hand over my jaw, neatly trimmed just the way Saffron likes.

I fix Gerald with a firm stare. 'I did nothing, Father, except agree to marry the woman you chose for me.' I don't say the rest. That I fell head over heels in love with her as well.

We used to laugh about the nature of our relationship—how we both knew it was a heavy-handed set-up from our parents. How their interference was like something out of a nursery rhyme. Except we were going to have the last laugh, because we were in love.

We were in love.

When had I started believing in love? What kind of goddamned idiot fool have I become to worship at the altar of something so childish?

I snap the Scotch glass down against the table, a little louder and harder than I intend, and I see my mother jump in my peripheral vision.

I've been an idiot.

There's no such thing as love. No such thing as 'happily ever after'. No such thing as 'meant for each other'.

And suddenly, all I want is to get away from this. From my parents and their expectations, from this life I've been groomed all my life to lead. I want to get away from Saffy, from our wedding, from my damned broken heart.

I want to get drunk, and then I want to get laid—one way or another I'm going to forget Saffy ever existed.

I stumble a little as I head for the door. 'Where are you going?' My mother, behind me, is anxious-sounding.

'Get Alf to fire up the jet.' I hear my own words, slightly slurred.

'But why? You can't leave. What if Saffron comes looking for you?'

I prop an arm on the doorjamb for support, blinking at my mother for several long seconds. 'Then I won't fucking be here.'

CHAPTER ONE

Five years later, Sydney, Australia

OH, MY GOD. Oh, my God, Oh, my God. There's an ancient grandfather clock against the far wall and it ticks loudly, but I can barely hear it over the desperate rushing of blood in my ears. Am I really going to do this?

The intimate rooms are perfectly climate controlled—it's cool in here but that's not why my skin is marked with delicate goose bumps. I run my hands over my naked legs, waxed and oiled so they're smooth and soft in honour of this assignation.

It's not too late to change your mind, my brain shouts at me.

But I don't really want to change my mind. I made the decision to do this months ago, meticulously planning every detail in order to give myself one night of passion. To give myself a life—even just for one night. It's been too long since I've had anything even remotely resembling a life. Too long since I've let go and enjoyed myself.

I still have too much to do, too much to achieve and, despite the tremendous growth and success of the charity, I want more. I need more. Faster, bigger. My charity is my all, and I'm happy with that.

But my body. Oh, my body. Lately, something seems to have awoken in me, a curiosity, a need I no longer seem able to deny. I want to get laid. No, I want to have sex. Really fantastic sex, and then I want to change back into my signature gown, swan out of this room and become, once more, the woman the world expects me to be.

I flick my gaze to the clock across the room. There are three minutes to go. Three minutes until Nicholas Rothsmore the Third arrives to seduce me.

My heart bounces against my ribs. I swallow. I need more champagne. No. No more champagne. I only had two sips at the party—I know better than to get drunk at something like this.

It's work for me, not play—though I have perfected the art of looking as if I'm playing when I'm not.

But this? Being here in Room Six, the sumptuous décor the last word in elegance and sophistication, dressed only in lingerie, waiting for a man I know solely through the club's exclusive, private online forum?

My pulse notches up a gear.

I'm waiting to have sex with a stranger.

Not just a stranger.

I lie back against the bed, my eyes sweeping shut

as I picture the man in question. Nicholas Rothsmore the Third isn't just a man. He's unbelievably sexy, all tousled hair and rock-hard abs, and a firmly committed playboy. Who better to have one delicious sexual encounter with, no questions asked, before going back to my real life?

I lift a hand to check the bright pink wig is firmly in place, tucked all around the hairline as my stylist showed me, so there's no risk of movement. It's soft and silky, the hair falling in waves to my shoulders. My mask is bright silver and covers not just my eyes, but lower on my face as well, stopping just above my lips, in keeping with the masquerade ball theme downstairs. Of course, I have a separate mask stashed in the wardrobe across the room, as well as my distinctive couture gown, to avoid any likelihood that Nicholas recognises me, after.

After.

Such a delicious word loaded with promise. After this. After sex.

My heart is hammering so hard now I'm surprised it hasn't beaten a hole through the wall of my chest.

I can't have anyone know I'm doing this.

I *never* get involved with clients, and Nicholas is one of the club's most prominent members. The last thing I want is to do anything to undermine the club or my charity. Chance is the reason for all of this.

I doubt anyone has any idea how hard I work behind the scenes. On the surface, I'm Imogen Carmichael, entrepreneur and socialite—my mother's daughter. But behind closed doors, when other people my age are falling in love, getting married, having babies, or even just getting wasted and falling in and out of God knows whose bed, I'm working. I'm working on Chance, I'm working on it, for it, every waking minute, and there's still so much more to do. We're nationwide now, but I want more—there are children all over the world who need what we offer. I've been toying with the idea of opening a London branch for over six months now but I know it's going to take a lot of my time and spread me kind of thin.

That's my focus. That's my life.

It's why this night is perfect for me. It's one night, and with a guy I know to be as interested in serious relationships as I am. Which is to say, not at all. He's perfect one-night stand material, and excitement is shifting through me.

How long has it been since I was with a guy, anyway?

My lips tug downward as I consider that. At least three years. No! Nearly four. Jackson and I broke up just before Christmas.

Yes, it's been a long time and, at nearly thirty, if I don't take control of this, I'm going to grow my virginity back. That's a thing, right? I'm sure I read it in one of those glossy magazines at the airport lounge a while ago. Okay, maybe nothing that drastic, but I am in danger of forgetting what it's like to be touched, kissed, driven wild with pleasure.

And I miss sex. I don't want a relationship, though God knows there are times when I wish I had someone I could talk to, someone I could bounce ideas off. But I don't have the headspace for a boyfriend. Where would I even fit a relationship into my life? And what would that do to Chance?

One day, maybe. When the charity is big enough to run without me, when we're fully established—and not just in America, around the world—maybe then I'll open myself up to something more. But I'm a long way from that, and I'm not going to do anything that might risk what I've spent my life building. I owe it to Abbey to keep my focus, to make this a true success.

The quietest noise sounds, but it might as well have been the tolling of a bell. I'm hyperaware of everything in that moment and I sit up, then push to standing, the stilettos I kicked off by the bed waiting for me. I slip them on and catch my reflection in the mirror across the room.

Holy crap.

I look…like sex on legs. I look like someone who does this all the time. The corset is firm at my back and pushes my breasts up, like two pale orbs, and my legs are curvy and slim. The wig completes the look and the mask adds an element of decadence that is just perfect for The Billionaires' Club.

'Knock, knock.' His cultured British tone would be haughty if it weren't for the permanent husk that thickens his words. 'Is there a Miss Anonymous in there?' My tummy squeezes at his sexy, teasing voice.

'Yeah.' My own voice comes out high-pitched. I suck in a deep breath, cross the plush carpet to the door and grip the handle. It's cold beneath my touch. I count to ten slowly, a trick I learned in school, when my nerves used to get away from me.

Slowly, I draw the door inward, my heart unbearably loud and urgent now.

And at the sight of him, it skids to a stop.

A bead of anxiety runs through me. We planned this secretly on the forum, and my only condition was anonymity. He isn't to know who I am—in fact, I went out of my way to create the impression that I'm some bored housewife just looking to get my rocks off. Naturally, he had no objections to that—if I know one thing for certain about Nicholas it's that he doesn't do commitment or serious.

Which makes him perfect for this. For tonight.

'Come in,' I invite, waving my hand towards the room. These Intimate Rooms were designed with seduction in mind and they have everything a couple could need for a sensual encounter. The bed is bigger than a king, laid with thousand-thread-count sheets. There's a fridge stocked with the finest French champagne money can't buy, a luxurious en suite bathroom with a spa bath and fragrant oils, and members are invited to request a bespoke 'toy chest' if their tastes run in that direction.

Nicholas requested handcuffs and seeing that on

the booking sheet two days earlier made my body break out in a sweat. A good sweat. I haven't been able to stop thinking about it since.

He swaggers into the room, his navy-blue suit slim-fitting and flattering to his trim and toned frame. His eyes take in the room, though I'm sure he's been here before. He crosses to the window—the thick black velvet blinds are drawn for privacy. He flicks the blinds open a little, showing a slice of Sydney Harbour, the unique Opera House right outside the window.

I'm nervous.

Beyond nervous.

I'm full of doubts and desire in equal measure.

I have literally never done anything like this in my entire life.

My tummy loops into a billion knots.

'So.' He turns to face me, his lips flicking in the sexiest smile I've ever seen. My insides burst a little. 'What shall I call you?'

'Miss Anonymous is fine.' My voice sounds so prudish and disapproving. I force a smile.

'Anon for short?' he quips, moving to the fridge as he discards his jacket over the back of the black velvet armchair.

I nod quickly. 'Whatever.' My name doesn't matter.

'You seem nervous.'

Crap. So much for seeming cool and in control. My lips curve into a small smile; his eyes drop to them. My throat goes dry. 'I am, a little.' When all else is lost, go for honesty.

'Why?'

He lifts the top off the champagne expertly and pours two generous glasses. He turns to me, his eyes dragging down from the tip of my head and performing the slowest, most sensual inspection I can imagine. As his eyes shift over my body, I feel as though he's touching me even when he's on the other side of the room.

Slowly, so slowly, he lingers on the generous curves of my breasts, my nipped-in, corseted waist, my hips and lower, so heat flushes my cheeks and I'm grateful for the face mask I wear.

Lower, lower, over my legs, until, at my ankles, he grins. 'Nice shoes.'

I lift a foot, to dislodge one, but he shakes his head, his eyes flying to mine. 'Leave them on. For now.'

My pulse races. Anyone who knows me—who knows me as I really am—knows I'm not one to be told what to do. But for some reason, the idea of momentarily relinquishing control is kind of empowering and very appealing. I do as he says, leaving the shoes in place. He lifts a finger and bends it, signalling silently for me to join him.

I walk across to him with what I hope passes for a seductive stroll, a feline smile on my lips the closer I get. Here, just a foot or so away from him, I breathe in and taste the masculine fragrance he wears—

woody and alpine and intoxicatingly sensual. His shirt is crisp white and at the cuffs he wears shining black cufflinks, which I have every reason to suspect are diamonds.

When someone applies to join The Billionaires' Club, we run a detailed background check to maintain our exclusivity and privacy. I mean, membership comes with an annual fee of a million dollars, plus the buy-in, so I know the members can get their hands on serious cash, but we need to know more than that. Criminal records, credit history, scandals, *everything*.

So I know Nicholas Rothsmore's background, probably better than most who just presume he's a playboy bachelor living off his family's considerable wealth. Sure, he was born with the proverbial silver spoon but he's also smart as all get out and a crazy hard worker. Five years ago he arrived in New York to take over his family's American branch of the Rothsmore Group and in that time he's trebled their revenue and expanded beyond a blue-chip investment portfolio to a remarkable presence in the tech world.

Even without his family, he's a formidable and impressive entrepreneur. Then again, his silver-spoon start in life probably didn't hurt.

'Your eyes,' he murmurs, scanning my face thoughtfully, and my heart rate kicks up a gear, so that I doubt my veins are going to be able to hold the blood in place. 'They're so...'

Instinctively, I blink, shuttering my eyes from him. They're a very dark blue, the colour of the sky at dusk, and I know it's unusual. I don't want him to recognise me. 'No cheating,' I say, taking the champagne flute he offers, lifting it to my lips. 'This is secret.'

'Right.' His grin is pure devilish heat and his expression is one of amusement. 'Well, Miss Anonymous, what's your thing?'

'My thing?'

'Yeah. What are you into?'

I think about it for a moment. 'I don't have a lot of spare time. I guess, reading…'

'Fascinating.' His laugh is a slow vibration that travels around the room before landing at the base of my spine, sending little shards of awareness through my nerve endings. 'But I meant, in bed.' He takes a step forward, closing the distance between us, his fingers lifting to curl the edges of the wig, teasing the flossy pink strands between his thumb and forefinger.

'Right.' I slap my forehead exaggeratedly and my smile holds a silent apology. So much for acting as if I do this all the time. 'I'm…a little out of practice.'

'Are you?' His gaze flicks to my cleavage again, lingering there for so long a faint murmur escapes my lips. Heat travels along my body as though he's touched me.

All I can do is nod.

'Why is that?'

We'd agreed not to discuss anything personal. I think of how to answer in a way that won't give me away. 'I've been single awhile.'

His smile is just a lazy flicker of those sculpted lips, framed by a squared jaw and a brush of stubble. I like the stubble. I itch to feel it and rather than denying myself that impulse, I surrender to it, lifting my hand to his face so I can run my fingertips over his jaw.

It shouldn't be so sensual, but just the act of touching him like this is so illicit and sinful that I make a low, husky sound, my body trembling with the first flush of desire.

'So you *are* nervous?' He comes closer, so our bodies brush, and then he moves behind me, so close I can feel his nearness, his warmth, even though he doesn't quite touch me.

He dips his head forward, something I only realise when I feel his breath on my shoulder, warm and smelling of champagne.

My knees tremble.

'Look.' He lifts his hands to my shoulders and angles me slightly so I can see us in the mirror. The sight of myself in this costume—so different from my usual appearance—and Nicholas Rothsmore at my back, his long, tanned fingers curved over my pale shoulders, fills me with a need that demands indulgence.

'Tonight, we're just two people.' He speaks slowly,

the words buzzing right against my ear. 'Who came here to fuck.'

I swallow, my throat moving convulsively. His coarse description sends a *frisson* of awareness down my back, because he's right. This is physical, primal, animalistic. 'Right.' I went into the forum looking for this. I don't know why I'm panicking at the eleventh hour. I draw in a deep breath and smile slowly, calming my nerves.

'That's what you want?'

'Count on it.'

His hands move to my back, where a delicate lace ribbon holds the corset together. He loops a finger beneath the bow, watching me with a hint of mockery as he pulls on one loop, loosening it appreciably.

'You can stop this at any time, if you change your mind,' he murmurs, pulling on the other loop.

My breath snags in my throat. I shake my head slowly from side to side. No way on earth am I going to put a stop to this.

'Good,' he growls, easing the corset down so my breasts spill over the top. He stops moving and stares at me in the mirror, his eyes hot and possessive, glued to my body as though I'm the first woman he's ever seen.

Strangely, I don't feel at all self-conscious now, despite the fact I haven't been naked in front of anyone in a really long time. I'm someone who wears underwear even at the gym or the spa; when other women seem perfectly happy to strip down completely in the sauna or whatever, I'm buttoned up in the corner, sweating into my cotton.

I just don't really do the naked thing.

But here, in the privacy of this intimate room, wearing a mask, with a prearranged lover loosening my lingerie, I have no reluctance; not even a hint of hesitation. This is what we're here for. It's just a transaction.

Convenient, satisfying sex.

At least, I hope it's satisfying. His reputation sure as heck precedes him, but then, sometimes the myth is bigger than the man.

I don't chase that thought down; I don't have *time* to think about that. His hands are running up my sides, his eyes on mine in the mirror as he brings his hands around front to cup my breasts, his fingers finding my nipples and tweaking them so I let out a low growl, the pleasure from such a simple touch totally overwhelming.

'I don't want to stop it.' The words are squeezed from my throat, breathing and speaking almost completely beyond me.

'Good.' Another husky admission before his fingers are sliding into the corset, pushing it even lower until it hits my hips and then falls apart completely, leaving me standing in just a scrap of elastic and lace. His eyes hold mine as he slips a finger into the waistband of my thong and then flicks it. I jump a little, and laugh, the sting unexpected, and unexpectedly sensual. Especially when his hands caress the area almost instantly, soothing the flesh.

My pulse is trembling like a fire in my veins and heat is rushing my insides. He moves his hands around my hips; still watching me intently in the mirror, he slides one hand into the front of my thong. I'm so glad I waxed there too.

His fingers brush my flesh, finding my clit with expert precision, moving over it slowly at first, so I gasp because the touch is unfamiliar and for a second I fight an urge to ask him to stop, because I haven't been touched here in a really, really long time. And *never* like this. He is some kind of maestro because the very idea of objecting disappears from my mind almost instantly as I succumb to the blinding heat of this pleasure, this possession. It's just the lightest touch but flame explodes to molten lava and I'm burning up, heat in every cell of my body, every nerve ending.

His mouth drops to my shoulder, kissing my flesh there, moving closer to the nape of my neck. His breath is cool, his kiss warm, his touch perfect and suddenly pleasure is like a lightning rod, forking through me, so I have to bite down on my lip to stop from crying out.

'Don't be quiet,' he urges, and I blink, finding his eyes in the mirror. He's watching me with an intensity that robs me of breath, his steady grey gaze fascinating and intelligent and somehow all-seeing, so I feel as if beyond my arousal he must be comprehending so much more about me right now. As if he might be seeing into my buttoned-up soul, might be seeing all of my usual tensions and removing them from me.

And I don't care.

'Look,' he prompts, lifting one hand to my breast and cupping it, while his fingers work faster until I'm tumbling so close to the edge of a ravine that I can only exhale in short, shallow rasps. There's nothing to grab onto; nothing to save me from falling.

'Watch yourself,' he says more insistently, though it takes me several seconds to process his words because my brain is no longer firing on all cylinders. All of my blood is busy being pleasured inside my body, being lit on fire by his intensely skilled ministrations.

'Oh, my God.' The words tumble from my lips and then I'm groaning, tilting my head back but doing exactly as he said—watching me, us, this. Watching as he moves his hand and pleasure makes me blush and my nipples hard and then I can't watch any longer because I'm scrunching my face up and giving myself over completely to the total subjugation of sense and reason in place of white-hot desire.

I am falling, I am falling too fast to stop, and yet somehow I'm also flying, all the way to heaven.

I dig my nails into my palms and, because I am secret and he is not, I cry his name as I tumble over the edge. 'Nicholas,' I moan into the glamorous bedroom. 'Oh, God, Nicholas.'

It is a wave that won't stop, as if the last four years of celibacy have left me with a hyper-charged sex drive. How did I not realise that until now?

'Oh, this is going to be fun,' he drawls, his British so very sexy, so husky, so hot, and I laugh, because I've already had more pleasure than I bargained for. I can't imagine what else he can do with those clever, clever hands. And that mouth…my eyes drop to it in the mirror and it lifts into a knowing smirk.

'Oh, yes, that'll be fun too.'

My eyes jerk to his. He's watching me with what I think is amusement.

Normally, I might feel embarrassed at having been so completely lost to that amazing feeling, but I'm not. Because firstly, there's nothing wrong with sexual pleasure—and this is the man to know that. And secondly, he has no idea who I am! This is totally anonymous, totally secret, totally no-consequences, no-holds-barred sex.

That knowledge is empowering, so I spin where I'm standing and look up at him. Even though I'm tall, there's a height differential between us that means I have to look up.

'How come you're wearing clothes?' I murmur.

His shrug is pure indolent heat. 'I'm not sure.'

'Let's do something about that, shall we?'

His nostrils flare at the challenge in my words. My fingertips tremble a little as I begin to undo his buttons, concentrating hard on the task so afterwards I think I probably could have moved a little more seductively. Not that I can muster much energy to care, because now I'm eye height with his naked chest and it is a sight to behold.

The first thing I notice is a tattoo that runs above his left pec, near his heart. It reads, in a strong cursive script, *I am my own.* I trace it with my eyes, imagining what would lead someone to have that written over their heart. I don't ask. We're not here for that kind of inquisition.

'Holy crap.' It's just a whisper, so soft and hoarse in the silence of the room, with only the grandfather clock's metronomic beat for company, but he hears and he grins.

'Yeah?'

'Oh, yeah.' Now it's my turn to look a little mocking when I turn to face him. 'Like you don't already know.'

Because how could he not? While he's slim, he's also insanely toned, a buff chest loaded with muscles, eight firmly defined ridges calling out to be touched. I lift my fingers and trace over the pectoral definition, lingering on his own hair-roughened nipples, surprising myself when I flick one, just as he did with the elastic in my underpants, and he lets out a growl.

'Retaliation,' I simper, grinning as I move to the other.

His hand catches my wrist, his eyes flaring. 'Careful, Miss Anonymous.'

'Oh?' My fingertips tingle. With his hand clamped

around my wrist, his eyes watching me, I blink—a study in wide-eyed innocence. 'Why is that?'

'You're baiting me,' he points out.

'Yep.' And I flick his other nipple, so he tilts his head back, staring at the ceiling, his Adam's apple moving beneath his stubble. More than that, through the confines of his trousers, I feel his cock jerk and power rushes my veins. Power, desire and a surge of sheer, desperate attraction.

I drag my fingertips lower over his body, moving them in teasing circles over his washboard abs then out to his hips, up a little, and lower, to the soft leather belt that's threaded through his trousers.

Now my lack of speed is deliberate. I can tell it's driving him crazy and, hell, I love that. I loosen the clasp and pull on the edge of the belt, watching him as I slide it out of his belt loops. I drop it to the ground beside us then concentrate on the button and zipper, easing it down, pushing the sides apart.

Suddenly, and out of nowhere, I'm uncertain. He understands and takes over, kicking his shoes off and stepping out of his trousers at the same time. Only his dark grey boxer briefs remain.

'My turn,' he murmurs, and I don't understand what he means until he kneels at my feet, looking up at me as he slides my lace thong lower. I watch, the pink wig swishing against my shoulders as he uses my techniques against me, moving too, too slowly. Frustration gnaws at me. I don't want slow. I want to be naked and possessed by him.

I go to step out of my thong but his hands are firm around my thighs, holding me where I am. He makes a tsking noise in response to my silent expression of inquiry, and then he's slowly pushing the lace lower, so I have to stand there and wait until finally my thong is at my ankles and I can kick out of it.

I keep the shoes on and he makes no effort to remove them.

I can't think about my shoes though. He's kneeling before me and now his mouth is moving to my clit, and the pleasure I've been surfing since he walked in the room is dragging me away again, swallowing me into its midst, so I'm dropping off the edge of the earth, just pure sensation and feeling.

I can't believe I'm doing this, but the last thing I think before I come—this time against his mouth—is that wild, anonymous sex might be the hottest thing ever.

CHAPTER TWO

JESUS CHRIST, SHE is unbelievably responsive. I lift her up easily, carrying her across to the bed. Her breasts are soft against my chest and I'm searching for her lips, kissing her, tasting her sweetness as I bring her to the edge of the bed and drop her onto it.

She laughs, a sound so sexy that I swear it writes itself into my mind as though it were chiselled from stone. There's something about it, husky, sweet, laced with promise and heat. I don't give her a second to recover; my mouth chases hers and pushes her backwards, my body coming to lie over hers even as she scrambles higher up the bed so she's lying fully on it.

I trap her wrists with one of my hands, pinning them above her head so her beautiful round breasts are high and firm and then I bring my mouth down to one, sucking on a nipple, rolling it with my tongue, flipping it, my body weight holding her still as she writhes with pleasure. I smile against her pale skin and then move to her other breast, my spare hand plucking the nipple I just released, and I grind my hips so my rock-hard dick—that is giving me no end of grief right now, desperately needing to bury itself deep inside her—throbs and begs for release.

Soon.

We agreed to fuck, once. She was very specific about this. She wanted to get laid.

I can't be away from the party for long. It has to be efficient.

A quickie? It feels as if it should have been outlawed, given how damned sexy she is. This is not a woman who should ever be made love to quickly, unless it is a desperate preamble to a long, slow seduction.

She deserves to be explored and tasted and delighted until she is hoarse from crying out in pleasure.

As if my thoughts have conjured her voice, she spills my name into the air over and over, arching her back, begging me to take her.

I don't want to, though. I want to prolong this; I want to lose myself in her.

These rooms were built for privacy—not even a hint of the party downstairs reaches us, and I'm glad. I kind of hope she's forgotten that a thousand of the world's most well-heeled individuals are just a hundred or so metres away.

'Please,' she whimpers, but in a way that makes it clear it has nothing to do with her desire to re-join the party, or her worry that she might be missed. It's more than that. She needs me.

I push up on my elbows, staring down at her, but

I want to see more. I want to watch her come. More than just her expressive eyes and pouting lips, I want to see her whole face. I move my hand to the mask and begin to shift it but she jerks away and, from what I can see, her expression sobers instantly.

'No.' The word is deadly serious. 'It stays on.'

Shit. I forgot. Anonymity is part of the deal.

'Sorry.' I grimace. 'I just wanted to see you.'

Her smile is laced with pleasure. 'You can see enough.'

I arch a brow but inwardly I disagree. Still, it's better than nothing, and sure as hell better than I expected when I agreed to this.

I'm no stranger to random hook-ups, but something about this woman's approach fascinated me. Her desire for anonymity, and the fact she is new to the club—I haven't seen her profile on any of the forums before and thanks to networking I'm pretty familiar with most of the members.

So she is new. Someone who has just come into money?

No. I can't say how, but I can tell she's old money. Cultured. She has a certain air about her, a way of speaking that's instinctively familiar.

'You do realise we're here to sleep together?' she prompts, her brows lifting above the edge of the mask.

My laugh is immediate. 'Are you complaining?'

'Nope.' She digs her white teeth into the pillow of her lower lip and need rushes through me. Fuck, she's hot. So hot. I drop my head and pull her lower lip between my teeth, my whole body mashed to hers, her nakedness its own kind of torture, so close to me, so close and yet there's still a scrap of cotton between my cock and her sweet warmth and suddenly I'm done being patient and I'm done with the idea of making this last.

Sex is sex. She wants a wild time, and that's what I'm going to give her.

I push up onto my elbows. 'Stay here.'

There's a box of condoms in the bedside table. I pull it out and cross back to the bed. She's watching me in a way that fills me with a torrent of needs and I intend to indulge each and every one of them.

There's something about not knowing who she is that makes this even sexier. Except...

Ridiculously, for the first time, I wonder about her life outside this, outside this room and our agreement. 'You're not married?' I prompt, staring down at her as my lungs work overtime trying to suck in enough air to keep me alive.

'Married? I told you, I haven't done this in a long time.'

My smirk is to hide my cynicism. It doesn't work. 'I don't think celibacy and marriage are necessarily oxymoronic.'

She grins, and I hold my breath, needing her to tell me she's single. I like sex. I fucking love it, unapologetically, but there are some lines I will never cross, and fucking someone else's wife is one of them.

I like my women to be completely mine, even if it is just for one night.

'No, Nicholas.' The words are soft, sweet, and they run over my skin like oil. 'I'm not married.'

Good. But I don't feel a burst of relief—yet. 'Engaged? Seeing someone? I'm not getting in the middle of anything?'

Her teeth are gnawing at that perfect, full lower lip again. She pushes up to kneel and moves across the bed, somehow managing to look elegant and co-ordinated. Her hands connect with my chest and my breath hisses out of me.

'I am definitely not in a relationship with anyone. Except my remote control. And my MacBook.' She grins, and I feel a kick of curiosity about who she is outside this.

I ignore it.

Tonight isn't a prelude to anything except sex.

And I'm more than optimistic that this will prove satisfying.

In the back of my mind is my father's edict.

'Five years, Nicholas, and each year I expect you to come home wiser and ready to make me proud. And each year you disappoint me.'

I slide a finger into the box of condoms and pull a foil square out. Miss Anonymous takes it from my fingers, lifting it to her lips and tearing the top off. I watch with a racing heart as she pushes my boxers down, just low enough to release my cock, then her hand is cupping my length, her fingertips brushing my tip, delighting in the drop of cum she finds there.

'I'm so glad your reputation isn't exaggerated,' she teases, sliding the condom over me and easing it down my length. My breath hisses out of me as she snaps it at the base, then squeezes me in her palm, my cock jerking against her hand, my whole body standing to attention.

'I've had enough. Reading about you on that idiot gossip blog, seeing you with a different woman every goddamned night. If you'd married Saffron you'd have three kids by now.'

Everyone seems to have forgotten Saffy left me— for a firefighter from Bristol, as it turns out.

'If you're not married by the time you're thirty then you can forget about becoming Lord Rothsmore. You can forget about the whole damned thing.'

It has been distinctly tempting to tell him to go to hell with his bloody title and inheritance. As if I give a damn.

Except I do. I care about my mother, and I care about my father, I even care about the legacy into which I've been born. But more than that, I'm becoming a little bored of this lifestyle. What started off as rebellion has become an unbreakable habit and it's all just a bit too easy.

Miss Anonymous is right. My reputation precedes me. Women fall at my feet, doors open because of my name and the title I'm due to hold.

I'm ready for a challenge. I'm ready for something different and unexpected.

I've decided I'll go home soon—before I turn thirty—and show my parents that, heirs or not, I am someone they can be proud of. I am someone who can think with more than his dick.

But for now, for tonight, I'm going to enjoy being the man my reputation has made me.

'Exactly how long has it been?' I prompt as I find her lips, tangling my tongue with hers, pushing her head back, so she falls flat against the mattress once more.

Her eyes, expressive and somehow familiar, swirl with uncertainty and then they zip closed a little, hiding herself from me. 'A while.'

'A month?'

She laughs, a skittish sound. 'Longer.'

'Six weeks?'

She shakes her head.

'Jesus. Two months?'

Pink spreads across her décolletage. 'A bit more.'

I frown, hating the thought of that, and hating it for her—because she's so sensual, so responsive, so completely driven by desire. I can't imagine how she could go even a night without sex, let alone months.

I nudge her thighs apart with my knees, and push my tip to her entrance, running my fingers over the bright pink of her wig. 'Let's see what we can do about that, huh?'

She nods, no smile on her lips, but I feel her anticipation and I recognise it because it one hundred per cent matches my own. Her breath is held; the room is quiet except for the incessant ticking of the clock against the wall. Outside, Sydney sparkles, beautiful, old, subtropical.

My hands press against the bed on either side of her and I watch as I slide inside her, slowly at first, but her muscles are so freaking tight that I lose my control for a second. Instinct takes over and I thrust deep inside her, grunting as I drop my head and kiss her hard, mimicking the thrust of my body, the tease of our flesh, the taste of her.

She lifts her hips, rolling them, and I have to fight to stop myself from going faster and harder and losing this.

This is sublime.

'Fuck me,' she whispers, her hands in my hair, driving through it urgently, and I grind my teeth together and do what we both want, thrusting into her hard, quickly, until she's moaning over and over and then she's pushing at my chest, trying to roll me over.

She's not strong enough but I flip anyway, turning onto my back and dragging her with me, so I get to look up and see her full, round breasts moving with every thrust, as she lifts up and down my length, taking me deep inside her.

She moves fast, running her hands over her own body, and I am totally transfixed by the sight of this, of her. She is stunning, fascinating, wanton, sexy. She is everything in that moment.

I dig my fingers into her hips, holding her down low on my shaft, and then I buck, taking control once more, driving into her until her cries are louder and hoarser and she's falling apart again, and I'm so close to coming, but I don't. I can't. I won't.

I hold on, I keep myself on edge, steadying myself with monumental discipline and effort, and then I push up to sitting so I can run my tongue over her delightful breasts once more, chasing circles around her nipples, teasing her flesh, sucking her deep into my mouth and teasing her until her hips are jerking frantically and I can feel how close she is.

But so am I and I don't want it to end. Yet.

I hold her still, pressing a light kiss to her lips before rolling us once more, so I'm on top, staring down at her eyes, running my gaze over the mask and trying to imagine what she looks like beneath it.

I make do with tracing the outline of her mouth with my tongue and she whimpers beneath me. I run my tongue lower, over the divot in her chin then lower to her décolletage, and the valley between her breasts, and then I push my cock deeper inside her, thrilling in the power of this possession, in how well we fit together, in how maddeningly mind-blowing this is.

It has to be the anonymity and the sheer directness of this. While I never take a woman to bed who wants more than one night, there's still a bit of dancing around to do. Dinner, flirtation, conversation. This, boiling down an encounter to the truth of sex, is rare.

And I like it. I could become addicted to the idea

of walking into a private room and finding a gorgeous woman dressed in lingerie waiting for me to drive her wild.

Yeah, this is fucking near perfect.

She cries my name and it drags me back to the present, back to what we're doing. The clock is ticking across the room and it matches my internal chronometer, the one that's telling me it's time to go home and face the music, to pick up the mantle my father wishes to pass on.

It's time to stop enjoying nights like this, time to stop fucking around and settle down.

But for now, for this night, I have a beautiful woman in my arms, I'm buried deep inside her and I am going to enjoy the rush of power as I drown in pleasure. There is only this, right now.

I watch him from across the crowded party. The wig and mask have been disposed of. I'm myself again: Imogen Carmichael, founder of The Billionaires' Club, founder of the Chance charity—strait-laced, professional, no-nonsense. I'm the woman everyone wants to talk to and I only have eyes for him.

He looks the same as always. Disastrously handsome, confident, cocky, hot, and, now that I've felt his body up close to mine, I can't look at him without feeling a rush of desire, a slick of heat between my legs.

He's talking to Minette Gray, the daughter of a Mexican mining magnate who's launched a successful Hollywood career for herself. She's stunning, with a mane of long, silky black hair and skin like crushed onyx, eyes that glisten and bright red lipstick. I look at them and for a second I'm transfixed by what a striking pair they make. In the background, beyond the floor-to-ceiling windows, the lights of Sydney sparkle like something out of a movie. I shift my gaze to them, refusing to acknowledge the sharp stab of jealousy that hits me out of nowhere.

Nicholas Rothsmore is a Player with a capital 'P'. Isn't that why I chose him to be my very casual, very temporary lover?

I needed someone who'd be good in bed, discreet and wouldn't particularly care about my 'no questions asked' demand for hot, anonymous sex.

Check, check, check.

Her laugh reaches me across the room and I jerk my eyes back to them on autopilot. He's leaning closer, whispering in her ear.

Shit.

I spin away, pushing down the unwelcome sense of possessiveness that steals through me, focussing on business. That's what I'm good at. It's who I am.

My eyes skate across the room. There are Hollywood A-listers, Grammy-Award-winning singers and musicians, Tony-Award-winning stage actors, royalty, sultans, billionaires, media tycoons. Anyone who's anyone is here, and a tingle of pride shimmies through me because this is all because of me—and all for Abbey.

I think of my best friend, as I often do, of the way

she died, the pain she felt, and I square my shoulders. I might have sacrificed a personal life but it's been worth it.

Nicholas Rothsmore was fun, but that's over now.

I pull my phone from my clutch and load up The Billionaires' Club app that runs the forums. Miss Anonymous has a profile with a picture of a stiletto—I have a predilection for heels. She's served her purpose now. I'm done with Miss Anonymous, done with the future Lord Rothsmore.

I click into the brief bio and scroll to the bottom, where a red button invites me to 'delete profile'.

I click and she's gone. Miss Anonymous has had her fun and now it's time to get on with my life.

If cities were animals, New York would be a gazelle. Fast, nimble, elegant, stunning. I stare down at this adopted city of mine, contemplating the first solo Saturday night I've had in…for ever.

It's been a week since Sydney, and I've been flat out closing the Hewitson merger, but that's done now. Usually, I mark my business triumphs with the kind of partying that would make my grandparents roll over in their graves.

Champagne, women, music.

I frown, surveying the empty penthouse. Only the kitchen lights are on, so it looks somehow more cavernous than normal.

I won.

This deal has been in the works for three years.

Three years of meetings, negotiations, hard slog and now it's with the lawyers and I can relax. And celebrate.

Out of nowhere, I close my eyes and remember what I was doing this time last week. I remember her pale body splayed against the dark sheets of the Intimate Rooms in the Sydney base of The Billionaires' Club and my body is tighter than granite, aching, not just for sex but for *her*.

Miss Anonymous.

I was right that not knowing her name was part of the appeal, but now the not knowing is driving me crazy. Because I want to see her again.

I want to fuck her again.

A smile lifts my lips, because I don't just want to fuck her, I want to have her every which way until she's incoherent with pleasure.

In one month, I turn thirty and England beckons. Lord Rothsmore awaits. In one month, I'll become the man my parents want me to be—or something more like him, anyway. But for the next four weeks I'm still a free agent, and I know just how I want to spend it.

Determination fires my step. I stride indoors, the temperature change marked. My cell phone is across the room. I lift it, loading up the app and selecting our private message conversation.

Except it's no longer a conversation with an exchange of words. My comments remain but hers are gone. Italics proclaim *These messages have been deleted*.

I hadn't expected that. Why?

Okay, that's weird. But it doesn't change how I feel and what I want.

'Fancy round two, Miss Anonymous?'

I figure her American accent makes it likely she lives here in the States. I can get my helicopter to my jet and travel *anywhere*. The minute I think it, I realise how desperate I am to see her again.

Even though I've spent the last five years fucking my way around the world, I freely admit last weekend was the best sex I've ever had. There was something so illicit and hot about it.

Her mask, her hair, her body…

I groan into the night air, looking back at the screen.

Message undeliverable

What?

With a frown, I click out of our message chat and surf to her profile instead. It doesn't come up when I type 'Miss Anonymous'. Adrenalin shifts in my gut.

I go to the list of members using the app and scroll through it slowly, my eyes looking for the stiletto she used as a profile picture. Which makes me think of the sky-high shoes she wore as I ran my hands over her clit, feeling her pulsing beneath me as she exploded with pleasure, and I'm so close to coming at just that memory.

I have to find her.

But where the hell is she?

She can't have left the club. It's not like that. The entry process is gruelling and elaborate. No one signs up and leaves.

So?

Her profile might have been anonymous but it must have been created by a legitimate member of the club. Even the online avatars are vetted. So who the hell is she? And where did she go?

CHAPTER THREE

'IMOGEN? THERE'S A Mr Rothsmore here to see you.'

Oh, my God. In the midst of studying the floor plans for a new school Chance will be funding in a couple of years, I jump so hard I bang my knee against the edge of my desk. Pain radiates through me. I ignore it, scrambling for the receiver of my desk phone.

'What did you say?' My voice comes out completely different.

'A Mr Nicholas Rothsmore,' says my loyal assistant—a woman to whom I offered a job after we met in a shelter for battered women that Chance was involved in supporting; she speaks slowly, as if I might have misunderstood. 'He has a membership enquiry.'

Oh, my God.

'I'm in the middle of something,' I demur, wincing, because The Billionaires' Club is founded on three tenets: exclusivity, privacy and exceptional customer service. My door is always open to members. 'I only have a few minutes.'

'I'll send him in.' She disconnects the call and I stand up quickly, my mind spinning. I have about ten seconds to get my thoughts in order.

I'm wearing a cream suit made up of a pencil skirt and a fitted blazer, with a lemon-yellow silk camisole beneath. No bra and my traitorous nipples are already straining against the soft fabric in anticipation of the fact he's about to be here in my office, my sanctuary. I look around quickly for anything that could give me away.

I've had a manicure since the ball—the nails that were bright pink are now a muted beige. I took great care that night to remove any identifying jewellery. My lips were painted bright red whereas now they bear just a hint of gloss, and my long hair tumbles in waves over one shoulder. I pull on it and then remember my eyes…that he remarked on.

Crapola.

I swing around behind my desk and grab my handbag, lifting my oversized Jackie O–style black sunglasses out and pushing them onto my face right as Emily opens the door.

'Mr Rothsmore,' she announces, a slightly bemused look crossing her face as she sees me in my disguise.

My voice! Oh, crap. He's heard me talk. No, he's heard me scream, over and over. Argh!

'Thank you, Emily.' I spent a lot of time with my grandparents, just outside St Louis, so the southern drawl isn't much of a stretch.

Her bemusement increases. 'Would you like anything to drink?' she prompts.

'We won't have time for that,' I say, still in a voice that hums with the Deep South. 'I've only got a few minutes.'

Emily's trying not to laugh. Crap.

At least Nicholas doesn't look any the wiser.

'Well, if *y'all* change your mind,' she says, with a wink at me right before she pulls the door shut behind her, leaving me alone with sex god Nicholas Rothsmore in the middle of my Manhattan office. I'm grateful the lenses of my glasses are darkly reflective, so I can stare at him without him having any idea.

He's wearing jeans today, low-slung and faded, with a long-sleeved black T-shirt. It's snowing out, so I imagine he's left a jacket somewhere, and I imagine it to be distressed leather, something that goes with this billionaire-bad-boy-about-town look.

I manage not to drool, but my tummy is clenching with serious lust.

'Imogen.' His voice is crisp, professional, but that doesn't matter, I hear it filtered through lips that have kissed me all over, sucked my nipples until pleasure exploded through me, and I find myself unable to push those memories away. My breasts ache now and heat fires low in my abdomen.

He crosses the room, extending a hand for me to shake, and my pulse shoots up a thousand notches; my body temperature skyrockets.

Act natural. Act natural.

I skirt around my desk, holding my own hand out, and I realise my fingers are trembling, just a little but enough for me to feel incredibly self-conscious. He doesn't appear to notice as he shakes my hand.

'Ignore the glasses,' I explain a little stiltedly. 'I had an operation.'

An operation? On what? My corneas?

If he thinks it's a weird excuse, he doesn't say anything. Maybe he presumes I had a big weekend and am wearing sunnies to cope with the hangover.

'I need your help.'

Straight to it, then.

'Sure, have a seat.'

'I'm fine.' He ranges to the windows, his stride long and lean, his body powerful. I mean, he looks powerful and sexy and yet I imagine him naked and my knees almost buckle beneath me.

He stares out at the city, snow falling fast beyond my window, the buildings lit up despite the fact it's mid-afternoon.

'Well, Mr Rothsmore, how can I help you?'

'I was at the masquerade last weekend,' he murmurs, still not looking at me. And I'm glad, because it means I get to look at him. And keep looking. At his broad shoulders, his narrow hips, his firm ass, his long legs. Legs that have straddled me, legs that have pressed hard against mine.

He turns around and again I'm glad for the glasses. He's waiting for me to speak. I swallow,

bringing much-needed moisture to my mouth.
'Yes?'

A single word, husky and dry.

'I met a woman there. I didn't get her name but
I'd like to speak to her. Can you put me in touch?'

My heart hammers like nobody's business. I'm
dying inside. 'I...'

My pulse is thready in my veins.

'You know privacy is one of the member guaran-
tees,' I hear myself saying, moving to the bar across
the room and pouring myself a mineral water. I take
a sip to buy time.

'Yes,' he agrees, his eyes narrowing slightly.

'That guarantee benefits everybody.' I move to my
desk, propping my hip against it with what I hope
passes for nonchalance.

'Nonetheless, the club is about networking and I
have a *proposition* I'd like to make her.'

I swallow, desire flushing through me. This isn't
how it's supposed to be! One night, no strings, no
more. But, God, I want to push him to the floor and
kiss him, hard, and beg him to make love to me. I
sweep my eyes shut for a second.

Safe in the knowledge I've deleted Miss Anonymous from our forums, I shrug. 'Have you checked
the app?'

'She's not there, despite the fact we exchanged
messages. I'd appreciate it if you could have someone
from IT locate her and give me the details.'

I'm floored. And kind of flattered. 'That would definitely be against membership rules.'

'And you don't break the rules, ever?' he prompts, lifting a brow, and he's just so perfectly rakish that my heart does a funny little tremble. I definitely broke the rules last weekend, even if they're just rules of my own creation.

'Rarely,' I say with a small smile, which I quickly flatten. I smiled a *lot* that night. I can't give myself away. In fact, I really need to wrap this up. As much as I don't want him to go, he has to.

That night was an aberration. An itch I needed to scratch, and I scratched it. A lot.

'Then perhaps this will be one of the occasions you will?'

I am instantly reminded that he is from a very wealthy, very ancient British family, a member of the aristocracy. He speaks with an authority and arrogance that would usually piss me off, but coming from Nicholas it is incredibly hot.

'I'm afraid not.'

His eyes narrow. I suspect he doesn't often get told 'no'.

'Not even if I make it worth your while?'

My heart turns over in my chest. 'What are you suggesting?'

'A million-dollar donation to Chance. For a name.'

My sharp intake of breath is involuntary. It takes me several seconds to process this. My fingers tremble. I curve them around the water glass and sip, needing to process this.

'A million dollars.' He's found his way to my Achilles heel and I'm sure he knows it.

Because I make it a policy of taking whatever I can for the charity. Even my parents' donations, when I have mostly wanted to tell them to go to hell and take their 'too little, too late' conscience-pricking gifts with them.

I take everything that's offered because I know the charity is now the wall that stands between life and death for so many helpless, impoverished children out there.

'For a name,' he murmurs, his hands in his pockets as he watches me intently.

'Who is she?'

'I only know that she's single,' he says with a grimace that signals frustration.

'That probably accounts for seventy-five per cent of our female membership.'

He scowls at me. It shouldn't be hot but it is.

'We exchanged messages. She's deleted them, and disappeared off the forums.'

I can't tell him the truth. But that doesn't stop me from asking, 'Why do you want to find her?'

He stares at me for several long seconds, a muscle twisting in the base of his jaw. 'It's personal.'

I dip my head forward, trying to slow my breathing, hoping my cheeks won't be too pink. 'So is the member's information. If you want me to look into our records and find out who she is, then I'll need more to go on.'

His eyes stick to me for a long time and I want to rip off my glasses so I can look him right in the eyes. I want to rip his clothes off. I want to fuck him right here.

Oh, my God.

What's happening to me? I've been single for four years and it never bothered me, but now I can't be in the same room with a man without wanting to leap into bed. Not bed. Desk. Floor. Window. And not *a* man. *This* man.

'Fine,' he grunts. 'We spent time together in the Intimate Rooms.'

There's a part of me that deeply appreciates his discretion, even though he doesn't know I'm Miss Anonymous. I'm glad he's not going into all the sordid details of what we shared. I appreciate that he's respecting our privacy.

'That's what the rooms are for.'

'I'd like to see her again.'

The room is suddenly a void, as if a black hole has opened up and swallowed us. The atmosphere grows thick, the air is heavy in my chest. Everything's different.

'Why?'

His eyes explode with strength. 'That is also personal.'

I swallow, desire unfurling in my gut like a slow-slithering snake. I want him. I want him so badly.

But that's crazy. I don't do relationships, and I particularly don't do relationships with men like this. Entitled, wealthy, spoiled, arrogant.

Even when they're savant-like in bed.

I clench my hand into a fist to ball up my own temptations.

I have to get rid of him before I do something really stupid. Like giving in to this.

One night. That was all it was meant to be.

'If she's deleted her profile, it suggests she doesn't want to be found, Mr Rothsmore.' His name in my mouth is so sexy. I want to kiss it against his skin.

I watched him get dressed on Saturday night. I lay in bed sated and so full of pleasure, and I watched as he pulled on his shorts, his trousers, donning the tuxedo he'd had on earlier. Even after sleeping together, that simple act of voyeurism felt strangely intimate.

'Perhaps.' His eyes narrow.

'In which case, I can't help you.'

'For a million dollars, you're not willing to discover who she is?'

I wait a moment.

He pulls a card from his pocket. It's jet black, matte, thick, with gold writing across the front. As he brings it closer I make out his name and, beneath it, a series of numbers.

'I'll tell you what, Imogen. You find her and ask her to call me. Whether she does or doesn't, the million dollars is yours regardless.'

I stare at the card, the trap he's unknowingly set one I refuse to enter. Because it's dishonest. I can't take his money under these circumstances. I mean, the woman he's looking for is standing right in front of him.

'A million dollars? You must have shared something pretty special.'

Damn it! Why the heck did I ask that? I jackknife off the edge of the desk, leaving his card where he's placed it.

'You could say that.'

Oh, God. I didn't need to hear that. Temptation is slicing through me.

And yet, he's loaded. Seriously loaded. A million dollars isn't even small change to him. It's the lint in his pocket after he's got rid of his small change.

And Chance is my life's purpose.

I toy with the morality of this, mentally tossing it back and forth.

'I'll try to find her,' I say, quietly.

It seems to placate him. He nods, moving towards the door. 'Then I won't take up more of your time. You'll let me know, one way or another?'

His hand curves around the handle. He's leaving. I swallow back an urge to shout the truth at him.

'Count on it.'

Count on it.

Her words jam against me, hard, holding me completely still. I'm back in Sydney, in the Intimate Rooms.

'That's what you want?' I asked her.

'Count on it.'

Count on it. Common enough, I guess, but no.

I spin around, catching her staring at me. Except it's impossible to tell because of those damned glasses she's been wearing.

Suspicion moves quickly to certainty.

I shut the door and stride across the room, and it's so unexpected that she doesn't even have time to react. I stand before her for a second, and now I look at her lips and I kick myself for not realising sooner.

I lift a hand to the glasses and pull them from her face before she can comprehend what I'm doing.

Those eyes, eyes that have stared into mine as pleasure made her wild with insanity and desire, look back at me, heavy with surprise now. Those lips that I have tasted and dragged between my teeth form a perfect 'O'.

'Miss Anonymous,' I drawl, and before she can answer I lift my hand around to the base of her skull and pull her head forward. I'm kissing her, kissing her first with exploration to test my theory, even when I know I'm right. And as I feel her familiar mouth, taste her sweetness, my kiss turns hard and heavy with censure for trying to hide from me, for lying to me, for being about to let me walk away.

She makes a strangled noise into my mouth and I swallow it; my body, denied the pleasure of hers for nine long nights, throbs with a need that will not be suppressed.

And whatever impulse had prompted her to try to get rid of me, it's gone now, as her hands lift urgently, pushing at my shirt, running it up my body, so her palms connect with my naked chest, her fingertips finding their way back to paths she explored last weekend.

'You were going to fucking hide from me.' I curve my hands around her ass, lifting her onto the edge of her table, spreading her legs. The skirt she's wearing splits with an almighty sound and she laughs, that husky sound having been imprinted on my memory in some strange way.

'It was meant to be one night, we agreed,' she says, tilting her head back so I can run my mouth down her throat, my teeth lightly nipping at the flesh on her collarbone. I feel her tremble beneath me and I have no time for the sensual seduction I thought I'd be engaging in. It's been nine nights and I don't think I've gone that long without sex since—

Well, since ever.

I reach into my back pocket, pulling my wallet out and flicking it open to find a condom without breaking our kiss. I move higher between her legs; the skirt splits more. I don't fucking care.

I undo the button of my jeans and slide the zip down, freeing my rock-hard, aching cock. I shift for a second, just long enough to rip the packet open and push the condom down my length, and then I lift my head to stare at her for a long second, my eyes laced with a thousand and one feelings—anger, annoyance, heat, need, mockery, impatience.

'You were going to fucking let me walk away just now?'

She bites down on her lip and in response moves forward, her hands against my chest, her face tilted, her lips seeking mine. I deny her that kiss, instead lifting her off the edge of the desk, using my hands to push the scrap of lace at her core aside, and sliding her onto my cock, stifling a moan as her muscles squeeze me so tight I convulse a little.

I take one step across her office and push her back against the thick, cold glass, bracing her there as I push into her hard. The eyes that meet mine are the same—exactly the same. And she knew it! Those fucking glasses.

Anger that she wanted to hide from me crests in my gut and I kiss her, pressing her head against the glass as my body takes command of hers. She is crying my name into my mouth, over and over, her nails digging into my shoulders, her heels pressed to my back.

Her muscles tighten, her whole body vibrates and her cries get louder and faster. At the moment she comes I let go of my own control, I stop fighting this, exploding with a guttural roar, pushing myself hard against her as I come buried deep inside her; finally feeling this release and giving myself over to it completely.

It is fast. It is animalistic. It is bliss.

I hold her, locked between the glass window and my frame, my body weight keeping her where she is, unwilling to put distance between us yet.

I push my head up, my cock still inside her, and fix her with an assessing gaze. 'What game are you playing, Imogen?'

Her throat moves as she swallows. 'Game?' It's husky, the southern accent forgotten, and her voice just as I remember it from Sydney.

'Does fucking members without their knowledge give you a thrill?'

Her spectacular, memorable eyes widen. 'No!' Her denial is sharp and fierce. 'I've never done that before. You were the first. And the last.'

Given my own attitudes to sex, it feels faintly chauvinistic that I'm relieved at that, but I am. I don't like the idea that she uses her position to find her way into bed with members.

'Why did you lie to me?'

'I didn't.' She drops her eyes. I shift my hips, my dick already growing hard again, surprising her so she jerks her attention back to me quickly.

'We agreed to a night. That's the deal we had. It's all I wanted.'

My laugh is spontaneous and deep, a sound of disbelief. 'You didn't want this?'

I have the satisfaction of seeing her cheeks flush pink. 'I...shouldn't have.'

'Why not?'

She shakes her head, and slowly she shifts before

me, her expression going from sexy deer in the head-lights to the force of nature I know her to be——the woman who set all this up off her own back, who's created an unbelievable empire.

'Because I meant what I said in our messages. I just needed to have sex.' More heat in her cheeks but she doesn't blink away from me now. 'I hadn't been with anyone in ages and I felt like I'd forgot-ten what intimacy is like.' She lifts her shoulders. 'I wanted to get laid. And let's face it, you're some-what of an expert in the meaningless sex depart-ment.'

She's right. I've made one-night stands an art form and my reputation makes sure everyone knows it. So why does it piss me off royally that she says it so casually?

I make no apologies for the way I live my life. This is who I am. I've tried to fit myself into a dif-ferent mould before, to be Lord Rothsmore In Wait-ing, and it was an abject failure.

At least when I get back to England this time I'll have a better idea of who I really am.

'You weren't supposed to come looking for me,' she says.

I roll my hips once more, enjoying the look of heat that shifts over her features. Desire flares between us, a flame too bright and searing to ignore.

'Why did you come looking for me?'

That's a great question. The thing about one-night stands is that they're *always* one night. That was what we'd agreed. I'm the one who wants to shift the goalposts, to make this something else.

Except, it's not as if I'd be changing the terms of our deal substantially. She wanted casual, no-strings sex. We obviously still have chemistry. So why not have fun until I leave? It's exactly the kind of relationship I do. Never commitment, never serious, never more than great sex, and lots of it. I am the king of casual fun, and suddenly it feels like a month of that with Imogen would be a lot like bliss.

'You know who I am,' I murmur, and with her back propped against the glass, her legs wrapped around my waist, I separate the lapels of her blazer so I can see the skimpy yellow singlet top thing she's got on underneath. It's soft like silk. I slide my hands under it; her skin is warm to the touch. She's not wearing a bra. My dick is hard again. Rock hard, as if I didn't have sex just minutes ago. My palms curve over her breasts, tormenting her nipples just how she likes it.

It was only one night but I learned a lot about her and I'm not ashamed of using it to get my way.

Her eyes hook to mine, powerful and yet powerless, lost as well as found.

'You know who I am,' I say again, and drop my head to take one of her nipples into my mouth through the flimsy fabric. It adds an extra layer of eroticism to something that's already pretty damned hot. I press my teeth to her nipple, just enough to make her draw in a sharp breath of pleasure.

'Yes.'

It's not clear what she's saying 'yes' to.

'You know I am due to inherit my father's title, the estate, the whole thing.'

She groans, nodding.

'In one month, I'm due back in England to take up my place in that life.' I'm surprised how flat the words sound—the usual derision not in evidence. 'I have only weeks left in Manhattan.'

Another gurgling noise as I transfer my mouth to her other breast and give it the same little bite. Her insides squeeze my cock so tight. I need more of her. All of her.

Impatiently, I push at her blazer and she pulls her arms from it, understanding that I need all of her, all of this. The camisole follows, the wet patches from my mouth visible as it scrunches to the ground at our feet. I have to put her down to get the tattered skirt from her body and I drag it off her with the lace thong, leaving both on the floor before spinning her around so her back is to me.

I push her forward at the hips, so her arms are braced against the windows, and I take the briefest second to imprint this memory on my mind—the sight of her naked ass, how hot she looks from behind. I spread her legs with my knee, and bring one hand around to her breasts, keeping it clamped there as my other holds her hips steady. I take her from behind quickly, thrusting into her, our voices mingling at the total possession of this, the rightness of my being buried deep inside her. The hand on her hip travels lightly to her clit, and I run it over her cluster of nerves as I move deeper and harder inside her.

My voice is music, deep and throaty, taking over the room. There's no clock here ticking as a background accompaniment to this passion, but the desire is just as intense and just as overwhelming.

I forget that we're in her office, I forget there's a secretary just down the hallway. I forget everything except how this feels, how badly I need her, how it's been nine nights of tormenting, snatched memories, of how I didn't even want to go out and hook up with someone else because I didn't think it could live up to this.

I am angry at that—angry at my dependence on being with her—but I am also thrilled because I've found Miss Anonymous and I have four weeks in which to enjoy her.

So long as she agrees...

CHAPTER FOUR

WHAT THE HECK just happened?

I press my overheated forehead to the glass, staring down—way down—at Manhattan. My office is on the ninety-second floor of this glass and steel monolith. Believe me, I'd have preferred to cut costs and rent something cheaper, but my parents own two floors of this building and gave me a great deal on rent—besides which, my clients expect a certain air of wealth and prestige. The whole Billionaires' Club is predicated on the idea of unattainable wealth and prestige, so I can't exactly have my office headquarters in some three-storey brick walk-up in Brooklyn.

His breathing is ragged, just like my own. I stay right where I am, pleasure like fireworks just beneath my skin, exploding fast at my pulse points. I stare down at the snow-covered city, thinking of the time I went to visit Meemaw and Pa. I'd heard about them, but had barely spent more than an hour in their company. My mother worked hard to distance herself from her working-class roots. She'd married Hollywood royalty, she was a theatre queen and she wasn't going to have the fact that she came from an ordinary family in the south do anything to harm her carefully cultivated image. I didn't have those hang-ups, and right after Abbey died, I just felt as if I needed to see my grandparents, to spend time with them. I wanted the authenticity their life offered; I wanted to be as far from my parents and their set as possible.

So I went to Meemaw's, and only a day or two after I arrived, a tornado crossed town. It was loud and fierce and so fast. It must have lasted only two or three minutes before it moved away again and the most surreal, unnatural silence followed.

That's what's happening now.

Silence, but weird and unnatural and, contrasted with our earlier passion, it is freakishly quiet in my office.

And I have no idea what to say, which makes me even more freaked out because I pride myself on being able to fill difficult silences and cover awkwardness with a quip or a joke.

Now, I've got nothing.

I'm just a tangle of nerves and excitement. My whole body feels as if it's been stretched in a thousand directions, stretched by the speed with which my blood has terrorised it.

His hands on my back are gentle now, inquisitive, returning me to the here and now with a slow, sweet touch. He curves his palms over my shoulders and turns me around to face him.

It makes it so much harder to kick my brain into gear because one look at his face and I'm melting. What the heck is wrong with me? I don't *do* rich guys. I find all that money off-putting and there's no mistaking Nicholas Rothsmore's background of privilege and wealth. It is in the strength of his spine, the confident tilt of his chin, the sophistication of his eyes, the dimple of his chin that for some reason screams aristocracy.

But there's also something hard-worn about him, something broken and devil-may-care. Something that tells me he's a risk-taker and an adventurer, that he might have been born to fit the mould of a privileged aristocrat but that he's worked hard to fight his way free of it.

That alone keeps me rooted to the spot, unable to look away from a face that I have been seeing in my dreams since we snatched an hour together in Sydney.

'I'm...'

He lifts a finger and presses it to my lips, his dark brows knitting together as if I'm a puzzle he's trying to solve.

'I didn't expect to see you again,' I say against his finger. When he doesn't move it, I dart my tongue out and flick it. His eyes flare wide and power rushes through my body.

This is bigger than me, bigger than him.

'You made pretty sure of that.'

'Not quite.' I bite the soft flesh of his finger now,

and he presses it to my lips, so I roll my tongue over it and feel his cock jerk against me.

He's like the Energizer Bunny of sex. Then again, apparently I am too, because desire ignites inside me, and I wish we were anywhere but my office.

My office!

'Oh, crap.' I press my hand to his chest and push him back, everything forgotten except the fact Emily and I have an extremely casual relationship and she walks in whenever she needs anything. Not to mention I've just been screaming like a banshee at the top of my lungs.

I sidestep him and move away as if he's explosive dynamite and I'm right in its trajectory. I need space. Space to think and I definitely absolutely need to get dressed.

'That was…completely unprofessional.' I lift a hand and smooth my hair over one shoulder, my fingers grazing my nipples by accident, so I have to spin away or risk him seeing my instant physical reaction to the simple touch.

'It was also completely fucking great.'

A smile curves my lips. There's a bathroom across my office—I work long hours and frequently have to attend Billionaires' Club events, which I go to directly from here. Fortunately for me, there's also a wardrobe and it's always stocked with an array of outfits. I pull out a black pantsuit and a silk camisole, trying not to think about what Emily will say when she notices the obvious change of clothes, pulling the silk top on quickly to dispense with the whole nakedness thing.

I spin around to find him watching me with an expression I can only describe as indolent. He's like some kind of crack cocaine to me—I'm high on him and already craving my next fix.

I stare across at him—he's pulled his boxers back on but there's still an expanse of toned abs and tanned skin—and my mouth goes dry, my stomach loops and my fingers tingle.

'I don't do this.'

He lifts a thick, dark brow, his expression quirking with curiosity. 'Do what?'

'This.' I gesture from him to me. 'Sleep with clients. Sleep with *anyone*.'

He laughs, the sound bouncing around my office. My pulse trembles. 'You weren't a virgin.'

I jerk my head. 'Yeah, but…'

He begins to prowl towards me.

'It had been a while.'

I told him that in Sydney. There's no point in denying it.

'What's "a while"?'

I swallow, my throat bone dry. I wave my hand in the air in what I hope passes as some kind of descriptor of time. He catches it in his, lacing our fingers together and holding it at my side.

Up close, I look at him—really look at him—in a way I haven't had the luxury of doing yet. I notice things that previously passed me by. Not because they didn't warrant notice, but because there's so much of him that demands attention: his square jaw; his perfectly sculpted lips; the little indent above his mouth, forming a bridge to his nose; a nose that is straight and strong—patrician, appropriately, given his pedigree—but that has a bump halfway down, as if it's been broken at some point. His lashes are thick and dark and clumpy, and close up it almost looks as if he's wearing eyeliner. He's not, but that's the effect the weight of his lashes combines to create. He has a silvery scar near his hairline—a single, trembling line about an inch long, very faint and, going by the shimmery paleness of it, earned long ago, perhaps even as a boy.

My tummy swoops. 'Oh, you know, years.'

'Years?' The word is like a curse, and his brow dips as if he can't even comprehend this concept. I can't really blame him—standing here in a post-orgasm glow, I have no idea why I've denied myself this for as long as I have.

I go to pull away but his hand squeezes mine. 'Years?' Softer, gentler, less shocked, more wondering.

'Yeah.' I don't meet his eyes. I hate feeling like this. Most people look at me with awe and it's pushed my vulnerabilities deep inside me. But suddenly, I feel gauche and insecure; I feel like the gangly, solitary teen I was after Abbey died and I realised I had no one who really knew me.

I make an effort to straighten and transform into Imogen Carmichael, entrepreneur, philanthropist.

'It's not a big deal, okay?'

'I beg to differ. Are you some kind of masochist? Or nun?'

'Clearly not the latter.'

'So why the hell have you been single so long?'

I square my shoulders but make no effort to pull my hand away from his. I like touching him. That should set alarm bells off inside my brain. Maybe it does. I ignore them, though, staying right where I am, his naked torso with that cursive script tattoo inked over his heart calling to me.

'I've been busy,' I point out, waving my free hand around the office.

'But sex is…'

'Yeah, yeah.' I roll my eyes. 'To *you*, sex is like breathing. I get it.'

'I was going to say,' he interrupts, a little gruffly, 'that it's an instinct. And it's more than sex, it's companionship. It's falling asleep in someone's arms, it's having someone to laugh with.'

'Says you, Mr Manhattan Playboy?'

He lifts his defined shoulders. 'So? A varied sex life doesn't mean I don't still enjoy those perks.'

It's an admission I didn't expect. Our eyes connect and something electrifies my pulse. 'With a different woman every night, right?'

His eyes hold mine unflinchingly and I admire him for his lack of apology. Why should he apologise? He's a renowned bachelor; he lives as he preaches. Everyone who sleeps with him knows what they're getting.

Great sex.

Lots of it.

But just for a night or so.

I knew that—it's why I approached him, specifically, in the forums. I didn't want the complication of a guy who might want more from me.

Which somewhat begs the question as to why he's here.

And why I don't feel more annoyed about it.

'You like sex,' he says, as if I'm a puzzle he wants to work out.

My cheeks flush. Because up until a week ago, I didn't know how *much* I like sex. I've only been with two guys. My college boyfriend, who it turns out was using me to access my mother's production company connections, and Jackson, who was 'great on paper' but a complete dud in real life. It's a shame it took me six months to work that one out.

In any event, the sex with both was…nice. At best.

'Apparently,' I murmur, scanning his face.

I had no idea it could be so completely mind-blowing. I mean, I've read my fair share of romance novels and watched movies where the women just have to be kissed on the nose to go into a full-blown orgasm, and I've always thought it was a stupid fantasy.

Not so much now.

'You came looking for sex,' he prompts, and I get a glimpse of the determination that's made Nicholas Rothsmore such a success in business, away from his family's prestigious standing in society. He has a needle-sharp focus and he's using it to sift through my soul.

'Yes.' I jut my chin out unapologetically.

'Why?'

I open my mouth to answer and then shake my head. 'I told you, it's been a while.'

'So why now?' he persists.

My eyes drop away from his, skimming the walls of my office. This place is my home away from home and yet it's nothing like the real me. Elegant Scandinavian furniture, obvious signs of wealth and success. It's what my clients expect.

'I guess…' I search for an answer. The truth is, it wasn't one thing or another. People in the club have been pairing off lately. There've been engagements and rumoured weddings, and I guess it's made me realise how far I am from that. It's the knowledge that I'm approaching thirty and that happy couple life is nowhere near being on my horizon. But mostly, it was desire. Curiosity. Loneliness—the kind that permeates me on a cellular level, so I could no longer ignore it.

He squeezes my hand so I jerk my attention back to his face.

'I just wanted to get laid.' The admission is bare-faced, if only a fraction of the complex knot of emotions that led me into the Intimate Room. 'And then get on with my life.'

'Ah.' He grins, just a flash, but I have the strangest—and most unpleasant—sensation that he's laughing at me. 'Sex isn't a part of your real life?'

I shake my head. 'This is…' I wave around the office. 'My business. The club. The charity. That takes pretty much all my time and energy. It's hard to meet anyone, but—'

'But?' he prompts, when I don't finish the sentence.

My teeth press into my lower lip as I think that through. 'But, I'm twenty-nine and I have barely been in a relationship. I mean, a couple of guys but nothing serious, nothing that could ever go anywhere.'

He's quiet, listening attentively.

'And suddenly, everyone seems to be pairing off, like the club has become its own kind of Noah's Ark or something.'

He laughs gruffly.

'I'm almost thirty and I have no social life to speak of.' I grimace. 'I haven't dated in four years. The guy I have the most frequent conversations with is my doorman, Mr Silverstein, and he's seventy-five years old and very happily married. My parents won't get off my back about being single. It doesn't matter that I've built all this, they really only care about me getting married and having babies—not so many that I ruin my figure, mind you.' I pause to roll my eyes, making the mental excuses for my mother that I always bring to the fore when I'm frustrated with her. How she's an aging Hollywood starlet who sees youth and beauty as her greatest assets—and both are shifting away from how she wants them to be. 'But more than that, I'm…getting used to being alone.' I swallow, the raw truth of the confession surprising me.

'It's not that I want a relationship.' The very idea fills me with panic. 'There's no way I could fit one in. I barely have time to workout in the day. I have to get a manicurist to come to the office if I need my nails done.' I shake my head, hating how entitled that sounds, resisting an urge to explain it's part of the whole image thing my clients expect me to project.

'So our night in Sydney was…what? Your sexual equivalent to an in-office manicure?' he teases.

Heat blooms in my cheeks.

'Dial-a-Fuck?' he pushes, and I laugh, shaking my head.

'Honestly? I was seriously starting to worry I might have forgotten how to even do sex.' I laugh, and am relieved when he does too.

'So… Dial-a-Fuck meets sex refresher course?'

'Sex for Beginners,' I agree with a wink.

'Well, Miss Carmichael, I'm delighted to say you passed, with flying colours.'

'Thank you, sir.'

Silence hums around us, buzzing like paparazzi at fashion week. I hold my breath and wait, though I have no idea what I'm waiting for.

'Why did you come here?'

His brows lift, just a little. 'I was looking for you.'

Heat spreads through my body.

'Why?'

His hands lift to my hair, flicking it between his fingers. 'You suit blonde.' His smile is somehow self-deprecating. 'Then again, you also suit pink.'

I laugh. 'Did you come here to discuss my hair?'

'No.' His eyes pierce mine. 'I came here to find Miss Anonymous.'

'Why?'

'Because last week was the best sex I've ever had, and I haven't been able to stop thinking about you. I want more. More of her, you, this. And I think you do too.'

My jaw drops, my heart stops, my pulse cracks like a frozen river.

'Nicholas—'

His name rushes from my lips, too much air, too much feeling. It's too much. If sex were a college degree, this guy would hold several PhDs. He really thinks I'm the best? The best he's ever had? Pride soars in my chest, and, more than that, the addiction centres of my brain are going into overdrive because he's damned right. I do want more of this.

But… 'We agreed it would just be one night.'

'That was before.' He shrugs away the objection, as though it doesn't matter.

'But you're not… Neither of us wants… I mean, what are you saying?'

'I'm glad you asked,' he says teasingly, pulling me closer, wrapping his arms behind my back so our bodies are cleaved together in a way that is both sexy and intimate. 'I came here wanting to fuck Miss Anonymous again, and I did. And still I want more. And now, I think I can see a way for both of us to get what we want.'

'What's that?' I sound as if I've run a marathon.

'Go out with me.'

Panic spirals through me and I shake my head on instinct. 'I don't date, Nicholas. I didn't mean to imply that I want that…'

'Relax.' He grins, and something fizzes in my gut. 'I don't mean for real.'

'What do you mean?'

'You haven't dated in a long time, and that seems like a waste. So date me. Play with me. Fuck me.' He says the last in a voice that is so deep it rumbles right through my bones. 'I'm moving home in a month and, suddenly, I can't think of any way I'd rather spend what remains of my time in New York than with you.'

His voice whips against me, seductive and intense. But I hold onto Chance, to what I owe Abbey, to the single-minded focus this business takes to run. 'I can't.' My tone is clipped, strange-sounding in the

midst of our conversation and what we've just done.
'I don't have time to date.'

'That's a cop-out.' His words are a little mocking.

'I'm sorry you feel that way, but it's the truth. I
work really hard, and I can't spare the time to fill
your last few weeks here in New York.'

'You're saying you'd rather work than do more
of this?' He lifts a brow and, damn it, he is so hot,
and I want him, and he knows it. He knows what
he's doing to me. I swallow, frustration biting into
my belly.

'Look, Nicholas, I appreciate the offer.' I wince,
knowing it sounds like some kind of real-estate
merger. 'But this was only meant to be one night.
I hadn't—'

'Had sex in a really long time,' he supplies, a
smile on his lips, as if he's teasing me, and a smile
twitches on my own lips in response.

'I haven't had a *life* in a really long time. No
friends, no boyfriend, I barely see my family—
though I can't say that's a bad thing, actually—but
I got… I know it's kind of sad to admit this, I got
lonely, okay? I just wanted one night to be like a
regular woman in her twenties. And it was great.
You were great. But that's all it can be between us.
I can't afford to get distracted.'

'Great. I don't want to distract you.' He wiggles
his brows. 'At least, not beyond this month.'

'Nicholas,' I groan, lifting my hands to my face

and covering my eyes. 'I can't do it. This all means too much to me—'

'I get it.' I remove my hands to find him watching me. 'Your work is important to you. But you just said you haven't had a life in a really long time. So why not give yourself one? Just for a few weeks.'

His words catch in my chest. I frown.

'I'm not talking about a relationship, and I'm not talking about long-term. I'm literally talking about you and me, doing more of this.' He gestures towards my desk and the window that still bears my handprints. 'Dating for a few weeks, having fun, all kinds of fun, until it's time for me to leave.'

'And then what?'

'Then, I go back to my life, and you can go back to working twenty-two hours a day and pretending you're not a red-blooded woman.'

It's crazy. But what's craziest of all is that it makes sense. It's everything I wanted and never thought I could have. A relationship with clear boundaries, limits on what we get from one another and a stop point that would make it impossible for this to overshadow my real life in any way. It's exactly the kind of relationship I would create, if I thought there was any likelihood I'd find a guy to go along with it.

It feels almost too good to be true. 'You want to date me?'

'Well, I want to fuck you,' he says with a devilish

grin that takes any impertinence out of his correction. 'But you *should* be dated. And I'm pretty good at the whole dating thing.'

My heart kicks up a notch. 'And not at all arrogant with it, right?'

'It's not arrogant if it's true.'

I roll my eyes again but stifle a laugh. 'I suppose you have a point.'

'So? Four weeks of debauched fun. What say you, Miss Carmichael?'

My body unequivocally and enthusiastically says 'yes'. A thousand times over, yes. But I have to think this through. I'm not someone who jumps off the deep end without looking at every angle first. 'I don't date clients.'

'Ever?' Then, before I can answer, 'Right, you're a date virgin.'

'I am not!' I splutter, laughing. 'I have dated.'

'A millennium ago.'

'Shut up.' I punch his shoulder playfully but his eyes flare in a way that promises it could very quickly go from playful to something else entirely if I'm not careful.

'No one has to know about this.'

'Yeah, right.' Could we actually keep this a secret? Is that remotely feasible?

'What? You're planning on taking out a full-page ad?'

'No, but, you're kind of recognisable, and so am I.' Temptation is dragging me towards the line of acceptance, though. 'Why don't we just, you know, sleep together? My apartment has a basement garage, you can come and go and no one needs to know…'

'No.' He lifts a hand, curving it around my cheek, his eyes flaring with mine. 'It's obvious you're a total novice and need a first-rate education. I'm going to take you out.'

'Wine and dine me?'

'Yes.'

Heat soars in my chest.

'It wouldn't work. I can't have people talking. This matters too much to me.' Once more, I wave my hand around my office, indicating the club.

'I respect that.' He studies me for a beat. 'I promise I won't do anything that could damage your reputation in the club. Scout's honour.'

I laugh, because he is far from a Scout. 'Dating you would do that though.' And it would. Not just because I'm me, but because he's Nicholas Rothsmore and his reputation would be enough to drag me towards scandal—just the kind of scandal I promise my members the club will help them avoid.

'So we'll keep it secret.' He says it as if it's simple.

Before I can ask him exactly how he proposes to do that, he pulls me closer, tighter, so our bodies meld and thought becomes a little harder.

'I saw something on the forums about the Christmas gala,' he murmurs, his eyes sweeping my face.

'That we're looking for donations of time?'

He nods, then drops his head so his lips buzz mine

so lightly it's a form of torture. I push up on my tip-toes without meaning to, so my face is closer, wanting an actual kiss.

He pulls back, just a little, teasing me, tempting me. Frustration kicks in my abdomen.

'So?'

'So,' he murmurs, buzzing my lips again, then sliding a hand between my legs so I sway forward and exhale softly. 'If anyone runs into us, we'll tell them I'm helping with the Christmas gala.' His fingers brush my clit and I dig my fingers into his shoulder, holding on for dear life as he stirs my body to a new fever pitch.

It's so plausible. Members with certain expertise often volunteer their time or resources when it comes to organising events. Ellie Little recently provided a heap of supercars for a member event. This isn't unprecedented.

People would believe it.

Probably.

He slides a single finger inside my core and my knees threaten to buckle. His arm clamps around my back as if he *knows* somehow.

'Think about it,' he murmurs in my ear before sucking my lobe into his mouth, teasing it between his teeth. 'How else will you know what really…' he moves his finger deeper, brushing his thumb over my clit; my breath hurts '…really…' he bites his teeth down on my earlobe and I make a sound of total surrender '…great dating feels like?'

I hold him as he moves faster and pleasure is like a tidal wave swirling around me. I'm not sure I care about dating so much as sex, and sex specifically with Nicholas, but at the same time I'm completely intrigued.

Pleasure is making thought almost impossible, so I ask the first thing that occurs to me before I lose myself utterly in this moment. 'Why would you do this?'

'Beyond the fact the sex with you is fucking fantastic?'

I nod, tilting my head back, staring at my ceiling as everything explodes in my chest.

'Because in a month I will become the man who's going to be Lord Rothsmore and any kind of social life will be a distant memory.' I cling on tighter as my eyes fill with stars. 'This month with you will be like my very own goodbye party to my real life.'

If I weren't cresting over a wave of sublime release, I might almost have felt sorry for him, I might have paid more attention to the heaviness in his voice. But I cannot think properly, I cannot act as I normally would. I cry out his name and tip over the edge, my eyes blinking open to find him watching me with an intensity that takes my breath away.

'Say yes,' he prompts, a smile flickering across his lips, as though he knows I'll agree—how can I not?

My throat is parched, my body awash with a

shock of feelings, but I nod, jerkily. In that moment, I would have agreed to give him my soul; I would have agreed to anything he asked of me. We have thirty days, not one thousand and one, and yet sex, I think, has become my Scheherazade's tale, and he is the master storyteller, intriguing me more and more with each and every encounter…

CHAPTER FIVE

WELL... THAT WAS UNEXPECTED.

I settle into the luxurious leather of my limo, staring out at Manhattan as I cut across town. I can still smell her on my skin, on my hands, taste her in my mouth. Desire slides across me like warm water, and I throw my head back, squeeze my eyes shut and exhale.

Miss Anonymous is Miss Imogen Carmichael.

I've met her before, but only briefly, and while I thought she was attractive, I haven't really given her a second thought. I focus on that memory now, remembering the way she was with me, the same way she is with everyone in the exclusive club. Friendly, but in a way I instinctively understood to be guarded. She is exceptional at seeming warm without giving much of herself away.

She's calm and measured, and the club is a testament to that. It's a behemoth of an organisation and she oversees all aspects of it, an impressive tribute to her hard work.

What is unexpected is the heat that runs just beneath her surface. The passion that makes her lose herself in the moment just as completely as I do—if not more so. She's driven by instincts, and her instincts are fire and flame.

It isn't that I haven't had good sex. I have. But she's on a whole other level. There's nothing practised about her, there's nothing overthought or contrived. She does as she feels, and she feels as she needs, and her body answers mine in every way.

It's utterly surreal.

It must have been, for me to suggest we date.

Date! What the actual fuck?

I don't date. I screw. I screw beautiful, available, temporary lovers then move on. A week here and there, sometimes longer, but always on my terms, and always only if my lovers understand my ballgame. I don't do promises, I don't do hearts and candles, love, promises of a future. If I date a woman, it's because she knows how temporary and superficial it will be.

One day, I'll marry, someone like Saffy, except I'll never make the mistake of falling in love with them again. The pain of Saffy's desertion has been muted by the passage of time but it's still there, a pressure in my solar plexus whenever I remember it. When I think of how it felt to stand in front of the church and realise that she simply wasn't going to show. It's a pain that only grew when, a month later, I learned she'd fallen in love with someone else. While I was preparing for our wedding, she was working out how to leave me for some new guy.

I feel my tattoo restlessly. *I am my own.*

I'd forgotten that for a while. I'd let the union my parents had pushed me into, had championed and supported, become something else in my mind, so I'd actually let myself fall *in love* with Saffron. So much so that I was devastated when we broke up. Devastated, humiliated, burned to a crisp.

Never again.

When I get married, it will be to someone who wants the title I can give her and the money at my disposal, who understands that, beyond polite companionship, I'm not offering anything more and that, beyond a need for a couple of heirs, I'm not looking for anything further.

It makes me see my parents' marriage through a new light. I used to think their lovelessness was kind of sad—the way they wasp their way through life. Now, I get it. It's a practical marriage. They married because it made sense, they had their son and heir to carry on the family name and probably never touched each other again.

Yeah, it's a well-worn blueprint for marriage in their circles, in my circle, and I have no doubt my own will be just like it.

But until then, for one month, I'm going to enjoy Imogen Carmichael, and I'm going to make it one of the best months of her life. I'm going to take dating to the next level, set the bar so fucking high for the poor next guy that he has to spend the rest of his life working to make her as happy and fulfilled as I have in these four weeks.

Why? Because I'm Nicholas Rothsmore and I'm always, without fail, the best at everything I do, and now that includes dating Imogen.

A box arrives the following afternoon. It's gunmetal-grey with white cursive script embossed across the top, proclaiming the name of an exclusive Manhattan lingerie boutique. My breath immediately speeds up. I ignore Emily's curious glance as I take it from her, moving to my desk and placing it carefully on the corner.

'RSVPs are coming thick and fast,' I say. 'Ticket payments are way ahead of where we were at this time last year.'

But, curious or not, Emily is all professionalism. She consults her clipboard for a moment. 'And donations are great too. Sir Bennet Alwin has donated a guided tour of Australia's Great Barrier Reef on his own personal submersible.'

'I wouldn't mind winning that,' I say with a smile. He's one of the leading naturalists of our time, and the Great Barrier Reef is regrettably a dying wonder of the world.

'You can bid,' she points out.

It's true, there's nothing to preclude me from entering the auction bidding, but, much like dating members, I have my own little set of rules that stands me apart from the other club members. In the past, I've matched donations for items that can be replicated, so the charity wins twice.

'I might. What else?'

'There's the private performance by the London Philharmonic, the flight over the Baltic in Yuri Ostromonov's helicopter, the private cruise of the Antarctic and the custom diamond choker from Alec Minton.'

'Wow. That's quite a haul.'

'That's just in the last week.'

I shake my head, floored by people's generosity, even when I know half of it is about advertising and the kudos that comes from being visibly associated with The Billionaires' Club.

'Seriously, you should see my inbox. It's overflowing with offers.'

'Great. Well, let me know if you need me to wade in.'

'Nope, I've got this. The caterer asked you to go by some time this week to review the menu. You're free Friday afternoon.'

My heart notches up a bit. Before Nicholas left, he turned and said, 'Friday night. I'll be in touch with details.'

But the afternoon is a separate matter. I nod, turning away in case the heat in my blood has converted to pink cheeks. 'Sounds good. Send me a meeting invite once it's confirmed.'

'Done.'

As soon as I'm alone, I cross the room and lift the box, running my finger over the embossed text with a small smile. My fingers shake as I pull on the satin ribbon. It loosens then drops to the floor, just a spool of white against the carpet.

I lift the lid slowly, placing it on the desk. There's a gold sticker joining two sides of tissue paper together. I slide my finger under it, easing it up, deliberately moving slowly to counteract my body's impatience, needing to control my instincts—which shout at me to rip the damned paper and see what's inside.

The paper lifts and a delicate cream silk fabric sits inside, perfectly nestled, so I have to lift it out to see what it is. My breath hitches not at the beauty of the lingerie, though it is stunning, so much as at the idea that he, Nicholas Rothsmore, bought it for me.

I hold it up a little higher, skimming my eyes over the delicate spaghetti straps, which lead to a low V of lace. I can tell that when I wear it, my breasts will be visible through the frothy, twisting swirls. Silk kisses lace and it falls in soft folds down to what I guess will be my hips when I finally put on the exquisite piece. I spin, looking back to the box, and smile, because there are matching briefs, silk and lace, with ribbons at the side, so they can be undone with no more than a slight tug.

Anticipation supercharges my blood. I'm about to lay the lingerie back in the box and stuff the lid on when I catch sight of an envelope in the bottom.

Intrigued, I reach for it, opening the back and lifting out a single piece of thick card.

It bears his name at the top, and a coat of arms, which, I imagine, belong to his ancient family. I stare at it for a moment, making out a lion, a spiky-looking flower and a bird with a full and impressive plume of feathers.

Aristocratic guys I generally avoid like the plague. And with good reason. All my experience has made me wary of people with too much money, but at least people who've had to work to earn it or fight to keep it have some appreciation for the value of it and an understanding for what life is like for those who don't; the liberties and choices many are deprived of because of a lack of financial viability.

But it's the lords and the sirs, the counts and the barons who are, by far, the most…wankery. In fact, the only member I've expelled from the club was a lord with an impeccable reputation, but we discovered he'd drugged a waitress at a club event—one of our members had found them in the Intimate Rooms just in time—but, God, it could have been so much worse.

Not that all the guys with titles are bad. They're just definitely not my type.

I have no idea what my type is, but it's not Nicholas.

That gives me a sense of relief because I don't want to get involved with anyone right now, and so the only way I can really date him is because I know it will go nowhere.

Miss Anonymous—
I'll pick you up at eight o'clock.
Wear this.
N

It's so simple, so completely to the point, but my heart stammers as though he's breathed the words into my ear, and I need to sit down for a second to regroup. His handwriting is bold and confident, just like him, and he uses—what else?—a fountain pen. I lift it to my lips without thinking and breathe deeply, as though I might somehow catch a lingering hint of *him* on the card.

Friday is still three nights away and suddenly the wait feels excruciating.

Fortunately, I'm flat out too busy to pine or anticipate…*much*. Wednesday will be spent doing membership interviews and vetting, Thursday will be planning out next year's events and schedules, making sure we have something seriously incredible planned for each month. Right now, The Billionaires' Club is the hottest ticket in the world—my waiting list is a mile long.

It's a great position to be in but it's also dangerous territory—someone else could set up and start taking my business if I don't make sure our offering is consistently *better*. Extra is my middle name.

We've got Egypt on the calendar next year, including the kind of money-can't-buy access to the Pyramids of Giza followed by a starlit dinner right beneath the Sphinx, with delicacies from all over the world being flown in for members. Imagine a carpet of stars, a thousand candles lighting the way and one of the world's best jazz musicians crooning some beautiful music all evening long. Followed by a night in a tent that, once you're inside, is more like a six-star hotel.

It's taken a huge amount of work to organise— dealing with the authorities and making sure we're not violating any local customs or laws—but this is what people pay their million dollars a year for. Oh, the ticket price itself is extra on top, but without being a member, you don't get a look-in.

On Friday, I meet with the gala caterers to do a small tasting of the menu, as well as the wines, and go over the running of the night, explaining when we'll serve which courses and why.

It's a busy day, and I'm glad for that, glad that by the time six o'clock rolls around I've barely had time to stop, let alone think about Nicholas.

Okay, that's a lie. I've barely stopped thinking about him but in a 'back of my mind' kind of way. But as I lather myself in the shower then towel off before smoothing oil over my hairless legs, all I can think about is the next few hours and the certainty that soon his hands will be where my hands are.

My pulse fires at just the thought. When I slip on the lingerie he sent me, my body is already a field of live wires so my breasts tingle and my stomach twists.

I stare at myself in the mirror, still nowhere near ready, but wanting to stay just like this. Not to go out so much as to stay in. I wish I hadn't agreed to date him, only to sleep with him. Except I'm actually a little excited to see what a guy like Nicholas has planned.

And sex is happening.

I just have to wait a few more hours.

Is this completely crazy? I don't get involved with members. Even though The Billionaires' Club is my creation, my baby, and I'm prominent in the community, there's a distance between me and everyone else. I have to oversee things, to make sure it goes smoothly. I have to run the business side of things and manage membership difficulties.

I can't be seen fooling around with someone in the club.

This *has* to stay private. And it has to be brief. He said he's going back to England in a month, but that's no real impediment to us seeing each other. I mean, the club has rooms all over the world; we host events everywhere. He attends most of them, like all of the members. So I'm bound to see him again, often enough that we could keep this going on a semi-permanent basis.

And then what?

I see him slinking off to the Intimate Rooms with someone else? I hear along the grapevine he's getting married to Lady Asher Cumber-something-or-other?

Because that's how this plays out.

And if I don't retain a bit of control here, I'll get hurt. I might seem, on the outside, as if I have everything ordered in my life, but loneliness is pervasive and powerful, and the temptation of being one half of a pair might lead me to forget the sense in all this.

I'll have to be clear with him from the outset, and clear with myself too. With a small smile curving my lips, I think of the tattoo above his heart and reach for a pen. *I am my own.* I write the words hastily on the back of a store receipt and stick it to my dressing table mirror.

It's a good incantation. I'm going to say it often. Just in case.

It's snowing again and cold out. With no idea what we're doing or where we're going, I dress with versatility in mind. A pair of slim-fitting black leather trousers paired with a silk shirt with long, bell sleeves that falls off one shoulder and is a dirty gold in colour. I like it because the colour flatters my skin, the softness of the fabric hugs my curves and makes it pretty obvious I'm not wearing a bra, and when the sleeve drops over one shoulder, you can see the hint of lace from the camisole he sent me.

I take a few minutes to style my hair, curling it with my wand so it falls in big loose waves over one shoulder. Make-up is simple—as always—just a slick of mascara and the bright red lipstick I wore the night we fucked in Sydney.

My heart is pounding like a bird trapped in a too-small cage.

There are still twenty minutes to go. Waiting is killing me.

I pace through to the kitchen and pour a Chardonnay, press play on my phone so soft piano music connects to the speakers that are wired through my apartment, filling the space with beautiful, calming jazz. It helps, but I'm still looking at the clock every ten seconds.

'This is ridiculous,' I groan, pacing across the lounge for my handbag. On a whim, I swap it for a small gold clutch that matches my shirt and opt for my faux fur coat, wrapping it around my shoulders as I pace back to the kitchen.

Shoes! I need shoes.

Damn it.

I can only laugh at myself and my state of nervousness as I survey my extensive collection of stilettos. Again, with no idea what we're doing, I should probably choose a shoe for all occasions.

But as I remember the way he looked at my stilettos that night in Sydney, a wild impulse has me pulling out one of my favourite pairs. Supple leather, a pointed toe, and a heel so high and spindly it's a wonder they don't snap in two, gives me a few extra inches in height and a mega-boost in confidence.

I add a couple of bangles on a whim, and have three big gulps of wine then stand perfectly still and wait. I breathe in, I breathe out, I empty my mind, I still my trembling—all the tricks the psychologist taught me right after Abbey died, after I'd started having panic attacks.

I don't have the attacks any more but I still get flushes of anxiety, especially when I have to speak at an event. No one would ever know—I pride myself on presenting the image of a calm and collected entrepreneur, but in no small part my success at faking a confidence I don't feel comes from this arsenal of stress-management techniques.

My buzzer rings.

My heart leaps to my throat.

I spin and stalk across the lounge, adrenalin pumping through me as I lift the phone off the cradle. 'Hello?' Just a husk.

'Miss Anonymous?'

My smile is broad and instinctive. 'I'll be right down.'

I hang up, take one last look at myself and exhale slowly—it does nothing to quell the butterflies rampaging my stomach. They chase me as I exit the apartment and descend in the lift.

'Good night, Mr Silverstein.' I smile as I approach the door. He pulls it inward, a kind smile cracking the lines that form his face.

He lets out a low whistle. 'You look mighty pretty, Miss Carmichael.'

He has a southern drawl a lot like my pa's. It softens my heart whenever I speak to him.

'Thanks.'

'Got a club function?'

I nod, because it's easier than admitting the truth—that I have a sort of date.

'Have fun, be safe,'

He says the same thing every time I go out at night. I like it. Even though I'm long past the point of needing protecting, it's still nice to feel as if someone cares.

Nicholas is waiting just outside, standing on the kerb, the back door of his low-set black car open. A driver sits behind the wheel. I don't know what I'd expected. A motorbike, maybe? Not necessarily this. But most people I know are chauffeured around. In fact, I'm probably an anomaly for the fact I use cabs or the subway.

As I step onto the kerb, his eyes trail their way over me, slowly, dragging heat and electricity wherever he looks. My heart stutters, my stomach dives.

Anxiety is back, pulsing through my veins. I refuse to show it.

He takes a step towards me, and another, and my pulse races, my heart twists.

'You look good enough to eat,' he murmurs, holding a hand out to me. I place mine in it; sparks dance the length of my limbs, and my eyes widen in recognition of the strength of this attraction and connection.

'I'll hold you to that.'

His eyes show amusement, but he doesn't laugh.

Heat explodes between us. I stay where I am; he doesn't move either. We're separated by several feet, but holding hands, just staring at each other.

He's wearing beige trousers, a white shirt and a dark blue jacket, with brown shoes. He looks handsome, sexy, stylish and wealthy.

I wish he weren't wearing anything.

'What are we doing tonight?' I hear myself ask, my lips shifting into a slight smile.

'Ah. It's a surprise.' He jerks on my hand a little, pulling me towards him, and he kisses me on the cheek. It's so chaste and weirdly sweet that a different kind of heat, a warmth, flows through me. And then, a whisper in my ear, just low enough for me to catch, 'But I promise it's going to end in my bed.'

CHAPTER SIX

LA CHAMBRE IS one of Manhattan's chicest, hardest-to-get-into clubs. But I went to school with one of the owners, so my entry is guaranteed, any time.

I chose to start our night here for a few reasons. Obviously, because it's exclusive, we can relax in privacy. It's also named the French word for *bedroom* because its central design feature is that it feels like an extremely sumptuous and classy series of bedrooms. Each private booth is filled with velvet cushions, soft seats that recline fully, and privacy curtains for intimate moments.

The food and wine are second to none, and the lighting is dim. But more than that, I've done my research. The head chef of La Chambre consults for Est Il Est, the company that has a long history of catering Billionaires' Club events. Meaning we can totally pass this off as research if anyone from the club sees us.

'It's like a grand bedroom.' She looks at me with those huge dark blue eyes, and I can't tell if she's laughing at or judging me. A little of both, I think.

For someone who's so wildly abandoned in bed, she's incredibly strait-laced when out of it. Yes, I see a hint of disapproval curve her lips and I ache to reach around and kiss it away.

And I will, later. For now, we're in the dating portion of our night.

Besides, I've found myself wondering about Imogen this week, about more than just what makes her tick in the bedroom. She's young to be so incredibly successful, and while I know she has the backing of her parents' wealth behind her, she also has the work ethic of someone determined to make it on their own. I should know—I share that trait.

'Ah, Mr Rothsmore.' The maître d' bows as he approaches us, a gesture of servitude I can't stand but know I'll have to learn to live with. 'Welcome back. I've reserved your usual table.'

I nod. 'Thank you, Jake.'

He leads us through the restaurant and the hand I place in the small of Imogen's back is purely friendly, even when I want to dip my palm a little lower, trailing my fingers over the delicate curve of her rear in those—God help me—leather trousers. As if she needed to get any hotter.

My 'usual' table is at the back of the restaurant, a booth that's set away from the others. The chairs are actually a wrap-around banquette, comfortable and soft. I watch as Imogen shrugs out of her coat and hands it to Jake, then wish I hadn't watched because the delicate shrug of her shoulders—one bare from where her silk shirt has slipped down—is enough to make my cock hard against my pants in a way that's almost painful. Then, I see just a few millimetres of lace and know she's wearing the twin set I bought for her and I'm pretty much done for.

'Everything okay?' she murmurs, batting her eyelids at me as she sits down. I order a bottle of champagne—my friend's private vineyard supplies a Legacy collection for special clients—and a soda for myself, then give her the full force of my attention.

'That depends. How do you define okay?'

'You look pale, suddenly,' she murmurs, her delicious lips quirking at the edges.

'Funny, that, given the fact my blood has rushed south all of a sudden.'

She dips her head forward, her blonde hair forming a curtain that blocks me from seeing her face. Impatience has me reaching down and pushing it behind her ear so I can see her properly. Her eyes lift to mine, meeting them with a mix of emotions I can't fathom.

'You come here often?' she queries and something shifts in my gut. A doubt? Does she not like the restaurant?

'From time to time. Have you ever been?'

She looks around, her expression impossible to decipher. 'Nope.'

I sit beside her rather than across the table. It's not my usual play but I don't really want to be separated from her. Once Jake brings our drinks, I'll have him draw the curtains. Our knees brush beneath the table. She jumps a little. I smile.

'You're nervous again.'

Her eyes flex to mine. 'A little.'

'Why?' I lift my finger to her perfectly painted, beautifully shaped lips. 'Don't tell me. Because you haven't done this in a really long time.' Her eyelashes are incredibly long, like wings hovering just above eyes. They flutter as a bird might flap and I stare at her, transfixed, until Jake reappears with the drinks. He places them on the table and, without looking at him, I say, 'Close the curtains.'

'Yes, sir.'

Imogen's eyes flare, anticipation in their depths. I shouldn't play with her—she's too sweet and way too inexperienced—but I pull away from her a little. 'We don't want anyone to see us.'

Her lips part a little. 'See us doing what?'

It's just a question but it might as well be an invitation to lift her up and fuck her right here on this table.

I'm seriously tempted. But I've got the night planned and, for a reason I can't really fathom, I care about showing her what her social life should be like. Maybe it's like passing a baton, enlisting an apprentice right before I hang up my New York shoes and go back to England?

'Dating, of course.' I grin.

'Right.' She swallows, her delicate, pale throat

tensing with the gesture. 'I've been thinking about that.'

Something switches inside her, and the nerves are gone. She sits a little straighter, reaching for the champagne glass without sipping it in what I now recognise is a prop technique. She likes to hold something. To stop herself fidgeting?

Her fingers curve around the stem. 'Go on,' I prompt, matching her gesture, pulling my own soda tumbler towards me.

'This whole dating thing.' She pauses, a furrow on her brow. 'We need to discuss it further.'

My lips quirk but I take a drink to hide the smile. I don't think she'd like to feel as if I'm laughing at her. And I'm not, really, more just thinking how cute she is like this—trying to bring her impressive business mind to a social agreement.

'Okay, so discuss it.'

'I'm serious,' she murmurs, her eyes forcing mine to hold hers.

'What is it?'

'I was thinking, earlier, about how crazy this is and I think we need to have some more rules in place.'

'Rules?' I jerk my brows without meaning to. 'Out of nowhere, I'm thinking of a headmistress and I've got to tell you, Imogen, it's very hot.'

She grins, leaning forward and pressing her hand to my shoulder. 'Maybe later, Mr Rothsmore.'

Oh, crap. Role play. With her? Suddenly, she has about a thousand upper hands as I start to imagine her in all sorts of costumes and can barely think straight.

'My business means everything to me,' she says, her smile slowly falling from her face. 'It's not just… It isn't just something I've worked really hard to build. It means a lot. To a lot of people. And part of that is my image. I really can't have anyone find out about us.'

'We've already dealt with this.'

'I know.' She nods a little jerkily. 'But what we didn't talk about is what happens after.'

After? 'In a month?' I never think more than a day ahead. Even planning to see her until I leave was somewhat paradigm-shifting for my mentality. Planning beyond that is not something I have the skillset for.

She nods. 'We'll see each other again. It's inevitable.'

'So?' I lift a brow. 'That's kind of fun.'

'No.' It's like a whip, cracking across me. 'I don't want this to be something that goes on, where we see each other in Monaco and decide to pick up where we left off.' A *moue* of disapproval shifts over her lips. 'That's messy and inelegant and definitely leaves room for discovery.'

Her summation is adamant, but she has a very good point. I could see me spying her from across the room at an event and finding an excuse to drag her into a hallway to have some fun, only to be seen by a passing member. It's risky.

'We need a line in the sand,' she goes on carefully, as though she's thinking on the fly. 'The Christmas gala should be our last night together. After that, we're civil, polite strangers. If you see me at an event, you say "hi", and keep moving.'

There's nothing in her suggestion that worries me. I know what my future holds and it is far away from Imogen Carmichael and this wonderful world she's created.

'Fine.' It's easy to agree to that.

Seeing her obvious relief dents my pride a little.

'Okay.' Her smile is bright. 'So privacy and a hard stop point.' She nods. 'Good.'

'You forgot the third rule,' I say, unable to explain why something is firing in my chest that feels a lot like impatience.

'Did I? What's that?' She's businesslike again, focussed on me and what she could have missed.

'A whole lotta fun in between.' I swoop my head down and kiss her, swallowing her surprise and laughing deep in my throat. Yeah, this is going to be fun all right.

He kisses as if it's a sport and he holds all the world records in it. He kisses as if his sole purpose for being is getting me off. He kisses as if he were meant to be doing this.

I surrender to him, lifting a hand and curling it in his shirt, clutching onto him in case he gets it into his head to stop what he's doing. I don't want him to stop. Beneath the table, I lift one leg a little, onto his knee, and his hand curves around the leather, keeping it hooked there, his tongue duelling with mine as he kisses me harder, his other hand lifting to the back of my head and pushing through my hair, holding me right where I am.

I have no intention of going anywhere.

My head spins, afterwards, when he lifts away from me. He really is the quintessential English nobleman, so handsome, so swarthy and fancy yet masculine all at once. There's something cultured and inaccessible about him that even someone like me, who grew up with Hollywood royalty and can generally move in all circles, finds intimidating yet fascinating.

'Are you hungry?'

Am I? 'I think I was when I was at home but, I've gotta say, Nicholas, you have a habit of pushing such considerations way down my list.'

He laughs. 'I'm glad.'

I reach for his hand, putting mine over it without really thinking about it—funny how such a gesture can become natural so quickly.

'So England, huh?'

Something sharp crosses his expression. Something very un-Nicholas that makes me feel concern for him, or worried for him. Something.

'Yes.'

Okay, there's definitely something here. Curiosity shifts inside me. 'You're not looking forward to going home?'

He lifts his shoulders. 'It's home,' he says after a moment. 'I always knew I'd move back, eventually.'

'How long have you been in New York?'

'Five years.'

'That's right.' I remember reading this in his file. 'You came here after—' I stop what I'm saying, but not in time. His eyes zip to mine, his expression dark.

'After my fiancée left me at the altar?'

I grimace. 'Sorry.'

He flips his hand over and squeezes mine, then reaches for his drink. 'It was for the best.'

It's a comment designed to move conversation on, to shut down worry and any further line of enquiry. I don't succumb to it. 'Why?'

He takes a drink. 'We weren't well suited.'

I don't know much about his fiancée. I can't even remember her name.

'Saffron,' he supplies and I realise I've spoken my thoughts aloud.

'She's not in the club?' Though our membership has grown, I know every member by name and sight and there are no Saffrons. We have a Pearl and a Cinnamon, though.

'No. It's not her thing.' His smile is indulgent.

'No?'

'No.'

Hmm. Another closed door. I don't really like closed doors. 'Why not?'

'Apart from the fact she ditched me in front of five hundred of our nearest and dearest?'

'But why? Why did she dump you?'

'That's the billion-pound question,' he drawls, and for a second, his face is in the shadow of an almighty rain cloud and I want to draw the sun back out.

'You never found out?'

'Why she left me?' He shakes his head. 'But I can guess.'

'Why, then?'

'She was like a bird in an aviary,' he says, after a moment. 'Beautiful, smart, funny, but completely defined by who she was, who her parents were, by what was expected of her.'

'And that's marrying someone like you?'

'Yes.' He dips his head forward. 'She hated it. I didn't realise how much until she left me.'

'Hate it or not, it's still a pretty shitty thing to do.' I wince. 'Sorry.'

'No, you're right. I think she knows that. The problem is, she did love me, but she hated what marrying me would mean more.'

Something makes my voice a little high-pitched. 'And you loved her?'

His eyes are swirling with emotion when they meet mine. 'I did, or I thought I did. I don't know. I have to tell you, the whole thing turned me off love and marriage for life.' His laugh is husky.

'So you're a dedicated bachelor?'

'I wish.' He rolls his eyes and he's Nicholas

Rothsmore, playboy, careless sex god, once more, so I relax, relieved I haven't sent him into some kind of grief spin by making him talk about his ex. 'I have been recalled to the manor.' He grins, showing me he's joking, only there's an edge to his words.

'Rothsmore Manor?' I tease.

He shakes his head. 'Actually, our country seat is Becksworth Hall.'

Somewhere I remember reading that. 'It sounds very grand,' I tease.

'Oh, it is.'

'Like something out of *Pride and Prejudice*?'

'Pemberley has nothing on Becksworth.'

I laugh. 'Tell about it.'

'Not much to tell. If you've seen one grand country home, you've seen them all. Ancient, huge, imposing, miles of windows, stables, a lake for trout fishing, strawberry patches for summer picnics.'

I can't help my sigh. 'That sounds idyllic.'

'In some ways.'

'Not in others?'

But he's done being questioned.

'What about you?'

'What about me?' My turn to sip my champagne and buy time. It's delicious. Crisp and fruity all at once, with enthusiastic bubbles that tickle my mouth as I swirl it around.

'You're from New York?'

'God, no, I wish.' I laugh. 'I'm a Cali Girl. Can't you tell?'

His eyes sweep my face, my hair, my golden skin and he grins. 'Now that you mention it…'

Heat fires in my veins, as hot as any day on a Malibu beach.

'So why New York?'

'I like it here.'

He reaches forward and tucks my hair behind my ear. 'It seems a little unfair for you to demand me to open the wounds of my past and you not tell me about something as simple as a geographical shift?' He says it in a way that's light-hearted but I feel his will of iron beneath the words.

Only he doesn't know. He doesn't understand that my move to New York was bound up in the wounds of my own past. How linked it all is to Abbey and a need to flee LA.

I don't realise I'm frowning until he reaches over and rubs his finger across my lips.

'It made sense, for the business,' I obfuscate. And I think he knows I'm not being completely honest, but he lets it go.

'Where'd you get the idea from?'

'For The Billionaires' Club?'

He dips his head once in a sign of encouragement.

'From a friend of mine—an actress, who was complaining about even the best bars being paparazzi haunts, and wanting to just get away. To have somewhere to let her hair down without having it splashed over the papers the next day.'

'I would imagine a lot of actresses live for the attention of the paparazzi.'

'You're wrong,' I say quickly. 'That attention can be used to build an image, sure, but it's a double-edged sword. And not being able to escape that hounding, it's horrifying. Everyone deserves to be able to switch off their "persona" and just be themselves for a while.'

He's watching me in a way that gives me goose bumps and makes my head feel light, because he's looking at me as though he sees the real me, deep inside who I am, beyond my own 'persona'.

'You're speaking from experience?'

'Sort of. Not really. I like to fly beneath the radar as much as possible, but my parents, on the other hand…'

He waits, encouragingly, as if he doesn't know about them. And maybe he doesn't. I forget sometimes that I'm out of the East Coast bubble.

'My mother's an actress. Or was. Now I guess she's a socialite. She never met a camera she didn't like.'

Wow. I sound so bitter. So serious. And I am— God knows I carry a lot of resentments but I usually do a much better job of hiding them. It's hard to hide things from Nicholas.

I force a smile to my face. 'The club was only meant to be for a few people, but it just took off.

I started with a single venue here in Manhattan but…'

'You found a gap in the market, and the market rose to meet it.'

It sounds so cynical when, actually, it wasn't at all. 'I studied business at college—I thought I'd get a job out this way but, once I got here, I found I didn't really want to spend my time working hard to make rich people even richer.' I smile to take the sting out of the statement. 'Then, the club took on a life all of its own.'

'And you have your charity too, right?'

My smile now is natural. 'Chance, yeah.'

'It does something for kids?'

'Excuse me, sir?' a voice calls from beyond the curtains.

'Yes?' Impatience curves Nicholas's expression.

The curtains open and the waiter reappears, placing a platter on the table top. 'Compliments of the chef.'

Oysters—one of my favourites—with a variety of toppings, and caviar atop thinly sliced cucumber. It breaks the serious mood that had descended on us, and I'm glad. Glad for the reprieve. We promised each other a whole lot of fun and talking about broken engagements and my parents is hardly fun.

Beneath the table, I brush my hand over his knee. He turns to look at me slowly, but that doesn't stop the slash of heat that steals across my body.

Dating was his idea and I really liked it but now

all I want is to be back in bed with him, exploring the desire that fogs the air around us.

I am hungry only for Nicholas Rothsmore.

CHAPTER SEVEN

I'M NOT SURE if it's the champagne I've been drinking, or the incredibly decadent Belgian mousse we shared after dinner, or the fact we're walking hand in hand through New York with the lights of the Brooklyn Bridge twinkling in the background, snow dusting down from an inky black sky, and Christmas lights twinkling overhead, but suddenly I feel as if I'm floating.

'So, is this a normal first date, Nicholas?'

His fingers squeeze mine. I love how he does that, as if it's his way of agreeing with me or something. 'I mean, we've already had sex on two separate occasions, so I'm not sure we can classify this as a first date?'

'No, no, no,' I demur with a grin. 'Those weren't dates. It was fucking.' Champagne has taken away any of my usual tendencies to hesitate. 'And you told me fucking is different from dating.'

His laugh is like a caress. I close my eyes and let it wash over me.

'It is.'

'But you don't really date.'

It's not a question; I know the answer.

'I date,' he corrects, pausing before leading us across the street.

'Oh, yeah?'

'Sure. I date like this—when I know it's just for fun, with no chance of becoming more than what it is.' His eyes meet mine for the briefest second. 'But not a lot of women are interested in that.'

'Really?' I pull a face. 'Because you're such a catch they insist on a wedding ring on the first night?'

He laughs. 'Something like that.'

'I can actually kind of believe it.'

'I wasn't serious.' He drops my hand so he can put his in the small of my back, guiding me further down the street. It's a perfect, perfect New York winter's night. Bundled up in my jacket, with Nicholas at my side, I feel warm, safe and as if I just don't want the night to end. 'It's just hard to meet someone who understands that I really, truly don't want to get involved.'

'Beyond sex.' I am definitely emboldened by champagne.

'Yeah.'

I look up at him thoughtfully. 'Is that what the tattoo means?' I blink and see those words *I am my own* written over his heart.

He doesn't pretend to misunderstand me. 'The tattoo means a lot of things.'

'Yeah?' Curiosity barbs in my chest.

His smile is self-deprecating. 'About a year after the wedding—the wedding that never happened—' he laughs '—my dad came to New York and he was livid. I don't think I've ever seen him like that. We argued—which we don't do. It's very un-British.' He grins, so sexy, so full of passion that I think Nicholas flies in the face of any stereotype regarding stiff, unfeeling upper lips.

'What did you fight about?'

'My lifestyle, which he hated. The nickname "Playboy of Manhattan", which people delighted in calling me.' He expels a sigh. 'He did everything he could to get me to go home, but at the same time I think he knew the business here needed me. So in the end, he issued an ultimatum. Sow my wild oats, get the partying out of my system. Then, at thirty, get married and come home to settle down.'

'And you're nearly thirty?'

He nods. 'It's time to face the music.'

'So, what, you go home and get married, sometime next year?'

For a second, something like fire flashes in his eyes, and then he shrugs. 'That's the deal we made.'

'Wow. So, what, like a dynastic marriage?' I'm kind of joking; the whole idea sounds so preposterous and so unlike Nicholas that it *has* to be a joke.

But his look sparks with something like muted anger. 'Yes.'

I stop walking. 'You can't be serious.'

He lifts his shoulders, staring down at me with eyes that seem to hold an entire universe in their depths.

'"You have been born to privilege, Nicholas. It is not for you to abandon this family's legacy on a whim."'

He is impersonating someone, putting on an even toffier accent.

'But surely you can carry on a family legacy while marrying who you choose…?'

'I would choose to stay single,' he corrects, turning again so we're shoulder to shoulder, taking a step forward. I move with him.

'Why?'

'Because I like being single. I like working hard. Playing harder. I don't want to get married. I don't want to have children. These are things my parents expect of me, but they don't reflect my wishes.'

My heart shifts a little inside my chest. 'Have you explained that to them?'

'My parents?'

'No, your secretary.'

He laughs. 'Has anyone ever told you that you have a smart mouth?'

I gape, because I don't. I really, actually don't. I'm very careful with what I say, moderating my language, aware that I am the representative of Chance and The Billionaires' Club everywhere I go. But there's something about Nicholas that makes me feel completely at ease, as if I can relax completely.

'Did I offend you?'

His laugh is uproarious. 'Do I look like I'm made of glass?'

I smile, relieved. 'I don't know why, but I feel like I can say anything to you,' I explain, simply.

His gaze hooks to mine again, probing. 'It's because of the stop point. We both know this is an aberration. Not real. Out of step with the lives we're both going to lead. So we can let go and have fun without worrying about any kind of consequences or future.'

That makes sense.

'I have told my parents, on several occasions, what I think of their expectations and their title, and even their fortunes.'

'Really?'

He's quiet, deep in thought. 'Except I do care,' he says, after a moment. To our right, a ferry boat passes under the bridge, bleating its low, thundering horn as it goes. The snow falls a little thicker now, landing on the bridge of my nose. I dash it away. 'Not about the money—I have made more than enough on my own. But the title is something that matters.'

We've slowed right down without meaning to. We put one foot in front of the other, but slowly. 'I was raised to care about it, and I do. There's so much history wrapped up in it, so much of my family's past. And there's a responsibility there to shepherd the title, the estate, the fortune on to a new recipient.'

It rankles my American sensibilities. I can't understand any of that old British aristocracy stuff. 'That's the way these things work, I guess.'

'Yes. I didn't much care for it when I was younger but now, at nearly thirty, I feel the weight of it in a new way. I don't want to be where my family's claim on the title ends.'

'Naturally.'

'You really think so? Sometimes I can't believe I actually give a shit.'

I laugh. 'I can. I can see that. Legacies are important. They should be protected.'

'And you? Is there some family tradition your parents are desperate for you to carry on?'

I bite down on my lip, thinking about that for a second before shaking my head. 'Not really.'

'They must be proud of you?'

'You think?'

'Sure. Why not?'

I wrinkle my nose. 'They're not easy to please.' I don't feel like talking about them. As much as I've come to a place in my life where I accept the limitations of my relationship with Mom and Dad, it still hurts. It hurts in a way I'll probably never get over.

After Abbey died, I needed them in a different way. I needed them to be there for me, to make things better, and they weren't. They just couldn't.

They've never really been there for me since— they just don't get me.

'Even when you're running a global empire, trading in luxury and world-class networking events?'

'Even then,' I quip, shutting down his line of questioning with a tight-lipped smile. 'Where, exactly, are we going?'

'We're nearly there.'

'Nearly where?'

'Don't like surprises?'

'I like some surprises.'

'Speaking of which,' he murmurs, surprising me by bundling me into his arms and pushing me against a wall. My breath catches in my throat, my face tilting towards him. 'Did you get the box I sent you?'

A smile lifts the corners of my lips. 'Which box would that be?' I feign ignorance.

'A little box of silk and lace, and a rather delightfully placed ribbon, if memory serves...'

'Ah.' I can't stop the smile that spreads over my face. 'You're just going to have to wait and see.'

'Haven't I been waiting a decade already?' he groans, dropping his head forward and brushing his lips over mine. Desire sets up camp in my belly.

'Did you choose the lingerie yourself?' I can't help asking.

His face is serious. 'Of course. Did you think I had my assistant do it?'

'Or your driver,' I tease.

'Edward can cross town in fifteen minutes flat but I don't think he and I share the same taste in women's apparel.'

'I'm glad to hear it.'

'You don't like Edward's taste either?'

I laugh. 'I don't think I've even clapped eyes on the man. I just meant I like the idea of you going into a boutique and picking something out. For me.'

'Ah.' He nods, sagely, his own mouth quirking into a delicious smile. 'I did.' He drops his head a little closer, so his breath teases my cheek. 'You know what else I did?'

My heart rate accelerates. 'What?'

'I ran my fingers over it.'

Heat pools between my legs.

'I imagined you in it.'

God. I feel weak-kneed.

'And then...'

I hold my breath, waiting. Desire is like a moth inside me, my blood the flame to which it's drawn. I feel the wings beating through my veins, hollowing me out from under my skin.

'Yeah?' My voice is just a croak.

'I went home and jacked off, imagining you in it.'

'Oh, God.' It's a tremulous acknowledgement of one of the sexiest images I've ever had planted in my brain.

He's smiling; I'm not. I'm burning up. I can no longer wait to be with him. I look around us—we are practically alone, save for the cars hurtling past and the occasional jogger out for a late-night run.

'I want to go home with you.'

He nods.

'Now.'

He laughs. 'I'm glad to hear it.'

'Wherever you were taking me, scrap it. I just want to get in a cab and go back to yours.'

'I'm taking you there now.'

I push away from the wall, my expression showing him I mean business. 'Good, then let's go.'

A few minutes later, he leads me across the street and towards the Hudson.

'You live on the water?'

I wrack my brain, trying to remember his address details from the paperwork, and come up empty. Someone better at this than I am might have taken the time to pull his file out for review, to re-familiarise themselves with his bio. But it never occurred to me and, actually, I'm kind of glad, because it's nice learning about Nicholas straight from the horse's mouth, rather than having a heap of his life story stored in my memory banks.

'I don't.'

'Then why are we going down here?'

'Just a second.' He grins, and I know he likes this—knowing something I don't. His hand curves around mine. He must feel the way my pulse is rabbiting in my wrist.

We pass a big building with a sign that proclaims MANHATTAN HELICOPTER RIDES in shining red letters.

But the office is boarded up. Further along there are a couple of security guys, and several sleek black helicopters. Nicholas holds something up and one of the security guys waves us through.

'Good evening, Mr Rothsmore.'

He dips his head in silent acknowledgement, shepherding me past more of the helicopters before changing course and weaving us between two. We approach one, larger than the rest, with *Rothsmore Group* emblazoned across the tail.

'What is this?'

'A helicopter.'

I roll my eyes. 'No kidding.'

'I thought it'd be the fastest way back to my place.'

I laugh, a little unsteadily. 'You're going to pilot the thing?'

He leans closer, so I smell his intoxicating fragrance, and my gut rolls in a way that I am learning to get used to. 'It's not my first time.'

He holds the door open for me, then supports my hand as I step up into the helicopter. Inside, it's like a cross between a private jet and a spaceship. The interior is all beige leather with shining wood panelling. I take the co-pilot's seat, but behind us there's a cabin with four deep armchairs facing towards a central table. Each has a thick black seat belt coming from both shoulders into a latch between the legs.

I reach for the clip and hook it in place, the pressure between my legs exacerbating an already fraught central nervous system.

Despite all of the events I've organised for the club, this is actually my first time in a helicopter.

I have to say I'm a little afraid of the whole idea. I mean, they're so un-aerodynamic…how can a helicopter possibly hope to survive if something goes wrong with it? They're like a dead weight on the atmosphere, pure drag. At least a plane *looks* as if it should glide, even if the rational part of me knows that an aeroplane is also a dead weight.

My point being, I thought I'd be afraid, climbing into this thing, but the second Nicholas takes the seat beside me, I relax. I smile. More than that, my insides buzz and hum with excitement.

This is going to be fun—and that's what we're all about.

New York glitters beneath us. The world-famous bridge cuts over the darkness of the Hudson, the only void of light in what appears to be a sparkler as we get higher over the city.

I am torn between looking at the view and looking at Nicholas, who flies the helicopter as though he does so every day. And perhaps he does.

I note the strength and capability of his hands as he manages the controls, pushing levers while he manoeuvres the navigation stick. Perhaps he feels me watching him because he shifts to look at me, his eyes pinning me to the spot, and his smile, though slow to spread, is as if it's poured from hot lava, pure sex appeal and dynamism.

I swallow and look away, butterflies now rampant in my stomach. He begins to bring the helicopter in lower, over the city proper, and another void looms before us. Central Park, I recognise from the surrounding buildings. I'm on the Upper East Side, a little further north, but he lowers the helicopter down gently, onto the roof of a high rise that must be just south of the park. Billionaires' Row—that figures.

A cursory look from my window shows three other helicopters on the roof. He unhooks his seat belt then reaches across; before I realise what he's doing, his hand is between my legs. My face jerks towards him, and a low, soft breath escapes me as desire floods my system.

I might have expected him to look teasingly but he doesn't. His face is serious, tense. There is an air of urgency in his movements now. The seat belt slides loose but his hand stays between my legs, and, with his eyes latched to mine, he begins to move his fingers, so that, through the leather of my trousers and the silk of the underwear he bought with me in mind, I feel a surge of pleasure forming, building, like a wave rushing to shore.

'These pants are seriously fucking sexy, but, God, how I wish you were wearing a skirt,' he mutters in his inimitable accent, his voice deep, like a growl.

I can't respond. I bite down on my lip and tilt my head back, my legs moving a little wider apart.

He makes a sound of impatience and his hand shifts up so he can slide it inside the leather and silk and touch my flesh, my hot, wet flesh, his fingers finding their way easily, constrained by the tightness of my trousers but in no way hampered in their effectiveness.

'Fuck.' The word bites out from my mouth; desperation is swirling through me. Intensity fires in my soul and before I realise what I'm doing, I push up from the seat, dislodging his hand, straddling him in his seat. His cock is hard between my legs and, despite the layers of clothing separating us, I grind myself down on him, groaning at the waves of pleasure that fill me.

I kiss him, hard; his hands tangle in my hair, pulling at it, pulling me down so our lips are entwined, and I grind harder, the power of this something I'll never forget. Pleasure is shifting, building, running like sand through fingers, I am tipping over the edge and I can't stop. I whimper as I feel the release starting, tingling low in my gut, and I move faster, more desperately.

He's speaking, words that are so low I don't catch them, but the tone of his voice adds an extra layer to my needs. His hand curves around to my arse, holding me down as he pushes up, thrusting as if we're having sex, and we sort of are, despite the regrettable lack of penetration.

Pleasure bursts like a sunray, slicing me with heat. I moan, low in my throat, as I tip right over the edge, my nails digging into his shoulder, my body shivering.

My breath is ragged. I lift up, blinking, bringing him into focus. His expression is like a mask of concentration, his skin flushed, his pupils dilated. My own release was intense but now I crave something else, something more. I want to make him feel like I do. I move quickly, back to my seat.

The cockpit isn't huge and as I climb back into place, my shoe flicks something.

'Shoot. Sorry.'

He angles his face to mine, his lips lifting at the corners.

'Imogen, you could smash the windscreen right now and I wouldn't give a shit.'

I don't answer. Instead, I reach across and undo his trousers, my eyes flicking to his, checking for his reaction. As though he might stop what I'm about to do. I free his cock, wrapping my hand around it and pulling it from his boxers, drawing my hand up and down a few times, pumping him until I feel a hint of his cum leak out.

He's watching me with an intensity that makes my blood simmer all over again and I want him properly, not in a cockpit, somewhere I can relish and savour every damned move.

That will come.

But first, this.

I bend forward but, before I do, I catch the glint of speculation in his eyes and smile to myself. I've surprised him. He wasn't expecting this. I like that, so much.

I start slow, flicking his tip with my tongue, chasing a bead of cum, tasting its salt, letting a small

sigh escape before I run my tongue over him a little
more, his hard tip smooth beneath my exploration.
He groans and my name is somewhere in that groan,
almost indiscernible. I open my mouth and move
down his shaft, slowly at first, exploring him with
my tongue, lifting up and looking at him, so I see
the tortured look on his features. I take him deep this
time, faster, and bring my hand to his base, moving
in time with my mouth, fast.

'Imogen, fuck, do you have any idea what you're
doing to me?'

I don't stop.

'I'm so fucking close,' he groans, moving down
in the seat a little further.

I move my hand down a little, cupping his balls,
and then I take his cock into my mouth completely,
so I taste him right at the back of my throat.

His hand comes to my head, his fingers there
light, no pressure, more as though he just needs to
hold onto something. To me.

My stomach does a funny little dive.

I move faster, and now his hand on my hair is almost pulling me away.

'I'm going to come,' he says, warning in his voice.

I flicker my eyes to his, a smile on my lips.

His eyes narrow. 'You're sure?'

In response, I take him inside me with a fevered
intensity so I feel the beginning of his spasm, the
urgency of his movements as his hips lift a little so
he thrusts into my open mouth, his hand on my arse,
his fingers digging into my flesh as he begins to spill

his seed. I keep him deep, I take him all, I hold him while he loses his control, and he holds me, his hands on my body as if he can't possibly take them off.

It is the hottest thing I've ever done—and it's just the beginning.

CHAPTER EIGHT

'The Orville-Greens are coming, and the Weiss-inghams too.'

My father lists two families who have daughters a few years younger than I am. 'The Sinclairs, Morialtos, Lyons.'

I grip the phone more tightly, telling myself not to react.

I've been expecting this.

'It's going to be a New Year to remember. A new beginning.'

I expel a harsh breath, reaching for my coffee. It's a bleak, grey day, and I have more to do than I can put into words.

'Anyway, we can go over the details at Christmas. You're still planning to be home for Christmas?'

I hear the apprehension in his voice and a fissure of sympathy opens up inside my impatient chest. Because at the root of all his bluster, my dad is worried. He's worried about the family's future, he's worried about the fact they're getting older and have no grandchildren, and he's worried about me—that I'm going to waste my life with a string of different women, never doing the 'responsible' thing and taking up the reins of the Rothsmore estate.

'Great.' It's too curt. I soften it slightly. 'Yeah, I'll be there. How's Mother?'

'Planning the party, you know.' My father's tone is a little weary. 'In her element.'

It's true. My mother is never happier than when she has a social event looming, particularly in the grounds of Becksworth Hall. I can just picture it, strung with fairy lights, marquees set up with braziers of fire to keep guests warm; an orchestra serenading people as they arrive; a field given over to cars and helicopters; the guest rooms full to the brim.

And this time, a bevy of eligible women for me to choose a bride.

The thought bothers me more than it should. I've known this was coming. I'm almost thirty—how long did I expect I could put this off for?

Out of nowhere, I think of Saffron, of how against our union I was at the start, how much I resented being set up and pushed into a relationship by my parents. It had felt wrong at the start, but we'd been well matched. They'd been right.

Well, half-right.

Saffy hadn't seen the appeal, evidently.

That was five years ago and I'm different now. I have no intention of getting involved with anyone I don't feel I'm compatible with. I'm not looking for love this time. That's where I went wrong with Saffron; I see it clearly now. I bought into a fairy tale, a myth, where I should have simply seen it as a dynastic union, just as Imogen said.

Imogen.

Out of nowhere, my storm clouds lift and I'm smiling, my eyes sweeping shut so all I can see is her pale blonde head descending on my cock, feel the sweeping warmth of her mouth around my flesh, the flicker of her tongue, impatient and hungry, teasing me to a desperate release.

'Dad, I have to go.'

'But—'

'Later.'

I disconnect the call and surrender to the memory, pushing back in my leather chair, staring at the ceiling of my office, my body harder than black diamonds. Imogen is everywhere—my memory, my mind, my senses, my soul.

The blow job in the cockpit was just the beginning. Neither of us was sated by that release, as fucking amazing as it was. I reach for my phone on autopilot, flicking open our chat window.

I can't stop thinking about you and your extraordinarily talented mouth.

I smile as I send the message.

A minute later, she responds.

My mouth and I are glad to hear it.

My smile stretches. I drink my coffee, but half an hour later I send her another message on the spur of the moment.

Busy later?

I see three little dots appear as she starts to type, then they disappear.

It's a few hours before she messages back.

What do you have in mind?

My gut kicks. Dating. We're dating. Not just fucking, though that's a given.

I'll pick you up at seven?

Another surprise?

Great question. What shall we do? I look towards the windows, which frame a panoramic view of Wall Street. The sky is woolly. It's freezing too. I can think of one surefire way to stave off coldness.

Dating, idiot. Dating.

I open up a browser and type in a few questions. Five entries down, the search engine has provided the perfect solution for me. I type a message.

Yes. Bring a bikini.

;) Have you looked outside?

Trust me.

She doesn't reply.

I click on the link and open the booking form,

then place my phone down, thoughts of Imogen and the night ahead already making the idea of an afternoon's work damned near impossible.

Seven o'clock can't come soon enough.

I love to swim. I was on my college team, and it's one of the few activities I regularly make time for. There's something about it I find meditative and calming, and I find being underwater, away from noise and other people, is also an excellent opportunity for deep thinking. I have at least three quarters of my ideas while submerged in my apartment complex's huge swimming pool.

Usually, I wear a one-piece, a habit that's a hangover from my college team days.

But for tonight, I've chosen a barely there string bikini, bright red. It felt bizarre pulling it out of the drawer given the weather—we're in the midst of a cold snap that feels as if it'll never end.

But his premise has intrigued me.

More than I wanted it to. I had a huge afternoon with some investors in the charity and I had to concentrate—almost impossible with my phone buzzing in my pocket and the memories of a few nights ago shifting against me.

I'm wearing the bikini beneath a black jersey dress and a floor-length trench coat, with a pair of gold stilettos. My hair is pinned into a bun high on my head, loose and casual.

The buzzer sounds and I move towards it. 'I'll be right down.'

'Okay.' Even that single word made up of two

syllables, spoken through telephone cabling at a distance of forty odd floors of concrete, has the power to double the speed of my pulse.

I grab my bag and sling it over my shoulder, moving quickly to the elevator.

Mr Silverstein looks at me thoughtfully as I click my way across the marbled lobby.

'Good evening, Miss Carmichael.'

'Hi, Mr Silverstein. Keeping warm?' I nod to the inclement weather—it's dark now, but the glass has a frost to it showing that the temperature is arctic.

'As warm as can be, ma'am. Out again?'

I nod, my eyes darting to the revolving door. I see his dark car parked right outside. My heart soars. 'Yeah.'

'Take care, miss.'

I smile, because for the first time in years, I'm doing exactly that. Taking care of myself. My needs. My wants. Things I hadn't even realised I felt or needed to tend to. And, sure, in three weeks there'll be the Christmas gala ball and this will end, and my time with Nicholas Rothsmore will be like an island in my life, girt by water and isolation on all sides, but it will still be there—a month of hazy, heady sex, of total indulgence and hedonism, a secret, joyous letting down of my hair.

'Goodnight.'

He opens the door for me and I don't look back.

Nicholas steps out of the car as soon as I appear on the pavement, his eyes crinkling at the corners with the force of his smile. 'Did you bring your swimming costume?'

'Did you expect me to be wearing only a swimsuit?' I tease. 'It's kind of cold, or hadn't you noticed?'

He pulls me to him abruptly, suddenly, jerking my body to his and wrapping his arms around my midsection so I'm tight to his hardness, contoured perfectly. 'Is it?'

Heat belies my statement. I feel it as surely as if the sun had burst out from the other side of the earth, channelling the heat of a few weeks ago, in Sydney.

He releases me just as abruptly, but not before he's placed a quick kiss on my forehead—just enough to send need lurching through me.

'You look beautiful.'

'Thank you.'

He opens the back door to his limo and I step in, noting there's a small box of my favourite champagne truffles on the back seat.

Once we're in and the car is moving, he hands them over.

'For me?'

He grins. 'Second date.'

'Ah.' I take them, dipping my head forward with a smile. 'Perfect.'

'Never date a guy who doesn't bring you truffles.'

'Duly noted.'

'How are you?'

His question, so simple—just a basic function of civility and etiquette—etches through me because of the way in which he asks it. As if he really cares about the answer.

'Good. Busy day. You?'

'Less busy than it should have been, thanks to some very distracting fantasies I struggled to ignore.'

My ego bursts, higher than an eagle. 'Lovely.'

'Yes, just what I was thinking.'

'Are you wearing trunks as well?'

He nods.

'So we're going swimming?'

'Later.'

'Seriously?'

'Yep.'

I laugh. 'International Man of Mystery?'

'Something like that.'

Curiosity grows. Even when the car slows to a stop, I have no idea where we are or where we're going. The door is opened by a driver, Edward, I think Nicholas had said his name was.

'Thanks.' I look around for any kind of clue. There's nothing.

'This way.' Nicholas puts a hand in the small of my back and leads me to a black door in a brick wall.

'I feel like you're taking me to some kind of Mafia hideout.'

His laugh dances across my spine like tiny little needles. 'More fun, less chance of death.'

'Glad to hear it.'

The door opens as we approach; presumably there's a security camera monitoring activity.

A woman wearing a sleek black dress greets us. 'Mr Rothsmore?'

He nods.

'Welcome to Uden Syn.' She pronounces the name with an accent, but even if she hadn't, the words would still have meant nothing to me.

'Miss Carmichael?' She holds a hand out for my coat. Nicholas's hands are at my shoulders, helping me out of it. A frisson of anticipation warms my belly.

In fact, I'm warm all over, and while that might have something to do with Nicholas, it's also this place. We're in a small corridor, dimly lit, but very, very warm. The heating must be switched to full.

'Do you have your phone?'

Nicholas offers his and she waves it over a device in her pocket. 'Your phone will now open the door to your room. Take your clothes off and leave them in the locker provided, then head in.'

Alarm has me jolting my eyes to Nicholas's. I did give him a blow job in the cockpit of the helicopter, and we did sleep together in the Intimate Rooms of the Sydney club, but that's a far cry from engaging in some kind of public orgy.

'Is this some kind of sex club?' I demand in a low whisper as he guides me down the corridor.

When we reach a door with the number eleven on it, he shoots me a look before swiping his phone.

'I'm serious, Nicholas,' I whisper despite the fact we're now alone in an elegant if somewhat utilitarian room. It's big enough for a chair, a wardrobe, and, as with the corridor, it's dimly lit and super warm.

'Do you think I'd bring you to a sex club?' he prompts with a lifted brow, shifting out of his shirt. The subtle lighting casts his handsome face in shadow, highlighting the planes and angles there.

'I don't know.'

He kicks out of his shoes. 'Public sex isn't really my thing.'

'It isn't?'

'Well, public sex with *you* could be,' he says with a slow wink. 'But not sharing you with other people. This isn't an orgy.'

I'm relieved, though, ultimately, not surprised. He wouldn't bring me somewhere like that. Not without talking to me first. I don't know what came over me.

I smile, relaxing and surrendering to this once more.

It takes us a minute to get undressed. His trunks are black briefs that perfectly cup and display his impressive cock, his tight ass. I can't help but stare, and he clearly notices, if his grin is anything to go by.

'Let's go.' He takes my hand in his and I fight an urge to tell him I'd rather stay. Right here. The chair looks sturdy enough to take us both.

When we push into the next room, it takes my eyes a second to adjust, and then to compute what they're seeing. We're not alone, but it's not some weird sex club thing—put your keys in the bowl. There's low, throbbing music surrounding us, and about twelve other people are dotted through the room, paired off, and painting each other. The only light in here is a black light, and the paint comes up as neon, glow-in-the-dark, on their bodies. And they're painted *all over*.

I'm bowled over. This looks *fun*. And different.

'Welcome, Mr Rothsmore. Here's your station, this way.' Someone appears wearing a bright outfit so they're visible, their teeth gleaming bright blue. He guides us across the room to a table with a shining line around it to delineate it is set up with paints. Each has an iridescent dot for accessibility.

'This is seriously cool,' I say appreciatively, after the waiter has gone through the rules and explained how it all works. A minute later, a bright bottle of wine is brought and two glasses, etched with paint so we can see them clearly in the room.

'Who first?' Nicholas teases.

'You.' I smile, and he returns it—I can tell because his teeth almost blind me.

I reach for one of the brushes and some paint, staring slowly, putting some paint on his cheek.

'How does it feel?' My eyes dart to his.

'Cold and mushy.'

I grin. 'It was your idea.'

'I may need to rethink it.'

'No, don't. I like it.' I smile again, dotting some paint over his shoulder. In just my bikini, my breasts are tingling, straining against the insufficient material. I work my way across his back, swirling paint—

different colours throw different lights in here—and then lower, to the expanse of flesh just above the waistband of his bathers. I feel his breath grow shallow, and I can't resist curving my hand around to his front, feeling his cock, secure in the anonymity the darkness of the room affords.

He's hard, and I'm not surprised. Being this close, touching without touching, is seriously hot. There's even something about the paint, its wetness, the sound of it against his body, the gentle persistence of colouring his skin, that has me aching for him.

I slip my hand inside his trunks and I feel his breath snag. 'I thought you weren't into public sex,' he observes, *sotto voce.*

'So did I.' But I pull my hand out of his pants, snaking it over his chest, to a just-painted nipple. I tweak it and then pull away, laughing softly at the paint on my fingertips.

'Caught, red-handed,' I quip.

He grabs my hand in his and holds it towards my chest, running my fingers down my abdomen, towards my own bikini briefs. At the elastic, he steps closer, and drops his head so he can whisper in my ear, 'Later tonight, I want to watch you get yourself off.'

Pleasure vibrates through my gut.

'I… I haven't ever done that before.' I'm glad he can't see the mad flush in my cheeks. 'In front of someone else, I mean.'

'Don't worry, I'll be there to lend you a hand if

you need it,' he promises, and I want to go, I want to have him, now.

But he's intent on torturing me, clearly, because when he starts to paint my body, he's so much better, slower, more devastatingly sensual than I was with him. He drags the paintbrush but with a feather-light touch, so I want to beg him to press harder. He trails a hint of colour over my shoulders, my arms, then back up to under my arms and the flesh at the side of my breast, so I make a soft whimpering sound. I see his smile, but it's just a flash, then he's back to concentrating.

I reach for a glass of wine while he works, needing to do something to steady my fluttering nerves.

He kneels at my feet, his mouth so close to my clit that I ache to push forward, to feel him there, his lips against me—knowing that it will come tonight. Later. Soon.

He drags the brush higher, lightly, over my calves, to my knees, the backs of my knees, my inner thighs, and as he paints with one hand, in the cover of the room's darkness, he uses his other to push aside the Lycra of my briefs and slide a finger inside my wet, pulsing heat. I gasp, loudly, so he freezes, looking up at me.

'Not. A. Sound.'

The words ring with a quiet authority I don't think of ignoring. I don't want to. I nod, gripping the wine glass and taking another fortifying sip before assuming a position that I hope seems normal.

As he moves the paintbrush over my legs, he moves his finger inside me, and I resist an urge—just—to buck back and forth. This isn't designed to get me off. He's teasing me—again. Torturing me. He knows how close I am to exploding and yet he's pulling away, his touch too light, too brief.

'Nicholas…' His name comes from my lips like a snatch of need. I hear my desperation and am unable to care.

'Yes, Imogen?' His smile shifts over his face.

'Please.' Just a simple word, but it means everything because I need him in a way that had bowled me over. I thought one night would be enough. I thought *once* would be enough, but it wasn't. It couldn't be.

'You want this?' he murmurs, moving his finger back inside me. No, two fingers now, and it's instantly more fulfilling, more promising, but still…

I nod, running my hands through his hair. He draws the brush around my back, kneeling higher now, blocking me more from sight, so I do what I'd wanted earlier and move my hips to get greater purchase, to feel more of him.

'You have to be patient,' he teases, except I can hear his own urgency and I get it. He wants me as badly as I want him.

'That's physically impossible.'

His laugh is low and husky. 'Then I probably shouldn't tell you that I plan to take you home and fuck you until your voice is hoarse?'

'Oh, God.' The promise is so erotic. 'What else?'

'How I'm going to run my tongue along here…' he draws his fingers out and in '…to taste you as you come? How I'm going to make you come again and again and I'm going to watch you, listen to you begging me for more, begging me until you can't think straight.'

'I'm already there,' I promise throatily.

His laugh is a dismissal. 'You only think you are, Imogen. Believe me, it gets worse.'

He is right.

We stay for another hour, and by the time we leave, my body is in a state of sensual torture. There's no helicopter waiting for us tonight. We take his car, and I don't sit too close because I feel as if one touch, now we're alone, will result in a complete explosion, and a short car ride isn't the place to satisfy that. I sit on the edge of my seat, staring out of the window at New York, the invisible paint we'd used in the black-lit room dry now and any hint of it concealed by the clothes we've put back on.

But not being able to see something doesn't remove the evidence of it and I feel every brush stroke in the fibres of my soul.

The driver brings the car into a basement garage and I expel a sigh of relief that Nicholas clearly hears, if his soft laugh is anything to go by.

But I'm not amused.

I'm alive with feelings that are new to me and seriously intense.

I am fuelled by a hunger that I insist on owning.

Edward opens the doors and we step out, my smile polite, my mind elsewhere.

We reach the elevator and the doors open after only a second. I contemplate jumping him but for the same reason I resisted in the car, I keep my distance now, aware that he's watching me, trying to decode me.

He has no idea what he's unleashed.

But he's about to find out.

The doors ping open into his apartment and the details I recall from last time flitter in my mind once more—the triple-height ceilings, a wall of pure glass, a balcony overlooking Central Park with a swimming pool and a hot tub. I know from the tour he gave me last time that there's an indoor squash court down the corridor, a yoga studio he's converted into a gym, four bedrooms, five bathrooms and two separate staff rooms, which he has vacant.

'I don't like living with other people, even if they're at the end of the corridor.'

I get his point. I hate it too. I have a cleaner who comes once a fortnight and that suits me just fine.

As soon as the front door clicks shut, I turn around to face him, my breath dragged from my lungs, the rasping sound filling the elegant Jeffersonian lobby.

'Didn't you say you were going to fuck me so hard I couldn't speak?' I demand, crossing my arms over my chest.

His expression shows surprise but only for a moment, then he's sweeping across the tiles, scooping me up over one shoulder as if I weigh nothing and carrying me to my heaven, my desperation, the sweetest torture I've ever known—his bedroom.

CHAPTER NINE

'OH, MY GOD.'

I must have fallen asleep. I push up onto my elbows to find Nicholas watching me, that unbearably sexy grin on his too-handsome face, and my heart does a painful little catapult against my ribs.

'What time is it?' I reach across the bed for his wrist and the platinum gold watch he always wears. 'It's seven o'clock? Why didn't you wake me?'

I push the sheet back, looking around for my underpants before remembering I only have paint-smeared bikini bottoms to put on. And they're in the lounge.

'Because it was more fun to watch you sleep,' he says, his voice frustratingly relaxed despite my obvious panic.

And I'm panicking, for no reason I can easily pinpoint. Yes, I need to get to work, yes, I have meetings in an hour. But it's more than that.

For some reason, spending the night feels like crossing a line that mentally I wasn't willing to cross. It is a bigger surrendering of myself than I

intended. Another line in the sand, one I hadn't realised I wanted to abide by.

'I'm serious, Nic.' The diminutive of his name
slips out, but not for the first time. As soon as I say
it I have a vivid recollection of crying the shortened
version of his name over and over again, as pleasure
racked my body in a way I almost couldn't process.

'You got somewhere you have to be?'

I pull a face. 'It's seven o'clock on a Wednesday
morning. What do you think?'

'I think you should cancel it and come back to
bed,' he murmurs, patting the matte black sheets.
As a further enticement, he pushes the sheet back,
revealing his rock-hard, naked body.

Predictably, my insides squeeze. And despite my
panic, a smile spreads over my face. 'I can't,' I say,
in an almost whining tone. 'Help me find my bikini.'

His laugh is low, a rumble. 'Oh, no, Miss Anonymous. I have no intention of aiding your escape. In
fact, if I had my way, you'd be tied to this bed so I
could have my very evil way with you some more.'

Okay.

I have meetings. But there's also this. I stop looking for my bathers and give Nicholas the full force
of my attention. At his mention of tying me up, I remember something from our night in Sydney.

'You ordered handcuffs.'

He lifts a brow, his expression teasing, silently
prompting me to continue.

'In Sydney.' Heat blooms in my face. 'You had

handcuffs put in the toy chest,' I remind him. 'But we didn't…'

He stands up, his dick at a ninety-degree angle to the rest of him, his haunches so strong and capable. 'Yes?'

He likes teasing me. I get it. I suck in a breath and assume my very best kickass CEO expression. 'We didn't use handcuffs.'

'No.' He shrugs nonchalantly, his naked body next to mine now.

'Why not?' It's breathy—all of me is consumed by his closeness.

'I wasn't sure you were ready.'

Indignation flares inside me. 'Oh, really?'

'Hmm,' he agrees, and then he's lifting me up, wrapping my legs around his waist and carrying me easily through his bedroom to the tiled adjoining bathroom.

'What are you doing?' Though it's self-explanatory when he flicks on the shower taps and steps past the wide glass wall.

'Helping you get ready for work.' He grins, and when he eases me onto his cock, I give up pretending I want to be anywhere but here.

'I thought we were talking about handcuffs,' I murmur as water douses me from overhead, plastering my hair to my face.

'Let's see.' His eyes probe mine and then he takes another step so my back connects with the tiled wall and one of his hands captures both of my wrists, pinning them over my head. It's just him, and yet his grip is vice-like. I couldn't easily wriggle free, even if I wanted to.

There's a challenge on his features as he thrusts inside me and there's something almost painfully erotic about not being able to touch him. I surrender to the strength of this feeling as he thrusts hard and deep, filling me, awakening barely rested needs.

My ankles dig into his back and I hold on as though my life depends on it until I'm coming around him. I go to pull my hands free but he shakes his head, dropping his mouth to my breasts and pulling one of my tight, sensitive nipples between his teeth. I shake all over, the pleasure doing funny things to me.

My orgasm is intense, and even as I come he continues to torment my breasts and hold my arms high above my head so there is no reprieve from the pleasure, no relief from this insanity.

I drop my head to his shoulder as my tortured breath ravages my body and then he's easing my feet to the floor, pulling out of me gently, letting my arms go all at once. It's a strange desertion. He's still rock hard.

'You didn't…finish,' I murmur, hating that I can still feel so embarrassed after all we've shared.

'Mmm…' he murmurs, biting my earlobe. 'As much as my parents are desperate for me to get married and have kids, I don't think they have a New York–based heir in mind.'

'Oh, my God.' It is a shocking wake-up call. 'I didn't even think…'

'I did. A bit too late,' he says with a self-deprecating shake of his head.

'I'm on the pill,' I say, to reassure myself as much as him.

'And I'm clean.' He shrugs. 'Still, I'd rather not take the risk.'

Why does that make my gut clench—and not in a good way?

I paste a smile on my face and reach for the body wash. 'And now, I really do have to get ready for work.'

He runs his mouth over my cheek, capturing my lips, his smile sweet and slow. 'Coffee?'

My heart lurches. 'Thanks.'

I lather myself all over, my body so completely raw and tender that everywhere I touch is like an erotic shadow of last night. My breasts are pink from the brush of his stubble, my inner thighs too, and I have a row of hickeys across my hip, leading towards my buttocks.

He was right to pull out, not to come. He's sure as hell right to protect us from any unwanted consequences.

But just the mention of that has made me think about a future that I would have said, two weeks ago, I don't actually want. A future filled with the laugh of a small person, the dependence of a child, the love of a little one.

I'm not maternal—I have no idea what being maternal even looks like, since my mother wasn't and I suspect I'm even less so. I don't have anything to go on. And yet, at the mention of little Rothsmore heirs, something very close to my ovaries fired to life in a way that has taken my breath away.

Thank God we agreed this was just going to last a month. I can't imagine much worse than being with Nicholas Rothsmore for real, allowing myself to do something really stupid and fall in love with him.

And there is such a risk there, because he's too good at this. He's charming and funny, sophisticated and smart, so damned thoughtful and, as for his bedroom prowess, there's no need to wonder why he's earned the nickname 'the Playboy of Manhattan'.

But only a fool would fall in love with Nicholas Rothsmore, and I'm no fool. Reassured, I step out of the shower and towel myself down. When I step into his bedroom, my eyes are transfixed firstly by the stunning view of Central Park, and then by a bag on the foot of the bed. I recognise the distinctive thick black paper with the embossed white logo. Curious, I reach in and pull out a lingerie twin set. My smile hurts my cheeks.

Pale cream and the most delicate lace, it antagonises my already sensitive body, the lace so raw on my nipples that I gasp as I move, every single shift of my flesh reminding me of his possession of my body.

I suspect this is something he foresaw.

When I slip into the kitchen a few minutes later, his knowing smile confirms my suspicions.

'Thank you for this.' I wave a hand over my flesh.

He shrugged. 'It seemed like a wise precaution, given the whole paint-on-body situation.'

'I didn't mean to fall asleep,' I say, reaching for the coffee. He's made it black, which is strange, because that's just how I have it. I sip it and let out a small moan of appreciation.

'Good?' he prompts over the rim of his own mug.

'Shh,' I tease. 'Let me drink this, then we'll talk.'

We drink our coffee in silence, my little ritual one I'm glad to observe, even side by side with Nicholas.

'I didn't mean to stay over,' I reiterate, a few minutes later, placing the empty coffee cup in the sink.

'Why?'

'I just didn't plan on it.' I shrug.

'We were up *late*.' He says the word with emphasis.

I think it was about two when I last saw the time. 'I remember.'

'It would have been kind of dumb to slink home at that hour.'

'Nonetheless,' I murmur, my voice a little icy, 'I prefer to sleep in my own bed.'

His face shifts with something like amusement and then he shrugs. 'Sure, if you'd like.'

I'm slightly mollified, but not completely. Our conversation from earlier sits inside me like the sharp edge of a blade and I can't really say why.

'Do you have much on today?'

'Yeah.' I nod, looking around for my clothes. They're arranged on the edge of a chair. I stride to them, pulling the dress on over my head only to find him watching me with a small smile on his face. My blood pounds through me. 'You?'

'Sure.' He shrugs. 'But I'd like to see you tonight.'

Tonight. Pleasure sounds in my head, pleasure so intense it almost drowns out the warning bells. Because he is ever so slightly too much for me to handle. Because I would fully believe it if a doctor told me he had the addictive properties of a drug and that I was already way over quota.

'Not tonight,' I say, shifting into my coat, then looking around for my handbag. It's on the kitchen bench. I lift it over my shoulder, checking I have everything.

'Tomorrow night?'

My heart is hammering. I keep my head bent so he doesn't see the way I'm shaking. 'I'll message you.'

He nods, a frown on his face that he quickly erases.

'I don't have my bikini,' I say, when I reach the door.

'Leave them. Next time, we'll use the hot tub.'

It conjures images that are too hot to forget.

I smile and nod, pushing down on my doubts as to the wisdom of this. 'Sounds fun.' I lift up and press a kiss to his lips then turn and walk away, needing a bit of space and a bit of time.

And maybe he gets that, because I don't hear from him at all that day. Nor the next. By Friday afternoon I'm starting to worry I've done something stupid and ruined this.

And it is truly the best sex I've ever had, but, more than that, I'm having fun.

Why did I get so bogged down in worrying about the future when we've both been clear about what we do and don't want?

Because I'm a worrier. It's what I do. If it were a job, I'd be supremely qualified.

Before I can regret it, I pull my phone out of my handbag and pull up our message chat.

Is it my turn to plan a date?

I have a pounding in my throat as I send it, and a nervousness that seems somewhat ridiculous. But when he hasn't replied an hour later, I'm having to fight not to send another text.

It's six o'clock when finally a message buzzes in.

What a day. Hot tub? Beer? Takeout?

My smile is so huge I feel as if it's splitting my face in two.

Perfect. See you soon?

His answer is immediate.

The sooner the better.

I breathe out, relief rushing through me. Everything's fine; nothing to worry about, whatsoever.

CHAPTER TEN

THREE DAYS AND I feel as though I haven't seen her in three years. It's just like that first godawful week, after Sydney, when I had no idea who the fuck Miss Anonymous really was and I worried I might never learn. That I might never see her again, nor know the pleasure of her beautiful, sensual body.

I am beyond impatient.

I have had to fight hard not to message her, but I had the feeling when she left on Wednesday morning that she needed a bit of space, and the last thing I want is to pressure her. This is all about fun—for her and for me.

Fortunately, things exploded at work, which kept me busy. Still, I must have checked my phone eleven billion times. My bed smells like her, sweet and lightly fragranced, so I have lain awake at night and remembered *everything* we shared.

She arrives a little after seven and I prowl to the door, buzzing her up and waiting impatiently.

When she walks in, I groan and pull her into my arms, smiling as I kiss her, holding her tight to my body, breathing her in, tasting her, feeling her, needing her, wanting her, loving this.

'Hey.' My greeting, minutes later, is gruff.

'Hey yourself.' Hers is breathless.

I want to drag her to bed and never leave, but already the sex thing is taking over from what was meant to be a casual flirtation, some harmless dating fun.

I have to slow that down a bit, as much as that idea is akin to scrubbing my skin with acid.

'What do you feel like?'

Her cheeks rush with pink in that way she has.

'For dinner,' I clarify, grinning, anticipation tightening my gut, and in all parts of me, as I look forward to how I know this night will end.

'Oh.' She bites down on her lower lip; I brush my thumb over her flesh, so she parts her mouth and bites the pad of my thumb instead. 'Pizza?'

'A girl after my own heart.'

'There's a great place just a few blocks away.'

'I'll get delivery.' I move towards the kitchen bench, lifting my phone and loading the app. I place an order for a few different ones. When I turn around, she's stripped down to her underwear, her eyes locked to mine with an intensity that almost bowls me over.

'Hot tub?'

Hell to the yeah. I nod, affecting an air of calm nonchalance. 'Go ahead. It's warm. I'll grab some beers.'

I hear her squawk as she steps out onto the balcony—it's just below zero out there. I turn around just in time to see her running across the tiles and up the one step before sliding in over the edge, so just her head bobs up. The relief on her face takes my breath away.

So does the fact she's here, in my penthouse, her smile, her eyes, her body, her laugh.

I spin away and yank out some beers, cracking the tops of them as I walk, placing hers on the edge of the hot tub.

'Oh, thank God, it's real beer.'

'What did you expect?'

'Tepid lager?' she says with an impish grin.

I laugh, stripping out of my clothes, down to my jocks, and stepping over the edge of the spa. She's watching me with undisguised hunger and my dick reacts accordingly.

'It did take me a while but it turns out I've developed a taste for your beer.'

She sips from her bottle, moving to one of the seats on the edge of the tub. Manhattan sparkles beneath us, an array of little tiny lights that make up a thriving island metropolis.

'Do you think you'll miss it?'

'American beer?'

'New York,' she corrects, smiling.

'Yeah.' I'm surprised by how deep the word comes out, and troubled seeming.

'I can't imagine not living here,' she says, simply.

'You don't miss home?'

'LA?' Her face is one of disgust. 'I miss it during the winter,' she says after a second. 'And I miss some people. And I guess there's always a nostalgia for where you grew up, so that on certain days I find myself thinking about the way the light would hit my bedroom wall, and I long to go back. Not to LA but to when I was a teenager and everything was so much simpler.'

It's a fascinating statement.

'In what way is your life no longer simple?'

'Are you kidding? My life is a study in clean simplicity,' she says with a self-deprecating smile. 'No mess, no fuss, no complications. I mean that people aren't simple. Life is messy and complicated, no matter how hard you try to fight that. I can control only so much, you know?'

'You sound like someone who's been hurt,' I prompt with curiosity, swimming across to her and taking the seat right beside her, careful not to touch because touching Imogen invariably leads to much, much more.

'Not really.' But she's lying.

'Imogen?'

Her eyes fix to mine, her pupils huge, swallowing up almost all of her icy blue. 'I'm just speaking generally,' she says unconvincingly, after a lengthy pause.

There's more to it, I'm sure of it. 'As you get older,' I say, sipping my beer, 'things do get more complex.'

'Yes.' She smiles, a little uneasily. 'You come to understand people and their motivations better.'

We're quiet a moment, reflective.

'So what happens when you go home?' It's a clunky attempt to change the topic but I let it go. My wheels are turning, wondering what she was thinking about a minute ago, and we'll come back to it later, when she's a little more relaxed, less guarded.

'What do you mean?'

'I mean, do you become the Playboy of London?'

Frustration nips at my heels, a frustration that's hard to fathom. 'No, I expect not.'

'I can't really see you hanging up your bachelor shoes.'

'It's been five years since what would have been my wedding day,' I say with a shrug. 'Five years of the kind of pace of life that would wear anyone down.'

'You're over it?'

I shake my head, surprised to realise that I'm speaking the truth. 'I'm ready for the next phase of my life.'

Her eyes skim my face, perhaps trying to see if I'm being honest.

'I wouldn't necessarily be going home,' I continue, 'if it weren't for my father's demands.'

'Demands?' she prompts, moving to close the space between us. 'You don't seem like someone *anyone* could make demands of.'

'His insistence, then.'

'Same deal.' She laughs softly.

'He's my father,' I point out. 'He holds a certain power.'

'I can understand that,' she says, her forehead crinkling with her frown. 'Even when I'm some-one who's turned disobedience into an art form.' It's said lightly, with a curve of her lips, but I feel there's more to it.

'You? Miss Strait-Laced?'

'Do I really seem that strait-laced to you?' she points out with a slow, tempting wink.

'Not in bed,' I assure her. 'But everywhere else.'

She opens her mouth but closes it again, grimac-ing slightly.

'That wasn't a criticism.'

'I know. And you're right. This...' she waves from her chest to mine, inadvertently drawing my gaze downwards '...is the craziest thing I've done in years—probably since I put as much of my trust fund as I could get my hands on into the charity.'

So many questions fire in my mind. 'So how have you disobeyed your parents?' I ask the question in a voice that rings with amusement because I think she's probably, at twenty-nine, beyond the point of giving too much of a shit what her mom and dad think of her. And yet, look at me. A grown man, the same age, about to leap the Atlantic to placate my father's expectations of me.

'In every way,' she says simply. 'My life is a study in parental disappointment.'

'Surely not.' I'm not joking now. 'Look at what you've achieved. They must be proud of you?'

'Proud?' She shakes her head on a small laugh. 'Proud is what they would have been if I'd married the CEO of Alpine Moor TV at twenty-three, like they wanted. Proud is what they'd be if I'd pursued the modelling career my mom desperately tried to line up for me. Proud is what they'd be if I'd stayed home in LA and troubled myself with my mom's hospital benefits.'

'But you're doing something so much bigger,' I point out. 'Look at the business you've built, and the charity you're funding.'

'Yes, but I deal with underprivileged kids, which is definitely not the kind of charity my mom thinks I should be championing.'

'No?'

'Oh, no. My mom would much rather I raise money to help embattled hedge-fund managers maintain their country club memberships.'

She's being sarcastic but I feel her resentment burning from her in waves, her hatred for wealth and society, her derision for its constructs evident.

'A charity's a charity,' I say simply.

'I used to think that too.' Her smile is wistful. 'I used to be so proud of my mom and dad and the work they did. Or the work I *thought* they did. My mom was forever organising benefits, fundraising, sponsoring events.' She shakes her head mournfully.

'Ironically, I probably got some of my philanthropic aspirations from Mom.'

'Why is that ironic?'

'Because, as I got older, I realised that my mom and dad really only cared about supporting the causes that *sounded* good. They wouldn't go near domestic violence or women's shelters, nothing to do with providing homeless women with sanitary items. My mom was *mortified* when I suggested any such thing.'

Her words zing with anger, despite the fact we're talking about events that transpired a long time ago.

'Then there was the time I tried to fundraise for a charity that buys groceries for families on food stamps. My mom honestly threatened to disown me.' Her smile is just a tight imitation.

'I'd like to say I'm surprised,' I say, eventually. 'But that kind of attitude is pretty prevalent.'

'Yeah, only amongst the very, very wealthy.'

'Not everyone feels that way.'

'A lot do.' She shrugs. 'And I hate it.'

'I can tell.'

She looks at me appraisingly for several beats. 'Can I tell you something? In confidence?'

It annoys me that she even needs to check. 'Of course.'

'When I first built The Billionaires' Club, I used to get a perverse kind of pleasure from taking money from the super rich and funnelling it to support a cause most of them would be embarrassed to be associated with.'

'So the club was spite?' I murmur, a smile on my lips because it's so ridiculously badass I can't help loving that.

'No.' She shakes her head. 'It was five per cent spite.' And then she laughs, such a contrast to the mood of a moment ago that my insides glow with warmth.

'I think most of our membership is actually pretty cool. Sure, there are a few people who wouldn't know a social conscience if it grew legs and bit them on their jewelled rears,' she says with a flick of her brow. 'But I've been bowled over by some really amazing offers from some club members over the years. Chance wouldn't be what it is without the club. I can never resent the members for that.'

'Tell me about the charity.'

'What do you want to know?'

I don't really want to admit how little I know about it. I gather it's something to do with children, underprivileged children, but that's about it.

'Why start your own charity rather than working for one that's already up and running?'

'Control,' she answers, simply and passionately. 'And contacts. I have access to what the charity needs and I can cut out a lot of middlemen. Plus, I like to know that there's no top-heavy administrative board or whatever. I run everything. It's my baby, my project.'

Her passion is overwhelming.

'Why children?' I prompt conversationally, but her face tightens, her eyes flashing away from me. She reaches for her beer, and I know she's using it to buy time. I wait with the appearance of patience as she sips her drink. But I'm not letting her move on.

'Imogen?'

She's upset. Her features are strained, her eyes showing a depth of emotion that I didn't expect.

Still, I don't let it go.

'You must care a great deal to have poured so much energy into it.'

'Yes.' A whisper, barely.

There's more here. A story she's not telling me and, for some reason, it feels vitally important that I know it.

'Why?'

'It's important,' she says quietly, simply, turning to face me once more, her eyes showing a profound pain.

'Lots of things are important. Why this?'

'There are almost sixteen million kids in America living in abject poverty, and that's with an incredibly low poverty line. I founded Chance for them. Because everyone deserves a chance and it's by no means guaranteed that everyone will get one. Our luck in life is predetermined at birth. Not just by wealth, by lots of factors, but financial security is a cornerstone of success. And there are sixteen million kids here, in the States, who struggle to get enough food to survive. Forget about books and sports, holidays, the safety of a good home and the comfort of parents who aren't worried about how they're going to keep the lights on.'

Her voice cracks and the passion she feels overwhelms me and makes me feel like a selfish git, all at once.

'This is a developed country, the envy of the world, and we have this vulnerable subset of society doing it so tough. I met a girl at an event last month who cried because I gave her a double pass to see a movie. She's never been to the cinema before.' She swallows, her eyes filling with tears. I feel as if a cement block has been dropped right onto my heart. I didn't expect this. And I *hate* seeing her upset. I hate even more that I've done this to her.

'I'm sorry,' she mumbles, beating me to the apology I want to offer. 'I just get so frustrated. The Billionaires' Club enables me to pour a fortune into the charity every year, but it still never feels like enough.'

'I bet you're making a huge difference,' I contradict gently.

'Maybe. I just want more, and I want it now.'

I pull her closer, into my arms, and press a kiss to her eyelid, tasting her salty tears, wishing them gone.

'I had this friend,' she says quietly against my chest. 'Abbey.'

I'm still, waiting for her to go on. It's started to snow, lightly, so the contrast in temperatures out of the spa and in is marked.

'She died, when I was a teenager.'

'I'm sorry.'

I feel her expression shift and I suspect it's a grimace. 'We were really tight, growing up. She lived just a block away and we spent almost every weekend together.' Her voice is grim, despite what sounds like happy memories. 'And then, when I was fifteen, the news broke that her dad had been charged with a federal crime—embezzlement. He'd set up a Ponzi scheme and taken people for billions. It wasn't Abbey's fault, but her whole life went down the drain. Her mom left, hooked up with some Swiss athlete and moved to Europe, her dad was locked up.'

'Shit. The poor thing.'

'I did what I could.' She lifts her face to mine, and I can tell she's back in the past, more than a decade ago, but the pain is just as real as if it were happening now. 'I had a credit card I maxed to cover what I could. I snuck her into our pool house to live. We did that for three months and no one ever knew. Then my dad found her.' Fury lashes her face, her look one of utter rage. 'And called social services. I was forbidden to see Abbey ever again. My credit card was cut up.'

Her tears are back; my heart breaks for her, and her friend.

'She was like a sister to me, I thought she was like a daughter to them, but when she needed help, they wouldn't do a damned thing because they were so ashamed of what Abbey's dad had done.'

'Jesus.'

'She ended up in foster care, but it wasn't pretty.' She swallows, turning away from me, focussing on a high rise across the street. It glows like a candle on this black New York night. 'In fact, it was downright awful. Her first foster father turned out to be a victim of her dad's scheme. He used to hit her.'

My stomach drops. 'I hope she pressed charges.'

'No.' It's a pained sound. 'She died.'

'He killed her?' My own fury is intense.

'He might as well have. She was miserable. She drank a big bottle of his vodka then went to watch the sunrise over Malibu. She was found at the bottom of the cliffs a day later.' A small sob escapes her and she covers it by reaching for her beer. My heart is breaking for Abbey, but also for Imogen, who comes across as so incredibly cool and professional but is, actually, very soft-hearted.

'My parents didn't let me go to the funeral. I think they were actually glad she was dead. They'd been worried about what kind of scandal she might drag me into.' The fury is back and I infinitely prefer it to her grief. 'I hated them after that. I mean, they're my parents, so I love them too, but I don't respect them, and I don't like them, and I hate what they stand for—or, rather, what they were too afraid to stand for.'

'I can understand why you feel that way.'

'Three years after founding Chance, *The New York Times* ran a profile about me. It was very flattering, full of praise for what I was doing. That was the first time my parents publicly acknowledged my work. After that, they started to donate, and even got their hoity-toity friends—the same ones who helped ruin Abbey's life—to hold benefits to raise money. You have no idea how it stung to take that cash.'

'Why did you?'

She fixes me with a look that is simple and sad, a surrender to pragmatism. 'Because that money could stop twenty kids from doing what Abbey did. We fund counsellors for at-risk kids—not just in-person sessions and drop-in clinics, but twenty-four-hour phone banks. The charity needs every penny it can get—I will never not accept donations, even from people who are so hypocritical it makes me sick.'

I lift a hand, running a finger over her cheek, studying her, somehow committing her and this to memory, because in the back of my mind I'm aware of the ticking of a time bomb, counting down to my future, our lives beyond this.

'I'm sorry about your friend.'

Her expression shifts to one of sadness, and then wistfulness. 'Me too.' She sighs, sips her beer. 'I wish I could have done more.'

'It sounds like you tried.'

'Yeah.'

'And you're doing so much for other kids like her.'

She nods, and pushes a smile to her face. 'Wow. I really tanked the mood, huh?'

'I'm glad you told me.'

'I don't know why I did. I don't really talk about Chance to members of the club.'

And despite the seriousness of our conversation, I can't help smiling. 'Is that what I am?'

'Uh huh.' She pushes up onto my lap, straddling me in the spa. I like her like this. Close and pliant in my arms; her body fits so perfectly with mine.

'One of the first kids I funded, in the first year of Chance, has just graduated medical school.' Her smile is bright. 'She was on the brink of dropping out of school when I met her. In fact, she kind of gave me the idea. I wanted to help her—not a little bit. A lot. I wanted to make it easy for her to study. She was so bright, so bright, and she just couldn't get a leg-up. That's what Chance does. You have to bring the attitude and the hope, but we will make it possible for dreams to come true.'

'I think you're amazing.' The words come from me before I can stop them, and I wish I hadn't said it, because it's the kind of compliment I usually avoid giving women, for the sense it creates of things meaning more to me than they do. I'm usually more careful.

Fortunately, Imogen doesn't really react. She makes a little face, an expression of mock coyness, and then pulls away from me, kicking across the hot tub to the other side.

'This is a nice touch, Lord Rothsmore.' Her smile

is back, and my heart relaxes—I hadn't realised how much I wanted to see her smile again.

'What's that?' My voice is deep and gruff.

'The hot tub, the lights, the snow.'

'I'll take credit for the hot tub but the rest is just this city.'

'It's quite the bachelor pad.' She looks over her shoulder to the cavernous living space. 'I can see how you got the reputation for being the Playboy of Manhattan.'

She wiggles her brows, flirty and teasing, light-hearted, except I feel something decidedly heavy flick through me.

'I'm really not so bad.'

'No judgement.' She lifts her hands in front of her. 'I don't care.'

There it is again. What do I want? For her to be jealous? That's kind of petty.

And stupid, given that I'm moving home in a few weeks with every intention of turning my lifestyle on its head completely, meeting someone who I can see a future with. A future that will look nothing like this. I'm not looking for someone I can laugh with and make love to all night long.

'Do you ever think how different your life would have been if your fiancée hadn't…?'

'Left me at the altar in front of our nearest and dearest?'

She winces. 'That must have sucked.'

I laugh, just a short, sharp noise of agreement. 'That's one word for it.'

'I'm serious. You must have been livid.'

'I was many things.' I drain my beer and place it on the edge of the hot tub.

'Like?'

'Livid, sure. Hurt. Heartbroken.' I catch the speculation that sweeps across her expression. 'That surprises you?'

'No, of course not.'

'You don't think I have a heart?' I can't resist probing, my voice light.

'Why would you say that?'

'When I said I was heartbroken you looked surprised.'

She shakes her head. 'You were getting married. It goes without saying you were in love with her.'

I give Manhattan my full focus for a minute, studying the beautiful, sparkling high-rises. Something inside me pulls tight—the thought of leaving this behind is not something I relish, even though I know the time has come.

'I wasn't really.' The admission isn't one I've ever made, even to myself. 'I wanted to love her. I suppose I thought that loving her would mean my parents hadn't masterminded the marriage. That it would have come down to Saffy and me being right for each other.' I grimace. 'At least she figured it out before we made it official.'

Imogen sits up a little higher, so her beautiful

breasts in that lace bra float on the surface of the water.

'Do you think you'd still be married, if she hadn't?'

'Probably. I didn't love her but I liked her a lot, and I respected her. We enjoyed one another's company. Our marriage made sense.'

'Do you ever speak to her?'

'No. Not for any reason—but I bear her no animosity.'

'You're far kinder than I would be. I mean, to leave someone on their wedding day—'

Her indignation is palpable.

'You think she should have married me just to avoid creating a scene?'

'Well, no. I guess ideally she should have realised how she felt before it was your wedding day.'

'It was a hard decision to make. She thought the wedding day would come and she'd feel okay about it. She didn't. She didn't know until she was living it.'

'Still.' Imogen's lips twist with disapproval and I want to bottle this part of her—her indignation and spark are so uniquely her, she is incredibly fiery. 'She deserves for you to hate her.'

I grin. 'To what end?'

'Because she embarrassed you?'

'I'm not so easily embarrassed,' I say with a lift of my shoulders. 'It sucked at the time. It was pretty shitty. So I went and got hammered. I got laid. And then I got on with my life.'

Imogen's eyes flare wide and I feel as if she wants to say something, but then she lets out a small sigh. 'Selfishly, I'm very glad she didn't marry you. It's been very nice having you as my sex toy for a while.'

It's so completely not what I expect that I burst out laughing. I'm still laughing when she crosses the hot tub and sits in my lap, and I laugh right up until she kisses me. I stop laughing, and I kiss her right back.

CHAPTER ELEVEN

SEVEN DATES. WE'VE had seven dates and more soul-bursting orgasms than I can possibly keep track of. I shift in the bed and look at Nicholas with a feeling that is a lot like dread.

He's sleeping, lightly, and I can't really blame him. It's some time before dawn, the night wrapping around New York even as the city insists on twinkling with its sparkly lights. We went to a Broadway show last night and I teased him beforehand, that it was a bit predictable.

He insisted it was a quintessential New York date and that I hadn't really lived until I'd been taken to a Broadway show. I prepared to tease him all night, that it was cheesy or schmaltzy or something, but then he went and made it all 'next level' and I got caught up in the fairy tale of the whole thing.

When he came to pick me up from my place, he brought a single red rose and a box of chocolate truffles—he's very cleverly discovered how much I love them. We rode in his limousine with classical music playing, and, on arrival at the theatre, we were escorted to a private box where champagne and sushi were brought to us. We had our own butler for the duration. Afterwards, we walked back to his place, talking and laughing the whole way.

He was right.

It was a new experience, a different experience, and one I'm so glad to have shared with him. I mean, I've been to shows before, obviously, but never like that. It was…lovely.

No, that's so bland. It was perfection. It was heart-stopping.

As was what happened after. My body hums and sings with the pleasures I experienced. Pleasures he gave me like gifts, beautiful little explosions of delight that have weaved their way into my soul.

The Christmas gala is one week away. I'm looking down the barrel of workplace mayhem as I make sure everything is organised for our biggest event of the year. While every Billionaires' Club party is a big deal, this is the one that draws almost the entire membership. It is our biggest fundraiser, a night not to be missed, and every year there's an expectation that it will get bigger and better.

And I think this year will be pretty epic—but I can't risk anything going wrong. Ordinarily, I wouldn't let anything rob me of my focus. And yet, Nicholas definitely does that, and I wouldn't, for all the stars in the sky, put a premature end to this.

I'm already dreading the gala purely for the fact it's our line in the sand, the end to what we're doing. I know how fast this week's going to go.

I contemplate reaching for him, running my hand over his taut stomach, and lower still, waking him with my hands or my mouth, drawing him none-too-gently from his sleep. But he's so peaceful and despite the fact tomorrow—no, today—is Sunday, I have to go down to one of the Chance facilities to give a talk. As tempted as I am for round two hundred, I know where my duties lie.

I push the sheet back with serious regrets and tip-toe out of his bed, out of his room, and I tell myself not to look back.

I sleep until midday then dress quickly—jeans and a sweater, a simple black coat and flats for today. I don't dress up for Chance sessions. The whole thing is to be relatable to these guys. They have enough adults in their lives that don't get them. I want them to see me as a friend, someone they can trust.

One of the things that's become harder as the charity's grown is that I get to do way less of this hands-on stuff than I'd like. I don't get to talk to as many of our kids, I don't get to meet them all. I've hired amazing staff, though, and I check in with them with enough regularity to know when things are working, and when they're not.

Where'd you go?

The text message from Nicholas comes through as I arrive at our Brooklyn Chance headquarters. I smile.

I didn't want to wake you, Sleeping Beauty.

I add an emoji with its tongue poking out.

Why didn't you stay?

But we've talked about that. I feel better not actually sleeping the night—which is a silly distinction, but one that somehow makes sense. Boundaries will be my saviour when all of him is a sink hole, drawing me closer, making me want him, making me need him in a way I definitely didn't expect.

I have a thing today.

A thing?

Alicia Waterman, the manager of this Chance facility, walks towards me, her no-nonsense air instantly reassuring. I only have time to dash out a quick reply.

I'm giving a talk to some Chance kids in Brooklyn. I'll call you later.

'Alicia.' I stuff my phone into the back pocket of my jeans. 'All good to go?'

'All ready.' She nods crisply, falling into step beside me. 'There's a huge turnout. Over two hundred.'

I let out a low whistle. 'That's great.'

'Will you have time afterwards for a quick sit-down? I need to talk to you about some of our vocational partners.'

'Uh oh. That doesn't sound good.'

Her smile is tight. 'I'm sure it will be fine; just a hiccough. I just need to go through some options.'

A presentiment of concern moves down my spine. 'You're sure?'

She grimaces. 'It'll wait.'

'Okay, fine. After.'

'You need anything?'

I survey the disused warehouse we've converted into a loft space. The high ceilings give it a feeling of freedom, and the office partitions are all on wheels, meaning for events like today we can move them around to open it right up.

My heart bursts as I step into the building.

Pride, unmistakable, is like a firefly dancing through my system. I did this. All these people are here because of me, and all of them have a chance because of me. And because of Abbey. I close my eyes and picture Abbey, and the ever-present sense of purpose has me pushing up towards the stage at the front of the room.

There's a lot of chatter but as I take the steps it quietens down a little. I stand at the lectern, push my phone onto silent, sip the water and begin to talk.

I love this—speaking to these kids. I used to get nervous but very quickly I realised that it's not about

me, it's about them. I'm here to tell them what they
need to hear, to give them what has been missing
in their lives.

I speak from the heart, and close everything else
out.

I didn't plan to come here, but when Imogen mes-
saged to say she was speaking at a Chance function,
curiosity got the better of me. Before I knew it, I'd
done a quick search and was flying my helicopter
towards Brooklyn.

It doesn't occur to me until I'm almost inside the
warehouse that she might not have wanted me to
come. I contemplate waiting outside, but that's just
dumb. She won't care.

Besides, I want to see this. I want to see what she
does when she's not facilitating a club where the
world's super-rich elite blow off steam.

The room is completely silent, despite the fact it's
full of kids. They're older kids, teens, mostly. I move
to the back of the room.

An efficient-looking woman with a clipboard and
short black hair regards me with a look of curiosity
and scepticism. I nod at her, as if I belong, and stand
against the wall.

My eyes fall on Imogen and something locks inside me.

'My meemaw used to have a saying.' She smiles,
naturally, comfortably, her eyes skimming the room,
and I can tell that she has a gift with this, with mak-

ing every single person in the space feel as though she's talking only to them. 'You can't see a dolphin when the water's choppy but that don't mean it's not there.' She does a perfect southern accent, as she did the day I came looking for Miss Anonymous. It makes me grin.

'I know you're all here today because the waters around you are choppy.' She takes a minute to let that sink in, her expression shifting so it's serious, sympathetic. I feel compassion bursting from her every pore. 'Maybe it's worse than choppy. Maybe you feel like you have a tsunami bearing down on you with nowhere to go. But that's not the case. Chance is your port in the storm, your anchor, your home and your family. You belong here with us, you're one of us, and we will do everything we can to help you.' Her eyes scan the room once more, and this time, they pass over me then skid back, surprise showing on her face for the briefest of moments so I feel a wedge of guilt, as if maybe I've driven her off course.

But she smiles, right at me, and my stomach soars, then she continues seamlessly. 'Just because the water's choppy doesn't mean there isn't a dolphin—you have a dolphin inside you, your future is out there, bright and waiting for you to grab it with both hands. I'm so proud of you all, and I'm thrilled you're a part of the Chance family. You belong here. Merry Christmas.'

The audience erupts, a huge applause that is almost deafening in this cavernous space. When she smiles, she looks so sweet and young, not at all like the founder of The Billionaires' Club.

She waves a hand and steps off the stage, and my pride in her catches me completely by surprise. I can't take credit for how good she is at this; it has nothing to do with me. And yet I feel an immense wave of warmth.

The woman with the clipboard takes the stage. She speaks for a few minutes, directing everyone to a table set up against the wall, loaded with pastries and hot chocolates. A better look shows there's a second table, which looks to be overflowing with coats and jumpers, all neatly folded, ready for new owners to take them home.

'What are you doing here?' She comes up from behind me, her smile bright and perfect.

I can't help it. I dip my head down and kiss her, so overwhelmed by how great she did, by the words she spoke, by the power she wields to make a true difference.

But she pulls away quickly, her eyes skittering around the room. 'Nicholas.' She shakes her head. 'Not here. There are people here who know me.'

Shit.

We're dating *secretly*. And I completely forgot. I forgot this is all kind of pretend. Not real. It's not my place to act like the doting boyfriend, which I'm definitely not.

I forgot myself for a second.

'Sorry,' I say, sincerely. 'I was just so proud of you.'

Her smile is back, her eyes twinkling. 'Seriously?'

'Yeah.' *Pull it together, you soppy bastard.* 'Christ, you were amazing up there.'

She blinks quickly, as if she's trying to combat tears or something. 'I have to talk to Alicia. Can you wait?'

'Yeah.' My voice is hoarse. 'I can wait.'

She squeezes my hand discreetly. 'Mingle.' Her smile is pure sensual promise. 'Eat something yummy.'

I lean a little closer. 'Oh, I intend to.'

Her cheeks glow and I laugh as she walks away, before doing just as she instructed, and find myself talking to a sixteen-year-old called Isaac, whose parents kicked him out of home when he came out to them as gay. He's smart and polite, and, when he tells me he was living on the streets until three months ago when someone told him about Chance, I feel like finding out where his parents are so I can go and give them some hard truths.

He introduces me to one of his friends, a girl called Bryony, whose parents died when she was thirteen. She was taken in by her aunt, but they fought non-stop. She ran away from home and ended up in Brooklyn, working as a prostitute until she found Chance.

My gut tightens.

These poor kids.

And their guardian angel, Imogen.

It's hard to fathom the effect this has on me—seeing for myself what she's doing, how hard she's worked to make a difference. I feel immediately impotent and completely selfish. I've worked my arse off these past five years but for what? To make myself richer? To make my family's already considerable fortune greater?

When this is how people live?

'Hey.' She appears at my side, and her smile is a little tighter now, her eyes less sparkly.

'Is everything okay?'

'Yeah.' Her eyes run over the room and before she can say anything else, a young teenager, maybe thirteen, comes bounding up to her.

'Imogen!' She puts her arms around Imogen's waist and Imogen dips down lower to wrap the girl in a proper hug.

'Sasha. I was hoping I'd see you today. How are you, sweetheart?'

'Good. I got something for you.'

'You did?' Imogen frowns. 'I'm pretty sure that's against the rules.'

'I know. But I saw it and I thought of you. Hang on. I'll be right back.'

'I'll be here.'

Imogen slides a glance at me. 'She's twelve. She became a part of Chance four years ago, when her parents were going through a divorce. Her mom was living in a car at the time. Sasha was stealing stuff from *bodegas* to get by.' She shakes her head wistfully.

Sasha appears a second later. 'Here.' She hands a small bag over. Imogen opens it and laughs, pulling out some saltwater taffy. 'I remember you saying you love it.' Sasha grins and Imogen nods.

'I do. So much. You've spoiled me.'

Sasha beams. I'm completely transfixed by Imogen's look of gratitude and surprise—that someone who does so much for so many should be genuinely chuffed by such a token gift. It's…charming. And… beautiful. No. Lovely.

She's lovely.

She quizzes Sasha. 'Did you get something to eat?'

'Uh-huh.'

'And a jacket?'

'No.'

'Go pick one out, honey.' Imogen waves towards the table. 'The forecast is for more snow this week.'

'I know. Merry Christmas.'

Another hug, and as Sasha disappears into the crowd again Imogen's eyes are moist. 'You ready to go?' she asks, looking up at me.

'Sure. You can leave already?'

'Yeah.' Her smile is dented. I wait until we're outside before I ask her what's going on.

I like that she doesn't try to fob me off. She could have, but, then again, I've come to know her pretty well and I don't think I'd be convinced by a lie.

Something's bothering her, something other than the sight of so many kids in need of Chance's support.

'It's our intern programme,' she says thoughtfully. 'We have a partnership with Eckerman Walsh for kids who want to move into finance. They take five Chance high school seniors a year on internships and help fund college for some. But they're going through a significant restructure and they've asked to put a pause on it for two years, while they right the ship.' She looks up at me, apology on her features. 'Sorry. I don't mean to bore you with that.'

'You're not,' I demur, instantly.

'I'll work it out. It's just that this year's kids were due to start in September and now they have nowhere to go. It'll be crushing.'

I don't even think about it. 'They can come to me.'

'What?' She's startled. 'What do you mean?'

'My office here. I run three hedge funds within my umbrella of companies. Let them come to Rothsmore Group for their internships. We'll take up the same terms as Eckerman Walsh, including college tuition. In fact, I could offer the same for each of the cities my fund has a presence. London, Rome, Sydney...'

'Nic...' She shakes her head from side to side so her blonde hair fluffs against her beautiful face. 'I can't let you do that.'

'Why not?'

'Because...' Her voice trails into the ether.

'Because?'

'Because, I feel like you're only offering because we're sleeping together.'

'I'm offering because I've just spent an hour of my life seeing that I've been a useless, selfish git, that there are incredible kids out there who deserve a better chance in life and you're giving it to them. I'm offering because I want to help in some small way that I can.'

Her mouth drops open. I look around quickly and steal a kiss, a kiss that makes me ache for her, a kiss that makes me feel things I can't compute.

'You said you never turn down donations to the charity,' I remind her.

'I know. But you're…you. I don't want you to think I'm taking advantage of you…'

'Oh, you're welcome to take advantage of me any time,' I tease, wiggling my eyebrows dramatically.

But she shakes her head, lifts a hand to my chest. 'It's so generous.'

'I can afford it.' I smile. 'And I insist. I *want* to do this.'

And I really, really do.

'So, your grandmother sounds pretty wise.' Imogen blinks up at me from the book she's reading. She likes to read. And I like watching her read. About five dates ago, she found her way to my library upstairs and has been working her way through the classics, just for fun.

'She was.' Imogen's smile is full of affection.

'Did she really used to say that? About the dolphin?'

'Yeah! Why? You thought I made it up?'

'I just haven't heard it before.'

'Oh, she had all these really neat sayings. Like, *"It don't matter how scratched up you are, you get back on the bike."*'

I laugh. 'I could have used that advice.'

'Why?'

'Oh, I came off my bike a long time ago and never rode again.'

She looks surprised. 'That doesn't sound like you. Quitting?'

'I wasn't afraid to ride again,' I clarify. 'I just didn't particularly like the feeling of crashing off it.'

'I can't say I blame you. Still, Meemaw would have insisted you keep riding.'

I smile. 'What else would she say?'

'Hmm… *"If you're careful, you only have to light a fire once."* Lots of them didn't make much sense, but she'd say them and Pa would look at me and roll his eyes. I miss them.'

'They're both gone?'

'Yeah.' She blinks away the memories.

'You were close?'

'Yeah.' Her eyes shift, as if she's running over memories. 'I started spending a fair bit of time with them, once I was a teenager. I used to go down there most summers. It was nice to get away from my parents, from Hollywood.' She lifts her shoulders. 'It was Meemaw who gave me the idea for Chance.

She used to say to me, *"There's a lot of bridges need building in this world—someone's always gotta place the first stone."'*

I smile. 'Meemaw sounds pretty smart.'

Imogen nods. 'The smartest. And you? Do you have grandparents?'

'No. My parents were in their forties when they had me. My father's parents were both gone, and my mother's only lived until I was maybe four or five. I never really knew them.'

'Was it a second marriage?'

I frown, not following.

'It seems kind of late in life to start a family?'

'Right. Actually, on the contrary, they were married quite young.' I reach over and brush some of her hair back, as if I can't help myself. 'They had fertility problems. A lot of miscarriages. A stillbirth. Then years of not being able to conceive. I think that's got a lot to do with why they're so damned keen for me to settle down and start a family of my own.' I wiggle my brows to downplay my frustrations. I do understand why my parents feel the way they do but that doesn't mean they don't drive me crazy.

'God, they must have doted on you,' she murmurs, watching me from narrowed eyes.

It's such an amusing observation that I laugh. 'Not at all. I mean, yes, my mother often describes my birth as some kind of miracle, but they're both by-products of their environment. They were glad to have me, grateful to have been able to produce an heir at last, but doting wasn't really in their vocabulary. I went to boarding school when I was seven years old. I only saw my mother and father on holidays, and, even then, they were frequently abroad.' I frown, because I don't often think back on that time. 'I liked school, though.'

Imogen's eyes crease with the sympathy that comes so quickly to her. She puts the book down and crosses the room, her eyes huge in her delicate face.

'You were too young to be sent away.'

I stare down at her, something moving in my gut. 'Was I?'

'Yes.'

I don't say anything; she's probably right.

'Promise me something.'

I nod slowly. I know that I would promise her just about anything.

'When you get married and have your little lords and ladies, don't send them away.'

I wonder why that thought fills me with a strange sense of acidity.

'I see it again and again in the kids I work with at Chance—all they really want is parents who are there, who love them.'

I imagine she's right about that. It seems to me that children have a universal set of needs and yet a lot of parents probably fail to meet them.

'Promise me,' she insists.

And I nod, because Imogen is asking something

of me and it's within my power to give it to her. 'I promise.'

She smiles, and it's as though the world is catching fire. My lungs snatch air deep inside them. Everything is frozen still inside me. She's the most beautiful person I've ever known, inside and out.

And in a matter of days I'll leave her for ever.

CHAPTER TWELVE

*December 21st, the Christmas Gala,
Billionaires' Clubrooms, Manhattan*

IT'S FINALLY TIME.

I stand in the middle of the ballroom and look around, taking it all in. The formalities are over, the auction concluded—we've raised twice what I'd hoped. The millions of dollars from ticket sales added to the auction revenue means I'll be able to fast-track the shelter I've had designed in Phoenix.

A lump forms in my throat, pride in what I've done, hope for the future of children making me feel, understandably, a little emotional. But it's more than that. It's the knowledge that this is my last night with Nicholas. That come what may, at the end of this evening, it will be the end for us.

A month ago, that made sense, but now, it feels a thousand shades of wrong. Everything inside me rails against the idea. I don't want tonight to be the last time I see him, but what other option is there? He has to go back to England. And if it were just a matter of work, maybe we could try a long-distance thing. I've been wanting to expand Chance to Europe—a London base would be a good start. Maybe I could get over my worries about what the membership will think if news breaks that I'm dating someone from within its ranks. Maybe I could make it work. But Nicholas is going home to find some aristocratic heiress and make a suitable match. There were a dozen reasons we gave our dating deal a time limit of one month, and none of those reasons has gone away.

Except I don't want it to end.

'Hey.' His voice behind me is the cherry on top.

I try my hardest to school my face into a mask of professional inquiry, but the second I turn around and see Nicholas Rothsmore in a tuxedo, my pulse shoots into overdrive and I feel as though I'm being driven at high speed around a hairpin bend.

I don't want this to end.

I want…what? What do I want?

'Nic…' I breathe his name into the room, needing nothing more than to crush my body to his and kiss him, hard, kiss him slow, kiss him all over.

'Quite the shindig.' His eyes probe mine and I have a feeling he's fighting a similar urge to mine; that he wants to pull me to him and kiss me.

My eyes drift to his watch. It will be at least an hour before I can leave. Emily, my assistant, will take care of everything after that; she is amazing.

'You having fun?' I murmur.

'I'll have more fun if you dance with me.'

I shake my head a little. 'I feel like that could be a giveaway.'

'I've seen you dance with at least five guys to-night.'

My heart turns over in my chest. 'Jealous, my lord?' I'm teasing him, a light-hearted joke, but his eyes narrow and he nods.

'Beyond belief.'

Blood fills my heart too fast; my chest hurts. What do I want from him? How can this night be the last one we spend together? 'That's work.'

'So? I'm work too. I'm your new internship partner, remember?'

Remember? I've thought of very little else since our lawyers rushed through the paperwork so this year's ballot of kids wouldn't miss their selections.

'You raise an excellent point.' And temptation makes me foolish. 'One dance.'

He holds his hands out, and I step into them, taking a position that would pass, if anyone cared to look carefully, as purely businesslike.

'I have been watching you,' he says slowly, the words brushing low against my ear, so no one else can hear. 'And trying to work out if this dress has a zip hidden somewhere.'

'Pre-emptive planning?' I prompt, my eyes running over his face.

'Yes. I intend to remove it from you just as soon as we get back to my apartment.'

My pulse races faster; my chest still hurts, as if it's being cracked wide apart. I don't want this to end. Ever.

The realisation slices through me like the sharpest blade of a knife.

'I want to strip the dress from you and carry you to the hot tub, pull you into the water and onto my cock. I want to fuck you there, first.'

I swallow, his imagery insanely erotic, but even that isn't enough to push my realisation from my mind.

I don't want Nicholas to go. I don't want 'us' to be over. And there *is* an 'us'. Despite our insistence that this is pretend dating, like an education for me and nothing more, I have done perhaps the most stupid thing in my life.

I've fallen in love with him.

I fell in love with a man. It was a trap. When we started this, I thought he was the opposite of everything I wanted. He's rich—he's going to be a *lord*, for Christ's sake—and he's shallow. He's meant to be, anyway, but he isn't. He's caring and sweet and compassionate and intelligent and fascinating and— *Oh, my God*.

I stop dancing for a second.

His eyes are skipping over my face. He's going to work out something's wrong.

'What else?' I start to dance again, lifting my lips into an approximation of a smile.

'There's a lid for every pot. You can't fight it when you find what fits.'

Meemaw used to say it about Pa, when she was frustrated by him, but always with a smile. As if he drove her crazy but she loved him completely.

'I want to spend some time saying goodbye to your beautiful breasts,' he groans, his voice a whisper that sends darts down my spine. But the words cause my heart to splinter into a billion pieces, because he's talking about saying goodbye as though he's totally fine with this.

My eyes sweep shut, and I know, in that moment, if anyone cared to look they'd see the face of a woman whose heart is being completely shattered.

'And this arse of yours.'

I have no idea how I hold it together. His words are making my body tremble with anticipation, but in the middle of my chest a cavity is being scraped out. I am hollow.

I am in love with a man who is wrong for me in every way. He's moving to another country. He's going to marry someone else and, even then, against his will—he would rather be single and continue to do what he's been doing these last five years.

What kind of an idiot falls in love with an unavailable playboy?

I look at him—I can't help it—and see a frown on his face. 'Are you okay?'

Shit. I don't even feel as if I can lie properly. 'I'm

fine. Just emotional. This event is the culmination of a lot of work.'

He visibly relaxes. 'I can see that.'

I love Nicholas Rothsmore. I don't know when I first started to love him, but somewhere along the way, I fell and I fell hard. It's like being struck by lightning; how does he not feel it?

Does he feel it?

His hand at my back shifts, just a little, closer towards my arse. I blink up at him and drop his hand, stepping backwards.

He doesn't feel it. He does this kind of thing all the time, and, even if he didn't, he learned his lesson from the first and last woman he let himself love.

He's built a wall around his heart that I don't think I can chip through.

'Imogen.' Orla, one of the club's Australian members, who I really like, catches me as she passes, oblivious to the explosions that are detonating inside my soul. 'You've outdone yourself.'

I zipper over my heart and take a breath, resuming my usual calm, unflappable exterior. 'You're having fun?'

'Oh, yes.' It's slightly breathy. Her eyes shift over me for a second and her cheeks flush. 'Definitely.' She puts a manicured hand on my wrist, her eyes shining. 'I've got some ideas for the next Sydney gala. I'll email you.'

I smile. Life goes on. Things move forward.

With or without Nicholas, the club will continue, the membership will grow, the charity will survive. But my heart won't recover. I have never been in love before, but I don't think you need to have first-hand experience to know that love has transformative powers.

I love Nicholas, and my life will never be the same after he leaves.

I have to tell him.

Orla slinks off, her beautiful dress caressing her frame. I watch her for a second and then turn back to Nicholas. His grin is pure, devilish playboy.

He doesn't love me, and all telling him will achieve is a premature end to this.

He won't take me home tonight; it will be over and I need that not to be the case.

One more night, one more night of fun and sex and pretending this is casual when I know it isn't. At least, not for me.

'I have to circulate,' I say softly.

'I expected as much.' But then, leaning even closer, 'You're sure you don't want to try out an Intimate Room? I can get some handcuffs…'

And despite my breaking heart, heat blooms through my body. 'Later.'

He laughs. 'Count on it.'

His use of the phrase I utter so often pulls at me, because it is this phrase that led him to discover I was Miss Anonymous. Would I take it back if I could? Would I make it so this never happened?

No. Not in a million years. Even as I feel my heart breaking, I know I would never wish we hadn't shared this. Nicholas has changed me, and I think for the better.

I continue to circulate, brushing past the billionaire property developers Ash Evans and Sebastian Dumont just in time to catch them shaking hands, Ash laughing at something Sebastian's muttered.

This is what the club promises its members. It's a safe place to do business, to network and to relax. It's a safe place but not, as it turns out, for me.

I run my tongue over his tattoo, hating it in that moment, because I don't want Nicholas to be his own. I want him to be mine. I flick his hair-roughened nipple, enjoying the feeling of his chest lifting, his breath snagging in his lungs as I move lower. His naked body is tanned against the matte black of his sheets. I kiss my way down his body, tasting his flesh, remembering everything I can about this, taking his hard cock into my mouth, absorbing the guttural oath he spills into the room as I move my mouth up and down, my nipples tingling, heat pooling between my legs.

I will never get sick of this. Him, me, naked. I want this to last for ever.

But it is already approaching dawn, and I hate that. Never have I wanted a night to last longer than I do this night.

I taste a hint of his salty pre-cum and then his hands are under my arms, pulling me up his body, his mouth seeking mine, his frame rolling me, so I'm on my back, his arousal hard between my legs. I arch my back and spread my legs wide, wordlessly begging him to take me, to make love to me, needing his body to console mine in the only way he can.

But he breaks the kiss and reaches across me. I hear a drawer and then something metallic. His hands curve around my wrists; he pulls them to the bedframe and then cold metal surrounds me. I pull on my hands. They're cuffed to the bed.

I stare up at him, my eyes wide, lips parted.

'Do you trust me?'

My stomach swirls with acid. 'With all my heart.'

His smile is sensual. A second later, his hands are trailing over my flesh, so light, barely touching me, and I'm crying his name out over and over. His mouth follows them, his tongue flicking my nipples, as he moves lower with his hands, spreading my legs to make way for his mouth.

His tongue is gentle at first, running over my seam, exploring me, rediscovering me. I thrash from side to side, my handcuffed wrists a new form of torture as I ache to touch him or touch myself, to do something to relieve this tidal wave of sensation.

'Please,' I groan, incapable of saying anything else. He keeps my legs pinned wide as he sucks my clit into his mouth and flicks it with his tongue. I am on fire; I am burning up. 'Please,' I whimper, needing him, needing more, needing everything.

He pulls away, up my body, his mouth finding my nipples, his hands roaming my skin freely, inquiringly, and I'm so hungry for him I can barely cope. I need to feel him inside me.

'I want you,' I beg.

'I know.' His smile is tighter now, tension on his face. He pauses, rolling a condom over his length, and hope is a beast inside me.

His eyes hold mine as he pushes his rock-hard arousal into my wet core; my muscles spasm around him and I jerk against the handcuffs, wanting to touch him now, to feel his muscles bunch beneath me as I run my hands over his skin.

His laugh is soft, a caress against my skin. He moves inside me, deeper, and I groan, surrendering to this completely. My body is an instrument and he plays me with perfection.

Dawn is coming. Even in winter, when the sun rises later, nothing staves off morning's eventual appearance. I watch him sleep, my own eyes heavy, my mind heavier, my heart a dead weight.

I love him, and I have no hope that he loves me back. For me, this has been completely unprecedented. For Nicholas, this is his life, his norm. I have no reason to think anything has changed for him since we started up with this, whereas all the boundaries of my world have shifted.

My eyes run over his beautiful face, disbelief curdling my insides.

This is so much harder than I thought it would be.

I shift in the bed.

A coffee will help.

I step out quietly, drawing one of his shirts from the wardrobe and pulling it over my nakedness as I prowl through to the kitchen.

It's snowed overnight. When I look down from the windows, I see the pavement is white like chalk, cars covered in a pale, sparkling blanket. I press a button on the coffee machine, cursing as it stirs to life. Even though it's quiet, it's not silent, and I look towards his bedroom door in time to see Nicholas shifting in bed. He looks for me and my heart groans, because I'm his first thought on waking.

How can this be the end?

He disappears from view and a second later steps into the lounge area, a pair of grey boxer shorts low on his hips. My eyes find his tattoo on autopilot; acid coats the inside of my mouth.

'Is it even morning?' he asks groggily, his face showing bemusement.

'I have to get going,' I say, my own voice tight like a wire that's been pulled too taut.

His eyes focus blearily on his watch. 'It's five o'clock.'

'I know.' I pull the coffee from the machine and cup it in my hands. I keep my back propped against the kitchen bench. I hope it looks nonchalant. I hope I seem better than I feel.

'Come back to bed.'

My heart groans. 'I can't.'

'Why?'

I swallow, focussing on the black liquid inside my cup. 'Because we said this would be the end. And I have to go.'

I don't think the stilted statements make much sense, and this is confirmed when I lift my attention to his face. 'Stay.'

'A few more hours?'

'No.' He frowns. 'I don't have to be in England until New Year's Eve. Spend Christmas with me.'

I feel as if I'm being stretched on the rack. 'What?'

'A week's extension on our original deal?' His tone is teasing.

Something shifts in my chest, something painful. 'Why?'

He shrugs his shoulders casually. 'Why not?'

My knees tremble. Fire spits through my veins. It's so close to what I want, but, now that I understand how I feel, being with Nicholas for another night—let alone seven—would just be too hard.

'Because, I can't.'

His expression is sceptical. I draw in a deep breath. 'I have to get back to my normal life,' I say emphatically—my normal life is my lifeline. It's the talisman for who I used to be. 'I have the Christmas drive for Chance, and the Christmas lunch I do every year.' I bite down on my lip, looking away from him because I can't bear to look into his eyes for another moment. 'I can't.'

The last word wobbles a little. I sip the coffee to stave off some kind of emotional scene.

'One more week.'

'No.' I am emphatic. I speak as if my life depends on it, and in many ways it does.

He's quiet a moment. 'I don't understand. Last night was...amazing. You're saying you don't want more of this?'

'We said a month,' I murmur. 'We were clear about this. The Christmas benefit was to be the end.'

'And that's what you want?'

I open my mouth to say something, but what can I say? That yes, I want more. I want too much more. How did this happen? The club and Chance have been my total priority for so long and I would have sworn they always would be, but now there's something— someone—else who matters just as much, and despite the fact I swore this would be fun and casual and no-strings, despite the fact I initially loved the boundaries we put in place, I want to push against them now. I'm in love with him, and I know he doesn't love me back, but, God, I can't ignore how I feel.

'Damn it, Imogen, it was an arbitrary line in the sand you decided on. Why can't we shift it by one fucking week?'

His anger sparks my own. I can no longer control my feelings, my rawness. 'Because a week isn't nearly enough, Nicholas. I don't want just one more week with you. I want a lifetime, okay?'

CHAPTER THIRTEEN

HER STATEMENT HANGS between us like a thousand and one daggers. I stare at her; nothing makes sense. I must have misunderstood.

'What are you talking about?'

She sips her coffee, her face pale, her features drawn.

She's so quiet and impatience is slicing through me.

'For God's sake, Imogen, that doesn't make sense. What do you mean?'

Her eyes are huge and hollow, emotions rushing through her that I can't comprehend. All I want is to keep this fun going—and it is fun. This last month has been one of the best of my life. I love spending time with Imogen. I love hanging out with her. God knows, I love fucking her.

'I'm in love with you.' Her eyes pierce me, accusation in them, anger too. I am silent, grappling with the words as though maybe I've misunderstood, as though I've magicked them up out of my deepest fears.

'What?'

Her smile is laced with self-condemnation. 'I fell in love with you. It was the last thing I thought would happen, and honestly I have no idea how it *did* happen. Without meaning to and without me even realising, somehow you've become a part of me. And I can't just pretend I don't love you, and go back to sleeping with and dating you and getting to know you when inside my heart is breaking.'

I'm silent. I'm completely floored.

'It's fine.' She smiles but her eyes look moist. 'I know you're not in love with me. I'm not telling you this because I'm hoping you'll get down on one knee and propose marriage.'

She swallows; I still can't speak.

'But I can't spend another week with you, sharing my life—my body—with you, knowing that you'll never be able to give me the one thing I really want.' She pauses for a second, her cheeks growing pink. 'I'm sorry to deprive you of a week of sex, but I have no doubt you can find someone else to fill your bed until you leave.'

My ears are filled with a screeching noise and everything in the room is too white, too bright, as if it's been overexposed or something.

'What?'

Fuck. That's not right. Focus. Concentrate. Say something better.

She shakes her head sadly and panic surges in my

chest. 'Imogen, you know…' I groan, drag a hand through my hair. 'It's not you.'

'But it is me. And it's the fact I fell in love with you, and you don't love me, and if I stay with you another night, I'm going to feel… I'm going to feel…a thousand things, and none of them good.'

'Love was never on my radar.' It's a stupid thing to say but I'm grappling with her statement, desperately trying to make sense of it.

Her eyes spit fire. 'Do you think it was on mine?'

'No.' My own frustration comes through in the word.

'Damn straight. I love that we had rules and boundaries and that this was—in theory—simple fun. But it's different now, everything's different, and I would hate myself if I didn't admit that. To myself, and to you.'

Her eyes close for a moment and I feel as if the ground has just swallowed me up. I'm falling and beneath me are the very fires of hell.

I hate hurting her. The realisation is like a punch in my gut. I'm hurting Imogen and this was always about helping her. About pleasuring her. And now I've hurt her and I can't believe that.

I need to make it better. I have to make her understand.

'You are incredible. Some guy, some day, is going to win the lottery when you fall for him.'

'But not you,' she murmurs, her eyes huge in her face. My chest kicks.

'Not me.'

She nods, but, God, her lip is trembling and I feel like a monster.

'Once, I believed in love, and it was a disaster.' I move closer, needing her to feel the sincerity of my words. 'I honestly believed I loved Saffy and when we broke up, it was like being woken from a dream I'll never find my way back to again. I don't *want* to find my way back there. I don't want to feel like that. I don't want to think I love someone. I don't want to give anyone else that power over me.' I lift a hand to her cheek and almost swear when she flinches out of my reach, as if I've shocked her with raw electricity.

'You are your own,' she says, but archly, with a hint of anger that I'm ridiculously glad about—I much prefer anger to the brokenness that confronted me a minute ago.

'Yes.' I am relieved. 'I'm my own, I belong only to myself, and that's the way I like it. I'm sorry, Imogen. I'm sorry if I did anything to make you hope for a future here. I thought I was clear—'

'Oh, you were.' The words are weary. 'Which just shows what an idiot I am.'

'No, Imogen…' But what can I say? She's right. Any woman who would fall in love with me needs her head examined. I try again. 'I think we should forget I suggested this.' I clench my jaw. 'I'll go back to England, as planned. I'm sorry. I didn't want this—I didn't have any idea you were developing feelings for me or I would have ended it sooner. I'm sorry,' I say again. Though it's manifestly insufficient, I have no idea what else I can say.

Silence wraps around us, a prickly, angry silence like the icy morning after a winter's storm.

'You are a goddamned coward, Lord Rothsmore.' She bites my future title out with disgust. Her statement crashes around me and I don't speak, because she needs to get this off her chest and I'm okay with that. I have to be—I'm breaking her heart. She finishes her coffee, placing the cup down hard on the bench top.

'You're too scared to let yourself feel this.' Her eyes lance me. 'You think you're the only person to be hurt? You think that means you need to put yourself in emotional stasis for the rest of your life? How is that even going to work? You're going to go home and make a sensible marriage and what? Feel nothing for your wife?'

I don't want to talk to Imogen about my future. Suddenly, the plans I've set in place chasm before me like an awful void. I grind my teeth together, trying to focus, trying to work out what I can say that will make this better.

I have to fix this.

'That's how it works,' I say quietly, calmly, even when I'm not calm.

'And that's what you want?'

I stare at her for several long seconds, pulling myself back mentally. 'I have accepted what is required of me,' I correct. 'And nothing is going to change that.'

She is so pale.

'I feel like we were clear about this from the start,' I say softly, and tears sparkle on her lashes.

'Hasn't anything changed for you since then?'

My gut churns hard. I shake my head. It can't. I can't do this. 'No.'

No. The word is emphatic. I look at him, my heart no longer in my chest. I have no idea what happened to it. Maybe it withered and died completely?

He doesn't love me. He doesn't want me—or at least, only for another week. I think about that, and wonder if I can shelve my own feelings, purely to squeeze every moment out of this that we possibly can. But there's no way.

I can't do it.

I move away from him, towards my ball gown that is discarded in the lounge, where he removed it last night. It's beautiful, but all I can think of is that it's what I wore on our last night together.

My throat feels as though it's been scraped with sandpaper.

'Imogen, listen to me.' His voice is gravelled. I don't stop what I'm doing. In fact, I move faster, pulling the dress up over my hips, discarding his shirt with my back to him. It's ridiculous to want to shield my nakedness, given what we've shared, and yet I do.

'I care about you, okay?' His voice is so deep, so

rough. 'If things had been different, maybe this could have worked out, but I'm not the guy you want me to be. I don't even believe in love, I don't believe in happy endings. I believe in *this*.'

When I look around, he's gesturing from his chest, towards me.

'I believe in the power of a resounding physical chemistry, and I believe in respect and civility. I believe in fun.'

'You have turned partying into an art form all so you can avoid feeling any kind of emotional connection with someone. You're living with your head in the sand and you don't even realise it.'

'And what exactly are you doing, Imogen? You haven't had sex or even dated a guy in four years and you tell me *I'm* the one who has my head in the sand?'

'I put my life on hold to run Chance,' I fire back, anger sharp in my mind. 'I don't have much of a social life but that's because I want to make the world better. You spend all your time having frivolous, meaningless affairs because you're shit scared of *feeling* anything for anyone. All because you loved someone once and she didn't want to marry you.'

'Jesus Christ,' he curses, his eyes sharp with fierce determination and frustration. 'This is spectacularly unreasonable.'

I suck in an indignant breath.

'Do you think you have any right to lecture me? You're the one who's moved the goalposts. You're shitty at me because I don't love you, when love wasn't even on the cards. Ever.'

I drop my head forward a second, his words like ice cubes, but ones I need to feel.

'I never expected you to love me. I'm just telling you why I can't spend another week with you.'

He holds my gaze even as I feel regret shift inside him.

'I told you to forget I suggested that. I'm sorry.'

I stiffen my spine, fixing him with my best Imogen Carmichael expression. I am the founder of The Billionaires' Club, founder of Chance, and I will not let him see how badly this is hurting me. Even as tears fill my throat, my eyes, my soul, I stare him down.

'So this is really what you want?'

A muscle jerks in his jaw and I sense his indecision, but I also sense his stubborn determination and I know what his answer will be, even before he says it. 'It has to be.'

'Don't. That's a cop-out.'

'Damn it.' He drags a hand through his hair. 'What do you want me to say? That I want you to go? That I'm sorry I hurt you and that I wish we hadn't got involved? That if I'd known we'd be having this conversation I would have left it with one perfect, sublime night in Sydney?'

His words are like knives, sailing through the air, each one slamming into me. He softens his voice but it's no less empathic. 'Do you want me to say that I don't love you? That I wish you didn't love me? That I don't believe in love, that I don't want it? That you and this has been great but it's not my real life any more than I am yours?'

A sob wells in my throat. I stare at him, unable to speak.

'This was never about love,' he adds for good measure. 'We both know that.'

I nod, slowly. I can feel a ticking time bomb in my chest; I have to get out of there before I cry.

But he's not prepared to let this go.

'I don't want it to end like this.'

Nor do I. I don't want it to end at all.

I steel myself to face him one last time and my heart almost gallops away from me. 'What difference does it make how it ends? It's over.'

I scoop up my bag and walk to the door with as much dignity as I can muster. I pull it open, holding my breath, wondering if he'll stop me, wondering if he'll say anything else. I'm still holding my breath at the elevator. The doors slide open and I step inside. The doors begin to slide shut and right as they're about to latch shut in the middle, his hand slides between them.

'Don't fucking go like this,' he groans, pulling me towards him, and, damn it, the tears I've been fighting are sliding down my cheeks. He pushes his hands into my hair, holding my face steady so he can look at me. 'Please don't cry.'

He is shocked. He didn't expect any of this.

So much of this is hard to understand, impossible to fathom, but there's one thing that always, without fail, makes sense. He kisses me and everything slides into place. Our kiss tastes of my tears. My body, my treacherous, traitorous, opportunistic body, melds to his, my hands lifting to encircle his neck, and he lifts me off the ground for a moment, holding me tight to him.

This is so perfect. I love him.

But he doesn't love me and there's no fix to that. This kiss is just delaying the inevitable.

A sob forms in my mouth and I break the kiss, pushing at his chest and wriggling to the floor.

'Don't.' The word is tremulous and soft, but it holds a mighty warning. 'Don't mess with me. You know how I feel and what I want. Don't look at me as though this is hard for you when it's all *because* of you.'

He takes a step back, his mouth open, shock on his features, and I take advantage of his response to reach across and press the button to close the elevator doors.

This time, he doesn't stop me.

'Lara Postlethwaite graduated with a first in philosophy. Did I tell you that?'

I look at my mother through a fog of Scotch and disbelief. The early evening light catches the books that line my parents' ancient library, making them appear to shimmer in gold, and all I can think of is

Imogen and the joy she took in my Manhattan library. The way she devoured book after book after book.

'I happen to know she thinks you're fascinating.' My mother's smile beams with maternal pride. A vulnerable ache forms in my chest.

My mother is growing older. I don't know why I haven't noticed before, but sitting by her and looking at her, I see not just a meddling society matron, but a woman who'll soon be seventy, who wants to know her son is married, that grandchildren are on their way. It's been easy to put all this matchmaking and expectation down to their concern for the title and the lineage. But what if there's more to it?

What if this is largely a case of a mother simply wanting to know her son is happy? Wanting to see that Saffy didn't ruin me for all other women?

'And I presume she'll be at the New Year's Eve ball?' my father chips in from across the room, his eyes meeting mine over the top of the broadsheet newspaper he's been reading for the better part of an hour.

'Oh, yes, m'dear.'

Perhaps my mother senses my lack of interest. Undeterred, she shifts in a slightly modified direction. 'Of course, Cynthia MacDougall is flying in and so looking forward to catching up with you.'

Cynthia I like. We have had a low-key flirtation going on for years. She's pretty and smart and doesn't really go in for all the aristocratic bullshit. She's personally wealthy enough that I know she's not a gold-digger, and I know she wants kids.

She'd be a good match for me; she definitely ticks the boxes of what I'm looking for.

So why does that very idea make me feel as though I'm being buried beneath a tennis court's worth of just-poured cement?

I recline in the seat, closing my eyes a moment, wishing it were so easy to drone out my mother's wittering about potential brides.

'I think a June wedding would be perfect, if you can make that timing work, darling.'

My gut is being squeezed in a vice.

I've been back in England three days and I feel as if I'm withering away into nothing. I stand abruptly and move to the windows, which perfectly frame a view over the east lawn towards the Kyoto garden and then the nearby stables.

I love this place. I have always felt at home here.

But not now. Right at this minute, I would do almost anything to be back in Manhattan, in the penthouse that was my bolthole when things turned bad with Saffy.

But I don't want to be there alone.

I press my hand to the glass, then drop my head forward, the cooling glass against my forehead bringing some kind of sharp sanity.

I want Imogen.

My insides groan.

I want her but I can't have her. I tried. I tried to

extend what we were and she didn't want that. I will never forget the sight of her face when she pushed me out of the elevator. Her tears—because of me.

Oh, God. I'd do anything to have her not cry. I'd do anything to fix this.

'I'm sorry to deprive you of a week of sex, but I have no doubt you can find someone else to fill your bed until you leave.'

As though what we were could be boiled down to a simple equation. Sex.

It was so much more than that. Because she was right, I could easily have found someone else to seduce for a night, if I'd just wanted to fuck some warm, willing body.

But I haven't wanted that. Not since Sydney. Not since I met Miss Anonymous and lost a part of myself to her.

I spent over a week on tenterhooks, as though my very survival depended on my ability to find her once more. I found her, and I held on as tight as I could for as long as I could. Even at the end, on that last morning, I offered what I could to prolong our farewell, because I wasn't ready to walk away from her.

Would I have been ready a week later? Would New Year's Eve have rolled around, and might I have hopped onto my jet and come here to England, to my parents' party, to meet the potential brides my parents had yet again selected?

'The Greenville on Strand could host it,' my

mother continues, a little hopefully, as though booking a suitable venue is of more concern than finding
someone to marry. 'The ballroom there has been re-
decorated and is quite perfect.'

Fuck. Fuckety-fuckety-fuck. The idea is anath-
ema to me.

Sleeping with someone else. Marrying someone
else. I only want Imogen.

I want her in a way that is filling me with boiling lava; I need her. I need her and I need her to
know that.

My face hurts from stretching this smile across it.
I look out on the sea of kids eating their Christmas lunches, their faces happy, the mood ebullient. I
alone am suffering. I stand in the background, watching the festivity as it overtakes the hall, knowing
that there are eighty-seven of these lunches being
held around the country for all the kids we support,
that Christmas is alive for the Chance community.

And usually this is my favourite day of the year.
I feel as if this is what Christmas is truly about—
the ability to give and make better the lives of those
who owe you nothing.

I know how important this day is but my heart is
too heavy to appreciate it. I find it almost impossible to enter into the spirit, so I keep my head down,
busying myself with the logistics I don't really need
to worry about. I clear tables and disappear into the
kitchen, filling the sink with warm sudsy water and

losing myself in the anonymity and pure, physical labour of washing dishes.

I take my time, the feeling of warm water on my gloved hands at least a little soothing. Staff move around me, chatting amongst themselves. I keep my back turned. I try to cheer myself, thinking about the incredible donation of gifts we received this year, gifts that made sure every child was spoiled with something truly lovely.

Ordinarily, I'd be walking on the clouds. But not today.

Not since he left.

I pause in my dishwashing, my eyes filling with tears once more. I'm such an idiot. What did I think? That I'd tell him I'd fallen in love and he'd leap into the air and exclaim, *Me too, darling!* Nicholas Rothsmore wasn't the 'fall in love' type—he showed me that again and again. All the love was coming from me, and it just proved what a fool I am.

'Bins are overflowing, Amy!' one of the wait staff calls to another.

'I'll do it.' I shuck the rubber gloves off and walk away from the sink, keeping my head dipped so no one speaks to me. I have to get it together. I have no interest in causing people to speculate on what's going on in my life.

I grab one of the bags out of the bin and tie it, carrying it carefully through the kitchen and banging out of the doors and onto the street. It's Christmas Day and it's deserted out here. Everyone's at home with their families, enjoying this perfect snowy Christmas.

I open the lid on the bin and drop the bag in it, then lift my head when I hear the closing of a car door.

And everything comes into a strange kind of focus, too bright, shaky, weirdly discordant. As though I'm looking through those old-fashioned 3D movie glasses.

Striding towards me dressed in jeans and a leather jacket is Nicholas Rothsmore, and damn if my heart doesn't rejoice even as I know I have to protect myself somehow.

Confusion sears me. Did he stay in New York? Is he here till New Year's, just as he said? Is this some Hail Mary, 'one last night' kind of booty call?

Nicholas Rothsmore is the love of my life but I swore I'd never see him again. So what the hell is he doing here now?

CHAPTER FOURTEEN

'Hi.'

He has this incredibly sexy, raspy quality to his voice, like a radio commentator or something. It makes my blood pound even as my stomach is dropping to my feet.

I find it hard to meet his eyes. 'What are you doing here?'

My throat is so dry. I swallow but it barely helps.

It's some consolation that he looks uncertain. Nervous? Apprehensive?

My stomach loops some more.

'I came to see you.'

I turn back to the building. Things are slowing down in there. I don't have to rush back—I'm superfluous now, here because I have nowhere else to be, no one else I want to spend this day with.

'What for?' The words are soft, showing my hurt, and I hate that. I hate how much he's hurt me. I hate that I let him.

He moves closer and I startle a little, wariness at

war with a deep-seated physical need. I shoot him what I hope passes for a warning glare.

His expression shifts.

'What do you want, Nicholas?'

A muscle jerks low at the base of his jaw. 'I have spent the last ten hours working out what the hell I would say to you and now I find I have no fucking idea where to start.'

'Tell me why you're here, on Christmas Day,' I demand, looking inside again.

'I came to see you,' he says, as if it's simple.

'Yeah, but why?'

'That's harder to explain.'

I grab hold of my anger, glad to feel it, glad to have some line of defence against the desire and wants that are ruining me from the inside out.

'Forget about it.' I spin away from him. 'It doesn't matter. You shouldn't have come.'

No. His response, when I told him I loved him, is burned into my consciousness. I will never forget it. I will never forget how that felt.

'Wait a moment.' He catches me, turns me around to face him, and my body jerks with recognition of this, of what he means to me. I wrench my hand free, glaring at him, wishing he could understand how much he's hurting me. 'Just let me get this out.'

But I'm done waiting. 'I don't think there's anything left to say, Nicholas. Unless you've had some kind of miraculous heart transplant?'

His jaw shifts, and I glare at him, waiting, but he says nothing for so long that I actually wonder if he's just here to hit me up for one last night before he leaves. My skin crawls. What started out as 'just sex' is now so much more that it would be an insult to even pretend we're not. Except that's what he did. It's galling and frustrating and hurtful and enraging, all at the same time.

'Please.' The single word brings me to a stop. I look at him with a growing sense of desperation. Doesn't he realise how hard this is for me? Doesn't he realise how much I hate this?

He must take my silence for consent, because a moment later he speaks, his voice thickened with concentration.

'My mother is in full planning mode, first for a New Year's Eve ball, which I gather is going to be a little more like the casting room of *The Bachelor*, with me as the prize.' He winces self-consciously. 'She's already got the wedding planned, now we just need to find someone for me to marry.'

Does he have any idea it's like being scratched all over? His words are vile. I hate them. I hate that he is here telling me this.

'We've discussed your obligations.' My voice simmers with contempt.

His own is gently placating. 'And six weeks ago, I was happy to go along with them. What did I care who I ended up married to? My only criterion was that it be someone I could stand spending time with.

In many ways, the less I had in common with her, the better. This was to be a straightforward arrangement. No muss, no fuss. Simple, right?'

'Undoubtedly.' I can't do this. I spin away from him again, needing to be alone, or at least away from him, breathing in frigid, ice-filled air. My lungs stutter.

He reaches for my elbow, spinning me around gently, insistently.

'And then I met you and, somehow, everything changed.'

I draw in a sharp breath.

'I don't know when it happened, but what I wanted when we started this has shifted and now I need so much more. From you, from my life, from my marriage. Everything's different, Imogen. Everything.'

The world stops spinning. This doesn't make sense.

'What?' I blink, wishing I didn't sound so completely non-comprehending. 'Wait.' I hold a hand up. 'This doesn't make sense. You left three days ago. After telling me you didn't love me, that you'd never love me.'

'I know that.' He runs a hand through his hair, his frustration and confusion barrelling towards me.

'I…' He draws in a breath, his eyes scanning my face, then he shakes his head, as if it's not quite what he meant, and starts again. 'When I was twelve, I came off my bike and I never rode again. I refused. I didn't like the way it felt to fall, so I gave up the pleasure of riding, which I had, up until then, loved very much.' He closes the distance and cups my face.

'You've told me that.'

His eyes gaze into mine. 'I hated the way Saffy made me feel. I hated being let down, hurt, burned, stripped raw in front of so many people. I felt worthless, Imogen. Worthless and unwanted. So I promised myself I would never fall in love again. That I would never be so gullible as to believe in love—what a stupid construct! But, Imogen, I left New York and I nearly turned my back on a whole lifetime of experiences and joy—a lifetime with you—because I was too scared to get hurt again.'

I can't get enough air in. His eyes drop to my lips, and there's a frown on his face, as if he has no idea where he stands with me.

'I fell in love with you, anyway, and I have been fighting it the whole time we've been together. I have not been able to put you out of my head for even a day. Not one single day, not an hour, in fact, since we met. I love you. I am obsessed with you, and I should have known that when you told me how you felt. I should have understood, but I have spent five years running from even the idea of love and I didn't know how to turn my back on that.'

His thumb pad brushes over my lips and I shudder. In a good way, I think. Or maybe just in an emotionally drained way because, despite the fact it's only been three days, I feel as if I have been strapped over a pile of burning coal and I'm so spent.

'It has been an agony and a form of torture to think of you going home to marry someone else,'

I mutter, my heart still so sore, so hurt, that I find forgiveness and understanding hard to muster, even in the face of what he's just said.

'I know.' He drops his forehead to mine, his warm breath fanning my face. 'I hate that. I am so sorry. The sight of you in the elevator, pushing me away, has replayed on my mind like some godawful ten-second clip since I left.'

'Left? You went home?'

He nods.

'And now you're back?'

'I couldn't stay there. I had to see you. I needed you to know, as soon as I realised, that I am head over heels in love with you. And not in a way I've ever felt before. This is so different. I feel as though if I don't spend the rest of my life with you, a part of me will die. I can't explain it. You're in my blood and my breath; you're a part of me.'

And for the first time in days, I exhale slowly and I smile. I smile in a natural way because I feel the first flicker of true happiness. In a very, very long time.

He drops a hand and laces his fingers through mine.

'I'm sorry I was so stupid.'

I laugh then, and shake my head. 'You were stupid.'

'Completely.'

'But you're done?'

'Being stupid? I can't promise that.' He grins and my heart stitches together a bit. 'But I will never hurt you again, Imogen. You are everything to me, and

I plan on spending the rest of my life showing you that. If you'll let me.'

Stars shift in my field of vision. 'I…don't…' I frown, and lick my lower lip. 'Are you…?'

'Asking you to become Lady Rothsmore and all that entails? Yes. Though not very well, evidently.'

I don't know what to say. I never thought I'd get married and not to someone with more money than Croesus, but here I am, head over heels in love with this man, and nothing matters beyond that. Not his title, his wealth, nothing. There is an imperative in me to agree to this—an imperative of my own making. My happiness is built on this conversation.

'I know I hurt you,' he says, mistaking my pause for doubt. 'I know I screwed up, monumentally, by letting you think, even for a second, that we were ever just about sex. When you told me I could find someone else to fuck for my last week in America, my God, Imogen, I wish you could have seen inside me and know how that made me feel.'

I shake my head urgently. 'Don't.' I lift a finger to his lips. 'I don't want to talk about that morning. We were both hurting.' I smile at him then, a smile that I think is laced with all my hopes for our future. 'There's no sense discussing the past when our future is waiting.'

His face shifts as comprehension dawns. 'Do you mean…is that a "yes"?'

I laugh and push up on my tiptoes so I can kiss my acceptance into his mouth. 'It's a hell yes.'

* * *

'They can't wait to meet you.' His expression is slightly sardonic.

I stand up, walking across the lounge. 'It's mutual.'

'I have, however, told them in no uncertain terms to cancel the booking for the wedding venue in June.' His expression is laced with affectionate exasperation.

I grimace. 'How did they take that?'

'They're thrilled to hear there is going to be a wedding of any kind.' He pulls me into his arms, moving his hips a little, dancing in time to the New Year's Eve broadcast that's on in the background.

'I can't believe this is happening,' I say, despite the fact we've spent the last week living like hermits in his penthouse, pretty much in bed the whole time, except when hunger called.

'It's happening.' He pulls me closer. Fireworks dance just beneath my skin. 'How do you feel about watching the fireworks from the hot tub?'

'I think that would be pretty perfect.'

It's perfect out—a bright night, filled with stars and light, too cold even for snow, but the hot tub is warm and luxurious. I sink into it, naked, sighing.

'I do love this city,' I say with a smile, catching his eye as he steps into the water.

'We can stay here, you know.'

It's about the hundredth time he's made that offer. I smile. 'I know.'

'I mean it, Imogen. I came back here fully expecting that if I was lucky enough for you to accept my proposal it would mean that we spent our life right here, in America.'

'I know. But I don't want that.'

'Seriously?'

'I love New York, but I'm ready for a change.' I move towards him so I can sit on his lap. 'I can run The Billionaires' Club from there, and I've been wanting to build a Chance presence in Europe for a long time. I've seriously been thinking about opening a Chance location in London. I don't know what's been holding me back but I do know nothing will stop me now.' I smile at him, my happiness pouring out of me. 'This is exciting for me, in lots of ways.'

'Yeah.' He grins and my heart flips over. I love how truly pumped he is for me—how proud he is. How much he wants me to pursue my dreams and see my future continue to revolve around helping others. 'And New York's only a quick flight away.'

'Perfect for weekends,' I agree, our life suddenly looking pretty damned blessed. And the thing is, having decided what I want most in life, I don't really feel like waiting. I've never been one to overthink or delay, anyway. 'You know, if your parents aren't expecting us for another week, maybe we could take a little detour on the way.'

'Yeah? Sydney?' he teases with an arched brow.

I smile. 'I was meaning more like Vegas.'

'Vegas?' He frowns and then, as comprehension

dawns, he smiles. 'You're thinking, what? The Little White Chapel?'

'Why not?'

'Why not in-fucking-deed?'

'Then we'd arrive in England already married. Unless you think your folks would hate to miss…'

'Oh, they'd be livid.' He grins. 'But only until they realise I'm finally married and "settled down". Besides, nothing will stop my mother from throwing you a "welcome to the family" party to end all parties.'

I expel a soft sigh, contentment bursting through me. I lift my hand out of the water, staring at the beautiful solitaire diamond Nicholas presented me with the day after Christmas. It's round, at least ten carats and fits me like a glove. Just like him.

'Then let's do it.' I smile, flipping over so I'm straddling him.

'Say no more, Lady Rothsmore.' He kisses me, slowly, sensually, and then pulls away. 'It's really what you want?'

I laugh, moving myself over him, taking him deep inside. 'Count on it.'

We arrive in England, man and wife, partners in every way. Despite the fact I've only been here a handful of times, with Nicholas by my side, I know that I've come home.

* * * * *

TURN ME ON

DYLAN ROSE

MILLS & BOON

CHAPTER ONE

IT SEEMED LIKE just another ordinary workday, but Faye would soon learn that there was a life-changing surprise in store for her. It was one o'clock on a Thursday and she was just about to close out of the document she was working on and head down for lunch. Her desk was in an open-plan maze of cubicles, with fluorescent overhead lighting and the constant buzz of her coworkers' chitchat. Every day at this time she made a point of leaving her editing work behind and taking the elevators down to the sprawling cafeteria in the building with its coffee bar, hot entrées and salad station. She had been working at *Amuse Bouche* for nearly ten years. It was her first job out of graduate school and over the time she'd been there, the magazine had become one of the world's most preeminent food and wine publications.

That's not to say she considered herself any kind of food expert. There had been a time when her palate had been more adventurous—when she couldn't imagine a better plan for a Sunday then to take the subway into the outer boroughs in search of the spiciest Indian food or the most delicious Thai noodles. But ever since things had ended with David, she had left all that behind in favor of bland foods: peanut butter and banana sandwiches were her new go-to. What was the point in making an elaborate meal when it was just her dining alone? Plus, she hated that now everyone who took a picture of their sandwich considered themselves a "foodie."

Faye pulled on her sweater, let the screensaver take over and grabbed her purse to head downstairs. She wasn't going so much for the food—although the selections were incredible—so much as she was just to take a walk and get a change of scenery. She'd lost almost twenty pounds since the breakup. And even though her skinny jeans were now her loose ones and stuff relegated to the back of the closet now fit, and she got second glances from men as she walked to work up Sixth Avenue, she was basically indifferent to the attention. And while part of her did imagine bumping into David and seeing him seeing her looking incredible, mostly she just felt so sad about the whole thing, even though it had been almost a year now since that fateful day.

Just as Faye turned to leave, she heard the familiar chirp of her desk phone. She knew it could only be one of two people: her boss or her mother. They were pretty much the only people who ever dialed her work number. All of her friends and contemporaries just texted. Faye preferred it because it was easier to delay responding. Calls were so immediate, and you had to actually talk to the person, which she was constantly trying to avoid. She knew if it was her mom, she would have to answer a series of questions that were all too familiar: Who was she seeing? Anyone worth a second date? What did she have lined up for the weekend? She hated the fact that she had instilled a grain of hope in her mom by telling her she was on Match, Tinder, Bumble and Plenty of Fish. The truth was, the only apps she had on her phone were her fitness tracker and an annoyingly addictive game where you pushed blocks around a grid. That was the extent of her dating life.

A quick glance revealed the name Beverly Rice flashing on the screen and Faye picked up the receiver, glad to delay the parent talk.

"Hi, Bev," Faye answered, greeting her boss by her preferred nickname. Bev was the editor in chief of *Amuse Bouche* and a legend in the New York publishing industry, known as much for her food and wine expertise as her iconic horn-rimmed glasses. Faye had started out as her assistant, and very quickly Bev had shepherded her into writing for the magazine. Now she considered Bev her mentor, and often stayed late nights to help her, long after the other staff members had gone on to happy hour when an issue was closing.

"Faye, can you come see me in my office?"

"Of course." Faye hung up the phone and smiled.

Her door was adjacent to Bev's, within earshot, but
Bev liked to keep things formal.

Taking her bag with her just in case there would
still be time for lunch, Faye rounded the corner past
the cloth-covered walls of the cubicles and found the
door to her boss's office ajar. Knocking lightly, she
made eye contact with Bev, who stood up from her
desk chair and waved Faye inside.

"Everything okay?" Faye asked, taking a seat in
one of the two chairs facing Bev's desk. The room
was tastefully decorated in muted neutral tones
and covers from the magazine's bestselling issues
adorned the walls. When Faye looked just past her
boss's head, she could see the sun streaming across
the midtown skyscrapers that surrounded them.

"Oh, yes," Bev said, sitting down and leaning
across her desk. She was about twenty years Faye's
senior, in her early fifties, with professionally blown-
out long brown hair and hard-earned physique which
she attributed to good genes and Pilates. "I have an
exciting assignment for you."

Faye instinctively perked up and sat up a little
straighter in her chair. Her first thought was the ru-
mored opening of a new restaurant by a *Top Chef*
contestant. For that, she would definitely forgo a
night of peanut butter sandwiches.

"I have two words for you," her bespectacled boss
said enticingly. "Gregor Wright."

Faye watched as Bev sat back in her chair and
waited for her reaction. Of course she knew Gregor

Wright. He was famous. In fact, she and David had spent many nights watching his cable show, *Globe-Trotting with Gregor*, where he visited different travel destinations, eating and drinking his way through under-the-radar hotspots. And although she never said it in front of David, Faye had a major crush on the tall and slender Gregor, always in his signature leather bomber jacket. The combination of his British accent and the facial hair that she could so easily imagine grazing against her lady parts was enough fodder for many a solo session with the hand-held showerhead in her steamy bathroom.

"Yes, I know him," Faye said with a nervous cough.

Bev sighed. "I know you *know* him. How would you like to *meet* him?"

"No!" Faye said adamantly and then quickly changed to a more measured tone. "I mean, it sounds interesting…" She saw Bev raise an eyebrow at her from behind her glasses, but she didn't care. The last thing she needed was to spend an afternoon inter-viewing a womanizer. An arrogant, sexy, intelligent famous person who could probably get most women to drop their panties by simply uttering their name in that crisp English voice of his.

"None of the other magazines have it," Bev said. "This could be major for you."

Faye twisted her long, platinum blond hair over her shoulder and smiled nervously at her boss. "I ap-preciate that, really, I do."

"I need you for this, Faye," Bev said insistently. "You're my best writer. And I know it's not my place to say, but maybe traveling for a few days would do you good."

Faye opened her mouth to protest her boss's gentle suggestion but instead her mouth hung agape. She wasn't quite sure what to say. Of course, the assignment was incredible. And she did deserve it. But she had heard the rumors about the women who encountered Gregor. It wasn't so much that he was persistent, but more that women were drawn to his aura. Getting caught up in a fantasy was just something she didn't need right now.

"Did you say days—as in, multiple days?"

Bev returned Faye's nonplussed expression with a knowing smirk. "A week, actually. In London."

Faye exhaled deeply and turned her gaze toward the windows. The sun was shining bright for what felt like the first time in weeks. It had been a long, cold New York City winter and today, for the first time, people were walking around without jackets. Spring was in the air.

But where was she? Still in emotional limbo over a guy who was long gone. And punishing herself with her bland diet and her austere lifestyle. Even her outfit was joyless. She looked down at her black trousers and pilled sweater and could just hear her mother saying how she was "hiding her beauty." But what if she wasn't ready for anyone to see it again? Maybe she would never be ready.

"What about Lindsay?"

Bev snorted.

"She's a good writer!"

"She's fine. But I don't want someone 'fine,' I want you." Bev reached into her desk and produced a file folder which she tossed across the desk to Faye. "Everything you need to know is in there. Your flight leaves out of JFK first thing tomorrow morning."

Later that night in her apartment, Faye sat on the living room couch. Even though she had kept almost everything when David had moved out, the place still felt weirdly empty without him there. There were some things she liked about living alone—for one, she could watch any of her "girlie" shows without snark or criticism. And now things were decorated the way she preferred—before she hadn't been able to display all of the framed pictures of her many travels with her girlfriends after college. Come to think of it, she hadn't traveled much in recent years as David was more of a homebody. Maybe the adventure would be a good thing, she told herself.

Her suitcase, which she had gotten out of storage in her building's basement after work, was in the middle of the room and she had multiple items of clothing piled on the bed. Faye stared off into space, lost in a reverie featuring Gregor from the episode of his show where he went stand-up paddle boarding in Turks and Caicos. She easily remembered how his lean, tanned body looked against the vibrant blue waters. He had worn a bike-shorts-length Speedo, but instead of looking ridiculous, as most men did in that skintight suit, he managed to pull it off and give his female viewership something very substantial to occupy their thoughts after the episode ended.

Angry at herself for letting her thoughts get away from her, she picked up the phone and called her sister, Eden, who was always her "in case of emergency" person.

"Hey," Eden answered right away, her voice sounding a little harried and tired, as per usual. She was three years older than Faye, and a married mom of three. Right now, she was probably in the middle of serving dinner to her army of boys.

"What do we think about Gregor Wright?" Faye asked her sister tentatively. Ever since they were kids, Eden was the barometer of cool for Faye. If she said anything negative, the trip would be off.

"Ooh, the hot guy from the Travel Channel?"

"Yeah. That's him," Faye said, with a slight tinge of disappointment in her voice. So there really was no getting off the hook for this.

"Are you interviewing him?" Eden asked enthusiastically. "Make sure to take a selfie. And do other things I would say if there were not children present," she added deviously.

"I'm flying out tomorrow to interview him at his home in London," Faye said. Saying it out loud for the first time that day suddenly made the trip seem all too real. "Anyway, I just wanted to let you know. In case I was in a plane crash or something."

"Geez. Positive outlook, sis."

"I know. I just worry…"

"About being alone with a sexy-as-hell famous man who's used to getting anything he wants?"

"Pretty much."

"Listen," Eden said, her voice sounding more serious. "You've suffered enough. You deserve to let yourself have a little fun."

"I know," Faye whispered, the events of the night it had all gone so very wrong flooding back to her. She swallowed hard, refusing to renege on the promise she'd made herself to not cry about this again.

Sensing her sister's mood, Eden switched to a perkier tone. "Well, make sure to take lots of pictures. Oh, and bring me back a souvenir."

"Like what?" Faye asked incredulously. Sometimes her big sister acted like she was five.

"You'll think of something."

Faye hung up the call with a smile forming on her lips. She looked at the picture of her and Eden on her refrigerator standing in a London phone booth on a family trip there as teenagers. Surrounding it was further evidence of the fact that she was a diehard anglophile—a Beatles postcard, a magnet from Harrods and another one featuring a Union Jack.

There was no denying it—London, and Gregor Wright, were calling.

* * *

After a fitful night's sleep—Faye could never sleep
the night before a flight—the alarm went off at 4 a.m.
She took a quick shower and did a last-minute check
of the apartment. She then lugged her suitcase down
the four flights of stairs, hoping not to disturb her
neighbors, before pushing her way out of the building and onto the sidewalk where she could hail a cab.

A short taxi ride later—there was almost no traf-
fic at this early hour—Faye went through security,
found her gate and settled into a seat with the file
folder on Gregor to wait for her boarding call. Ever
punctual, she always liked getting to the airport with
plenty of time to spare.

After a while, she looked up from an article about
Gregor's favorite Thanksgiving recipes, including
a roguish photo of him in an apron with three-day
stubble, to check out some of her fellow travelers.
There were plenty of people flying solo, presumably on business, a few families dressed in their
comfy sweats, their seats overflowing with bags
and snacks and amusements, and seated just across
from her, a young couple obviously on their hon-
eymoon. The woman was wearing tight jeans and
high-heeled boots and looked about the same age as
Faye, and she could tell from the sparkle in her eye
that she had to be a newlywed. Her husband, a tall
man dressed in a gray sweater and jeans, seemed
to dote on her. Faye smiled wanly in their direction. As hard as she tried, it wasn't easy to let go of

all the plans she had made for her life as a married woman. She would never admit it to anyone, but seeing other happy couples made her stomach churn. Other people in love only served to highlight how very alone she felt.

When it was finally time to board, Faye found herself seated near a window with an empty seat next to her. *Perfect!* she thought, wrapping the huge cashmere scarf she always brought on trips around her shoulders and fishing for Bev's file folder in her bag. But before she could settle in, she felt a tap on her shoulder. Turning around, she saw that it was the newlywed.

"So sorry to ask, but would you mind switching so we could sit together?" the woman asked.

Faye thought about saying no but decided that would be too mean.

"Okay," she said reluctantly, gathering up her things.

"Thank you so much!" the woman cried, over-enthusiastically.

Faye made her way into the aisle and squeezed past a burly man in a faux leather jacket to find the middle seat—with another just as large guy on the other side—that she had agreed to occupy for the next seven hours. And, to add insult to injury, she'd have to look at the heads of the happy couple right in front of her. Once the plane reached cruising altitude, they would probably be making out, or more.

Faye pulled out her file folder and was just about

to resign herself—not just to the seat, but most likely dying alone in a fourth-floor walk-up apartment, when she heard a voice call out her name.

"Faye? Faye Curry?"

Faye sat up straight and looked around the plane, confused. Her first thought was that she was in trouble. Had the TSA found radioactive materials in her checked luggage? No, of course they hadn't, she told herself.

"Excuse me? Is Faye here?"

As the voice got closer, she recognized a distinct British accent. And when a man with spiky brown hair, sunglasses and a leather bomber jacket appeared in the aisle, the hair on her arms stood up on end.

"Hello?" Faye said feebly, totally thrown off by the fact that Gregor was suddenly standing two feet away from her, yelling her name through a packed flight full of strangers.

"Sir, if you'll just return to first class, we can page your friend." A pretty flight attendant reached out her hand and tapped Gregor gently on the shoulder. Gregor turned to the flight attendant, lowered his sunglasses and gave her a smile.

"I'm sorry, love. I'll have this sorted in a moment."

The woman blushed, clearly mesmerized by his sparkling blue eyes and his warm tone of voice paired with that crisp accent.

Faye was fumbling with the materials spread out on her tray table. She wasn't even sure if Gregor had heard her, until he turned his gaze toward her. She felt his eyes land on a picture of himself—the Thanksgiving article. Faye blushed deeply and quickly shoved the pages into her bag.

"I'm Faye," she said, standing up and mustering her confidence. She thought she would have a day to get over the jet lag before meeting him—or at least a moment to freshen up in the washroom.

"Pleasure," Gregor said, reaching out his hand to her. For a moment, Faye thought they were going to shake, but then she felt him leading her out of her seat and into the aisle. His hand was large, almost completely covering her own, and slightly rough to the touch. Once she was out in the aisle next to him, they looked at each other for the first time, face-to-face.

"You're the writer."

"You're on my plane," Faye said, stating the obvious.

Gregor smiled. "Let's go ride up front, shall we?"

Faye grabbed her carry-on out of the overhead bin and followed Gregor up the aisle and past the curtain that partitioned off first class from the rest of the plane. Her mind was racing a mile a minute. She wasn't expecting to have to begin her interview so soon. And she also hadn't expected that Gregor would be this good-looking in person. She had hoped it would be like other celebrities she had met who looked amazing on TV but short with skinny bodies and big bobble heads in person. Gregor was, in fact, quite tall—well over six feet—with a nicely formed head and broad shoulders Faye could easily imagine wrapping her arms around if he were inside her…

Easy, girl! she cautioned herself. Not only would this line of thinking be extremely distracting from getting her assignment done, it was also against her journalistic code. Getting involved with a subject, no matter how rakishly sexy, was a very bad idea.

"Let me grab that for you," Gregor said, taking the carry-on from Faye and easily hoisting it into the overhead compartment. The first-class cabin was the complete opposite of the cramped economy seating Faye was used to. The seats were wide and luxurious, each with their own entertainment center. A flight attendant was offering champagne to the couple seated in the row across from the one Gregor had stopped in front of. Although she was nervous about having to be "on duty" for the flight, at least she'd be comfortable, she figured.

"After you."

Gregor had stepped aside and was gesturing for Faye to take the window seat.

"Thanks," she said, sliding into the seat and looking up expectantly as Gregor sat down next to her. "So how did you know I'd be on this flight?"

"Bev told me," he said matter-of-factly. "I realized I was going to be leaving New York at the same time and I have to admit, I wanted to check out who was going to be interviewing me."

Faye smiled nervously, wondering what Bev had told Gregor about her.

"Bev said you're her top writer at the magazine. That's a very big deal."

"I've been doing this for a long time," Faye said. "Well, not this exactly," she said, looking around at her very not-usual surroundings. "But it's what I love to do."

"She didn't tell me that you're also strikingly gorgeous," Gregor said and then quickly put a hand over his own mouth. "Sorry. Please tell me you're not going to sue me for sexual harassment?"

Coming from any other man it might have seemed crude, but from Gregor, it was totally disarming. Faye smiled and laughed girlishly at the suggestion.

"You're fine," she said, trying to maintain an even keel while her mind did an instant replay of him calling her gorgeous.

"So what do you want to know?" Gregor folded his hands in his lap and looked directly at Faye, waiting for her response.

"Umm," Faye stuttered. "How did you…?" Funny enough, her mind, which was normally filled with thoughtful and provocative questions, was running on an endless loop of shirtless Gregor up on that paddleboard.

"I'm kidding!" Gregor said, touching Faye's shoulder so naturally and letting out a laugh. "Plenty of time for business later." He turned his attention to the flight attendant who was passing by in the aisle and

Faye audibly breathed a sigh of relief. This whole situation was just too intense! "Can we get two glasses of champagne?"

"Absolutely, sir," the flight attendant responded in what Faye thought was a flirty tone. Moments later, they each had a real crystal glass in hand, filled to the top with fine, French bubbly.

"Cheers," Gregor said, clinking glasses with her and taking a big sip. "Preflight ritual," he said, holding up the glass by way of explanation.

Faye reached into her bag and pulled out the copies of her tabloid magazines. "These are mine," she said with a grin.

"Oooh!" Gregor said, raising his eyebrows with a devilish grin. "I love these. They're so sordid."

Faye's insides turned to butter in reaction to his wicked pronunciation of the word. Why did even normal, everyday words sound so sexual with a British accent? She could probably be happy with him reading the dictionary out loud to her for the entirety of the flight. Instead, Gregor had taken one of the magazines from her and was paging through it.

"This is my favorite!" he exclaimed. "'Stars, they're just like us.' Look, it's Matthew McConaughey eating a burrito!"

Faye laughed and looked over his shoulder at the picture. She couldn't help but quickly inhale the scent of his aftershave. It was clean and manly and sent a signal straight to her private area.

"Have you ever been caught for one of these?"

Gregor waved off the suggestion. "That's just for A-listers. No one wants to see me coming round the bend with a bog roll."

"I think that would be rather intriguing," Faye said, which made Gregor laugh.

"If my toilet papers are what you're interested in, this is going to be a terrible interview."

Faye looked down at the glass she was holding and realized she had finished off the champagne. She was feeling a little light-headed, though she wasn't sure if it was from the drink or the cabin air. The flight attendant collected their glasses in preparation for takeoff and Faye made sure her seat belt was fastened before turning her gaze out the window. They were headed for the runway.

"Next in line for takeoff," the captain announced over the PA system. "Flight attendants prepare for departure."

Faye wasn't so sure she was ready for departure, but here she was, buckled in next to a handsome celebrity, and ready to spend a week in London with him working on the story of her career. As the plane picked up speed, she felt Gregor place his hand on top of hers on the armrest that divided their seats. She looked over at him, but he was sitting all the way back in his seat with his eyes closed.

It was exciting, the feel of his skin on hers, and comforting, too. It had been too long since she'd been touched by a man, let alone one she felt so instantly attracted to. Faye steadied herself against the loud

noise of the engine and just as the plane became air-
borne, she felt Gregor squeeze her hand—hard. The
sudden pressure gave her a jolt and she felt the nerves
throughout her body tingle in anticipation—of what
she wasn't yet sure. But one thing was certain: there
was no turning back now.

CHAPTER TWO

GREGOR WASN'T A fan of air travel, but he had done it so often in his career that settling in for a New York to London flight was really no big deal. As he settled back in his seat, reclining it now that the seat belt light was off, his mind began to turn over the details of the meetings he had taken over the past few days in the city.

There was talk of launching a new show, a cookbook, even a podcast. And while he was grateful that viewers still wanted to see and hear more from him, the truth was that his heart just wasn't in it. Ever since things had gone so terribly wrong with Emily, his girlfriend of over five years, he'd been down in the dumps. His friends had tried to cheer him up with several wild nights out in London, Ibiza and even Paris, but nothing had changed his downtrodden mood. His knack for picking up the prettiest girl in the room was still intact. The problem was, those easy hookups just weren't a thrill anymore.

So when his dear, old friend Bev at the magazine had begged him for an exclusive interview, promising to set him up with her top reporter—who also happened to be dynamic and wildly attractive—he allowed himself to be convinced. Some time spent with a woman who could actually make intelligent conversation sounded pretty good. And besides, when it came to Bev, he knew that there was no stopping her from getting what she wanted. So with a little bit of skepticism in his heart, he had agreed to booking the same flight and opening up his home to a complete stranger.

After flipping through the channels on the in-flight TV, Gregor turned to see that his traveling companion was already fast asleep. He smiled to himself, thinking that Bev knew him better than he had realized. Physically, Faye was his type—blonde, American, fit but not rail thin, with curves in all the right places.

Making sure she was actually asleep, he stole a quick glance at her breasts, the outline of which were nicely visible through her sweater. A feeling started to stir inside him that necessitated him readjusting the front of his jeans. Gregor quickly averted his gaze and grabbed a copy of the free magazine in his seat pocket.

As he absentmindedly paged through it, Faye stirred and stretched and then curled her body into his side. Gregor looked over at her and exhaled with a deep sigh. She was smart and sexy, and there was also an earnestness about her that was totally refreshing. The thought of getting her naked in his bed was very, very appealing.

Keep it professional, old boy, he thought to himself, trying to focus on an article on fly-fishing. Just then, Faye languidly threw her arm across his chest, pressing her ample breasts into his side and making a gentle purring sound as she slept. Gregor rolled his eyes and suddenly felt completely helpless to resist the growing urge she was inadvertently awakening inside of him. As he leaned over to pull her shawl up over her, he accidentally inhaled the sweet scent of her hair—a mixture of jasmine and honeysuckle that went straight to his head, intoxicating him more than any glass of champagne ever could.

Just then, a flight attendant appeared next to him, the same one he thought was flirting with him earlier.

"Excuse me, sir, would your girlfriend like a blanket?" she asked in a hushed tone.

Gregor stuttered momentarily, wondering if he should correct her. "Yes. Thank you very much."

Clearly, this did not look like what it was—a strictly business relationship. Would he be able to keep it to that? he wondered. When the flight attendant returned with the blanket, he laid it across Faye so that some of it was covering his legs, too. Against his better judgment, he allowed himself to imagine the beautiful American reaching her hand out to touch the growing bulge in his jeans. He thought about what it would be like if she actually undid his zipper, releasing his hardness and stroking it, unbeknownst to their fellow passengers, under the privacy of that airline blanket. Gregor sat back in his seat again, closing his eyes and allowing himself to revel in that sweet fantasy. Faye seemed like a nice girl, which made it all the naughtier, imagining her doing such dirty things to him in public.

"Mmm-mmm…" Faye left like she had no control over the noises that were coming out of her mouth.

"Shhh!" Gregor said, squeezing her ass as he balanced her on the plane lavatory sink. The full length of his manliness was inside her, and she was wetter than she could ever remember being.

In such close quarters, she was forced to look directly into Gregor's sparkling blue eyes, which was not such a terrible thing except for the fact that it intensified all the sensations she was feeling, making it even more difficult to keep quiet and not arouse the suspicion of the other passengers.

Gregor kept a firm grip on her ass. His motions were quick and deliberate, his eyes flashing with lust as he expertly drilled her, clearly stifling his own need to grunt or make any kind of sound. Wanting to be somehow even closer to him, Faye tilted her pelvis upward so that with each stroke she could feel his body graze up against her clitoris, which sent shivers running up her spine. It was the most pleasurable feeling she had even known—the fullness of Gregor's manhood inside her combined with the friction against that sensitive nub of nerves. In a moment her hands were in his hair and she pressed her mouth into his shoulder, trying to stop herself from coming. It was no use, as her body exploded in the biggest orgasm she'd ever experienced.

"Oh!" Faye cried out, waking up groggy in her seat. When she realized she'd been dreaming she instinctively clenched her wrap up close around her throat, covering herself as best she could from the curious eyes of her neighbors in the first-class cabin, and the handsome man seated next to her.

"Someone had a nice nap," Gregor said devilishly, raising an eyebrow at her. Faye quickly sat up, mortified that she had been pressed up against a man she hardly knew. At least he didn't know what she'd been dreaming. Or she hoped she hadn't said anything in her sleep that would give him a clue.

"I'm so sorry," Faye said, reaching into her bag for the water bottle she'd purchased back at the terminal and taking a big sip. Her mouth was dry and she felt totally disoriented.

"Not at all," Gregor said kindly.

Faye reached for her bag again and this time, slung it over her shoulder. "Will you excuse me?"

Gregor stood up to allow Faye to pass into the aisle, but even as he tried to make room, their legs brushed up against each other's, causing Faye to recoil. It wasn't that she didn't enjoy being in close contact with the Englishman, it was that she was too afraid of revealing her not-so-mild attraction to him.

When she reached the bathroom, Faye pushed the door open and locked it behind her. Splashing cold water on her face, but being careful not to wet her mascara, she tried to snap herself out of whatever reverie she was indulging in. Grabbing some paper towels, she looked down at the sink and vividly recalled some of the key scenes from her very dirty dream about Gregor. And although the dream wasn't real, the reaction of her body was. She couldn't remember the last time she had felt so frustrated with herself and at the same time, so turned on.

So it was possible she could feel like this again! she thought to herself. After her wedding was canceled, it seemed like her nether regions had dried up like the Sahara. It startled her to think that Gregor could arouse such a primal, physical reaction in her. She was just getting used to leading a sexless existence, but here was proof that she could still get those butterfly feelings—and then some! Fixing her lip gloss and running a brush through her hair, the sensible side of Faye took over. Even if she had been turned on by a dream, that was much different from getting turned on in real life. She unlocked the door and made her way back toward her seat.

"Feeling better?" Gregor asked, flashing Faye a knowing look as she slid past him and took her seat.

"I'm fine, thank you," she responded. She looked down at Gregor's tray table and saw that he was reviewing the file folder Bev had given her.

"This is some pretty intense reading," he said, paging through the clippings. "Guy seems like a bit of a wanker."

"Hey! That's my research," Faye said defensively. "It must have fallen out of my bag."

Gregor closed the folder and looked Faye directly in the eyes. It was eerily just like in the dream. "Let's get one thing straight," he said, his tone turning serious. "If I'm going to do this interview, then it can't be any of these canned questions. No, 'what's your go-to recipe' or 'your favorite holiday destination' crap. I want us to have a real conversation. Does that make sense?"

"Of course," Faye said, sliding the folder off his tray table and back into her bag.

"I don't mean to criticize, it's just that I want this to be genuine," he said. Faye could see that he was struggling to put all his thoughts and feelings into words. "I'll make you a promise," he said, leaning in closer toward her, so much that she could smell that manly, heady scent of him again. "I'll be completely open with you. If you do the same with me."

Faye shifted in her seat, feeling just the slightest bit uncomfortable. "Well," she answered carefully, "this interview isn't about me. It's about you."

"True," Gregor said, his tone growing even more direct, "but if there's to be trust, I need to know that you're being honest with me."

"Okay," Faye acquiesced. "What do you want to know?"

Gregor leaned in to whisper in Faye's ear. He was so close, she could feel the bristle of his whiskers against her cheek. "When was the last time you were touched, I mean really touched?"

Faye's cheeks instinctively burned hot. "Excuse me?" she hissed in a hushed tone.

Gregor turned his head so that their eyes were locked on each other's. "I can tell when someone is lonely. I've met lots of people in my line of work. It's like a signal people send out when they need contact."

Faye's cheeks burned even hotter, not because Gregor was wrong, but because he was so very right.

"Maybe you're right, but it's still none of your business," she said. And with that, Faye reached into her bag, pulled out her headphones and turned her attention to the screen in front of her for the duration of the flight.

When the plane finally landed in Heathrow, Faye was looking cool, calm and collected on the outside, but inside she was completely stressed out. Somehow, she was no longer on speaking terms with the person she was supposed to be interviewing. She vowed to herself to keep her personal feelings out of it and focus on the task at hand.

As they walked from the gate to baggage claim, Faye wondered why Gregor was so intent on figuring her out. Maybe it was a way to deflect attention off himself. Was he afraid of revealing too much? Was there something in his past he'd rather forget? She watched as a little boy walking with his family dropped his stuffed animal. Without a second thought, Gregor grabbed the doll and sprinted toward the family, calling out to them until the little boy was reunited with his bear. Faye watched a second longer as the family recognized him. Gregor gamely posed for selfies with each of the family members, including the stuffed bear. So he was a good guy, too, Faye thought, almost wishing it wasn't so. If he was an asshole, it would be so much easier to dismiss him, to put thoughts of him out of her mind.

As they left the baggage claim, each with a suitcase, Gregor headed to the parking lot and Faye followed. By the time they reached his car, a glistening black Miata, she was happy to be inside and get warm. Sliding into the passenger seat, Faye looked out the window as Gregor started the engine.

"I'm sorry about what I said back there, about your…" Gregor started and then trailed off. "None of my bloody business."

"That's right," Faye said matter-of-factly, in the most curt tone she could muster. Still, she couldn't help but allow a smile to cross her lips. It was delightful, knowing he was worried he had offended her.

"What?" he asked, turning his attention from the road to her and back again.

Faye laughed and pushed him playfully on the arm.

"Hey!" he cried. "One of us is operating a motor vehicle. This is serious business."

"I'm sure," Faye said, reaching over to the console and turning on the radio. It was "I'm Alive" by

Love and Rockets. Faye started to sing and after a moment, Gregor joined in, tapping the beat on the steering wheel.

When the song ended, they smiled at each other in acknowledgment of the moment.

"So, don't you want to ask me about my sex life?" Gregor asked after a moment.

"Not really," Faye said, and watched amusedly as Gregor made a face. "How about this," she started, blushing slightly at the question she couldn't believe she was about to ask. "What's the strangest place you've ever made love?"

Gregor laughed at the question, throwing back his head. Faye loved the sound of his laugh, it was so devil-may-care and sexy.

"Easy!" Gregor said emphatically. "A bear cave at the zoo!"

Faye laughed. "With—a bear?"

"No!" Gregor yelled, smacking her on the leg. The slap sent a pleasurable sensation across her thigh and straight to her nether region. She put her hand on the spot he had touched and rubbed it. "With a young lady. It was ill-advised. For us and the bear."

"Thank God you're alright!"

"Yes, but I am banned by the Zoological Society of London for life. I think they have a security shot of my face midcoitus posted in the break room."

"I'm sure the bears needed therapy," Faye said, smiling at him.

"Indeed."

Faye looked out the window and saw the familiar buildings of London disappearing on the horizon. "Hey, why are we driving away from the city?"

Gregor paused a moment before answering.
"We're going to my country house. You'll like it.
It's much more intimate." Gregor must have felt Faye
giving him a look because he quickly added, "Less
noise. You'll have your own room, of course, and
access to the study."

Faye thought about protesting—after all this was
not according to plan. Bev's itinerary stated that she
would have her own room at The Savoy and that all
the interviews would take place in a meeting room
set aside for that exact purpose. Still, it was true that
she would probably get more out of Gregor if he were
allowed to roam free in his natural habitat. And anyway, she was curious to see how this globe-trotting
star lived when he wasn't filming. Often a person's
home told more stories about them, or inspired the
subject to open up like nowhere else.

Instead of complaining, Faye found another song
she liked on the radio and settled in for the drive.

It was late in the evening by the time they reached
the country roads leading to Gregor's residence, and
it was too dark outside for Faye to discern any of the
scenery. The only thing she could see was Gregor,
his strong profile lit up by the dashboard lights, his
face looking serious as he navigated the winding
roads. Seeing him like that made her wonder why
he had dropped out of the public eye over the past

few years. Was it something romantic? Or something related to a family member? There would be time for all of those questions when they got settled into the country house and had gotten a good night's sleep. The thought of sleeping in the same place as Gregor made Faye's heart skip a beat. Even if they would be in separate rooms, it would still be such close quarters. She wasn't sure if she wanted him to turn the car around and take her to the safe anonymity of her reserved hotel room, or to just pull over to the side of the road and make out with her furiously. She thought about what it would be like to slide over the console dividing their seats and straddle his lap. She imagined her hair falling over her face as she leaned over him, grinding her way to ecstasy on that lean, strong, beautiful body of his.

Faye let out a sigh and saw Gregor's eyes momentarily flicker from the road onto her and back again. They drove on into the night.

By the time they reached the cottage, Faye was feeling groggy from all the travel, but she perked up at the sight of the beautiful stone house. Even in the pitch black, she could see that it was surrounded by a beautiful English garden, with seemingly every possible variety of flower sprouting from the ground to decorate the gray slabs. Gregor came around to open the car door for her and when she stepped onto the gravel, she noticed just how peacefully still it was outside, her heels crunching against the rocks was the only sound she could hear. It had been a while since she'd left the city and she'd forgotten just how much quieter things were away from the subways and 24/7 delis.

"This is it," Gregor said, fishing in his bag for the key. "My humble abode." Gregor unlocked the door and flipped a switch that lit up the entryway and the living room. If the outside of the house was country-chic, the inside was definitely cozy-modern, with neutral colors, comfortable couches, a wide-screen TV and top-of-the-line Bose speakers. Faye could see the kitchen from where she was standing, and it looked like something from out of a magazine. It was like stepping into the most expensive choice on the Airbnb list, except that this was Gregor's home.

"Or not so humble," Faye commented, taking in the colorful artwork that adorned the walls. "Oh, my God. Is that a Warhol?"

Gregor smiled and seemed a little embarrassed by his own good fortune. "Yeah," he said casually, stroking his chin. "I bought it during my art phase. I've been thinking of selling it."

"It's fantastic," Faye said, marveling at the painting—and the whole place.

"I'll keep it, then," Gregor said.

"Do you mind showing me to my room? I'm a little tired," Faye said, suppressing a yawn.

"Of course," Gregor said, snapping to attention. "Right this way."

Faye followed Gregor down the hallway and into

a small bedroom. When he flicked on the lights, she saw a comfortable room painted white, with a beautiful area rug. There were colorful pillows on the bed and a small writing desk with a stool next to it.

"This should have everything you need. The loo's through there." He gestured to a door leading to a private bathroom. "Can I make you something? You must be starving."

"I think I'm just going to take a shower and crawl into bed," she said, plopping down on the fluffy white comforter. Then, thinking she didn't want to give him the wrong idea—or did she—she quickly stood up. "Thanks so much for having me in your home. It's really lovely."

"Anything you need, I'm just down the hall," Gregor said chivalrously. The two stood in awkward silence until Gregor cleared his throat. "Well, I'll leave you to it, then," he said, smiling at her as he shut the door behind him.

Faye stood there staring at the door for a beat and then lay down on the bed, this time breathing out a heavy sigh. It was exhausting, trying to look good in front of someone for that amount of time. She decided to take a long, hot shower and then get into bed and sleep for a very long time. She could worry about the interview tomorrow.

After doing some quick unpacking into the chest of drawers and reveling in a steamy, hot shower, Faye slipped into her pajamas—a pair of tiny shorts and matching camisole covered in pink and red flowers.

Noticing her phone, she saw there were a few text messages from Bev, asking how things were going and reminding Faye how important the story was for the magazine.

Faye understood why Bev was so concerned. With so much digital content available, magazines like *Amuse Bouche* really had to go the extra mile to grab readers' attention. It didn't help that three of their sister magazines had folded in the past two years. The pressure was on to deliver.

She also noticed there was a voice message from her mother. Faye had sent her a quick text, letting her know she'd be out of the country, and of course her mother had called her back and left several messages. She made a mental note to give her a call the next morning.

Faye took a cursory glance at her Facebook feed and noticed that David had posted a picture of himself with a group of friends at the beer garden. Even though her sister and friends had advised she unfollow him, Faye couldn't bring herself to do it. But they were right, it was torture, looking through his pictures, wondering if he was having more fun without her...

Faye clicked off the page and placed her phone, face down, on the nightstand.

But just as she was about to slip into the comfort of her bed, she felt her stomach growl. Deciding to head into the kitchen to see if there was any food, she opened the door to her room and slowly made her way down the hall. She turned the corner and saw there was a light on. Peeking her head around the corner, she watched for a moment as Gregor stood at the counter. He had on a T-shirt and lounge pants and looked even sexier than he had on the plane.

"Hey," Faye said, walking into the room. "We were thinking about the same thing!"

"Were we? I wasn't sure," Gregor said, raising an eyebrow at her.

Faye pointed to the ingredients strewn across the counter. "The food," she said, moving next to Gregor and looking more closely at what he was making. Then, throwing caution to the wind, she decided to make a huge confession. "Remember what you said on the plane? About my sex life? Well, you were right."

Gregor stopped what he was doing and gave Faye his full attention.

"The thing is, I just don't think I like sex anymore," she said, running a hand through her long blond hair. "At least, I didn't think I ever would again. Until earlier today."

Gregor's eyes lit up with desire and he moved toward her with laser focus.

"Wait," she said, holding out her hand when he was almost close enough to touch her. "I'm not sure we should do this. Even if it would be fun…"

Gregor put his hands around her waist and just when it looked like he was about to kiss her, he instead spoke directly into the side of her neck. She could feel the gentle bristle of his facial hair on her skin as he moved his lips.

"I just want you to feel pleasure," he whispered, his breath hot on her neck.

Faye nearly melted, her skin tingling in anticipation of that pleasure, but she somehow managed to maintain her composure.

"I'm a journalist, working on a story," she said, reminding Gregor of her creed. Or was she really trying to remind herself? She knew there was something she had learned in school about reporters needing to remain clearheaded, which was at the moment impossible to do, as Gregor planted openmouthed kisses along her neck.

"Wait," Faye said, breaking away from Gregor and trying hard to catch her breath. "I can't get involved with my subject. It's unethical."

"Is that really what you're concerned about?" Gregor said, pushing Faye's curtain of long blond hair behind her ear and looking directly in her eyes. Faye could see that this had been true all of his life. He was used to getting whatever he wanted, whenever he wanted it. But not this time.

"I never get involved with my subjects. It's my personal policy," Faye said, steeling herself. Every inch of her body was pulling toward this man's touch, but her mind held her back. Just as she was about to turn and head back to her room, his voice called her back.

"Wait," he said. "What if it's just about me showing you one of my skills? For your article."

Faye couldn't help but be intrigued. "And what
skill is that?"

As an answer, Gregor pushed all of the utensils
and ingredients off the countertop and easily lifted
Faye onto it so that she was seated directly in front of
him. She could feel the cool sensation of the marble
against the parts of her buttocks that were exposed
by her shorts. She breathed in deeply and kept eye
contact with Gregor as he moved in close enough
to kiss her, but then knelt down, looping his fingers
into the elastic waistband and lifting her up slightly
as he removed her shorts. Once he had undressed
her, he simply stood there, admiring the beauty of
her femininity.

Faye wasn't used to being so exposed. Any previous action she'd ever partaken in with other partners
was pretty much relegated to under the covers. But
in that moment, having it all out there made her feel
powerful and sexy. It also didn't hurt that Gregor was
looking at her with the most intense, lustful stare
she'd ever witnessed.

As he began kissing the insides of her thighs, she
grasped the edge of the counter to steady herself.
What was this man doing to her—and why was he
so good at it? she wondered. She admitted to herself that as soon as she heard she was interviewing
Gregor, she had hoped there would be a spark between them. But if anyone had told her he would be

pleasuring her on his kitchen counter, she definitely would not have believed it.

It was the same place he had probably prepared countless meals for dignitaries and celebrity friends, and now he was making a meal of her, hungrily biting at the soft flesh of her thighs, his fingers only lightly grazing across her most intimate area. It was this withholding that made her want his touch even more.

Faye groaned—it was an animalistic noise, begging for Gregor to put her out of her misery and give her the warm, tingly feeling she had gone without for too long. Gregor responded by pressing his mouth over her honeypot and flicking his tongue persistently over her clitoris. Faye threw back her head, her long hair trailing down her back as she closed her eyes and gave in to the feeling Gregor was bestowing upon her.

Coming in front of your interview subject seemed like the wrong thing to do, but Faye couldn't stop herself. As Faye felt herself begin to tremble, she raked her fingers through Gregor's hair, which she'd been wanting to touch ever since they had met and cried out, making a sound that came from somewhere deep in her belly. Pulling him toward her, she reached her climax and then teetered there for a few moments, her body quivering against his mouth. When she finally came down, he looked up at her with a satisfied smile.

Faye wasn't sure what she expected to happen

next—was he going to fuck her right there on the kitchen counter? Or maybe bring her back to his bedroom and make love to her for the rest of the night? She had no idea.

But instead of taking off his own pants, which Faye would have been highly curious to see, Gregor simply reached up and planted a sweet kiss on her forehead.

"Sleep well," he said before turning and retreating to his own bedroom.

CHAPTER THREE

GREGOR WAS AWAKE earlier than usual the next morning. Over the past year, he had allowed himself to sleep in, ignoring the flurry of business emails and texts to be answered. After a while of not responding to them, the offers for appearances had started to die down—and he was okay with that. Ever since Emily had run off with his supposed best friend, Erik, all of the fame and money suddenly seemed less important. He had been on TV so long, he wasn't even sure he could remember the reason he had wanted to cook and travel in the first place.

This morning was different. Something about this beautiful young reporter had stirred something in him. He had the overwhelming need to please her. She was smart, sharp as a knife and gorgeous—it was true. But he had been with plenty of smart, good-looking women before. Staring out his bedroom window at the perfectly manicured lawn, he decided that it was Faye's sincerity that was having this profound effect on him. She just seemed so genuine.

Suddenly he had a strange flash of him and Faye

with two kids, pushing a pram in Hyde Park. Gregor shivered. He had always been adamant about not wanting kids. It was one of the things that made him so attracted to Emily. She was always ready for the next party, never wanting to settle down. He had a strange feeling that something was shifting inside him. It was damn near disconcerting.

Feeling the pangs of hunger pinch at his stomach, he threw on some jeans and a T-shirt and made his way into the kitchen. The house was still quiet, so he assumed his guest was still asleep. Had it been a mistake to bring her here? he wondered. Not because he didn't trust her—he had trusted her fully from the first moment they had locked eyes—but because he wasn't sure if he wanted the world to know what had been going on with him.

Surveying the state of the kitchen—it was fully cleaned and spotless—Gregor shook his head and smiled, realizing Faye must have done it. How could she have had the presence of mind to clean a kitchen after what had transpired? He remembered how Faye had looked after he had given her an orgasm to end all orgasms—maybe his best work yet.

It had taken everything in him to not unleash his raging hard-on that he had been harboring since the airport and plunge it deep into that inviting opening of hers. Of course, his cock had been aching for her, particularly when she leaned on him in her sleep during the flight. Their scene in the kitchen was a total feat of restraint, as far as Gregor was concerned. He had gone back to his room and given himself release thinking about her gorgeous naked body, that was true. To Gregor, it was more important that she knew he was attentive to her than for him to get what he needed. It was a lesson he had learned firsthand long ago.

Her name was Marina and she was the chef in the restaurant where he had been a busboy at age eighteen. She was older—probably late thirties—and they'd spent many late nights together in the restaurant long after the dining room had closed. Marina was more than his lover, she was his mentor, teaching him everything she knew about sex and cooking. The two were not that dissimilar, really. They both required a heightened use of their senses, attention to detail, precision and the unwavering confidence to be bold in their choices and execution. He had gone from being a child that thought pleasuring a woman was something you had to do to get your own bits off, to an act to be savored in its own right, like prying open a luscious oyster and reveling in the sweet and tangy flesh as it slid down your throat.

He hadn't thought that way about food—or a woman—in a long time. In fact, everything in his life felt a bit stagnant. At first it had felt good to turn down shows and speaking engagements—it was freeing, really. But then he stopped answering when friends called, and even stopped cooking altogether. It was just him anyway, so what was the point?

As he scanned the kitchen area, he looked for

the tools he needed. He reached for the pan on the rack above the range and opened the subzero fridge, pulling out herbs, spices, anything he could get his hands on that would go together. He had the sudden urge to cook for this woman—to create something special and watch her consume it. He needed to see that look of happiness on her face and this was the one thing he knew he could do well.

After laboring over the stove for forty-five minutes, cooking an exquisite breakfast of eggs, vegetable and fruit, and brewing French-press coffee, he had hoped the aroma would have stirred Faye, but the house was just as quiet as when he had gotten up. Walking quietly down the hall toward the guest bedroom, he listened at the door for a moment for any signs of activity before cracking it open just the slightest bit and peeking his head inside.

The outline of Faye's body was visible in the bed, and all but a few strands of her blond hair were covered by the comforter. Gregor thought about waking her up, but instead decided to let her be. Opening the window, he reached out and plucked a peony from his garden and placed it on the pillow next to her before quietly taking leave of her room.

Faye tossed and turned and finally opened her eyes, feeling a little disoriented. For an instant, she had no idea where she was, but then the memories came flooding back. Of course. This was Gregor's house. And she was on assignment. But clearly that wasn't the only thing she was on. Faye blushed, remembering the spontaneous encounter between the two of them in the kitchen last night. Then a jolt of reality hit her. Would things be awkward? Would he want her to leave? Would she have to return to New York and face Bev without a story in hand?

Reaching over to the nightstand for her phone, Faye noticed a red flower resting on the pillow beside her. It was answer enough—so he was still thinking about her! She couldn't help but smile to herself. Gregor Wright, she thought to herself, laughing at the improbability of it all. The man she knew from TV was roughish, witty and adventurous. Gregor in real life was all of those things, too, but he was also kind and intelligent and very, very attentive. She wondered why he had ended their encounter so quickly.

Swinging her feet over the side of the bed, she quickly showered in the en suite bathroom and threw on a cream-colored, belted linen shirtdress, pulling her long hair into a simple chignon. As she opened the door to her bedroom, she noticed a wonderful aroma emanating from the kitchen. Having forgotten all about checking her phone, she realized she didn't even know what time it was.

"Good morning," Gregor said when she walked into the kitchen. He was sitting at the counter reading the newspaper and drinking coffee, and he had on a pair of reading glasses that somehow made him look even sexier. Glancing at the counter, she couldn't help but flash back on their very erotic encounter from the previous night.

"Sleep well?" Gregor asked.

"Very," she answered, sitting down beside him.

"Here, let me get you some breakfast," he offered, jumping up.

"Oh, please don't bother, I'm not much of a breakfast person." Faye saw Gregor's face drop and quickly realized that he had prepared this entire meal on her behalf. "I mean, yes, please."

Gregor smiled and poured coffee, eventually setting a beautifully plated breakfast in front of her.

"Do you cook like this for all your guests?" she asked, digging into the perfectly cooked omelet.

Gregor looked thoughtful. "I don't have many guests these days. But I do enjoy cooking for people I care about."

Faye returned Gregor's smile and took a sip of coffee—it was the richest, most luxurious roast she had ever tasted. Clearly, this man knew his way around the kitchen—and other things!

"Why is that? Why have you been so out of the public eye lately?"

Gregor chuckled to himself. "I see, so are we in interview mode now?"

"That is what I came here for," Faye replied, meeting his gaze.

"Very well," Gregor said. "I've been taking some time to figure out what I really want to do next."

"That's valid," said Faye, wishing she had brought out her recorder or at least a notebook.

"But off the record?" Gregor raised his eyebrows and looked at Faye. She nodded. "It's really lame, but I had my heart broken."

Faye was speechless for a moment, surprised by how open he was being. "Me, too," she offered.

"There is something I want to show you," Gregor said, his tone a little more positive. "Are you up for a drive?"

Moments later, the two of them were back in Gregor's car, driving down a twisty country road. In the daylight Faye could see just how beautiful the English countryside really was, and she felt thankful that Gregor had given her the chance to see beyond the city streets of London. As they passed emerald green hills and fields populated by horses and cows, Faye felt herself relax. There was so much beauty here, and she had a world-class tour guide to show it to her.

Shortly into their drive, they turned into a small village and Gregor parked the car in front of a simple redbrick building.

"It used to be a pub, but there was a fire and the owners never rebuilt," he explained, opening the door for her and leading her up to the main entrance. As they walked up the cobblestone steps, Gregor put his hand protectively on the small of Faye's back and she felt a shiver run up her spine. Just the touch of this man, even over her clothing, was enough to get her blood rushing to all the places she wanted him to stroke. The door was unlocked, and Gregor pushed his way in. "It needs a lot of work, but it has potential," he said as the two of them stood together in what was presumably the dining room, surveying their surroundings.

Faye nodded enthusiastically, but all she could see was a stone floor, exposed support beams and a few leftover booths that had seen better days. It was hard to envision the space as the bustling pub it had likely once been.

"My concept is a gastropub, it will be communal-style with new beers and wines introduced each week. It's something I've been thinking about for a long time."

"This isn't the first time you've visited here, is it?" Faye asked.

"I used to come here all the time with friends. Ever since the property was put up for sale—well, let's just say I've been interested."

"Well, I think you should go for it," Faye said decisively. "It sounds really exciting."

"I just don't know if people would be as enthusiastic as I am…"

Faye cut him off short. "Once my article runs, the whole world is going to want reservations." Boldly, she put her arms up on his shoulders, taking a moment to feel his muscular deltoids. He answered her touch by wrapping his arms around her waist and pulling her in toward him, so that their bodies were pressed together.

Wordlessly, Gregor leaned in and kissed her hard on the mouth, his hands roaming her body. Faye could feel the growing erection in his jeans, and she put her hands on his ass, pulling him toward her with urgency.

"This is the strangest interview I've ever done," she said, looking up at him when they came up for air.

Gregor smiled and left her side momentarily to bolt the front door to the pub shut.

Faye's insides tingled with anticipation as she watched Gregor walk toward her with a determined look. For someone who thought she wasn't interested in sex anymore, she surprisingly could not deny the ache between her legs that needed to be addressed, immediately. Maybe the problem was she just hadn't been having sex with the right person.

Gregor stood in front of her, piercing through all of her inhibitions with those crystal-clear blue eyes.

"I want you so badly," he said in that amazing British accent. Before she knew it, he was leading her to one of the remaining restaurant booths. Spinning her around, he bent her over the table. Pulling up the skirt of her dress, he wasted no time in removing the white lace bikini that stood between him and what he wanted. Faye savored every moment as she felt his rough hands grab the sides of her panties and slowly slide them down her legs, exposing her ample behind to him.

With her cheek on the old wood table and her

mind devoid of any thoughts other than Gregor, she made happy noises as he planted little kisses from her ass cheeks toward the insides of her thighs.

She wasn't sure if it was the unusual environment or just the fact that it was Gregor, but she found herself getting wetter. She instinctively pushed her behind out toward him, hoping he would give her what she so desperately needed.

Faye usually wasn't one for dirty talk but in that moment, she felt no shame in asking for what she wanted.

"Please…fuck me," she requested, her voice urgent and commanding.

Gregor made a noise that told Faye he was completely undone by what she had just said. Feeling the rough fabric of his jeans scratch against the back of her legs, she could tell that he was about to comply. With a quick unzip, no sooner had Faye arched her head up from the table than she felt the head of Gregor's smooth, warm cock pushing at her entrance. With a deep grunt, he easily slid his full length into her, and she arched her torso up even farther as she received him.

It seemed like Faye's whole body had been shocked awake by his entry. She hadn't even had a chance to see his penis or to hold it in her hand, but she could tell from the way her body was responding that it was nicely sized, just thick enough for her to feel totally filled up with him inside her.

With his hands on her hips, Gregor fucked Faye,

keeping a steady rhythm as he grunted and moaned, clearly as caught up in the frenzy of the moment as she was. Faye loved it even more when he let his hands explore, moving up to her breasts, which he squeezed, sending shivers through her body. Even though her nipples were still covered by the thin, linen fabric of her dress, they responded immediately to his touch, getting erect underneath the pads of his fingers.

Dizzy with lust, Faye pushed her ass out even farther and Gregor responded by quickening his pace. He was fucking her so fast and hard, she thought the old table might give out from beneath them. Reaching one hand under her, Gregor's fingers quickly found Faye's pleasure button and he flicked it repeatedly as he himself came to finish.

The combination of hearing Gregor come, along with the direct pressure he was providing her, made Faye's whole body seize up in orgasm. She let out a low growl, the likes of which she'd never heard come out of her mouth before, and finally collapsed down in exhaustion.

Gregor pulled Faye up toward him so that they were facing one another. He had a silly grin on his face and Faye felt the sudden urge to kiss him again—he looked so simultaneously pleased with himself and vulnerable.

"You can't talk like that if you want me to last very long," he said, pushing a strand of hair that was plastered to her cheek behind her ear.

"Like what?" Faye said innocently, batting her eyes at him.

"C'mon," Gregor said, taking her by the hand. "Let's go get some bangers."

"Didn't we just do that?"

"Cheeky," Gregor said, raising an eyebrow at her.

"Indeed," she said, happily following him outside and back to the car.

Sitting at an outside table at The Filly Inn, one of his favorite pubs in the area, Gregor felt satisfied for the first time in as long as he could remember. Not only did he have the company of Faye, a smart and gorgeous and sexy American, but he had his favorite meal in front of him to share with her: fish and chips and a pint. The sun was shining brightly, and it was as perfect a day as one could ask for. Bringing Faye to see the run-down building that really was his dream restaurant, he'd had no plans to do anything other than show her the space. But being with her had an effect on him. Just one come-hither look from her seemed to get his cock twitching and now his senses were on high alert in her presence.

She was an even better lover than he had anticipated. He loved the way she looked, the unabashed curves, the way she asked for exactly what she wanted. He had thought that maybe they would flirt but in deciding to let her interview him, he hadn't anticipated this strong of a connection. Now he wondered just how much of himself he was willing to expose. In a way, he had already started to let his guard down.

"This place is perfect," Faye said, looking around at the scenery. She had sunglasses on and Gregor watched as she dipped a chip into the little pool of ketchup on the side of her plate and slid it between her perfect pink lips. Oh, to be that chip! he thought to himself. And then, *Get a hold of yourself, man.* It was easy for Gregor to get carried away with whatever he was passionate about at the time.

For a while it had been his show, then Emily. Now he wasn't sure what he wanted to focus on. But he knew that Faye was a positive person, and showing her his plans for the future had just felt right in that moment. He got the sense that she was a kindred spirit.

"Thanks for taking me here," Faye said, raising her sunglasses. Her brown eyes were so deep, so sexy. He suddenly wished they were alone so he could go for round two.

"This is the best interview I've ever done, hands down," he said, draining the pint and placing it in front of him on the table.

"I bet you say that to all the pretty reporters," Faye said with a hint of sarcasm in her voice.

Gregor frowned. "No. Actually, I'm a one-woman sort of bloke."

Faye changed her expression to match Gregor's serious look.

"Does that surprise you?"

"No," Faye said quickly. "I think that's nice. I'm pretty much a serial relationship person, too." She stood up from the table and Gregor gave what must have been a concerned look.

"More lager," Faye said, holding up the empty glasses. He watched with admiration as she walked away from him, her silhouette so beautiful in her dress.

After she was out of sight, Gregor looked around at the other bar patrons. He loved that this was a place that, even if someone recognized him, he would be left alone. There weren't a lot of places left in the world where he could just be another bloke out for a pint, but this was one of them, and because of that he treasured the place.

That was the drawback of being a world traveler for a living—everyone knew you, or at least thought that they did. And thus, everyone wanted a piece of you, whether it was a moment to chat or a selfie or just having to answer the question, "Hey, aren't you…?"

After all these years, Gregor wasn't jaded about the privilege his job afforded him. After all, how many people got to jet off to exotic locales and be fed the world's greatest food to make a television show? But part of him just wanted a break from the grind. He wanted to get back to basics, to find the thing he was really passionate about. He wanted to remember why he had started off on this path in the beginning. He thought that just maybe, his restaurant idea was a way to do that. For a second, he let himself wonder what it would be like to run the place with Faye by his side. Not that he would expect her to give up her career and move to the other side of the world to serve upscale bangers and mash with him. But being in the space with her earlier had just felt so perfect, he couldn't let go of the fantasy.

Gregor looked up from his reverie to see Faye standing in the doorway of the pub talking to a man. He was tall, slightly older and his booming laugh was audible over the low rumble of chatter from the other pub patrons. It only took him a second to realize that it was Erik. Then, in about two seconds, his blood started to boil.

What was she doing talking to that ass? And why was he here? He hated The Filly Inn. They had even agreed after their big falling-out that it would remain Gregor's place.

Gregor watched as Erik helped Faye with the beers she was balancing. There was nothing he could do to avoid it—they were heading toward the table.

"Fancy seeing you here, mate," Erik said in a too-friendly tone when he was standing in front of him.

"Erik," Gregor said, unable to disguise the disappointment in his voice. It had been a year since they had crossed paths—not entirely by accident. He watched as the tall, prematurely gray-haired man he knew so well slid his glass of Guinness onto the table and took a seat in front of him.

"Seat's taken, man," Gregor said, his defenses up.

"I've met your girlfriend, she's lovely," he said, regarding Faye admiringly.

"She's not my girlfriend, she's a reporter. We're here working on a story so if you'd kindly…"

"Surely you have a minute for an old friend, mate." Erik looked expectantly at Gregor, but Gregor wasn't about to give him an opening. He knew from experience that if you gave Erik an opening, his tendency was to burst through it, taking everything he could grab.

"You're still not sore about all that are you?" Erik turned to Faye with a smile by way of explanation. "Stuff from the past. Ancient history, far's I'm concerned."

"It would be, to you," Gregor said quickly, trying his best to keep his anger in check. The story of his best friend stealing his long-term girlfriend out from under him was not something that he wanted in the article—or for Faye to know personally, given recent events.

"She left, mate," Erik said, shaking his head.

Gregor looked up unable to hide his surprise.

"It's true. I'm all alone again."

"I'd say I'm sorry but—"

"I know," Erik said, cutting him off. "But you're not." He took a long pull on his beer.

"That's not what I was going to say," Gregor corrected. "What are you doing out here anyway? I thought you detested The Filly."

"Not a bad place to throw back a pint on a gorgeous day," Erik said, trying to sound more cheerful. He turned to Faye. "And what brings the two of you down this way?"

"Gregor was showing me an empty space."

Gregor made hectic slashing motions across his throat, stopping Faye midsentence.

"We were just out for a drive," she said quietly.

"Ah…" Erik said, putting it together. "You were looking at the old Arms were you? Got a project in mind, then?"

"I wasn't and I don't," Gregor said curtly. "Now if you'll excuse us…"

Finally getting the message, Erik stood up and drained his beer. "Alright. I can tell when I'm not wanted," he laughed. "It was a pleasure meeting you," he said, taking Faye's hand.

"Nice to meet you, too," Faye said. Gregor couldn't help but roll his eyes.

"What was that all about?" Faye asked once Erik was gone.

"An old friend," Gregor said wistfully. "Former best friend. Until he stole the love of my life. At least, I thought she was."

Faye gasped and covered her mouth. "I'm so sorry, Gregor."

Gregor waved off her concern. "Ah, he's right. It's in the past. But I don't trust him. This is all off the record, I hope? I wasn't planning to tell you any of this. You have a way of making me want to open up."

"I'm sorry I mentioned anything…"

"You're fine," Gregor said, taking both of her hands in his and looking directly in her beautiful eyes. The wave of nausea he felt at seeing Erik lifted when she smiled at him. "More than fine," he said, adding just enough of a sultry tone to his voice that Faye smiled sexily back at him and squeezed his hands in hers. Maybe things were going to be alright after all.

CHAPTER FOUR

IT WAS 2 A.M. when Faye's phone started to buzz, jarring her out of a deep slumber. Blinking her eyes open, she looked at the name on her screen and decided to answer.

"Hello, Bev?" she said, unable to hide the exhaustion in her voice.

"Oh, honey, I'm sorry! The time difference! I completely forgot," her editor said apologetically.

"It's okay," said Faye, sitting up in bed with an array of pillows behind her. She actually was happy to hear a voice from back home, even if she had been soundly sleeping. She and Gregor had spent the rest of the day pub hopping and after a long walk, ended up at a small farm-to-table restaurant where he knew the owners and they'd been treated like royalty.

"Do you want to talk tomorrow?"

"No, no," Faye said, dismissing the thought.

"So, how's our friend, Gregor Wright?"

Faye thought for a moment and couldn't stop a smile from forming on her lips. "He's great!" she said. "Very nice. More introspective than I would have thought."

"Oh, is that so?" Bev asked, her voice dripping with innuendo. She knew her boss wanted some juicy gossip but there was no way she was going to give it to her.

"It's going well," Faye said vaguely. As Bev went on about other work projects Faye wondered for a second if it really was going well. At least she thought it was. When they had finally made it back to the house, they both instinctively retreated to their own rooms. Which was fine. After all, it wasn't like she was expecting to sleep in his bedroom with him. Although the thought of lying next to him, wrapped up in his arms, his leg slung over her naked body was quite appealing.

"Faye, are you getting all of this?"

Faye snapped back to reality and looked at the clock. She really did need to get some sleep if she was going to continue their interview in earnest the next morning.

"Actually, Bev, is it okay if I update you again tomorrow? I'm suddenly feeling really tired. Must be the jet lag."

"The jet lag or something else," Bev suggested.

Not biting, Faye thought to herself as she said goodbye and hung up the phone.

Faye rested her head on the pillow for a moment and was about to close her eyes when she thought of her mother. Since she was already awake, she hit the number in her favorites and waited patiently as the phone rang.

"Faye!" her mother answered. "Where are you? You had me worried sick. Eden says you're with some guy from television?"

"Mom, everything is fine," Faye tried assuring her. "I'm in London, in the countryside actually, interviewing Gregor Wright. Have you heard of him?"

Faye's mother snorted. "Heard of him? The man's sex on legs! I watch his show for masturbation material."

"Mother!" Faye gasped. Even though she was used to her mom talking this way, and in her older years actually found it quite funny and endearing, she never let on. In a way, it was their comedy act, with Faye playing the straight man.

"Oh, don't be such a prude. It's high time you had a good seeing to, especially after that loser David."

"Mom, please don't say that," Faye pleaded. It wasn't that her mother was wrong, she just didn't need to hear all of her inadequacies spelled out for her.

"Well, stay safe and let me know what happens," her mother said.

"Will do, Mom. You take care," Faye said gently. They exchanged kissing sounds before hanging up.

When she woke up the next morning, she showered and changed into a fitted, sleeveless top and dressy, wide-legged shorts. Even though her outfits were getting progressively skimpier, Faye rationalized that it was quite hot outside and she needed to feel comfortable.

Entering the kitchen, she saw that Gregor had already gone out, so she made herself some coffee and toast. While reading through the news on her phone she thought she heard a car pull up to the house. When Gregor didn't enter, she went to the door and opened it, only to see the taillights of a black Jaguar speeding away. She looked down and saw that there was an envelope on the doormat. Picking it up, she inspected the handwritten script that bore both her and Gregor's names. Just then, Gregor came jogging up from around the other side of the house.

"Good morning," Faye said, taking in the view of Gregor in his running shorts. He was sweaty and sexy, and she suddenly had the urge to put all thoughts of an interview aside and get up close and personal with every inch of his dripping body.

"Hello," he said, leaning in to kiss her cheek. When he did, Faye inhaled his masculine scent and found it so intoxicating it was hard to stand up. "You look lovely," he said, his gaze making its way down from her clavicle to her breasts.

Remembering the envelope she was holding, she held it out to him.

"What's this?"

"I have no idea," she said, "but I think it was dropped off in person. I saw a car pulling out just as you came back."

Gregor looked at the envelope with a curious

glance, turning it over. He then went inside and Faye followed him.

With the envelope torn open, Gregor sat down on one of the kitchen stools and read its contents. A frown formed on his lips.

"Everything okay?" Faye asked.

"It's from Erik. He's invited us to dinner tonight at his home."

"Well, that's very formal. He could have just texted, right?"

"That's just like him. He can't do anything without making a huge deal. Anyway, this is a big deal. We haven't spoken in a few years—well, before yesterday."

Faye tilted her head to the side and moved closer to Gregor. "It sounds to me like he wants to reconcile."

Gregor let out a big sigh.

"You've been close friends for a while, haven't you?"

"Since we were kids," Gregor said, his expression softening. "We both went to culinary school together. We were a team."

"So why did he betray you?"

Gregor stood up and paced around the kitchen. His nervous energy was palpable. "It's the way we always are. We end up fighting over women. This time one woman in particular." Gregor looked at Faye, waiting for a reaction.

"Ah," Faye said knowingly. "Emily?"

"They'd been sleeping together for an entire summer when I found out. The thing is, I don't think he even cared about her. Part of me thinks he did it for sport."

Faye got up and put her arms around him. "I'm so sorry. You must be heartbroken."

"Not anymore," Gregor said, shrugging it off. "In retrospect, we didn't belong together. She was a free spirit and even when we were together there was always someone else waiting on the sidelines."

Faye pulled Gregor in tighter and he let himself be hugged. Burrowing her face into the soft T-shirt covering his chest, she found it hard to imagine how any woman could give this up.

"I know how it feels. I went through the same thing recently, too," she said, not looking up at him.

Gregor pulled back and gazed at her. "Really? Faye, I'm so sorry that happened."

"Me, too," she said with a slight smile. "But let's focus on the here and now. Do you think you and Erik can move past this?"

Gregor looked contemplative. He ran his fingers through his hair and sighed again. "Honestly, I don't know. When we saw him at the pub he looked really out of it."

"If you want to go, I'm game," Faye said. It seemed like there was a lot of history there. Maybe this was the key to who Gregor really was, deep down. In any case, she was interested to see the two men together again. Their dynamic was volatile, but she could also imagine it being incredibly creative.

"If you'll be there, I'll consider it," he said, smiling.

"Great. But for now…"

"I know," Gregor said quickly. "You want to do the interview. Let me take a quick shower and then I'm all yours."

Faye smiled inwardly and resisted the urge to make a dirty pun. *Keep things professional*, the voice in her head said. *It's a little late for that, lady*, the other side of her brain retorted.

"Great," she said, sitting down at the table. "I'll set things up in here while you get ready."

"Back in a jiff," Gregor said, heading toward the back of the house.

Faye gathered her necessary materials—her digital voice recorder, notebook and notes—and put some water on the stove for tea. She wanted things to be as relaxed and as natural as possible. She knew if they weren't, Gregor would instinctively keep his guard up. He was so used to doing interviews at this point in his career, she understood he would have a series of stock answers he gave to the most common questions. She'd seen them after reading enough of the articles on him. Her mission was to break through his defenses, to get the real story on the real man. It was the only way her article would be worth anything to Bev, or to herself, really. It was a high standard to uphold but she knew there was no alternative.

"Faye! Faye!"

Faye dropped what she was doing and looked up in shock at hearing her name. Gregor was yelling from the back bedroom. Without thinking, she ran down the hall in the direction of his voice. She hadn't been inside his bedroom yet, but she didn't think twice to open the door, worried that he had fallen or was in some kind of danger. Looking past the un-made bed, she saw the light on in his bathroom and heard the rushing sound of water.

"Gregor, are you okay?" she called, pushing the door open, worried that he had fallen, or had had a heart attack even. Could you yell out while having a heart attack? She wasn't sure. The steam was so thick she could barely see the hand reach out of the shower. Before she knew what was happening, she was being pulled into a powerful stream of water.

Faye gasped, taking in a mouthful of water, and Gregor responded by pressing his mouth over hers, ravaging her with openmouthed kisses. Feeling his naked body pressed against hers, she couldn't have cared less about her outfit. With her hands on his ass, she pulled him closer and felt flushed with desire as the hot water cascaded over their bodies.

Gregor stared at Faye with desire in his eyes and moved his hands from her waist up to the buttons on the front of her shirt, which he quickly undid, freeing her breasts from their confinement. As the water hit her nipples, Gregor alternated between putting his mouth on each of them, flicking each of them with his tongue until Faye threw her head back in ecstasy. Each lick from Gregor's expert tongue sent signals straight to her core. Soon she couldn't tell the difference between the wetness coming from inside her body and the water washing over them.

Grabbing some shower gel from the ledge of the marble bathtub, Faye squirted some of the ginger-scented liquid in her hand and reached out to touch Gregor's formidable member. It was the first time she had gotten a good look at it, and it was lovely—nice-sized with a beautiful head that was just begging to be sucked on. But first she had something else to do.

As she started to work her hand with the gel in it up and down his shaft, Gregor steadied himself on the blue-and-white-tiled walls of the shower.

"What are you doing to me, Faye?" he asked, his eyes rolling back in his head.

"Cleaning up a very dirty boy," she said, quickening his strokes and watching him closely as his body responded to her touch.

Even though she had seen him on TV dressed down to his bathing suit, in person it was like discovering his body anew. She loved that he was tall and thin, with snaky hips that he knew how to move just right. He was lean enough that the creases leading from his hips to his cock were visible, which Faye found unspeakably sexy.

Allowing the water to rinse away the soap she had just applied, Faye knelt down and began licking long, lazy strokes around the head of Gregor's cock. When he sighed appreciatively, she couldn't help but smile to herself. She had forgotten how much she loved the feeling of giving someone pleasure, of being totally in control of their every response.

Taking the full length of him into her mouth, she moved up and down on him like a woman possessed with passion. Looking up at him, she met his gaze and this seemed to undo him. With a few quick thrusts, she could feel him coming, his balls seizing up and the result of her work filling the inside of her mouth, somehow tasting sweet and salty at the same time. Once she had taken every last drop he had to give, she stood up and kissed him, reveling in the hot water that rushed over them.

It was such a rush being with Gregor. It seemed like he was up for anything. And he was so unlike David in every way that it made Faye suddenly wonder how she had almost married someone so conservative. She flashed back on the time she had drawn a bath with rose petals and lay naked in it to celebrate their two-year dating anniversary. David had smiled and kissed her but, not wanting to get wet, asked her to come out and meet him in the bedroom. Gregor was the exact opposite. She had no idea what new adventure he was going to pull her into next. And she was pretty sure that if she presented herself naked in a bathtub to him, he would dive in immediately.

"Where are you going?" Gregor asked, a wicked tone in his voice. He had his fingers in the belt loops of Faye's shorts, which she realized she still had on.

Faye figured that their shower-time fun was over but she had no idea that it had just begun. After removing shorts and undies, which were now soaking, Gregor grabbed the detachable showerhead and turned it to the highest setting. Kissing Faye on the mouth, he pointed the showerhead directly at her womanhood. Faye had done this before, on her own, but never with another person holding it, and definitely no one as sexy as Gregor.

Trembling under the steady stream of water that was ricocheting off her most tender spot, Faye dug her nails into Gregor's shoulder as she tried to prepare herself for the onslaught of orgasm she was about to experience.

Faye kissed and bit at Gregor's lips as the rhythmic pulse of water hit her clitoris over and over. That was the thing about the showerhead—unlike when she used her hand, there was no wavering in pressure, no letting up. Faye was helpless to stop herself from coming, and Gregor furrowed his brow, watching her with serious eyes as she began to quiver under his guidance.

Faye held on to Gregor's forearms to steady herself as she rode the wave of pleasure. When she could finally breathe again, she looked up at him and he shut off the water.

"So much for getting any work done today," she said, smiling through the wet strands of hair plastered to her face. She didn't know how she looked but she felt incredible.

"You're amazing," Gregor said, handing her a fluffy brown towel that she wrapped around her body. "And anyway, this is the interview. Aren't you getting to know me?" He smiled devilishly.

Faye laughed. "I don't think this is what my editor had in mind," she said. "Or maybe it was."

"Bev does have a streak of the matchmaker in her," Gregor said, toweling off. Faye still couldn't help but marvel at his reflection in the mirror over the sink. It was no wonder they put him on TV. Like Mom said, he was sex on legs.

"So is this all a setup?" Faye asked, instinctively pulling her towel around her just a bit tighter.

Gregor tilted his head and gave her a forlorn look. "Of course not. Bev and I go way back. If I was going to talk to anyone it was going to be *Amuse Bouche*. The fact that her top editor was also a complete babe was just a happy coincidence."

Faye frowned, working out the backstory of everything he was saying. Then, letting down her guard, she pulled off her towel and whipped it at Gregor's ass.

"Hey!" he said, caught off guard before joining in the fun. Taking off his towel, he chased Faye all the way into the bedroom, where they spent the rest of the afternoon.

By the time the sun was setting, Gregor was having second thoughts about accepting Erik's invitation to dinner. Seeing him at the pub had brought on so many emotions—anger about the betrayal, yes, but mostly sadness about the loss of their friendship. If there was anyone who would understand what he was trying to do with the old pub it was Erik. He just didn't know if he could trust him.

Just as he was about to tell Faye that they should stay in and order takeaway, he looked up to see her emerge from her bedroom in a sleek black ensemble. Her dress was fitted and short, her heels sky-high and her blond hair was slicked back, which made her look like a Bond girl—one you would definitely risk giving up the microchip for a few hours in bed with.

"Wow," was all he could say when she smiled at him. His mouth hung agape and his body temperature was starting to rise. It was amazing how after so many months of being sad about Emily, his spirits were completely lifted by Faye. And she had so many qualities that his former lover didn't. There was a tenderness to her that told him that if the feeling with someone was right, she would give up everything to be with the person. That was not something he could have ever expected from Emily.

"All set?" Faye asked, straightening the collar on Gregor's crisp white oxford. Although he was still on the fence about going, he had to admit they made a striking couple.

"We can always leave after a drink if you're un-comfortable," he told her.

Faye smiled sympathetically, like she knew that this was just his way of giving himself an out. "Yeah, we'll play it by ear."

"Okay, then," Gregor said, grabbing the car keys.

He placed his hand on the small of Faye's back as she walked out the door toward the car. "Let's do this."

Gregor knew the drive to Erik's by heart—back when they had both experienced some success in the restaurant world they had purposely bought houses in the countryside near one another. *Close but not too close*, was the phrase Erik had used. Though they were both cooks by trade, Erik was really a restaurateur at heart while Gregor felt most at home in the kitchen. Unfortunately, the miles did not make up for the fact that their personal lives had become so intertwined. Too close for comfort, indeed, Gregor had often thought.

The part he never could understand was why he had gone for Emily. The two of them could have had any woman they wanted. Erik had all of London and beyond to choose from but he had made the conscious decision to break up his best friend's happy home. Or maybe it hadn't been so happy after all. In the days after their breakup, Gregor found himself examining the relationship from different angles, looking for cracks in the facade. Had she ever even loved him at all? He wasn't sure.

Glancing over at Faye in the passenger seat, Gregor felt comforted. For some reason, having her with him made him feel like it didn't matter what happened. So why was he headed toward this old friend's house when he could just take her out on the town? As they approached Erik's house, which was idiosyncratically modern, a smile crossed his lips. Seeing the light on in the kitchen, he recalled many nights of cooking there together, entertaining friends. Maybe it was that he knew Gregor better than any single person on earth. Or maybe, the good times still outweighed the bad.

Whatever the reason, he found himself standing with his date for the evening and pressing the doorbell that rang the theme to *Monty Python*. Faye smiled at Gregor and gripped his hand tightly just as they heard the door click open.

"Hello, you two," Erik said when he opened the door. He was looking more relaxed than he had at the pub and was wiping his hands on the apron tied around his waist.

"Hello again," Gregor said stiffly, feeling unsure what to do with himself. Erik held the door open and he and Faye entered the house.

"You look lovely," he said to Faye.

"Thanks," she said, proffering the bottle of wine they'd brought with them.

"God, it's good to see you," Erik said suddenly, pulling Gregor into a hearty embrace.

Gregor stood frozen at first, but then he relented, hugging his old friend the way they always had when some amount of time had passed.

"What is that smell?" Gregor asked, inhaling quickly and trying to suss out the barrage of aromas filling his nostrils.

"That's my take on shepherd's pie," Erik said proudly, gesturing for them to join him in the kitchen.

"How long have you two known each other?" Faye asked, taking a seat at the counter.

"Be careful," Gregor warned, reaching for the wine opener. "She's a reporter." He still knew where everything was kept in the kitchen, and as always, the place was immaculate.

"Ah, then I'd better not tell her about the time you were almost expelled for running naked in the school yard during recess?"

"What?" Faye laughed, looking back and forth between Gregor and Erik.

"Don't listen to him," Gregor said, pulling ingredients out of the fridge.

"What are you doing, mate?" Erik asked. "I've got everything under control."

"If Faye's going to see the real us, then we have to make the Scotch egg," Gregor said, lining up everything he needed.

"Ah, you're right, of course," Erik said, raising a glass. "Well, cheers to having you here. Both of you."

"Cheers," Gregor said, raising his own glass and looking back and forth between his best friend and the woman he couldn't get off his mind. Maybe it wouldn't be such a bad dinner after all.

CHAPTER FIVE

FAYE WAS SEATED in the living room holding a sambuca in one hand and a cigar in the other. Gregor and Erik had prepared a feast so elaborate, she could barely keep up with her notes on what everything was. It was by far the finest meal she'd ever eaten, and she could tell that it was made with love. The camaraderie between Gregor and Erik was so palpable, it was hard to imagine them not being friends. They worked together like brothers, making jokes at each other's expense, each trying to one-up the other with his food and his wit.

Now that the meal was finished, the dessert plates soaking in the sink, Faye placed a hand on her stomach and knew for a fact that she had gone a little too overboard.

"Faye, you look satisfied," Erik said, taking a sip of his drink.

"Satisfied and bloated," she said, placing her drink down. "Seriously, this was the most amazing meal."

"We should probably get going," Gregor said, placing his drink down and checking the time.

"Nonsense," Erik said with a wave of his hand. "You've both had too much to drink. Just hunker down in the spare room. Or take two rooms, if you prefer. I have to be up early tomorrow, but the place is yours."

Faye looked at Gregor, who shrugged. "Are you sure?" she asked.

"Absolutely," Erik said. "I wouldn't have it any other way. You remember where everything is?" Erik said, looking in Gregor's direction. Gregor nodded and stood up.

"I'll be right up," Faye said, carrying the empty glasses to the kitchen.

Gregor headed upstairs while Erik followed Faye, turning off the lights as he walked.

"You don't have to do that," he said, as Faye stacked dishes in the sink. "Maryann will come tomorrow."

"Thank you so much for everything," Faye said, smiling at Erik. He was tall and thin like Gregor, but that was where the similarities ended. Where Gregor had styled hair and crystal-blue eyes, Erik was more rugged looking, with a graying beard and dark brown eyes.

"It's good to have you both here," he said, leaning on the counter. "I'm glad to see him happy again."

Faye felt a little shocked that Erik seemed to be referring to their past relationship. She figured that was a topic that had to be off-limits for everyone.

"She must have been a wonderful woman," Faye said carefully.

"Not really," Erik said. "He deserves someone better. You're a gem, Faye."

Faye felt herself blush. "Well, if you'll excuse me, I'm exhausted."

"Sleep well," Erik said. She could feel his eyes on her as she turned to go and headed upstairs.

When Faye reached the top of the stairs, she noticed a light on in one of the rooms and assuming it was where Gregor was, she lightly tapped on the door before opening it.

"Well, hello!" Gregor was lying on the bed in just his underwear—a pair of black boxer-briefs that showed off the sinewy outline of his body. His blue eyes had that devilish come-hither look that Faye had noticed on television but gotten to know firsthand for herself these past few days.

"You look like you're up to something naughty," she said, sitting on the edge of the bed.

"Always," he said, reaching out for her. In one quick motion he pulled her on top of him. As they began to kiss, Faye could feel him getting hard underneath her and it triggered an almost immediate response. Her skin got more sensitive, her nipples went hard and she could feel that now-familiar wetness between her legs coming on. Where had he been all her life? Or better yet, why had it taken her so long to find out what really got her going?

Looking at Gregor, she felt a sudden surge of happiness. In a flash, she could imagine moving to England to be with him in his restaurant, having his little blue-eyed babies and writing books in the guest room of the cottage.

But those were thoughts for another time. Right now, the only thing she could focus on was him being inside her. Getting up off the bed, she unzipped her tight black dress and let it fall to the floor. With Gregor watching her intently, she reached behind her back and unfastened the black lace bra that she was wearing and slowly, teasingly pulled down the straps, still holding it to her chest as Gregor's expression grew more interested, more frustrated.

Unable to wait, he dove toward her and, pulling her close, roughly threw the bra aside, burying his face in her ample cleavage. Faye threw her head back and sighed, savoring the prickly scratches from his beard as his mouth grazed across her nipples. His strong hands kneaded her breasts. It was obvious that he couldn't get enough from the way he ravenously devoured her. Tossing her back on the bed, he slid down the length of her body, removing her panties in the process. Faye wasn't used to letting go like this, to allowing someone so much intimacy, but it felt like the most natural thing in the world to permit Gregor's wandering hands and mouth access to her pussy.

When it came to pleasuring a woman, he was clearly an expert. For the first time with any lover, Faye didn't feel the need to guide or direct. She just lay back and opened herself up to him, ready to enjoy what he was about to do to her.

Faye arched her body toward him, expecting to feel the scratchiness of his beard clamp down on her sex, but Gregor had other ideas. Using just his fingers, he found her pleasure spot and began making circles around it, putting her into a dizzying state of ecstasy.

Faye tried to stop herself from making any noise, well aware that they were guests in someone's house, but it was difficult to remain silent as Gregor's fingers began to take more precise action—flicking her bead back and forth until she could no longer hold back. Feeling that ache that indicated she was close, she pushed her soaking sex farther toward him and he answered her request by increasing the speed and pressure of his fingers to a frenzied pace, so much so that she was powerless to stop the onslaught of shivers that ran up and down her body. Where most other men would have stopped, Gregor kept going, keeping up his persistent strokes on her clit while she rode a wave of pleasure that seemed to last for minutes, not seconds.

"Wow," she said quietly when she finally sat up to catch her breath. Gregor gave a self-satisfied little smile, knowing full well what he had done to her.

Faye could feel herself sweating from all the activity, but she knew she was far from finished. Pushing Gregor back on the bed, she slid down his body this time, pulling away the boxer-briefs to unleash his lovely cock. She positioned herself between his legs and gently began to graze her breasts up and down the length of it.

Gregor sighed as his cock sprang to attention. Faye took care to watch his expressions closely as she used her hands, breasts and mouth to give him the attention he so badly needed. By the time she had pushed his member between her breasts, sliding it up and down and knowing full well that this view could put him over the edge, he was rock hard, and she loved the fact that she could inspire this in him. His hands reached for her and pulled Faye on top of him. With his hands on her ass, he slid her down onto his hardness and she gasped the moment he entered her.

Here they were, naked and fucking in what was for Faye a near-stranger's house and it felt so naughty and delicious. Woman on top wasn't the position Faye was usually the most comfortable in, but in that moment, she sat up and allowed her whole body to be on display as she bounced up and down on Gregor's beautiful erection. She felt powerful, magnificent even, as her hair cascaded down her back and her large breasts swung around, up and down and every which way. How could she feel self-conscious with the worshipful look on Gregor's face? Reaching his hands up to massage her tits, which now seemed even fuller than usual, she could feel his cock begin to quiver inside her.

Gregor audibly grunted as he came, and Faye collapsed down on top of him, silencing him with an openmouthed kiss.

"Shhh!" she whispered into his mouth.

Finally coming down off his high, Gregor rolled onto his side and looked at Faye.

"You were incredible tonight," he said.

"So were you," she answered.

"No, I mean, at dinner. Thank you for encouraging me to come. It felt like the right thing to do."

Faye smiled and raked her fingers through Gregor's hair. It was astonishing to think that this experienced, worldly man was really tripped up by a childhood friendship.

"I'm glad I can help," she said, spooning into Gregor's body and allowing the sleepy feelings to take over.

The next morning, Faye slept late and after cleaning up in the bathroom attached to their rooms, she and Gregor made their way back down to the kitchen, following the aroma of coffee that called to them. Wearing the fluffy white guest robes they had found in the bathroom—*He thinks of every detail*, Gregor had said upon discovering them, shaking his head in wonder—they sat on the stools at the counter and dug into the fruit and pastries that were left for them next to a note on Erik's personal stationery.

"'Thank you both for a lovely evening,'" Faye read the note aloud as Gregor bit into a croissant. "'Had to be up and out early, stay as long as you like. Yours, Erik.'"

Faye put the note aside and sipped her coffee. The jolt of caffeine was just what she needed. She wasn't used to drinking or eating this much and she vowed to herself to take it a bit easier for the rest of her stay in London.

"There's somewhere I want to take you today, if you're up for a trip," Gregor said, draining the rest of his coffee and standing up.

"Will this help me gain some insights for my article?"

"Exactly," Gregor said, pointing at her. "Now let's go and get dressed."

Wearing last night's clothes, Faye and Gregor left Erik's house just as his housekeeper was pulling up.

"I'm afraid she has her work cut out for her," Faye said. She still hadn't felt right leaving a sink full of dishes after a dinner party.

"This is normal for Erik, throwing parties and having someone else clean up. Except that instead of an intimate gathering, it's usually over twenty people," Gregor explained as he held the car door open for Faye.

"What a lifestyle," Faye said, sliding into her seat. Gregor came around to the driver's side and sat down next to her. "And he never married, never had kids?"

Gregor shook his head. "We were both married to our work. It has to be like that, to be really successful."

"Do you still believe that?" Faye asked, hoping that her tone sounded neutral.

Gregor paused before answering. "I believe that

with the right person, you can do more than succeed, you can flourish," he said, giving Faye a smile as he started the ignition.

Gregor knew it was a risk, taking a woman he had just met to the Côte d'Azur, but somehow with Faye, it felt right. He turned it over in his mind: Was it because he wanted her to really understand him for the article, or was it something more?

As they sat together on his private plane, he watched her as she looked out the window. Of course, she had been stunned when he told her that was where they were going.

"I was thinking you were going to take me to your mother's house in Covent Garden."

Gregor had laughed. He was sure his mum would love to meet Faye, but if she really wanted to understand his cooking and his love of travel they had to go back to where it all began: a seaside village between Nice and Monaco.

This was one of the perks of being Gregor Wright. He could just leave at a moment's notice, decide he was going to the French Riviera, and minutes later a plan was being put into action. His producer on *Globe-Trotting with Gregor* had asked if they could film an episode there but somehow it felt too personal. He didn't want to share his special place with the world, not yet.

He thought if he ever did open that dream restaurant it would borrow elements from the small sea-

food restaurants he had grown up eating at as a boy.
He remembered at first thinking everything tasted
fishy and slimy but then slowly growing to love seafood, especially the bouillabaisse at La Pignatelle.

Gregor felt Faye place her hand on his leg and
turned to see she was still looking out the window.
Although his leg was covered in his jeans, it immediately triggered the memory of them being naked
together, his skin on hers, and his cock started to stir.
Clearly, she had no idea that a simple touch could
have that effect on him, but it was true. He had always liked sex, and had lots of it, but ever since
Faye had arrived it was like his senses had been re-
awakened. He couldn't tell if it was just that heady
feeling that came with getting to know someone
new—exploring each other's bodies, telling each
other your stories. But something inside him told
him that maybe this was something more.

Then again, he wondered, was Faye even available? Who was this ex that had hurt her, and was
she still hung up on him? His heart suddenly seized
with the awful thought that maybe this assignment
of hers was just an adventure, and that she was planning to go back to him when she touched down in
New York. A little journalism with a side of sex with
a famous guy…

That was always a deep insecurity for Gregor.
Being famous meant that it was never clear who was
in it for what they could get from you, and who was
really sincere. As crazy as it sounded, he often won-

dered if the women he hooked up with were doing it because they were attracted to him, or to the television personality. The Gregor on TV was him, of course, but a heightened version of himself. Deep down, he wanted someone who could see past all the lights and cameras and red carpets and premieres, and just love him for him.

Love. It was silly that he was thinking this way. *She's just here on assignment, mate*, he reminded himself, knowing full well he was only saying this to protect himself. In a few days she would be going home—that was a fact. Her job and her life were in New York, and if he was really going to open a restaurant—it wasn't a recipe for a relationship. Of course, he had the ability to jump on a plane when he wanted, but with the hours it would take to open a new place, he knew it wouldn't be often.

Gregor felt the plane beginning to make its descent and he took Faye's hand in his. She turned and smiled at him and then rested her head on his shoulder. For an instant, he let go of all his misgivings and worries and took a deep breath, allowing himself to enjoy the smell of her shampoo, which he had decided contained jasmine and rose. They were about to land, and the thought of taking her to the places that meant something to him was undeniably exciting.

"It is absolutely beautiful here," Faye said as they drove down the coast together. Gregor had someone drop off a car for them to use and now Faye was in the driver's seat, easily taking the twists and turns of the road and looking radiant with her hair tied back and a simple blue-and-white-striped dress. Of course, he had insisted that they put the top down on the car—the weather was warm and beautiful and he wanted her to get the full effect of driving through this idyllic scenery.

"Turn here," Gregor instructed, pointing to a small road off the main one that he recognized from his many childhood trips. His parents had started taking him here when he was just a baby, and it felt as familiar to him as the streets of London.

"Where are we going?" Faye asked, putting on her directional and making the turn.

"You'll see."

She briefly took her eyes off the road and raised an eyebrow at him. "Very mysterious."

"Indeed."

Being in this setting made Gregor want to take Faye back to his favorite hotel, La Réserve de Beaulieu. He would take her swimming, and then back to the suite he always stayed in. He imagined them kissing and peeling off one another's wet bathing suits... Gregor did his best to push the thought to the back of his mind, for now. Faye's body was so perfect, so womanly, that it elicited what he could only describe as a primal reaction in him. Seeing her large breasts perfectly displayed in her summer dress made him want to ask her to pull over to the side of the road so he could do all of the dirty things he was constantly imagining. But he also knew Faye had a story to write.

"Onward," he said, pointing out the next turn.

By the time they reached the small village where Gregor had spent his youth, it was late afternoon and Gregor's stomach was grumbling. Truth be told, he was always in the mood to eat, and he loved that Faye seemed to share his hearty and adventurous appetite.

"I think you love food almost as much as me," he said as they walked through the small village they had stopped at. Faye was drooling over all of the different food stalls, pulling Gregor back to look at the assortment of delicacies.

"Can't we eat?" she whined as he ushered her along.

"Soon," he promised. "There's something I want to show you first."

She made a disgruntled noise and followed along as they left the village and took a rocky path that led to a small residential area. Gregor took the street turns by heart, pausing here and there to get his bearings. He had been to the Riviera many times in recent years, but had not been back to Beaulieu-sur-Mer since he was probably twenty.

"This is it!" he said triumphantly as they turned a corner. He could see Faye looking around, confused.

"Follow me," he said, taking her hand to cross the street and pushing open the wrought iron gates that opened up onto a small but extremely lovely community garden.

"What is this place?" Faye asked in awe, looking around at the unexpected spray of lush greenery.

"Breathe in," Gregor said, placing a hand on Faye's abdomen. She closed her eyes and took a deep breath.

"Thyme, dill, cardamom." Faye blinked her eyes open and faced him. "Gregor, this place is incredible!"

"It's a community garden, the place where I learned everything about plants and spices. There was a local family, I played with their son. The parents took an interest and taught me how to cook on those long summer days."

Faye shook her head. She finally understood. "Was it Erik? Is that how you two met?"

"Yes," he said, smiling. "So we were literally brought up together."

Gregor put his arms around Faye's waist and pulled her close to him. "Thank you for being here with me."

"Just doing my job," she said. Gregor's face fell. "Only kidding. I'm really touched that you took me here. Seeing all of this would make me want to feed people, too."

"But you're already such an adventurous eater. And traveler," Gregor said, pushing her hair off the side of her cheek.

"Not really," she said, her tone growing more seriously. "Not lately."

"It has to do with your ex," Gregor said knowingly.

"Yeah…" Faye answered, her voice trailing off.

"After all that, I didn't have much of a taste for anything."

Gregor could tell she didn't want to discuss it any further, so he changed the topic.

"Are you still hungry?" he asked. "Because there's a place I know not far from here…"

"Let's go!" Faye said enthusiastically.

Gregor took Faye's hand and led her through the winding streets to a familiar doorway. It was still painted blue, and inside, he could see Sylvie presiding in the restaurant's open kitchen.

"*Mon chou!*" she cried when he walked through the door. She looked older, but still as hearty and beautiful as he'd remembered.

"It's wonderful to see you," he said as they hugged.

"So, you've brought your new girlfriend to see me," she said.

"I'm not his girlfriend. *Journaliste.*"

"Ah, I see," Sylvie said, showing them to a table.

She brought out an array of delicacies, from seafood to duck to dessert. By the time they were finished, they were both stuffed.

"If I keep eating like this, I'm going to have to buy all new clothes,"

"I think you look sexy as hell," Gregor said, leaning across the table. "More bread?"

Faye laughed and Gregor smiled. He couldn't wait to get back to the hotel he had reserved. It was the same place he always stayed, and he knew Faye would love it.

A quick drive later, they walked into the lobby of La Réserve and Faye gave a little gasp that thrilled Gregor. He loved the fact that he could impress her. They took the lift up to the room and once inside Faye went into the bathroom, taking an inordinately long amount of time. When she emerged, this time it was Gregor who gasped. She was a vision in a sexy lace bra and panty set.

"I thought it was a little French," she said. Gregor swallowed hard when he saw that she had left on her high heels. It was a touch that always enticed him.

Wrapping his arms around her small waist, he pulled her in for a long luxurious kiss.

"Will you excuse me for a moment?" he said, breaking away, his eyes gleaming with excitement.

"Sure," Faye said, looking confused. But Gregor didn't want to waste any more time. This visit, and Faye, had given him the courage to move forward with his plans.

In the living room, Gregor found his cell phone and dialed the number for the landlord of the Arms. On the third ring, Jon, the man he had met with in person, answered.

"Nice to hear from you!" he bellowed in a jolly tone.

"Look, I've been thinking... I'm ready to put a bid on this place."

"I'm sorry, mate."

"What do you mean?"

"Place went into contract this morning, an all-cash offer. Fellow just about your age. Looked and talked like you, too. I wonder if you know him."

Gregor tried hard to contain his anger. The thought of Erik stealing his girlfriend, and now, his business idea, was just too much to bear. With a loud grunt, he threw the cell phone down. It landed with a thud on the marble floor and he watched as the screen shattered into a million pieces.

CHAPTER SIX

FAYE WAS GETTING ANTSY. It wasn't every day that she presented herself to a man in French lingerie, and the moment she had done that with Gregor, he had excused himself from the room. Faye lay on the merlot satin duvet of the hotel bed and tried her best to push any insecurities from her mind. *It must be something important*, she told herself. *I'll just wait.*

Just then, her phone rang. She saw that it was her mother and against her better judgment, she decided to answer.

"How's it going there?" her mom asked. "Are you two going to give me a little British grandbaby?"

"How are you, Mom?" Faye asked, rolling her eyes.

"Don't roll your eyes. You already have the beginnings of crow's-feet. It'll just make it worse."

"I don't have crow's-feet, Mom," Faye said, standing up to look in the mirror and check her eyes.

"I know, but I do, so you will," her mom said with resignation in her voice. "How's the work going?"

"It's going," Faye said.

"Well, remember, life is not all about work," her mother counseled. "Make sure you make time for fun, too. That's the one thing I regret not doing more of."

"Okay, Mom, listen, I really need to go…"

"Make sure you call me again soon," her mom insisted before she hung up.

Faye sighed. She loved her mom, but their calls were exhausting. She lay back down on the bed and did her best to hold her sexiest pose. But she was starting to get cold. Reaching into Gregor's bag, she grabbed a sweatshirt, threw it on over her lacy lingerie, and got in under the luxurious covers. Once her hand had found the remote control on the nightstand, she flicked through the channels, trying to find something in English. Then there it was—her favorite romantic comedy of all time, *It Happened One Night*.

In college, one of her favorite pastimes was to hole up in the lounge with her girlfriends watching romantic comedies. They would speculate on who was going to get married first, who would have the most kids. Her friends always said Faye was destined to be married before thirty and to be a mom of three and back then she believed it. She had a whole future mapped out with David, but now things didn't look so certain.

But still. If she had just gotten married and everything went according to plan, she would never have had the chance to stand there in the French

Riviera, in Gregor's childhood garden, sharing that moment with him. She wasn't sure if he was that person for her, but she liked the person that she was when she was with him—confident, adventurous and, yes, fun.

She thought about how he had pulled her into the shower with him, and how he had really pulled her into a more exciting part of her life. She had been missing out on that spontaneity. Just as she was getting to the part in her memory of Gregor holding the showerhead on her, he appeared in the doorway. Faye could tell from the expression on his face that something wasn't right.

"Hey, are you okay?" she asked, clicking off the TV and sitting up in bed.

Gregor came around and sat down on the side of the bed closest to Faye.

"I've just had some terrible news," he said, his eyes looking sad and dejected.

Faye's heart nearly skipped a beat, not knowing what *bad news* meant in Gregor's world. Had someone close to him died? From the look on his face, she knew he was going to need her support.

"What is it?" she asked, her eyes wide.

"Someone's gone and bought the Arms out from under me!" Gregor exclaimed. As he said the words, the sad look on his face turned to something more like furious.

"What?" Faye blinked. "How is that even possible?"

"That's what I thought," Gregor said, turning

toward her, his voice growing more impassioned. "That place has been on the market for two years. Jon would have told me if I was bidding against someone. But apparently, he got an all-cash offer just this morning."

Faye didn't want to say what she was thinking. Could Gregor's friend really do something like this to him? Could he two-time him twice, first with Emily, and now this? Thankfully, Gregor filled the silence, saving Faye from having to ask the obvious question.

"It had to be Erik," Gregor said, looking at Faye intensely. "No one else knew about it."

"Ugh, I'm so sorry," Faye said, slipping her hand into his. For a moment, she thought Gregor was eyeing her skeptically. Of course, it made sense he might be suspicious. After all, she was a journalist. It was her job to take notes, report the facts, remain impartial. "You know I didn't tell anyone about your venture," she said carefully.

"Of course," Gregor said immediately. "That wasn't what I was thinking at all. If anyone's done something behind my back, it's Erik." Gregor got to his feet and paced the room. "Why didn't I see this coming?"

Faye got out of bed and went to Gregor, placing her hands on his chest. "Because you're a good person."

Gregor seemed to soften a little.

"You're trusting. And kind. And loving," she said,

not in the least bit worried about how forward her words must have seemed.

Instead of turning away, like many other men might have, Gregor pulled Faye closer, so that her face was resting on the strong chest muscles covered only by his light shirt.

"I'm so glad you're here with me," he said, moving his hand to the base of her neck and kissing her gently on the lips.

Faye kissed Gregor back, biting lightly at his lips. "I'm happy to be here, too," she said, giving in to the feeling of his kisses trailing down the side of her neck. Faye sighed, submitting to the sensations that were becoming more and more familiar the longer she spent with Gregor. As his hands wandered up underneath his own sweatshirt, he paused when he reached the strappy panties she had on just for this exact occasion.

"Is this my shirt?" he asked, stepping back to take a better look.

"It is," Faye confessed. "I hope you don't mind. I got cold."

"It suits you," he said, looking her up and down, his eyes hungry with desire. "But right now, I think you'd look much better with it off."

Without saying a word, Faye complied by pulling the oversize sweatshirt over her head to reveal her pert breasts, barely contained in the balconette bra. Gregor took in the sight of her and then spun her around. She knew he was looking at the special undies she had on—they were mocha colored, to match the bra, and in the back, several straps ran across her buttocks from the tiny sliver of fabric barely covering her most intimate area.

"Mmm…" Gregor sighed, kneeling down to kiss all of the exposed areas of her cheeks. Faye felt herself flush with desire. Gregor had a way of doing that—when it came to being with him, no tricks needed to get her in the mood. One touch from him was enough, and as he ran his finger up the length of the fabric from the top of her ass to her entrance, she felt herself getting wetter and wetter.

When she felt Gregor begin to plant kisses on her behind, she instinctively bent over the side of the bed, giving him full access to the fullness of her bottom. As he trailed his way from one cheek to the other and back, she quivered in anticipation of the moment he would pull down those special panties, and reward her with his extremely filling, and seemingly always-hard cock.

He must have read her thoughts, because Gregor suddenly stood up and pressed his crotch into her still-covered behind. Faye smiled to herself—she loved knowing that her body made Gregor this erect, this quickly. She didn't know if they matched as a couple just yet, but sexually, they were highly compatible. In fact, they seemed to be a perfect match.

Reaching his deft fingers into the straps on the side of the undies, Gregor finally removed her panties altogether. She paused for a moment and turned her head to see him removing his own clothing. She took in the sight of his lanky, sinewy body. The more she saw it, the more she craved it. Still bent over the edge of the bed, Faye looked straight ahead and steadied herself for Gregor's grand entrance, which sometimes felt like more than she was able to handle. She enjoyed the feeling of being so filled up by him—even though his member was large by any standards, he knew just how to use it to make her feel his presence inside her intensely.

"Please," she begged. "Fuck me now."

Faye was growing frustrated with lust, but thankfully Gregor attended to her request. As he stood up, she felt the head of his cock run down the crevice of her ass. She shivered, loving the fact that she had no idea what Gregor was going to do next.

All of her questions were answered when, in one mighty motion, he plunged himself into her wet softness.

"Ohh!" Faye cried out, hoping that she wasn't waking up the guests in the neighboring rooms, but also not really caring.

Gregor began steadily pumping as Faye encouraged him with wild calls of "Yes!" and a spontaneous reach-around to his balls. They were full and wonderful to hold and Faye enjoyed playfully slapping them as Gregor fucked her.

"You're going to make me come if you keep doing

that," he growled at her. But that didn't stop Faye from persisting in her playful slaps.

Gregor made an animalistic noise, and grabbing her by her long blond hair, he plunged into her with more force than he had previously used, causing her body to arch up toward his.

"Oh!" she cried out at the same time she could feel him coming inside her. She loved the feeling of his cock quivering in her and spilling out all of that come that she knew was just for her.

When they had both finally caught their breaths, Faye lay down on her back, her body heaving with the intensity of their activity. Gregor lay down naked beside her and propped up on one arm. He caressed each of her breasts, which were now totally spilling over the top of her rather unsupportive bra. He didn't seem to mind a bit and luxuriated in playing with her round pink pert nipples that seemed to tighten and harden to his every touch.

Reaching her hand down to her pussy, Faye let Gregor watch as she brought herself to orgasm, using two fingers to flick at the sensitive little bead above her opening. Within seconds, her breath was ragged again, and she was arching, this time to her own hand, as her body shook with pleasure.

"You look really beautiful when you come," Gregor said, smiling at her. "Show me again," he whispered.

Faye knew that it would be easy to coax another orgasm with Gregor watching. His very presence made her body more alert, more sensitive. Looking directly in his eyes, this time she moved more rapidly, and grinding against the side of her own hand, she found her wave again. Gregor was definitely responsible for how intense that second orgasm felt—with his rough mouth biting and teasing at her nipples, it was easy for Faye to stay at that peak, and to push into that feeling of intense pleasure, instead of shying away from it.

"That was truly incredible," she said when she finally got up to go to the bathroom. There was so much the two of them needed to do the next day, but right now all Faye could think about was going to sleep.

Returning to the bed, she curled into the space next to Gregor's body and drifted off, feeling more content than she had in a long, long time.

The next morning, Gregor was up bright and early, his bag already packed. He would have loved nothing more than to spend several days in his favorite location with Faye, but there was business at home that needed his immediate attention.

He thought about calling or texting Erik with his cracked phone but knew his friend's tricks for avoidance. The best thing to do was to go and confront him in person. And he knew exactly where to find him.

Faye stirred in the sheets and Gregor sat down on the edge of the bed, feeling just the slightest bit guilty that he hoped it would rouse her. She looked so content and comfortable at La Réserve. He loved that she had responded so enthusiastically at the garden, and here, in his dream hotel, she seemed to fit in perfectly, too. The cynic in him wondered if she was just too good to be true, but he knew in his heart that Faye was definitely an honest person. In the past, finding out the news he got last night would have sent him into even more of a rage, but her presence was so calming, so reassuring. If there was a way to put a spin on a bad situation, Faye could find it. And that wasn't a bad quality to have in a partner.

"Wake up, sleepyhead," he said, gently pushing on her hip that was covered in the 800-thread-count Egyptian cotton sheets. He couldn't blame her for wanting to linger, but there was work to be done.

"You're dressed early," Faye said, sitting up in bed and stretching. She was naked and when she lifted her arms into the air, he got a fantastic glimpse of her amazing breasts. It was a sight that made him want to dive on top of her and spend the day between the sheets, but he held himself back.

"There's an appointment I need to get to back home," he said apologetically. "But the next time we come here, we'll stay longer, I promise."

The next time? He watched Faye's face for a reaction to this veiled offer of a second date—or rather, second vacation—but her expression remained unchanged. She looked a little tired, and happy. Gregor thought to himself that she looked even more beautiful with no makeup. He knew that annoyed some women when he said it, so he kept the thought to himself, but it was the truth.

"Well, you look very smart," Faye said, playfully smoothing the collar of his madras button-down. She shifted her body so that she was right in front of him and her nipples grazed the soft cotton of his shirt. "I guess I should start taking work a little more seriously, too."

Gregor reached out to grab her, but in a flash, she had gotten out of bed, cast off the sheet and was walking, stark naked, to the bathroom.

In a few hours' time, they had taken enough planes, trains and automobiles to get them back to where they had started their journey. Walking up the pavement to the pub Arms, Gregor felt Faye place a hand on his arm as they neared the entrance.

"How can you be sure he's here?" she asked.

"I know Erik," Gregor said definitively. "If he's gotten an idea in his head, he has to start working on it immediately."

"Unlike you who's more of a ruminator?" Faye asked with an arched eyebrow.

"Exactly," Gregor said. "You've figured us out."

"Are you sure this is the right way to go about things?"

Gregor thought for a moment. "Absolutely."

Pushing open the heavy door, he was unfazed to

see Erik standing over a set of blueprints, speaking with a well-dressed petite woman with short blond hair who he assumed was an architect.

"Working out all the details, then?" he said in lieu of hello. Erik and his worker both looked up from the table. And while the architect's face registered surprise, Erik made a sly face that told Gregor he was expecting him.

"Good to see you, mate," Erik said. "Dinner was a lot of fun. Hello, Faye," he said warmly, giving her his best smile. Faye was lingering close to the door and gave him a little wave.

"I didn't come here for dinner party chitchat," Gregor said, angry at himself that he was unable to hide his anger. "You stole this place out from under me!"

Erik rolled his eyes, a habit that Gregor always found dismissive and childish. "Will you excuse us for a moment?"

The architect nodded seriously and, rolling up her papers, marched quickly out the front door.

"What are you doing, crashing in here and causing a scene?" Erik said, matching Gregor's fighting words with a harsh tone.

"You were the only one I told about this place. You only got the idea from talking to me. You have no interest in opening a restaurant. Admit it," Gregor said pointedly.

Gregor's words hung in the air for a moment before Erik smiled and sat down in one of the remaining booths. Even in the heat of the argument, Gregor couldn't help but remember what he and Faye had done in that very booth, and the memory made him smile and glance toward the supportive woman standing in the doorway.

"I'll admit it—I wasn't thinking about opening a restaurant, but hearing you talk about it made me realize it really is a great idea. I think the area would benefit from it, and people would want to have this type of place. It could become a centerpiece of our community."

Gregor paced, running his hands through his hair. "So you went after my place?"

"It's not yours, it's mine," Erik said simply.

Gregor restrained himself from lunging at his cocky so-called friend.

"Listen," Erik said, gesturing for Gregor to sit down. "I know you, and I knew you weren't going to pull the trigger. So I did it for us. Of course I want you involved."

Gregor considered this for a moment. He sat down across from Erik and spoke slowly and clearly, so there could be no misunderstanding.

"I don't want to work for you. I don't want to work with you. I don't want anything to do with you!"

For the first time in the conversation, Erik actually looked surprised. Gregor stood up.

"I should have learned my lesson the first time with you."

"Gregor!" Erik shouted, but it was too late. Gregor

strode toward the door, passing Faye on his way out. He couldn't bear to make eye contact with her—the whole situation was so humiliating. It was just like with Emily, all over again. Why was it taking him so long to learn that Erik could not be trusted?

He could hear Faye's footsteps behind him and knew she was following. He didn't know what he was going to say to her. Was she going to put this in her profile of him, how he had handed over his best idea in years to a man who wasn't worthy of his trust? The thought of any magazine piece on him made him cringe. He should have waited until he had his life more together. He cursed himself for allowing Bev to convince him that this was a good idea.

"Hey!"

Gregor turned around and saw Faye running to catch up with him.

"Are you okay? That was pretty intense back there," she said, squinting at him in the bright sun. Gregor felt his anger soften a little. Faye had that effect on him.

"I'm a fool, Faye. A complete and utter fool."

Faye moved closer to him and took both of his hands in hers. "No, you're not. You're a smart, passionate man who likes to be careful and deliberate. Erik is just…"

"More bold, more spontaneous, more confident?" Gregor tried finishing her sentence with an appropriate adjective.

"Yeah, but he's also kind of an asshole," Faye said, tilting her head to the side and then smiling.

Gregor couldn't help himself—he had to laugh.

"Is there any chance you want to work with him? It sounds like that's what he had in mind?" she asked.

"I might have considered it but it's such a messed-up way of asking. It's like he needs to maintain the upper hand at all times. I'd be working for him."

"So don't do it," Faye said.

Just then, the architect got out of her car. She looked skeptically at Gregor and Faye as she passed them, and then scurried back into the pub.

"He's probably going to make it into some awful modern, minimalist space."

Faye stroked Gregor's forearm. "Why not do your own thing, then?"

Gregor shook his head. "There are no other spaces around here that would work. I've been going over it for the past year. It's my own damn fault for waiting so long."

When he said this, Gregor had the sudden thought that there was something he wanted to tell Faye. He couldn't put it into words, but he had the gripping fear that if he waited too long, she would go back to America, and he would lose his chance with her, too. The thought of losing both his dream space and her was too much to bear.

"There are other ways to get your food to people.

What about a food truck?" Faye said, the enthusiasm in her voice building.

Gregor squinted his eyes and stroked the stubble of his beard. Part of him hated how trendy food trucks had become. But he had to admit, it wasn't a bad idea.

"I'd need to get licensed. But… I'd be able to get it going before he could open the restaurant."

"I'm sure you'd get a ton of press," Faye said slyly, punching him playfully on the arm.

Even though just moments before he was in despair, he now found himself working out a menu in his head. Small versions of his favorite dishes. Portable, good quality food that people craved.

"I could even set up social media for you, so people could track your whereabouts," Faye offered.

"And you could work the window while I run the kitchen," Gregor said, pulling her close to him.

"Well, I am going back home in a two days," she said. Gregor's heart skipped a beat when she said this. The thought of Faye leaving so soon was depressing. In a short time she had become such an inspiration to him. He felt that when she was around, anything was truly possible.

"Maybe you can extend your trip," he said, putting his hand on the back of her neck and staring intensely into her eyes. He studied all of her features—her beautiful eyes, her small nose, her mouth that looked like two rose petals and widened when she smiled, which was often.

"Are you getting all of this down?" he asked and smiled just as he moved in to kiss her.

"I'm taking very good notes," she said, kissing him back and squeezing his ass as she did.

CHAPTER SEVEN

"FAYE, ARE YOU ever planning to come back to work?"

Faye held the phone away from her ear as she half listened to Bev complain how unorganized the office was without her over the past several weeks. She had agreed to let Faye stay in England an additional two weeks since the food truck that Gregor was opening was part of the story she was writing, but Bev wasn't too pleased about missing her favorite employee and confidante.

"I'll be back before you know it," Faye said gently, trying to assuage her boss's feelings of abandonment. It took going away for both of them to realize how much they relied on each other. But while Bev seemed to dislike the vibe in the office without her right-hand woman, Faye had to admit to herself that she loved the flexibility of working remotely and being out in the field.

"We're taking the truck for its first run today," Faye enthused. "I think we're going to get a really good crowd for opening day." Faye was standing outside the cottage and looked over at Gregor who was in the driveway, adding some finishing touches to what he had dubbed The Beast. They had found the truck for sale through a restaurant contact of Gregor's and transferred the permits. It had all happened quickly, since the inside of the truck was all ready to go. An artist Gregor knew had stayed up for two days straight working on the artwork for the outside of the truck, which featured a hungry beast emerging from the English countryside. His menu was simple—just three items, so he could execute it himself, with Faye working the front of the truck.

"Make sure you take notes, and lots of pictures," Bev said. Faye had opted not to tell her that she would actually be working in the truck and not just reporting. She didn't think it would be wise to tell her just how close she and Gregor had gotten, although she suspected that Bev already knew.

"I'll give you a full update soon," Faye promised before hanging up the phone.

As chance would have it, the phone rang again. It was Faye's mother and she answered.

"Are you having fun out there, dear?" she asked.

"I actually extended my work trip," Faye explained. "Gregor is opening a food truck and I'm helping him."

"Is he paying you for that?" she asked.

"Mom!" Faye shook her head. "I'm tagging along for research on my story. I'm not his employee."

"I'm just looking out for you, sweetie," she said,

her voice suddenly dripping with honey. "Are you two thinking of getting engaged?"

"Mom, I told you, I'm not getting married. Not ever," Faye said through gritted teeth. She knew that her mom wouldn't feel settled until both of her daughters were hitched, but Faye couldn't think about that. After her first horrible experience with almost being wed, she was in absolutely no hurry to go for a second turn.

"Okay, okay. You'll change your mind," her mother said matter-of-factly.

"How are things at home?" Faye asked, trying to change the subject.

"Boring. Maybe I need a trip to England."

"I'm sure travel would be good for you. You should ask some of your girlfriends to take a cruise with you."

"Bleh," her mom said, brushing off the idea. "I want to come where you are. Does Gregor have a good-looking father, preferably widowed but maybe divorced?"

"Okay, Mom. We're about to get going so let's talk later. Love you," she said before hanging up.

Tucking her phone in the back of her jeans pocket, she adjusted the red bandana in her hair. Her white tank top completed what she felt was the perfect look for working the window of Gregor's truck.

Marching up to the truck and stepping inside, she saw Gregor checking his supplies and watched for a moment as he seemed to be taking a mental inventory. It was sexy to see a man doing what he loved, and even though it was a scaled-down version of the restaurant he had been planning, Gregor was clearly in his element. Plus, the worn-out jeans and apron over his T-shirt suited him perfectly. Faye coughed to get his attention and he turned around and smiled at her.

"You look adorable," he said, wrapping his arms around her waist. The galley kitchen area in the truck was small and their bodies were pressed together in such close quarters.

"So do you," said Faye, adjusting his apron. "Is everything all ready?"

"As ready as it's going to be," he said, looking around at the setup. "I can't believe we're doing this."

"You're doing it, I'm just helping," Faye said.

"Well, I wouldn't have been able to do this without you. So thank you."

"Let's see if you're thanking me after the lunch rush."

"You're going to do fine," he said. "Just call out the orders and put the slips up here. You know what to do."

"And if I mess up?" she asked, batting her eyes at him.

Gregor's eyes took on a devilish look. "Then I'll have to give you a spanking later," he said naughtily, cupping her ass in his hands and pulling her in toward him.

Faye squealed in delight as Gregor squeezed her

buttocks as he started to kiss her neck. It was so exciting, being on this adventure with him, and she couldn't believe that not only was she writing his story, she was now also becoming a part of it.

On the ride into town, Faye looked out the window at the beautiful countryside and tried to imagine herself living there. Of course, it was just a fantasy, but she thought she could get used to this life of gardens and pubs and home-cooked dinners. She realized that over the past week she'd hardly given much thought at all to her life in New York City. Her apartment was nice—very cozy and it suited her well, and she loved sitting out on the fire escape in the summer with a glass of wine and listening to her neighbors talk, play music, fight and laugh.

But ever since David, she had started to think about what it would be like to leave New York for somewhere new. It was a thought that surprised her, since she'd thought for a long time that it was the place she would always call home. After college, she'd moved out there by herself. She was a Midwestern girl with *Sex and the City* dreams, and she loved the fact that all of her friends were impressed that she rode the subway to her job in publishing and went out for drinks with her coworkers at places way fancier than the local chain restaurants they were used to frequenting. Faye felt like a New Yorker, but she was also open to finding a new home—with the right person.

Looking over at Gregor in the driver's seat, his

gaze fixed on the road, she knew he was a little on edge for their opening, and that his adrenaline was running high. Hers was, too, and she so badly wanted to see him succeed. Then a sobering and distressing thought crossed her mind. If the food truck was a success, Gregor would be off and running. She wanted the best for him, but she also knew that if he reentered the media's consciousness, especially with a successful new venture, he would have little time for a personal life. She sighed, knowing all that he had to gain, and all she had to lose. At least it would make a good story, she told herself, which was cold comfort in the moment.

Faye had started to think like that in the past few years. She tried to look at her own personal situations, her triumphs and tragedies, and make them into novels or movies in which she was the main character. Maybe it was the writer in her, or maybe it just helped to detach from reality sometimes.

In today's scenario, she was the girlfriend of a wildly popular travel show host, and she was on location with him for his latest venture. She tried to imagine what it would be like to really be with Gregor. Would they be a celebrity couple? She hated the idea of having her personal life scrutinized by the media, even though she was a part of it. And the red carpets would certainly be fun, and the clothes! The designer dresses, the parties, all of it, would obviously be amazing. But how would she maintain a closeness with someone who belonged to the whole world?

When Gregor pulled the truck up to the curb right outside a busy park Faye knew that it was go time. They had their permit and in a short time, the lunch crowd would hit. She had tweeted out a few hints on Gregor's behalf, being careful to strike a balance between intriguing his fans and creating a full-on frenzy. Looking out the window, she could see members of the local media hanging out with their cameras, ready to get the perfect shot of Gregor busy at his craft. She had a gut feeling that this was going to go well, that they were both in the place they needed to be.

"Almost done setting up if you want to open the window," Gregor called to Faye. She turned around and pulled open the hatch on the window where she would be taking the orders and almost fell backward when she saw the magnitude of the crowd that had assembled on the other side of the truck since they had parked.

"Gregor!" she called frantically. "I think you're going to want to see this."

Gregor looked up from his perfectly chopped scallions and wiped his hands on his apron. Stepping up to the window and looking out next to Faye, a barrage of camera flashes went off and the crowd, which was now snaking around at least three blocks, erupted in cheers.

Faye watched the look of calm on Gregor's face morph into something more like stunned surprise.

"That's a lot of hungry people," he said in a daze as the cameras kept flashing.

"Maybe I should have been a little more subtle with my Instagram posts," Faye said. She wondered if they would even be able to handle a crowd of this size. She hoped that people wouldn't go away hungry, or worse, hungry and angry.

"Alright, let's get to it!" Gregor yelled to the crowd. "Are you guys ready for some great food?"

The crowd cheered in excitement as Gregor went back into the truck and assumed his post at the grill. Faye smirked at him, thinking that he was such a ham, but he was too focused on getting orders out to even notice. It was the first time she had seen him in "performance mode" since they were together and she had to admit it was a little disconcerting, how easily he could switch on the charm.

The next few hours passed in a frenzy with Faye yelling out orders, clipping tickets to the board and Gregor shuttling out his painstakingly prepared creations. The temperature in the truck had to be one hundred degrees, and with the combination of the oven going and the nonstop orders to fill, Faye found herself a sweaty mess by the time they served the last seafood bun and announced to the crowd that they were out of ingredients and had to close up.

"That was incredible!" Gregor said as Faye closed the catering window. They were finally alone, and somehow he seemed even more energized than when the night had begun. Lifting her up in his arms, he spun her around as best he could inside the close quarters of the truck and kissed her. "Thanks for all your hard work tonight."

"It was my pleasure," Faye said, smiling. It was good to see Gregor in his element, doing what made him happy. "You were like a machine!"

"It's what I do," he said with a shrug. "Wait, that sounded really arrogant."

"Very un-British of you," Faye laughed. She wiped some kitchen grease from the side of his cheek. "You have every right to be very proud." Just as she reached up to kiss him, there was a knock on the door of the truck.

"Let me just tell them we're all sold out," Gregor said. "Actually, maybe you want to tell them?"

Faye nodded. She understood that if he opened the door, Gregor would be pulled into interviews, or at the very least selfies with fans. And she wanted him all to herself.

Even though she was about to drop from exhaustion, she was also turned on by seeing Gregor work masterfully at his craft. She had never even realized how sexy this could be—watching someone do what they're good at was actually a bigger turn-on than being wooed with flowers or poetry. It was like Gregor had allowed her to see his true self that night, and that was so revealing, so intimate. And not only that, she had been a big part of what they had done here—together.

Even though she had been hurt badly in the past, she now found she was allowing herself to daydream about a future with this man. She didn't know what it would look like, with living on different continents, but for love she would be willing to work it out.

Love. Neither of them had uttered the word, but the feeling had been shared in their actions, in their kindness and caring toward one another. Faye had to think that this was more than sex—although that aspect of her relationship with Gregor was pretty damn excellent. No other man had made her feel this much like herself before. It was like he had some magic touch. Maybe it was that he made her feel so confident in herself that nothing felt like it was off-limits. With him, she could go to the highest places because she knew he wasn't judging her. In fact, it seemed like he was almost worshipful of her, but not in a weird way. When they lay together in bed after sex, she felt secure and something else she hadn't felt in a long, long time—happy.

There was another sharp rap on the door and Faye opened the door to see a small crowd of people all huddled together, smiling and laughing.

"I'm sorry, we're all done for tonight," Faye said professionally.

"Get your arse out here, ya bugger!" the man standing at the front of the group yelled into the truck. Must be drunk, Faye thought to herself as she started to close the door on him. Just then, she felt Gregor come up behind her.

"Hey!" he yelled with familiarity. "You made it!"

"'Course we did," said another guy in the group.

"These are my mates," he said, turning to Faye.

Faye blushed, embarrassed that she had just treated Gregor's friends like random customers.

"I'm sorry," she said.

"No worries," Gregor said quickly. "This is Faye Curry, she's a writer for *Amuse Bouche*."

Faye bristled a little at the introduction. She didn't expect Gregor to introduce her as his girlfriend, that would have been absurd. It was just that what he said made their relationship sound so formal, so businesslike.

The friends stood there and nodded, and then the guy who had yelled took one step up into the truck.

"We're all going down to The Filly to celebrate you. You coming?"

Gregor looked to Faye.

"We should go!" she said, trying a little too hard to sound enthusiastic. What she really wanted was to continue the sweaty kissing session they had just begun, to bring things back to his place and maybe get in that lovely shower of his together again before heading off to bed. But it was his night, and it was right that he should celebrate.

"Great!" Gregor said excitedly. "We'll meet you there in a bit."

On the drive over to The Filly Inn, Gregor and

Faye didn't speak much, they were both so exhausted from the night of cooking and serving. Faye's mind was abuzz with how they could market the food truck, maybe translate the idea into an actual restaurant, but these were conversations for another time. She was just glad that he had gotten his confidence back after the blow of having the pub bought out from under him by Erik. Maybe sometimes not getting what you wanted really did lead to something better than you could ever have imagined. She guessed that was true for her, too. If anyone would have told her that not marrying David would lead her to the place she was right now, sitting in a food truck she had helped create with a famous TV personality and chef, she never would have believed it.

"Thanks again for all your help tonight," Gregor said, breaking the silence as they drove down a dark, winding road with no streetlights toward the next town where The Filly was located. "For everything," he said, putting his hand on Faye's jean-clad thigh and squeezing. Her legs were already hot and sticky from the unbearable temperature while they were running service, but somehow Gregor's touch made her feel even hotter, but in a good way.

She felt a little wistful when they finally pulled into the parking lot of The Filly. It was greedy, but she wanted Gregor all to herself.

"Are you sure this is okay?" he asked when he switched off the engine.

"Absolutely," she said, nodding affirmatively. "I look like hell, but I don't think anyone's looking at me."

Gregor put his hands on the sides of Faye's sweaty cheeks. "I'm looking at you. And you're gorgeous," he said. And even though her mascara was smudged and her white tank top was now grease stained, Faye believed him. In fact, this was the most beautiful she had felt in a long time.

"Let's go," she said, hopping out of the truck and taking Gregor's hand as they walked into the pub.

The Filly had a different vibe from the first time Faye had been there with Gregor. During the day it was an open, sun-soaked place with beers flowing and young couples and families playing outside in the grass. Walking in now, the room was glowing with faux lamplights and it was so crowded that bodies were pressed together like at a dance club. Faye grasped Gregor's arm as he led her through the crowd and toward a table in the back, an area she hadn't even noticed on her first visit. They spotted Gregor's friends, none of whom she had any background on, and when they saw them coming, they cheered.

"All hail the chef!" shouted the burly man who had been at the front of the group by the truck.

"Faye, this is Tom," Gregor said, wrapping an arm around his friend.

"Lovely to meet you, Faye," Tom said, making space at the table for the two of them. The table was already filled with half-empty glasses and pitchers of beer. "What can I get you to drink?"

"Beer sounds fantastic," Faye said, and it really did, she was so hot and dying of thirst.

Tom disappeared to retrieve more glasses while Gregor got pulled into a conversation with one of his friends on the other side of him. Faye looked around at the other bar patrons. She loved just being in the middle of somewhere and observing all of the dynamics, the little comments and gestures between people. She liked to imagine who was on a first date, and who had been together for years. There was a couple in a neighboring booth who looked so tired, yet happy. She imagined that it was their first night out after having a baby. Another couple sat at the bar, their legs touching as they talked. Judging by the way he attended to her, and how she leaned in to him, Faye decided it was definitely a first date.

It had been a long time since she'd even had to think about dating. She couldn't exactly call what she and Gregor were doing dating, but at least it was a reminder of how it felt to get to know someone new. She shuddered at the thought of going on all the dating apps her mother and friends were always recommending. Meeting someone through just living your life seemed like the better way to go, at least for her.

Tom returned with extra glasses and poured Faye a beer.

"Thanks," she said, raising her glass. "Cheers!"

"Cheers!" he said, clinking glasses with her. "So you're working on a story about Gregor?"

"Yes," Faye said carefully. She never liked to reveal too much about her work to people, especially before it was even completed. "The readers of our magazine love Gregor."

"Everyone loves Gregor!" he said, clapping a hand down on his pal's shoulder. Gregor was still in conversation with the other end of the table but he turned around and smiled at Tom, and then mouthed the words *Are you okay?* to Faye. She nodded affirmatively.

"He's a real comeback kid," Tom said, draining his beer and pouring himself another one.

"Tonight was a big success," Faye agreed. "I hope it can be the beginning of something really exciting for him."

Faye watched Tom's expression suddenly change. She followed his eyes toward the door of the pub where a tall redhead in a jean skirt and biker jacket stood.

"Shit," Tom whispered as the woman saw their table and started walking toward them.

"Who's that?" Faye asked, wiping the sweat from her brow with the back of her hand. She was still perspiring from all the hard work, and it was warm inside the pub.

"That's Emily," Tom said with a sense of foreboding in his voice. "Broke Gregor's heart. What the hell is she doing here?"

Faye's eyes widened as she checked out the approaching woman. There was no denying it—she was gorgeous, with long legs, flawless skin and that mane of long red hair. She took a giant gulp of her beer.

"But they've been done for a while, right?" Faye asked, hating the crack in her voice. She saw Emily approach Gregor and watched a series of emotions play out across his face—shock, confusion, reluctance—but then Emily touched his arm and his look softened, and they came together for a hug. The embrace certainly wasn't passionate, but it was enough to make the hairs on Faye's arms stand up.

"Ah, some things never change," Tom said, shaking his head. "Especially with a beauty like that."

"Does she still live around here?" Faye asked. She watched as Gregor made room for Emily at the table and poured her a beer. They were smiling at one another.

"No," Tom said. "But Emily's a girl who gets what she wants. Not surprising that she'd want him back, especially after tonight."

"Indeed," Faye said, quickly draining her beer as Tom watched with surprise. She looked over at Gregor and Emily again, willing him to turn around and look at her, to give her some type of sign that he wasn't falling for his ex, that he was hers and not interested in this fair-weather person. But Gregor was deep in conversation, and she could see the history of their physical relationship from their body language. Gregor was turned toward her and she instinctively mirrored each of his movements as they talked and laughed.

"I'm gonna go get some fresh air," Faye said, standing up. "Will you excuse me?" she said to Tom. He nodded. Faye pulled a few pounds from her fanny pack and threw them on the table. If Gregor noticed her walking out, he didn't try to stop her.

Outside the pub there were still plenty of people lingering around, and Faye just wanted to be alone. She felt like she was going to be sick. She hated it when people used the word *triggering*, but she knew that was exactly what was happening to her. Seeing Gregor with his ex brought back all the terrible memories of David, how she had trusted him totally, and how he had betrayed her on what was supposed to be the happiest day of their lives.

Faye looked back at the door, willing Gregor to walk through it, to come after her and tell her that he didn't have feelings for Emily, that she was the one he wanted. But the longer she waited the more apparent it became that this wasn't going to happen.

All Faye wanted was to get away from the situation but she was trapped. Then she spotted it—a taxicab letting a group of people out at the pub. Before they could close the door, she ran up to it and leaned in to talk to the driver.

"Can you take me all the way to London—The Savoy?" she asked. The driver gave her a quick nod. Faye glanced back at the pub one last time and then hopped into the cab and closed the door. As they pulled away out onto the dirt road, she leaned back against the seat and closed her eyes, feeling hot tears fill them even though she tried squinting them back. She had done her job. She had enough to go on for her article. She just couldn't believe that this was the end of their story, but it felt like this was where the road ended for her and Gregor.

As they drove into the night, Faye pulled out her cell phone and dialed Eden's number. The phone rang and rang, but uncharacteristically, there was no answer. Eden always took Faye's calls, especially while she had been away. Giving up, Faye pressed End Call and stared at the screen of her phone, wondering what to do next.

She toyed with the idea of calling her mother. She knew that it was a bad idea. Her mom would likely tell her she was to blame for things going wrong. But in that moment, she just wanted to hear a familiar voice. So against her better judgment she dialed her.

"Faye!" her mom answered. "It must be late there! Is everything alright?"

Being asked that question, Faye became totally undone. "No," she cried. "I think Gregor might want to get back with his ex-girlfriend," she said, giving voice to her greatest fear. Of course, when she said it out loud, the thought occurred to her that she might be overreacting. It wouldn't be the first time she had blown a situation out of proportion, letting her imagination run away with her.

"Darling, I'm so sorry," Faye's mom said gently. Her voice was kinder than Faye had expected. "Why don't you come home?"

Home. The thought sounded appealing to Faye.

"Get the next flight, I'll meet you at the airport. You've been through so much, you need to be with family," she insisted.

Faye nodded in agreement but didn't say a word.

"Honey, are you there?" her mom asked.

"I'm here," Faye finally answered. "Okay."

"Good, then it's settled. I'll see you as soon as tomorrow. Send me the flight info when you have it."

Faye hung up the phone. She knew that if she had talked to Eden instead, the conversation might have gone in a totally different direction. While Faye's mom wanted to protect her, Eden was usually the one to encourage her to take a deep breath and assess the situation before acting. She would tell Faye to ask herself if what she was feeling was in response to something real or imagined.

Fear. False evidence appearing real, she could just hear her sister saying. Resting her head back on the upholstery, Faye began to search for flights and then stopped to look out the window. She wasn't sure if she wanted to go home but she was sure of one thing—she couldn't stay here, not where she wasn't wanted.

CHAPTER EIGHT

IT WAS A GOOD half hour or so before Gregor looked up from his conversation and noticed that Faye was no longer at the table. His eyes darted around the bar, and he wondered if she had gone to the loo, but part of him started to worry. Emily had been talking non-stop and he had been too polite to excuse himself from their catch-up session, or more like her catch-up. Being overly polite was one of his flaws. It was in his British blood, but he just didn't know how to be rude, especially to a woman, even if she had been terrible to him.

Emily was telling him how lonely she'd been since they had broken up, and though part of Gregor still felt that familiar tug toward her, that spark of physical attraction, he quickly realized that it was simply a habit. His life was actually going great. But at the moment, he couldn't find the one woman who had helped him turn things around.

"Tom, have you seen Faye?" he yelled across the table.

Tom, who was completely drunk by now, nodded

his head slowly. "I think she went outside," he said in a slurred voice.

Gregor stood up from the table and Emily quickly stood up, too.

"I'm so sorry, my friend's gone missing. Will you excuse me?" he said.

"I'll help you find her!" Emily volunteered.

Gregor wished she wouldn't, but he didn't know what to say.

"What's she look like?"

Gregor thought about Faye for a moment, and the first thing he saw were her dark brown eyes. He needed so desperately to see them right now. But maybe she was right outside, and he was overreacting.

"Blonde, short, pretty," he said, trying to sound perfunctory.

"Ah, just your type," Emily said playfully, giving him a little punch on the arm that he thought was too flirty.

Gregor pushed his way out toward the door and finally made his way outside.

"She's gone," he said with certainty. Gregor pulled out his new cell phone and hit redial on Faye's number. The phone rang and rang but there was no answer.

"Everything alright?"

Gregor felt Emily snake her arms around him from behind. He turned toward her and gently removed her hands from his body.

"No. I need to go find my friend." Gregor knew

she might go back to the cottage. But there was one place he felt certain she was headed. Pulling out his keys, he jumped into the truck, but when he tried to start the engine, it wouldn't turn over. "Fuck!" he yelled, hitting the steering wheel with both hands. Jumping down from the cab, he paced in front of his broken-down beast, thinking of what to do next.

"I can give you a lift," Emily said, dangling her own set of keys in the air like bait. Gregor hesitated. He knew that Faye seeing him with Emily had probably upset her. He thought of his friends back inside the pub, all likely too plastered to drive. He weighed the pros and cons of accepting anything from Emily.

"Okay," he said reluctantly, not wanting to waste any time waiting for a car service. "Let's go."

Emily smiled like she had gotten what she wanted, and a paranoid part of Gregor wondered if she had done something to his truck just to orchestrate this very scenario. He shook the thought off and tried to keep his focus where it needed to be—on finding Faye.

Gregor knew which car was Emily's and quickly hopped in when she opened the doors. But instead of making conversation on the drive back to his house, he kept trying Faye's number, hoping she would pick up. Getting no response, he sent a series of text messages.

I need to speak to you.

Where have you gone?

Please pick up.

There was no response to any of them.

By the time they pulled into his driveway, Gregor had the sinking feeling that Faye was really gone for good. The situation was a total misunderstanding, of course, but he could have taken more care to check in with her during the evening.

He was so wrapped up in wondering where she was and if she was okay, that he barely noticed when Emily pulled into his driveway, turned off the ignition and sat staring at him.

"So, here we are," she said.

Gregor wasn't sure what she was up to, but he had no time to play games.

"Thanks so much for the ride, I really appreciate it," he said, undoing his seat belt.

"Don't rush off," Emily said, reaching a hand out and placing it suggestively on Gregor's upper thigh. "Wherever she went, I'm sure she's just fine. She's a big girl."

"I really ought to get going," Gregor said, gently removing her hand from his leg. It would have been easy enough to let Emily stir up those old feelings, but he was quickly realizing that the only woman he really wanted was the one he had spent the last few weeks with. She was the person who helped him and supported him, encouraged his dreams. Not to mention turned him on in a major way!

"Gregor," Emily said, calling him back as he reached for the door handle. "I miss you."

Gregor paused. A year ago, it would have been the only words he had wanted to hear. But now it was strange how her words actually meant so little. He had finally moved on.

"Emily, you and I had so many problems. The main one being you let yourself be seduced by my supposed best friend…"

"Loser never had the nerve to even do anything," Emily muttered.

"What?" Gregor was confused. Wasn't Erik the one who had tried to steal Emily, who had taken her to bed despite the fact that she was engaged to him?

"Never mind," Emily said, her expression suddenly going cold. "Go chase your American. I'm sure she'll make you very happy."

"Yes!" Gregor said, ignoring the sarcasm in Emily's tone. "Yes, I think she will!"

Even though she didn't mean it, it was the truest thing he had heard in a long time. Faye could make him happy, and he had to find her.

Once Emily was gone—for good this time, he thought—Gregor got a few things from inside the house before hopping in his car and starting the engine. He thought he knew where to find Faye and he was going to take a chance and follow his instincts.

The drive down darkened roads in the middle of the night should have been exhausting, especially after the crazy day he had just had opening his food truck for the first time, but Gregor was wide-awake. He didn't need to stop for caffeine because he was running on pure adrenaline. The thought crossed his mind that maybe Faye had gone to the airport, but he hoped that wasn't the case. He had to believe that she had some of the same feelings he was experiencing. Besides, there was unfinished business with her article. He pressed his foot down on the accelerator, driving carefully but fast, into the night.

When he finally arrived in the Strand, the city was mostly asleep. It was completely dark apart from the twinkling lights of The Savoy where he knew Faye had a reserved room. He was so glad he hadn't let her stay there when they'd first met. Having her at the cottage felt like the most natural thing in the world.

The valet was off duty, so Gregor parked the car himself and marched into the opulent lobby where the desk was quiet. Ringing the bell on the counter, he waited a moment until a young woman emerged from the back office.

"Good evening," she said sleepily, before taking a good look at Gregor's face. "Mr. Wright!" she said, suddenly recognizing him. "Welcome. Do we have a reservation for you?"

"No," Gregor said, smiling his most charming smile. "But my friend Ms. Faye Curry is here, I'm supposed to meet her at her room."

The desk attendant typed quickly on her computer

and then nodded her head. "Yes, she's in room 1404. In fact, she left an extra key for you."

Gregor raised his eyebrow at this. So Faye had hoped he would show up! His heart leaped in his chest as the attendant slid the plastic card across the counter to him.

"Any luggage?" she asked.

"I'm all set," Gregor said, unable to hide the ear-to-ear grin that was emerging on his face.

Gregor rode the lift up to Faye's floor and when he got to the correct room, he quietly opened the door. He could see Faye's form lying in bed. He wasn't sure if she was awake or not, but without hesitating, he kicked off his shoes, pulled up the covers and slid in next to her.

"You came," she whispered.

Gregor put his mouth on the spot on Faye's neck he loved to kiss. "Of course I did."

Faye turned to Gregor. "I'm sorry if I—"

"It's okay," Gregor interrupted. "Things with me and her—it's really over for good. I know that now."

Even in the darkness of the room, he could see Faye smile at him. "I got scared. My fiancé—he walked out on me on our wedding day. For someone else."

Gregor didn't even know this man who had done this to her, but he still felt the fury rise up inside him. "You don't deserve to be treated like that. I would never do that. Faye," he said, brushing her blond hair off her cheek. "I'm not him."

Faye ran her hand over the side of Gregor's stubbly cheek. "I know," she said, leaning in and kissing him passionately.

Up until that moment, Gregor hadn't even noticed that Faye was completely naked. But now she pushed her body closer to him and his hands wandered from her back all the way down the length of her gorgeous body.

"I want you so badly," he growled.

Faye didn't say a word, but by the glow of the slightly open shades that let in the streetlights, he could see that her eyes were saying *Take me.* He waited as her hands worked quickly to help him remove his T-shirt and jeans, and soon they were totally naked and holding one another, face-to-face.

Faye reached her hand down to Gregor's cock, which was stirring. He allowed her to stroke him in that capable, firm way that she had that never failed to send the blood rushing into the part of him he so desperately wanted inside her. Gregor put his face into the softness of Faye's breasts and began to kiss them gently as she continued her steady strokes on his hardening member. When he couldn't wait any longer to be one with her, Gregor slid his body on top of hers. As Faye wrapped her legs around his waist, his fingers found the entrance to her honeypot. As usual, the whole area between her thighs was dripping wet. He loved that she was always ready to welcome him, and this time he was extra hard. Needing to be inside her more than anything, he pushed the head of his cock into the soft folds of her pussy and immediately, she received the entire length of him.

Gregor let out a guttural noise as he plunged into her. It was a relief, being inside her, and her hips arched up toward him, her way of showing that she wanted him to fuck her.

Their mouths devoured each other hungrily as Gregor pushed into her, working up a steady rhythm.

"Mmm," Faye said, making happy, satisfied noises every time Gregor pumped into her. Putting her hands on his back she pulled him into her even deeper and he almost came, feeling her nails dig into the flesh just below his shoulder blades. He had never been with someone who seemed to love sex as much as Faye did. And now that he knew her story, he could see why she had been reluctant to trust. As she wrapped her legs around him tighter, he mentally vowed to always be good to this amazing woman.

Gregor pulled Faye up to him so they were sitting face-to-face, his hardness still inside her. Faye squeezed her legs around Gregor's waist even tighter so that their bodies were completely intertwined. Kissing each other, he grabbed her behind in his hands, as she began grinding on him. The fact that they were making eye contact felt so intimate, but what really took him over the edge was when Faye started to bounce up and down. With her breasts grazing his chest and her sweet pussy welcoming him with every movement, he was helpless to do anything but let go.

The feeling started in his cock but then radiated through the rest of his body—a swell of good feelings that sent a forceful surge of come up from his balls and into Faye's tightness.

"Ohhh!" he cried out as they rocked together.

Knowing not to stop until he had gotten every last drop out of him, Faye grinded her hips into him even more, which was both pleasurable and painful in a good way. His body had never felt so alive, so sensitive. He didn't want to disconnect from her, not ever again. But he knew there was something he wanted to do for her.

Finally, as they lay back on the pillows, Gregor reached his hand down to Faye's opening. When she arched up toward him, he knew he had found her clit, and he began making quick circles around her sensitive little bud as she writhed on the bed in pleasure.

When he knew she was getting close, Gregor took his other hand and plunged two fingers into her sticky, wet opening while he continued to flick and rub her pleasure button.

"Gregor," she called, as he quickened his precise little strokes. He could feel her body clamping down around his fingers, pulsing and tightening, and within moments, the look on her face coupled with the fact that she was shaking, told him that Faye was coming for him.

When it came to giving her pleasure, he also knew not to back off too soon. He was now rubbing her clit with an almost rough stroke and pushed her hips toward him, her body begging for more.

As much as he loved coming, it still wasn't as great as watching her orgasm from his touch. He loved making her body beg for more, and when it came to sex, her appetite was unquenchable. He loved that she loved the two things he also couldn't get enough of: sex and food.

When Faye's burst of orgasm finally began to subside, the two of them lay back on the pillows side by side, basking in the happy, sweaty glow of what they had just done.

That night, Gregor slept more soundly than he could recently recall, his body wrapped around Faye's. In the morning, he woke up early and lay there for a moment, content to just be near the woman who made him feel so complete.

"Hey," he said softly when Faye finally began to stir. She sat up, leaned her head on one hand and looked at him for a long time before speaking.

"I'm glad you're here," she said, running her fingers through his messy hair.

"I'm glad I'm here, too," he said, gazing back at her. "I had a feeling you might come here."

"This is where I was supposed to be from the beginning."

"But if you never came to the cottage…"

"We would have missed out on a lot of fun," she laughed.

"And getting to know each other," he added.

Gregor wasn't sure if this was more than just sex to Faye. He hoped she was feeling the same connection he was, but he didn't want to assume anything.

Faye smiled at Gregor and leaned in to nuzzle her head against his bare chest.

"Do you think you'd ever see yourself leaving New York permanently? I know you're a city girl, but the UK has a lot to offer."

Faye laughed and kissed Gregor's chest.

"I think I'm just getting used to enjoying life again. I was so wrapped up in what I didn't have for so long. It feels wonderful to be free."

"He really hurt you…" Gregor's voice trailed off. He didn't want to pressure Faye to talk about her ex, but he knew that it was there, simmering under the surface.

"More than I care to remember," Faye said, turning away from Gregor and resting her head on the pillow. He watched as she stared up at the ceiling above their bed, and he could see her remembering what had happened.

"It was my wedding day. I was already in my dress when it happened. We were going to observe the tradition of not seeing each other before the ceremony. David and I."

Gregor bristled when she spoke his name.

"I was so excited to see him, though, so I thought I'd surprise him in the groom's suite. Then I got the surprise of my life."

"Ugh, he was with someone in there? The fucker!"

Gregor said. He couldn't help but feel violated on her behalf.

"His coworker. They were doing it right there, up against the wall. He was wearing the tux he was supposed to marry me in. That didn't happen."

Gregor laid his head down next to Faye's.

"That must have been awful."

"It was. So humiliating." Faye's voice grew more impassioned as she went on. "Having to call things off. All of my relatives that had flown in, the gifts, the flowers. But the worst part of it all was that I really loved him. I trusted him."

Gregor didn't know what to say so he simply stroked Faye's forehead and planted a kiss on it.

"You deserve better than that," he said matter-of-factly. "I hope you know that."

"Well, it messed me up for a really long time."

"And now?" Gregor said hopefully.

"I just know I'll never get married," Faye said, her eyes looking steely. He could see that she was hurting underneath her tough exterior. "It's just not for me."

"Oh," Gregor said, sitting up in bed. He wasn't sure what to make of all this. "I thought we were really connecting."

He felt Faye reach a hand out to him, and he turned toward her.

"We are. I just need time to be on my own. To figure out who I am—not as part of a couple, but as a person."

Gregor nodded. He was silent for a while before he leaned down and kissed her gently on the lips.

"You know, I'm not him, Faye."

"I know," she whispered, and kissed him back, pressing her mouth to his with urgency.

"Come back home with me," Gregor implored. "You can write and relax and I'll make you delicious food. What more could you want?"

"It sounds perfect," Faye said looking up at him. "But I have a story to write. I need some time alone to do that."

Gregor's face must have fallen, because she quickly added, "I'm not going anywhere. I'll rebook my ticket, I promise."

"Okay," he said, hesitant to go back to the countryside without her next to him.

"Are you going to try and get The Beast up and running for tonight?" she asked enthusiastically.

"Maybe," he said, considering it. "Maybe I will."

"You should," she said with certainty in her voice. "And I'll be here writing. And then in a few days we can meet and catch up."

"That sounds great," he said with a smile. "But I don't know if I can go a few days without seeing you." Gregor pulled her on top of him and she squealed in delight.

"I'm sure you'll survive," she said, as he began to kiss her neck on the spot that he knew sent signals straight to her lady parts. If he was going to have to leave, he might as well do it with a bang, he figured.

"Are you really ready to go again?" she asked with a raised eyebrow.

Being ready was one problem Gregor never seemed to have.

If Faye needed space to work, he would give it to her. But not before giving her something to think about while he was away.

CHAPTER NINE

FAYE HAD A hard time saying goodbye to Gregor, but she knew herself well enough to know that if she returned to the cottage with him, she wouldn't get a word of writing done on her article. Gregor made it too tempting to relax and enjoy herself. She could easily imagine spending the next week going from his bed to the kitchen and back again without a care in the world. It was a big departure from the type of life she'd been leading up until the trip, and she loved that he had brought out this more hedonistic, carefree side to her. In fact, she loved that he made her want to enjoy life. In her previous relationships, she always felt like she had to adjust her own opinions, wants and needs to her partner. But with Gregor, things felt more in sync.

Still, she knew she needed the time and space to get her work done. Bev had been calling and emailing daily since she told her she was extending her trip. Part of the reason for the calls was to check on the article status—she knew it was going to be the cover story for the issue they were getting ready to close back home. But she was also well aware that Bev wanted the gossip on Gregor. She'd kept quiet on anything regarding her own relationship with him. Bev may have successfully played matchmaker with them, but that didn't mean she needed to share the dirty details with her boss.

Faye was still in her robe and it was the middle of the afternoon, so she decided to take a shower, get dressed and go downstairs to get something to eat before starting in on her work in earnest. She also made a quick call to her mother, telling her not to expect her home just yet. She had her work cut out for her compiling all of the notes, pictures and memories from the conversations she and Gregor had about everything from his favorite meal (fish and chips), to his most memorable episode of his television show (visiting an ashram in India), to his biggest hope and dream (his restaurant, of course), but also to "find true love" which made Faye simultaneously blush and worry when he had said it to her over dinner in the French Riviera. Part of her wondered if she was that person, the woman he had been looking for all this time.

Another more serious part of her worried that if it was her, things wouldn't work out. After all, they were from two different worlds. He was a celebrity, and she was a journalist whose byline likely no one but the most well-read food connoisseurs recognized. He was British, and seemed so at home there, and she was a New Yorker through and through.

And besides, even if they could overcome those admittedly huge issues, there was his crazy schedule to contend with. Even if he wasn't filming the show, he would certainly be pulled into public appearances across the globe, and although she loved travel, she certainly wasn't ready to take on a lifestyle like that.

Once she had showered and changed into a pair of drawstring denim pants and a Parisian red-and-white-striped top, Faye twisted her wet hair into a bun and went down to the café in the hotel to get some coffee and lunch.

The lobby of The Savoy was opulent and well-appointed and filled with mostly business travelers. She was immediately seated in the mostly empty restaurant at a nice table near the window overlooking the city street. Faye didn't feel the usual need to occupy herself by looking at her phone or a book. Instead, she looked out onto the street and people watched.

It occurred to her that although she had been single for about a year in New York, she had never really taken herself out to eat like this, had never let herself enjoy the peaceful pleasure of a solo meal in a place that wasn't quick service. There were a lot of pleasurable things she had denied herself in this period of mourning for her marriage that never was.

Now, looking back, she realized that it was a waste of time, and that she had in fact been punishing herself for having gotten into a bad situation.

She now knew there was no time for that. Food, experiences—life—were here to be enjoyed while she had the chance.

The waitress came by to take her order and Faye selected a healthy salad—an antidote to all of the rich eating and drinking she'd been doing. It was time to sober up and put her work hat on, otherwise she wouldn't have a job to go back to once she touched down in New York.

Just as she was about to continue watching the passersby on the street, she heard her phone ping and instinctively reached into her bag to check it. Her pulse quickened when she saw that it was a message from Bev. By now, she really should have been further along on her article, but with all the drama of the last few days, she was way behind. Reluctantly opening up the message, she saw that Bev had sent a picture of herself in a classic-looking, one-shouldered black dress. Too much for a first date? was the message. Faye smiled and typed furiously into her phone. Who is he? You look fantastic! she replied, adding a smiley face emoji.

Bev hadn't dated in years and it was so surprising—and hopeful—to see her putting herself out there. Faye shook her head in disbelief. So instead of checking up on her work or her love life, her boss was actually out there taking a chance herself! For a second, Bev's bold move made Faye regret telling Gregor to leave. She knew she had done it for the right reasons—she needed space to get back on track, to get her work done...but

now the doubtful thoughts started to creep in. What
if he had taken it as a blow off? And what was it he
had said about changing your life for true love? Faye
felt like smacking herself. This amazing man was lay-
ing it all out there for her, basically telling her that he
loved her, and she had told him to…leave?

Faye suddenly knew that she needed to talk to
someone, the only person who could guide her in
this type of situation.

"Excuse me, could I take this to go?" Faye sig-
naled the waitress, indicated her untouched salad.
The waitress nodded and in moments, returned with
her meal boxed up. Faye left a tip and headed toward the elevators. Inside her room, she worked
diligently, outlining the article and completing the
first half of it before taking a break to dial her sister's number.

"Hey! How's London?" Eden answered enthusiastically. "Are you having a great time? How's
Gregor?"

"Eden…" Faye began. She didn't have to say anything else for her sister to know that something's
wrong.

"Oh, honey, what happened? Tell me all about it,"
she said soothingly. She could just picture her sister
sitting on the couch in her living room. Alan and the
kids must have been out somewhere since there was
no background noise.

"I think I may have just blown off the love of my
life," Faye said, trying to hold back the tears. Her

big sister had guided her ever since that awful day of her never-to-be wedding. When everything went down, she was the first person Faye turned to, and she handled everything with precision and class, telling the guests what to do and where to go and keeping Faye protected from any unnecessary questions or attention.

Now the situation was totally different—but Eden was still the one person Faye could always rely on.

"And I acted totally jealous and crazy," Faye continued.

"Hold on a minute, slow down," Eden interrupted. "So you like him?"

"Yeah."

"And he likes you, I take it?"

Faye swallowed hard. "I think he might even love me." She surprised herself by saying it out loud, but when she did, the words didn't sound totally absurd. In fact, they fit.

"Faye, if you think this could be something real, don't push it away," Eden advised over the phone. Even though they were thousands of miles apart, Faye felt like she was close by as she listened. "You deserve happiness."

Eden had hit the nail on the head. After everything that had happened to her, deep down, Faye didn't really believe that happiness was possible. Intellectually, she knew she had done nothing wrong, but there was still this feeling that she couldn't shake, a voice that told her she was unworthy, that she couldn't truly be loved.

"He seems very genuine," Faye admitted to her sis. "I hope I'm not making a mistake."

"If something feels right, run to it," Eden advised. "You have to trust yourself on this."

Faye nodded. "Thanks for talking me through it," she said, feeling worlds more calm than before she had called. "Everything okay there?"

"Oh, same old," Eden said in a blasé tone. "No torrid affairs with TV stars—though the day is still young."

"Nice," Faye said, starting to laugh.

"Don't forget to bring me something," Eden reminded her.

"Okay," Faye said, saying her goodbyes and ending the call.

Sitting on the edge of the bed, she thought about texting Gregor and telling him to come back, but just then she saw that she had a voice message, one that must have come in while she was talking with Eden. Pressing Play on the message, she expected to hear the low timbre of Gregor's manly voice, but instead it was a different man speaking, whose voice she didn't recognize at first.

"Faye, please return this call as soon as possible," said the voice. "It's Erik. I know that Gregor doesn't want to speak to me, but it's imperative that you call me back."

Faye replayed the message twice, considered calling Gregor, and then impulsively hit the call back button on her phone.

"Hello," Erik answered on the second ring.

"Erik…it's Faye, is everything alright?" She felt slightly disloyal making the call, but part of her, maybe the journalist in her, needed to know what the story was.

"Faye, I know you have no reason to believe me, but before you write your story on Gregor, there's more that you need to know. Can you come to the restaurant tonight? I'll be there all evening, working."

Faye coughed nervously. "Er, I'm here in London, so I'm not sure—"

"Faye," Erik interrupted in a voice that made her sit up and take notice. "This is a matter of great importance. Can you come?"

Faye didn't know what excuse to give, but the truth was, part of her wanted to go and meet with Erik, to get to the bottom of this mystery behind their lifelong friendship.

"I'll be there," she said before hanging up the call.

An hour later, Faye was in a rental car, unused to driving on the wrong side of the road, and hoping she could make it to the restaurant before the sun went down so she wouldn't have to drive on those winding dirt roads in the dark.

For most of the trip, she hadn't taken notes. It seemed so natural to just talk to Gregor, to be with him and listen to his observations, to absorb the dif-

ferent sounds, smells and tastes that comprised his
life. But now, on the way to meet Erik, she had her
notebook and digital recorder in her bag on the passenger seat. She wanted to make sure she got the
facts straight. She was writing the life story of the
man she loved after all.

Love. Faye toyed with the idea as she exited off
the highway and turned onto the winding country
streets she was slowly becoming very familiar with.
It was a word she had once used to describe her feelings toward David. But that had been all wrong. She
had given her love to someone who wasn't worthy
of it. But this time, she was more sure of herself.
She knew that she didn't need Gregor to have the
life she wanted. She had proven she could survive
on her own. And now she was doing more than just
surviving—she was thriving. That was the feeling
she got around Gregor.

As she turned down another road, and then yet another, she traced the path by heart back to the restaurant Gregor had showed her when she first arrived.
Pulling up in front of what was once the abandoned
pub, Faye could hardly recognize it now. The frame
was still the same, but everything else about it was
now modern, from the door to the sign that hung
above it. Erik had clearly spent some money and
done a total renovation in an extremely short period
of time. She hated to admit it, but he had really good
taste. At least judging from the outside, she was sure
he had a hit on his hands.

Faye walked up to the entrance and hesitantly pushed open the door. The restaurant had undergone a total transformation since she had last seen it. There was an open kitchen plan and the booths had all been refurbished. Erik was seated in one of the booths, talking on the phone. She made her way over to him.

"Faye, thank you for coming," he said, ending his phone call and gesturing for her to sit across from him. Faye had never been alone with him, but sitting directly across from him, she had a chance to study his features more closely. He had captivating dark brown eyes, thin lips and a winning smile she wasn't sure whether or not to trust. Her guard was certainly up from the stories Gregor had told her, but she also knew there was a closeness between the two men, more like brothers than friends. Well aware that she was probably stepping outside the territory she should be treading, she chose her words very carefully.

"You've done an amazing job here, and in such a short time," she said, looking around the restaurant. The decor managed to be simultaneously modern but also included some retro hints at the past. She could easily see it being a destination spot, but also the place you always went to if you were a local.

"When I have a vision for something, there's no stopping me," Erik said, smiling at her compliment. "Full speed ahead."

"Congratulations," she said, hoping he would get to the real reason she was sitting there.

"It looks great, but there's a problem," Erik said, furrowing his brow. "I don't have the right person to help me."

Faye wasn't sure what he was getting at. "You mean Gregor?"

"The place doesn't work without him. It's got to be a team effort. Me and him, the dynamic duo. Otherwise, it's a restaurant, yeah, but there's no magic."

Faye tilted her head to the side and tried to size Erik up. Was he being sincere, or just playing her for some other reason? "You do realize that you pretty much stole this place out from under him, right? That turning this space into a high-end restaurant was his idea. We discussed it that night, at your house."

Erik shook his head and ran his fingers through his hair in a gesture of frustration.

"What can I say, Faye? He's always the one who gets everything. The TV gigs, the great jobs, the amazing women." Erik looked up from the table and met Faye's gaze. "He's very lucky to have you."

"So is this what this place is all about? You were jealous so you stole his idea?"

"No," Erik said quickly. "My hope was that we could do it together."

"I don't think he sees it that way," Faye said, trying to understand where Erik was coming from. If he really wanted Gregor on board, it seemed that stealing his idea from him was getting off on the wrong foot, to say the least.

"I wasn't trying to take this from him," Erik said. "Just the opposite."

"But this isn't the first time you've taken something—or someone from him, right?"

Faye's eyes searched Erik's for signs of guilt, or any sign of emotion.

Instead of answering, Erik got up from the table and returned with a bottle of bourbon and two glasses. Wordlessly, he poured them each a drink.

"I'm going to tell you something I've never told anyone before," he said, taking a swig of the golden-hued liquor, presumably for courage. "Everyone thinks that I stole Emily from Gregor, but that wasn't the case."

Faye looked up at Erik with interest as he continued his story.

"It was right before Gregor was set to propose. She came to me, looking to stay the night. I told her no. If you know Emily, she's not one to take no for an answer. She said that she and I were meant to be together. But of course, I told her I could never do that to my best friend. The next day she left, and I let him believe that I had seduced her."

Faye's eyes brightened as she put it together. "So, Gregor would believe that you had betrayed him rather than have his heart broken by the woman he loved," she said, finishing his thought.

Erik raised his glass. "Exactly," he said, holding it to his lips and drinking. "But it backfired. I think he ended up hating both of us. He was only supposed to hate me."

Faye took a big swallow of her own drink. "That may be the saddest, sweetest thing I've ever heard," she said.

"It was hard at first, having him so angry at me. But in a way, it was just easier for him to think I was a pig than to tell him that she wasn't in love with him."

"Sometimes it's hard to watch the people you love get hurt," Faye said, understanding where he was coming from. "But if I've learned anything over this past year, it's that you have to let people go through it. There's no saving other people from the pain. You just have to be there to support them when they fall down. Like my sister did for me."

"You're right," Erik said sullenly. "I've made a complete mess of this. Faye, I need your help. Can you talk to him for me? I need him here, to make this restaurant work. Without him, it just doesn't make sense. But more importantly, I need my friend back."

Faye was touched by the request. Oddly, she felt that she could really sympathize with Erik. She was also the kind of person who would rather take the blame than make waves. But now she understood that this was no way to go about life. You had to be honest, not just to others, but first and foremost, to yourself.

"I'll see what I can do," she said, standing up from the table.

"Thank you," Erik said, giving her a spontaneous hug. "Where are you headed from here?"

"I suppose I'll go over to Gregor's," she said, thinking out loud. "We were on a little bit of a break—so I could get some work done—but I miss him," she said, trying not to sound too sugary sweet but pretty sure her voice was dripping with it anyway.

"You guys go well together," Erik said. "Like I said, he's lucky to have you."

"I'm lucky, too," Faye said, and really meant it.

"Do you need a lift?" he asked, walking her toward the door.

"No, I've got my rental," she said.

Erik opened the door and they stepped outside into the warm night. "I think it's quitting time for me," he said. "Not much more I can do tonight."

"Give yourself a break," she said, patting him on the arm. "It'll come together. Just like with the food truck. I didn't think we'd pull it off, and then somehow it all worked out."

"I heard that was pretty amazing," Erik said, smiling. "Are you sure he'll want to come work here when he has that going on?"

"I think that the two of you create electricity when you're together," she said. "If that night at your house was any indication, together you'll be taking all of England by storm."

"I think you're right," Erik said, pulling Faye in for another hug. "Thanks again for coming," he said.

All of the pent-up energy was suddenly released

in Erik's embrace and Faye hugged him back. "It'll be okay, you'll see," she reassured him.

Just as they were about to break away from one another, they heard footsteps and a voice. Faye looked up to see Gregor standing there, watching them.

"I thought you were in London?" he said to Faye, his eyes steely and his voice devoid of emotion.

Faye opened her mouth to try and explain what she was doing, why she was standing there hugging his best friend but she was so stunned that no sounds came out. Instead, she stood looking at Gregor with her mouth agape.

It was Erik who broke the silence.

"Mate, it's not what you—"

"It's exactly what I think!" Gregor said, cutting him off. "And to think, I came here to see if you wanted to reconcile."

Erik and Faye tried to move toward him, but he backed away.

"Don't," Gregor said, holding his hands out in a defensive gesture. "We've done this before," he said, looking directly at Erik. "I should have learned my lesson with you the first time. Or the second!"

"Gregor!" Faye said, tears of frustration welling up in her eyes.

"I didn't expect this from you," he said, eyeing her with what she felt was disdain. "You, of all people."

Gregor turned and went back to his car and Faye stood on the steps of the restaurant, still speechless and wondering what had just happened. She watched, helpless to do anything, as the man she loved sped away in a fury, into the night, leaving her and Erik standing there in the wake of his misdirected anger. She and Gregor both knew all too well what it was like to have trust broken, and for both of them, that instinct to run would always be there. In that moment, she knew there was only one thing she could do that mattered: find Gregor and make things right again.

CHAPTER TEN

GREGOR WAS ALMOST too angry to see straight. His foot hit the accelerator extra hard as he took the twists and turns of the road back toward the cottage faster than he knew he should but he didn't care about being cautious. The only thing that mattered to him was getting back to his house. That was his safe place where the world couldn't bother him.

He had gone to Erik's hoping to patch things up and was shocked to see Faye there. What was she doing? His mind offered up different scenarios, each one more horrible than the next. Faye and Erik conspiring against him. Faye and Erik having sex in the very booth where they had, before the restaurant was renovated. Faye and Erik laughing at what an idiot he was, for actually thinking he had a best friend and a woman who truly cared about him.

A voice in his head told him not to jump to conclusions, but it was an easy leap to take, especially given his history with Erik. Why had he wanted to trust him again? he wondered. Was he a glutton for punishment? It didn't make sense that Faye would betray him, after opening up about how badly she was hurt by her fiancé. He tried to tell himself that maybe he was just overreacting. But the vision of the two of them embracing on the steps of the restaurant was now etched in his mind. What were they up to anyway?

There were no streetlights on the road home, and Gregor put his high beams on so that he could see better as he navigated the sharp twists and turns. His pulse raced as he tried to quiet the stream of negative thoughts that were running through his mind. He reached down to turn on the radio, hoping it would distract him, and in that split second, he lost control of the car and found himself skidding sideways off the road.

Time seemed to stand still as he slowly opened his eyes. The car had come to a stop in a field. He checked his body. He was alive, but the car was badly damaged, that much he could tell. He went to try and move out of his seat, but a voice stopped him.

"Stay still, stay still," someone insisted.

He blinked his eyes again and could see a woman standing over him with a halo of blond hair. Faye.

"Are you okay?" she asked.

Gregor took inventory of his body again. It seemed like nothing hurt. "I think so."

"Thank God," Faye whispered. She planted a gentle kiss on his head. "Don't move. I called an ambulance. Help is on the way."

"What happened?" Gregor asked, still groggy on

the details. The last thing he remembered was reaching to turn the radio on.

"You hit a tree and spun out," Faye explained. "You must have taken the turn really fast."

"I just wanted to get away," Gregor said. "Thank you for stopping for me."

"Of course," Faye said, stroking his cheek. "I was chasing you. I needed to tell you that what you saw back there was not what you think."

"I know that now," Gregor said, feeling simultaneously foolish and relieved. Of course things weren't always what they seemed at first glance. "I should have asked before reacting like that."

"We both have a history of people hurting us. It makes sense that you'd be suspicious. I was, too, remember?"

Gregor tried to say something but then he heard the faint sound of a siren. Instead, he and Faye just looked into each other's eyes.

"It's going to be okay," Faye whispered as the siren's blare grew closer.

Even though his car was wrecked and he wasn't sure if there would be any lasting damage to his body, for the first time he could remember, Gregor believed that this was true.

When the doctor finally came into the room to see Gregor, he and Faye had been talking and resting for hours. An initial check didn't show any broken bones or damage, and for that Faye was thankful. She felt guilty that Gregor had been speeding due to his worry over her, but he told her not to blame herself.

"It's my own neurosis that got me here, not you," he insisted.

Faye stepped out into the waiting room to give Gregor a moment of privacy and dialed her sister's number.

"Hey," Eden answered. "How's things in London town?"

"Eden, Gregor's been in an accident," she said, covering the phone with her hand. She didn't want the word to get out to the tabloids. The last thing they needed was people knowing what had happened. "Please, you can't tell anyone about this," she added.

"Of course not," Eden said. "Is he alright?"

"I think so," said Faye. "It just really shook me up."

"I can imagine," Eden said soothingly. "Are you there with him now?"

"The doctor's just checking him. This whole thing made me realize how much I care about him. If anything ever happened to him…"

"I know," Eden said. Faye could imagine her sister nodding her head in understanding. They had lost their father in a plane accident when they were teenagers, so accidents always put them on high alert. It was because of their father's sudden death that they both understood how fleeting life was, how you had to tell people that you loved them and not take anyone for granted.

"Well, I'm glad you found someone that you care so much about," Eden said, her voice sounding more cheerful.

"That's just like you, always seeing the bright side of things," Faye said.

"It's like you, too!" Eden insisted. "You're a positive person, Faye. Gregor is lucky to have you in his corner."

"Thanks," Faye said to her sister. "Well, I should probably go check on him now."

"Go do what you need to do. I'm here if you need me."

"Thanks again," Faye said. Hanging up the call, she returned to the room where Gregor was finishing up with the doctor.

"Hello," the doctor greeted her, shaking Faye's hand. "I'm sorry to meet you under these circumstances. Your husband is going to be okay. You're both very lucky."

"He's not—" Faye began to correct her, before Gregor interjected.

"The missus has been taking good care of me," he said grandly. "She's the reason I'm alive," he said, giving Faye a furtive wink.

Faye smiled and sat off to the side while the doctor made a few notes on Gregor's chart. His clothes had been removed and he was in a hospital gown, but somehow still managed to look incredibly sexy.

"Everything looks as it should be," said the doctor. "You may have some mild soreness for the next few days. No strenuous activity. Stay home, take it easy. You're very lucky," she said pointedly to Gregor. "Had another gent in here who took that same bend, he was in traction for a month."

Gregor visibly shuttered at the thought. Faye knew that situations like this could really put things in perspective. She hoped that it would make Gregor calm down and see that she wasn't out to do the wrong thing by him. In fact, she wanted nothing more than to see him succeed and thrive. It was quickly becoming apparent to her that this man's well-being was more important to her than any magazine article. If something bad had happened after such a silly misunderstanding with Erik, she wouldn't have been able to live with herself.

"I assume your wife will be home for the next week to see after you?" she asked.

Faye didn't respond at first. She had still planned to go back to London to finish the article. But she could see that this would have to come second to being there for Gregor. He looked at her and waited for her response.

"Of course I'll be there," she said, and Gregor smiled. Being there for him was the right thing to do, and it was also what she wanted to do. It dawned on her that the thought of anyone else caring for him while he recovered just didn't seem right. Maybe they were each other's person. It was nice to think there was someone there for you when you needed them.

The doctor left the room and Faye sat on the edge of the bed next to Gregor's legs.

"You don't have to do this, you know," he said. "I know that you planned to take time to be alone and work, if you want to go back to your hotel."

"I know I don't have to, I want to. Is that okay with you, if I'm there?" she asked.

Gregor answered by pulling her on top of him. "It's more than okay," he said biting her lower lip. "Much more than okay." He kissed her passionately, and she could feel something stirring under his hospital gown.

"Hey!" she protested, pretending to be scandalized. "I thought the doctor said no strenuous activity!"

"I'm not going to do anything," Gregor said into the side of her neck. The feeling of his breath there sent shivers running down her spine. "You're going to be doing all the work."

Faye laughed and reached down underneath his gown. If she had any worries about his body, they were completely erased, feeling the strong and large reaction he was having to her being on top of him.

"This gown is super sexy, by the way," she said, pulling it up as she kissed him.

"Ahem."

Faye and Gregor both looked up from the hospital bed to see a stern-faced nurse standing in the doorway. She didn't look too amused by their activities.

"Your pants, sir," she said in a very upper-crust

British accent. Faye did her best to stifle the laughter that was about to escape from her mouth. Still she was a little disappointed that they couldn't continue. Making love in a hospital bed did sound kind of strange, but when it came to Gregor the surroundings were secondary. In that moment of knowing he was okay, she felt the sudden urge to celebrate. She wanted nothing more than to tear off that hospital gown and have her way with him. She couldn't imagine anything more life affirming than making love to the man that she had almost lost.

"Thank you," Gregor said in a low, gracious voice. He sat up in the bed, nearly knocking Faye onto the floor.

"Oh, my goodness, I'm sorry," he said, extending a hand out to her.

"I'm fine," Faye said, steadying herself.

"And your discharge papers to sign," said the nurse, proffering a large stack of forms.

"Thank you, this is great," Gregor said, resting the papers on Faye's back and going through each page and signing. Faye's senses stirred feeling Gregor press the pen onto her back through the paper. She wanted to get him out of there so she could get Gregor home and do all of the things she was imagining. Of course that included taking care of him, cooking for him and monitoring his condition. And she also needed to allow enough time for herself to finish her article. But more immediately it involved needing to feel his skin on hers, to connect, with nothing at all separating their bodies. That was the top thing she had in mind for this man.

When the chore was completed, the nurse took her leave from the room.

"Are you ready to get out of here?" Faye asked, almost breathless from her wandering thoughts.

"Absolutely," Gregor said, swinging his feet over the side of the bed and getting dressed. "Are you okay?" he asked, looking at her quizzically. "You sound a little out of breath."

"I'm good. More than good." She smiled.

"Are you sure you don't need some oxygen?" he teased.

"I need something more than that," she murmured, putting a hand on his now-clothed leg.

"Should I take this with me?" he asked, holding up the hospital gown. "This turning you on?" he asked, raising an eyebrow.

"Kinky!" Faye laughed, taking the gown and tossing it into the laundry bin.

Even though he insisted he was fine, the hospital made him ride out to the parking lot in a wheelchair. The same nurse pushed while Faye walked alongside them. Every time Gregor looked over at her, she gave him a reassuring wink and a smile.

"I'm just parked right over here," Faye said, indicating to the nurse that the car was within reasonable walking distance.

The nurse nodded and unceremoniously deposited Gregor onto the sidewalk. She then turned the wheelchair around and went back through the hospital's automatic sliding glass doors.

Faye put her arm around Gregor as they walked to her rental car. She thought he seemed steady enough, but she didn't want to take any chances.

"Faye, this isn't necessary, I'm fine," Gregor said, reaching to open the door to the car himself.

"I just want to make sure you're okay," she said. "You're supposed to rest. Doctor's orders, remember," she said with a little wink. "And…" she added in a softer voice "…you're kind of important to me."

Gregor smiled and slid into the passenger seat.

Turning the key in the ignition, she started the car up and pulled away from the hospital, heading toward home.

"Are you going to make me stay in bed all weekend?" Gregor called from his bedroom.

Faye was in the kitchen, putting together a meal from whatever she could find in the refrigerator. It was a lot of pressure, feeding a famous chef and lifelong foodie.

"Be right in," she called in answer to his question. Adding a pot of tea to the tray she had filled—she'd gotten into drinking it in addition to her morning coffee—she smiled to herself, happy to have someone she cared about to look after, even if Gregor wasn't really that injured.

When she entered his bedroom, Gregor was in full-on relaxation mode. He was in his pajamas, sitting up in bed with the television on, his cell phone in hand and the curtains drawn.

"Wow," Faye said, taking in the scene. "I thought you were feeling just fine?"

"Well, doctor's orders, right?" Gregor said, raising an eyebrow and patting the empty spot next to him on the bed. "You made me food? You're the best!"

"It's nothing much," Faye said, shyly placing the tray on the bedside table next to him. She sat down on the bed next to Gregor as he surveyed her presentation.

"Peanut butter and banana sandwiches?" Gregor gave her a stunned look. "This is my absolute favorite."

"It always makes me feel better, too," Faye said, pleased with herself for doing the right thing. She was so glad she hadn't attempted to make anything fancy. She could sense that today was going to be all about getting cozy, and what was cozier than her PB and B sandwiches?

As Gregor reached for a sandwich, Faye put her hand out to stop him.

"Before you eat, there's something else you need that's going to make you feel a lot better," she said seductively. Standing up at the side of the bed, she removed her shirt, pants and underwear, until she was completely naked. She watched as Gregor took in the view of her body, which she now felt totally confident putting on display. Being Gregor's lover had taught her how truly sexy she was. Instead of diving directly under the covers, like she had done in the past, she was happy, turned on even, to stand there, being the object of her man's desire.

Just when it looked like Gregor was about to reach for her, she found her entryway point under the covers. Sliding in between the sheets, she made her way up the length of Gregor's strong legs, making sure to graze her breasts against his thighs as she homed in on the area between his legs. Gregor's cock was already getting hard from her little display, and Faye's mission was to give him an orgasm that would erase all of the doubt and bad feelings of the past few days.

She knew that she could make Gregor feel good. In fact, she was becoming an expert at finding the places on his body that were his most erogenous zones. She knew that if she touched his inner thighs, especially with her nipples, it made him gasp for breath. She also knew that the feeling of her long hair across his chest made him crazy with desire. She felt like an explorer, eager to learn more about what made Gregor experience pleasure. She wanted to give him every good sensation that she could, and she loved knowing that she was the one who could provide him with this level of ecstasy.

"What are you doing to me?" Gregor moaned as Faye took his hardness in her mouth, using her hands and her breasts to stroke his shaft and balls as she licked the length of him, slowly and deliberately. She couldn't remember a more satisfying activity and she took her time, making sure he really felt every sensation she was providing him with.

"Get up here," Gregor said, pulling hungrily at her until she acquiesced, and allowed him to pull her on top of him so they were face-to-face, their bodies pressed against one another's.

Faye straddled Gregor's lap and, sitting upright, slowly lowered herself down onto his cock. They both sighed when she came to the point where he was totally inside her. And even though it felt like home, having him there, she knew that she had work to do. Faye pulled herself up, her hands steadied on Gregor's chest, until only the tip of him was inside her lips, and then with full force, she sat down again, once more happy to feel the fullness of him in her body.

Throwing back her head, she reveled in the feeling of being filled up by Gregor. She loved how his manhood stretched her to her limits and made her want to do things she had only ever fantasized about. She began to bounce up and down at a steady pace, her softness encompassing his hard-as-a-rock member. She could feel her own juices dripping down onto his thighs and she wasn't in the least bit ashamed that she was this wet, this turned on, by a good fucking.

Woman on top was quickly becoming Faye's favorite position for sex, and this time, she owned it, allowing him to lie back and take in a perfect view of her full breasts bouncing in the air as she continued moving up and down on his erection. Locking eyes with Gregor during sex was such a turn-on. It was as if he really saw her, not just her looks, but straight down to the core of who she really was as a person. Anyway, fully nude and perched on top of him, there was no hiding anything, so she simply enjoyed the ride.

Faye hoped that this would be the time they could reach their climax together. She knew it wasn't something that usually happened, but in that moment, she was craving that connection. Making Gregor come would be easy—so easy in fact that she worried he wouldn't be able to hold off if she didn't join him soon. Angling her body so that every time she moved toward him, her clit grazed the hardness of his body was enough to do the trick. As she watched Gregor go from happy to ecstatic, she brought herself to the height of pleasure, grinding against his body until she, too, screamed out in orgasm.

"Oohhh!" Faye cried just as Gregor let out a hurried, "Yes, yes, don't stop."

Their bodies both shaking, Faye loved that they were experiencing that ecstasy together at the same time, and she tried to stay at her peak as long as possible. In fact, every time she moved her hips toward his body, she felt more waves of pleasure roll in, until she was so dizzy with that heady feeling that she collapsed, exhausted on top of him.

"That was incredible," Gregor whispered. He sounded out of breath and for a second, Faye started to worry.

"Are you sure you're alright?" she asked, sitting up to wipe his brow and make sure his pupils were of normal size.

"I'm more than alright," Gregor said languidly.

"Seriously," Faye said, rolling over and lying next to him. "You scared me badly last night."

"It scared me, too," Gregor said, holding her in his arms. "I don't want to ever be apart from you. I don't care if you think it's too soon to say something like that. It's the truth."

Faye didn't hesitate to share her feelings this time. "I want to be with you, too," she said, curling in toward Gregor's long, lean body. She wanted to stay like that forever, their limbs intertwined, their bodies sweaty and satisfied.

"Stay, then," Gregor said. The way he uttered it, it made it sound so simple. She had a life back home in New York, a job, friends. She wasn't sure what to tell him.

"I'll stay until the article is done," she said, not wanting to give him false hope. A big part of her wanted to just say she would do anything to be with him, but she knew that wasn't what she needed, to make sure she was okay for herself.

"Okay," Gregor said. "I'm not going anywhere," he promised.

Over the next few days, Faye slept in Gregor's bed, but spent days working in the guest room. For the first time on the trip, the words began to flow easily, and she found the story of Gregor's life telling itself as she sat at the small desk by the window in her room, typing.

Every now and then she would pause, either to take tea with Gregor in the garden, or to bring him peanut butter and banana sandwiches. But the majority of her days were spent working, and it felt great to be nearing the end of what would hopefully be her most important piece of work for the magazine.

"When are you going to let me read it?"

She and Gregor were sitting outside together, sipping tea and not saying much, which was okay since they were truly comfortable with each other, no matter if they were chatting away or just silent.

"I told you, not until it's finished," she said, repeating the same thing she told him every time he tried to sneak a look at her notes or her laptop screen.

"I just hope you're not making me look like some insane, washed-up former TV star," he said, scrutinizing her face for clues.

"Exactly!" Faye said, laughing. "You'll be offered a spot on reality TV after this in no time."

"Celebrity rehab? Weight loss?" Gregor speculated with a smile.

"Oh, everything," Faye said jokingly.

"But really, in all seriousness, what was it that Erik told you about me?" he asked as they finished their drinks, their empty cups and saucers scattered across the wrought iron table that overlooked the amazing English garden.

"Good things only," Faye said.

"You're not going to tell me, are you?" Gregor said in an annoyed tone of voice.

Faye nodded.

"Then there's only one reasonable course of action," Gregor said, pulling Faye up out of her chair and lying her across his lap. When she felt the palm of his hand strike her buttocks, she let out a surprised little yelp. She and Gregor laughed.

"Let me get back to work!" she protested, but Gregor clearly had other plans in mind for her.

"Not yet," he growled, reaching up her flimsy, short sundress.

CHAPTER ELEVEN

GREGOR WAS HAVING a hard time staying away from Faye while she wrote. For one thing, it was difficult having her in such close proximity but not being able to spend all of his time with her. He loved this stage of a relationship, when you only wanted to be with that one person all of the time. Everything Faye said and did was fascinating to him. But he had a feeling that even when the newness of the relationship wore off, he'd still be all over her, all the time. She was everything he had hoped for in a partner—sexy, smart, kind and caring.

The other reason he found himself lingering outside the door to the guest room where Faye had taken to working was that he was highly curious about what she was writing about him. Part of him wanted her to forgo writing the article. Now that they were involved, he imagined it would be difficult for Faye to remain impartial while writing about him. He wasn't really worried that she would portray him in a negative light. He feared that she knew him too well, and that his most private thoughts and feelings would be exposed to the world. He wasn't sure he was ready for that. He wasn't even sure what his next professional move was going to be. Sure, the food truck had been fun, and he could probably make a killing doing it, but was that what he really wanted?

In a way, driving around in a truck was the opposite of what he wanted, which was to be settled down. He'd spent almost the last twenty years touring every corner of the globe on his television show. And although he still enjoyed meeting new people and having those unique experiences that came from traveling, what he really wanted was to stay put for a while—to cook Sunday dinners and spend afternoons in his garden. Sharing those experiences with Faye—especially the ones they had taken to having in his backyard—was what he really craved.

It stood to reason, then, that he had an important question to ask her. Gregor walked into the backyard and strolled alongside the rosebushes. Faye was busy typing away in her room and had planned to take a break to have lunch with him soon. *I want her to stay*, he thought to himself. He knew it was a long shot—asking her to upend her life in New York and move to a sleepy village in the English countryside. Part of him thought it was an absurd question to even ask her. But another, more hopeful part wondered if she might say yes.

Gregor chose the most vibrant rose he could find—the one with the deepest red hue—and plucked it, being careful not to prick himself on the thorns. It occurred to him that love was a lot like that—after all he had been through, he still wanted to go for it, still wanted to take the chance of getting hurt, because the good parts made it worth it.

"Lunch is ready!"

Gregor was shaken out of his reverie when he heard Faye call to him from the window. Her face was bright, and he could see she had on a simple white T-shirt with her long hair in a ponytail. Even though she looked dynamite when she was all dressed up, this was the Faye he preferred: dressed casually with her natural beauty shining through.

"Be right in," he called, hiding the flower behind his back. As he walked toward the house, he tried to work up his nerve to ask her the one question he needed an answer to—would she give it all up and stay here with him, and really make a life together? Or invite him to live with her, if that was the only way they could make it work? These were big questions, so he took an extra deep breath before entering the house.

"Food will be right out," Faye said. She had her back to him and was checking on a quiche in the oven. "Just have a seat," she said.

"Thanks," said Gregor. He wasn't used to Faye waiting on him like this. In fact, he sort of liked the dynamic that he was the one to do the cooking. It was his way of taking care of her, of showing his love. Sitting down at the counter, he noticed a stack of papers on his place setting.

"You finished?" he asked, sitting down and paging through the papers.

Faye turned to him and smiled.

"It's finished!" she said.

Gregor went to her and lifted her up and spun her around before planting a long kiss on her lips.

"You may want to read it first before you do that," she said, looking a little trepidatious.

Gregor put her down but kept his arms looped around her waist. "I'm sure whatever you wrote, it's the truth."

Faye tilted her head to the side. "Read it, and if you don't want me to send it, I won't," she said seriously.

Gregor picked up the pages and sat down at the counter. "I appreciate that, but wouldn't that mean your job?"

Faye nodded gravely. So she was willing to put him above the assignment. Even though he told himself not to get too excited, his heart soared.

"Us being okay is more important to me than an article," she said. "Although this could really be like, a career-making feature for me. But don't worry about that," she said quickly. "Just read it."

Gregor shifted in his seat, trying to get comfortable while he read the long portrait of himself that included everything from his childhood journeys to the French Riviera to the food truck. It was strange, reading such an intimate portrait of himself. Even though he had seen himself on television a million times, this was somehow stranger, to see himself laid out like that on the page. When he got to the part about Erik, he had to force himself to keep his emotions in check, and to keep reading without stopping to ask questions. When he finally finished the last sentence, Faye was standing in front of him. She had just placed the quiche on the counter. Her eyes looked expectant, like she was waiting for a verdict.

"It's beautiful," Gregor said, unable to find another word that better described her depiction of him.

"Thank you," Faye said, breathing a sigh of relief.

"You're a wonderful writer," he added. "That stuff about Erik…"

"It's all true," Faye said quickly. "He wanted you to know."

"So he has been a good friend all along. But why didn't he just tell me about Emily?"

"I think he didn't want to see you get your heart broken," Faye said. "He was trying to protect you, like…"

"Like a brother," Gregor finished her thought.

Faye nodded.

"I need to go speak to him," he said. Suddenly nothing else mattered except getting to his friend and making things right.

"Take the car, I'll stay here," Faye offered.

"No," Gregor said. "I want you to come with me. This involves you, too. Plus I need you to drive," he smiled sheepishly.

On the drive to the restaurant, Gregor suddenly

remembered the rose, and the question he had to ask Faye. He had wanted the moment to be intimate and perfect, but he also knew that if he put it off any longer, she would be gone before he knew it. After they pulled into the parking lot of the restaurant, he came around to the driver's side and opened the door for her. Leading her toward the steps of the restaurant, he took both of her hands in his.

"Faye, there's something I've been wanting to ask you," he began. Though he was never at a loss for words, in that moment, he felt like he could barely speak. He cleared his voice, hoping the words would come out right. "Stay."

Faye blinked in the sunlight and smiled at him.

"Stay…here?" she asked.

"In England. With me. What I'm saying is, I don't want you to leave. Not ever."

"Wow," Faye said. Gregor scrutinized her expression trying to figure out what she was thinking. "That's a big step," she said when she finally spoke.

"I know it is, and I understand what you'd be giving up," Gregor said carefully. "But I couldn't let you leave here without letting you know how I feel."

Faye threw herself into Gregor's arms and they hugged.

"You know this is hard for me," she said into his shoulder.

"I know," he said, nodding.

"Is it okay if I take some time to think about it?

I love you, Gregor, but this is a big decision. I have to make sure I'm really ready for it."

"Of course," he said, holding her back from him so he could get a better look at her. Even if she left, he decided he would never regret this moment. He took a mental picture of how she looked just then, her blond hair shining in the sun, her smile so radiant.

"Let's go in," she said, taking him by the hand. "You have some important business to attend to."

"Yes, I do," Gregor agreed.

Gregor led the way into the restaurant and immediately saw Erik sitting in a booth. He appeared to be crunching numbers on a calculator. He looked totally stressed out.

"Hey," Gregor said when he looked up. Erik met his gaze with a surprised look.

"Gregor," Erik said, standing up and going to him. "Glad to see you're okay."

"I'm fine," Gregor said, pulling Faye into his side, "mostly because of this one."

"She's a fantastic woman," Erik agreed, smiling at Faye.

"I'm going to leave you two alone for a moment," Faye said, excusing herself and heading toward the bathroom.

When they were alone, Erik gestured for Gregor to sit down with him at one of the tables.

"I read Faye's piece," Gregor said. "I never knew you did that for me, that Emily was the one who betrayed me, not you."

"I know it was a crazy way to do things, I was just trying to protect you from getting hurt," Erik explained. His voice, usually full of bravado, sounded quiet and serious.

"Unfortunately, none of us can be protected from the stuff that really hurts," Gregor said. "Especially when it comes to love."

"I know that now," Erik said. "And I'm sorry for the lies. Going forward, total honesty, okay?" he said, holding out his hand.

Gregor smiled and grasped his old friend's hand in his. "Well, maybe not total honesty. But for the most part," he laughed. "How's this place coming? It looks great."

Erik appeared nervous all over again at the mention of the restaurant. "Everything's great—on the outside. But internally, we're completely lost. And we're supposed to open in a week."

"Is it anything I can help with?" Gregor asked. He didn't want to seem like he was stepping in on Erik's venture, but he knew that this was probably his friend's way of asking for help.

"I need you in here, Gregor," Erik said. "Not as an employee. As a partner. That's the way it was always supposed to be with us. Don't you agree?"

"So what are you going to call it?"

Erik shook his head. "Rules? Because we break them?"

"Beaulieu-sur-Mer," Gregor said matter-of-factly.

"Perfect," said his friend.

Gregor nodded. "We're definitely stronger together."

"Yin and yang," said Erik.

"Peanut butter and…banana," said Gregor. His eye caught Faye's as she walked back into the main dining room.

"What have you two worked out?" Faye asked, putting her hands on her hips and looking back and forth from one man to the other. "Please tell me you've made up."

"We have," said Gregor, putting his arm around her. "And we've got a lot of work to do."

"Sounds like I do, too," Faye said.

"What do you mean?" asked Erik.

"I'll need to revise my article," she said with a smile. "It looks like you guys are at a new beginning."

"We are," Erik said, putting his arms around both of them.

The next week passed with lots of work and activity, getting the menu in order and rearranging the kitchen to accommodate both Erik and Gregor, working side by side. Faye could see that this was how things were meant to be. The two men complemented each other perfectly. Where Gregor was analytical, Erik threw caution to the wind. But sometimes they reversed roles, and when they did, they worked on intuition and passion and the results were incredible.

Faye thought that it wasn't just the food that was better when they collaborated—it was a different energy, the two of them together, that created a magical vibe.

It was two days before opening and they were still in the process of hiring the waitstaff, which Faye had volunteered to help with. Now that Gregor was settled in his position as owner/chef, she felt that her time was better served writing than slinging food. Nonetheless, she couldn't help but offer to lend a hand, especially since the guys were already so overwhelmed.

"Are we ready to start the interviews?" Faye asked. Gregor and Erik nodded. They were seated at a table and ready to hire their team. Faye had narrowed down the candidates and planned to let them meet only the most viable prospects for the job. The first person to enter the room was a young redhead. She was short, with large green eyes and a smile that was contagious to everyone in the room, especially Erik.

"Hi, I'm Janine," she said, locking eyes with him and extending her hand.

Both Faye and Gregor watched as the two of them began chatting and completely ignoring the fact that there was anyone else in the room.

"So maybe there's a happy ending for Erik, too," Faye leaned over and whispered to Gregor.

They both looked over at Erik and Janine, who were laughing together over some joke only they were in on.

"I'd say either the two of them need to get a room, or we should get out of here," Gregor whispered back.

Gregor took Faye's hand and led her into the kitchen.

There was so much Faye wanted to say to Gregor, but this wasn't the time for words. As soon as they were inside the large kitchen, Gregor led her to the back area by the sinks, the one area that was not in full view of the dining room. Pushing her up against the counter, he began to kiss her and unbutton her blouse, deftly opening each button down the front of her chambray shirt and finally, unclasping her bra. In one swift movement, his mouth was tasting her nipples, suckling them like sweet summer fruit. Faye felt herself getting turned on. The rough sensation of Gregor's five-day stubble, combined with the way his hands were cupping and squeezing her ass underneath her short skirt was all it took to make her feel oh so ready.

As they continued to kiss, Faye wrapped her arms around Gregor's strong shoulders, pulling him in closer as they devoured one another.

"Shouldn't we get out there?" Faye asked as Gregor lifted her up onto the counter.

"He's fine without us," Gregor said, removing Faye's panties. He was working quickly to get inside her. Faye was glad that she wasn't the only one who felt such an urgent need to be connected.

Part of her wondered what would happen if Erik or one of the other employees did walk in on them, but a bigger part of her was just focused on what was happening right then and there with Gregor. Grabbing his ass with both hands, she pulled him toward her. She was at just the right level for Gregor to enter her waiting opening.

Gregor made a guttural sound as he plunged in, and then out, and then in again.

Burying her face in his shoulder, Faye bit down hard, trying to stifle her own cries of pleasure as her man fucked her so well, she could feel it from her toes to the hair on the top of her head. Making love with Gregor was a full body experience, even when it was a quickie.

Just as Faye thought Gregor might be getting close, the kitchen doors swung open. Erik and the redhead stood there for a second before Erik spoke.

"Sorry, guys!" he said, ushering the applicant out the doors they had just come through.

"Shit!" Gregor disengaged from Faye and quickly pulled up his pants. He mouthed the word *Sorry* to Faye as he rushed out after Erik.

Faye was left sitting on the counter, and she had to laugh to herself. If anyone had told her a month ago that she would be having sex in a kitchen with a famous chef—and acting like a teenager getting caught in the act—she would have told them they were insane. But this was her life now, and she was loving every minute of it, even the totally embarrassing parts where innocent job applicants saw your vagina.

"You guys, I really want to apologize," Faye said once she had straightened out her clothes and gone back into the dining room.

Amazingly, Janine hadn't left. In fact, she had a knowing little smirk on her face.

"It's okay, nothing I haven't seen before working in the service industry," she said in an adorable British accent.

Faye breathed a sigh of relief. "Thanks," she said, grateful to this woman for not making her feel like a total crazy person.

Gregor and Erik were engaged in conversation and Janine moved closer to Faye.

"I remember what it's like when you first meet someone and you can't keep your hands off each other," Janine said with a wistful look in her eyes.

"So...you're single?" Faye asked.

"Very," she said, her eyes wandering toward Erik.

"But possibly not for long?" Faye asked, noticing her lingering gaze.

"He is really cute," she whispered to Faye.

"He's a really great guy, too," Faye said, leaning in. "I can vouch for that."

Gregor and Erik returned to where the women were standing and talking.

"Again, sincerest apologies," Gregor said, putting his hands in a prayer gesture.

"Don't worry about it," Janine said, waving him off.

"What about me?" Erik asked, looking at Gregor. "I'm scarred for life. The image of your arse is permanently etched into my consciousness."

"I'll pay for the hypnosis," Gregor said, throwing his arm around his buddy.

"So…" Faye said, trying to change the subject. She looked at Janine. "Is there any way you'd consider working with us? We'd love to have you."

Janine thought for a second. "It would be my pleasure," she said.

The three of them cheered and when they found out she had prior experience running front of the house at another restaurant, she was instantly promoted.

"Things are looking up," Gregor said on the drive back to the cottage later that night.

"I'd say we should finish what we started in the kitchen, but honestly, I'm so exhausted," Faye said.

"I can't believe I'm going to say this, but me, too," Gregor said.

They spent that night curled up together in Gregor's bedroom, and Faye fell into a deep, dreamless sleep.

On the opening night of Beaulieu-sur-Mer, Faye was stationed at the hostess stand, trying to keep all of the reservations on time and answering the phone, which had been ringing nonstop since they had arrived that morning.

Gregor and Erik were working hard in the kitchen, and Janine, wearing a tight black power dress, was striding through the dining room, making sure all of the servers were on point. Faye had decided to wear an off-the-shoulder white jumpsuit for the occasion, and Gregor had told her how beautiful she looked when he saw her walk past the kitchen.

"I'd kiss you, but I'd get you dirty," he said with a devilish grin.

"I think you already did that," she retorted, pulling his head toward her and kissing his cheek. Her lipstick left a red mark on his face, but she decided not to tell him.

The first hour of service was frantic and Faye hardly had a chance to even glance back at the kitchen to see how Gregor and Erik were doing. But judging by how happy and jovial the customers were when they left, she figured things were going well.

"It's crazy in here," Janine said, stopping by to bring Faye a glass of water. "If we can continue like this, I think the boys have a hit on their hands."

"Of course they do," Faye said confidently. Earlier that morning, before Gregor was even awake, she had sent Bev her final draft of the article, including a paragraph about him and Erik opening the restaurant together. "If these two manage to stick together, there's no telling what kind of magic they'll make," was the sentence she ended it on.

Now, as the service slowed down and the last few guests trickled out, she wondered if the same would be true for her and Gregor.

When they finally closed the doors, she saw Janine beckon her over toward the bar. An amazing giant slab of marble that Erik had insisted on in the design, it was indeed a grand bar, with twinkling lights interspersed between the bottles up on a magnificent glass shelf. Gregor and Erik emerged from the kitchen and the four of them sat down to toast their first successful night with a bottle of Krug.

"To many more," Gregor said, holding up his glass.

All of them cheered and drank. As Janine began to pour another round, Faye took Gregor by the arm and whispered to him.

"Can I speak to you alone? Outside?" she asked.

Gregor immediately excused the two of them and as they walked toward the door, Faye looked back to see Erik inching closer to Janine on his bar stool. She smiled, hoping that this might be the missing thing her new friend had been searching for.

"What did you want to talk about?" Gregor said once they were standing together outside on the steps. It was a beautiful warm night, the stars were sparkling in the sky and Faye looked up at her handsome man and said something that surprised her.

"I love you, Gregor," she said. It was so simple but it had taken so much effort to get here.

Gregor put his arms around her and brushed her hair off her face. "I love you, too," he said. "I'm going to miss you so much," he said with a look of longing and regret in his eyes.

"I'm not going anywhere," Faye said. She still wasn't sure what her life was going to look like here in England, but she knew that she had to take the chance. It was time to leap.

"Really?" Gregor's face broke out into a gigantic smile.

Faye nodded. "I'm staying. If you want me to."

Gregor lifted Faye off the ground and kissed her so long and hard, she felt her entire body vibrate. It was answer enough. With Gregor, she felt home, and it was the only place she wanted to be.

CHAPTER TWELVE

"ARE YOU SURE you have the guest room set up just the way I told you?" Faye was pacing around the house while Gregor worked on inflating a giant air mattress.

"Faye, you are supposed to be sitting down, remember?" Gregor reminded her.

Faye stopped what she was doing and remembered that he was right. Reluctantly, she sat down on the couch. She was a ball of nervous energy. In just a few minutes, her sister, Eden, and her family including the three boys would be arriving at the house for a visit. Even though she'd been there almost a year, it was the first time she had invited anyone to stay at the house. Of course she'd been back to New York a bunch of times. Last summer she had gone to empty out her apartment, shipping some things to the UK and putting the rest at her sister's house in Westchester.

She liked going back to New York City as a visitor, sometimes with Gregor along for the ride under the guise of business. But those opportunities to travel together were few and far between. The restaurant had taken off and Gregor and Erik were devoting most of their time and energy toward it. When she brought up the idea of inviting her family to come and stay, Gregor was all for it. Having them here at the house was important to her. If her sister approved of her home, it would make it feel all the more real.

Faye had only lived in apartments since graduating college and it felt like a luxury to spread out into an actual house. It didn't hurt that Gregor had great taste, so that had made it even easier for her to move right in. She turned her apartment in New York over to a friend who wanted to pick up the lease, so there was no backup plan. She decided it was better to be positive. She was planning for things to work out because she really wanted them to.

"I thought you said your sister was easygoing," Gregor said, checking the pantry. Faye had given him a list of food items the boys liked, and he had dutifully gone shopping for chicken nuggets, mac 'n' cheese and huge boxes of cereal—stuff he otherwise would never have brought into the house. She loved the fact that he was excited to meet her nephews— if anything, it gave her a good indication of the type of dad he would be someday.

"She is easygoing!" Faye insisted. It was true— her sister managed to stay sane in the face of chaos and Faye always wondered how she did it, especially raising three boys. She was more of the planner while Eden tended to take things as they came.

"Oh, so then it's you who's causing all of this fuss," Gregor concluded. Faye stood up and went over to Gregor, playfully punching him on the arm. *My God, he is handsome*, she thought to herself. Still, that didn't change the fact that she didn't want to be teased in this moment.

"Just bear with me, this is all new, and my sister's opinion means a lot," Faye confessed.

"I know," Gregor said, putting his arms around her. "But don't worry. I've got this. I'm a host. It's what I do, remember?"

Faye did remember. Since she'd been living with him, she never thought too much about "TV Gregor" or the fact that he was famous, unless they were out at a restaurant and strangers began staring at them. It always took Faye a moment to remember that they weren't looking at her because she had toilet paper stuck to her shoe or something. *Oh, right, I have a famous boyfriend*, she'd remember. At home, he was just plain old Gregor, the guy who weeded the garden, massaged her feet while they watched movies on the couch together and helped her kill insects whenever necessary. She always forgot that other people thought they knew who she was. But now she knew the real Gregor, and he knew her.

It was a Sunday, the day Gregor usually took off from the restaurant to spend at home. His hours were long, but that was okay because it gave Faye uninterrupted stretches of time to write whatever piece she was working on, or just wander and explore the different little villages near them and look for inspiration. She knew that if Gregor was around more, they would probably spend all day in bed together. A year in, it was still that type of relationship where they couldn't keep their hands off each other. Faye was sure that having the chance to miss each other while they worked was the key to keeping the spark alive. It made both of them want the other even more.

Walking around town, Faye definitely still stood out as "the American girl" but that was okay with her. In fact, she was enjoying being the one who was out of her normal territory. It was a great conversation opener and she found the locals to be welcome and curious.

And although she'd enjoyed meeting more of Gregor's friends, and even hosting dinner parties at their house, she couldn't wait for her own family to see where she had been living, to be a part of the life she was making here.

Faye heard the doorbell ring and she jumped up. But then she quickly remembered the doctor's orders and sat back down again.

"I'll get it," Gregor said, wiping his hands on a dish towel and striding toward the door. He had been cooking for the past day in anticipation of her family's arrival. When she heard the front door creek open, it took everything in Faye not to leap up and push him out of the way.

"Hello!" Faye heard Eden cry when she saw Gregor. "It's so great to see you," she shouted. She could see from where she was sitting that they were hugging, and Faye blushed a little. From the first time they had met in New York, she had told Eden specifically not to go overboard or refer to the fact that Gregor was famous in any way, shape or form, but it made sense that she couldn't help herself. To be honest, sometimes Faye got a little starstruck by Gregor. He was so dynamic. But then he'd do something normal like blow his nose, and she would realize, *Oh, yeah, the famous guy is the one on TV. This is the man I'm in love with.*

Of course, he still wasn't just some regular guy. Now that Beaulieu-sur-Mer had received a Michelin star, he and Erik were even more inundated by the press. Faye knew some of the reporters who had done interviews with him following the opening, and she was fine with that. Her own article had received many accolades and Bev had given her a new title, writer-at-large, which allowed her to be away from the office and basically writing something for them whenever inspiration struck. Faye felt she was done writing about Gregor and his work. Now she wanted to focus on writing her own story. It was shaping up to be a book, based on her own adventures. Much like her life, it was a work in progress.

And although it was initially strange not to wake up and go to an office every morning, she quickly got used to her new writer-at-large lifestyle, taking breakfast with Gregor when he was home, doing some yoga and gardening in between blocks of work and having the freedom a car gave her to get up and go when she wanted to.

Faye looked up to see Eden standing over her and Faye got teary-eyed when she saw her sister's face. The two of them looked exactly alike, except that Eden was a brunette. They often challenged strangers in bars to guess which was the older one, and people almost always decided they were twins. Since Eden was older by three years, she loved that, but what Faye really loved was just partying and having fun with the sister who had turned out to also be her best friend. Even though their lives were so different—Eden was a mom and Faye was running around the world—they always made time to see each other and connect.

Since Faye had moved, their regular visits had come to a stop, but they still tried to stay connected by FaceTime, text and even sending each other posts on Instagram. All that was fine, but having her big sister here was so much better than seeing her face on a tiny screen. Faye hugged her and Alan and all three of her nephews, each of whom seemed to have grown a foot since the last time she had seen them. She decided right then and there that she never wanted them to go home.

"Look at you," Eden said, eyeing Faye's stomach, which was now large enough to necessitate maternity clothes, which hadn't been the case the last time her sister had seen her. Faye was surprised that she loved being pregnant so much. That was probably due in some part to how worshipful Gregor had been of her from the moment she had taken the test after missing her period. He not only waited on her hand and foot, he seemed obsessed with her growing body, telling her how sexy and womanly she looked, even during the first trimester when she had broken out in acne to rival the spots she'd had when she was a teenager.

"I'll give you a pass on the belly rub since we're related," Faye said jokingly.

"No, seriously, Faye, you're huge," Eden said.

"I know," Faye said. "Just a few more weeks!" She had enjoyed being pregnant up until the last few weeks when it had gotten uncomfortable to sleep or even walk around for too long.

"Good job, man," said Alan, giving Gregor a fist bump. Gregor laughed and Faye smiled. Alan had gotten him right—Gregor was incredibly pleased with himself that he had gotten her knocked up! He had told her it was something he'd thought about but figured it was too late to do since he hadn't found his person. They both told each other that they considered themselves a family—with or without a child. But now they would both have a chance to be a family of three.

Just as Faye started to ask her sister about the plane ride, the doorbell rang again. Faye and Eden both looked up.

"I'll grab that," Gregor said, running toward the door.

"Who are you expecting?" asked Eden.

"Nobody!" said Faye, and it was the truth. Faye was confused. It wouldn't be the postman on a Sunday, so who could it be?

When the door opened, Faye heard the familiar voice of the woman who had known her all her life; the one who had raised her, corrected her, complimented her and embarrassed her in public at every given opportunity.

"Mrs. Curry," Gregor said jubilantly. "I'm so glad to meet you."

"Call me Gladys," said Faye's mom. "And it's wonderful to meet you, too. Aren't you a hot thing!" she said, making a playful grab for Gregor's ass.

"*Mom!*" both Faye and Eden yelled in unison.

Eden's eyes widened and she shot Faye a look of shock. "You invited Mom?" she whispered to her sister incredulously. "But she refuses to fly. Why didn't you tell me?"

"I didn't know she was coming! I swear!" Faye said, trying to hoist her body into a standing position.

"Darling!" Faye's mother entered the room. She was dressed to the nines even though she'd just come off a transatlantic flight. It was just like her to set the bar high.

"Don't get up!" she yelled at Faye, and then came and sat down next to her.

"Mom, so good to see you!" Faye said. She gave Gregor a questioning look.

"It turns out I don't mind flying on a private jet," said Gladys.

Gregor gave Faye an innocent shrug. *I thought she should be here*, Gregor mouthed so that only Faye could see.

"I knew this would happen for you one day," her mom said, patting her daughter's belly. Faye cringed. She hated being manhandled just because there was life growing inside her. "I never gave up hope."

"Well, thanks for that," Faye said evenly, trying hard not to overreact.

"Is that a Warhol?" Faye's mom's eyes wandered to the wall on the opposite side of the room and she stood up to take a closer look.

Faye knew she would immediately gravitate toward it if she ever visited and she loved that her mom was well versed when it came to all things to do with art and culture. Before she could offer her guests something to drink the doorbell rang again.

"Who is it now, the Queen?" Eden asked.

Gregor jogged to the door again. Faye saw him open the door to reveal a silver-haired woman in a tailored pantsuit. She looked just like Gregor, except with even higher cheekbones and a long, elegant neck.

"Mum, thanks for making the journey. Come and meet everyone," he said after giving her a lengthy embrace.

Faye tried again to stand up but then allowed Gregor's mom to come to her instead.

"Faye… I'm Helen. It's so nice to meet you," she said, taking Faye's hands.

"I've heard so much about you I feel like I already know you," said Faye.

Faye's own mother gave a little cough.

"Oh! And this is my mom, Gladys. And my sister, Eden, her husband, Alan, and that's Jack, Harry, and the little one is Zeke."

"Thank you all for being here today," Gregor said gallantly. "It really helps to warm up the home we've made together. And Gladys, Eden, I know Faye is very excited to see your faces. It's been a big transition, her moving here, as you know."

"Nah, I think she's always been a real English girl at heart," Eden said, giving her sister a hug.

"We're going to have a little party in the backyard," Faye told everyone. "If you want to get settled, I have a few things to do and then I'll join you all in a moment."

Gregor showed Faye's family to their rooms, and Faye went into the bedroom, formerly Gregor's, that the two of them now shared. She had added some feminine touches, like a vanity, some throw pillows and a writing desk that looked out onto the garden. There were so many beautiful spots for her to do her writing at the cottage, but this little desk was her favorite and she loved gazing out at the flowers while she wrote. Mustering up her energy, Faye took off the navy blue jersey dress she was wearing, the one that had become her uniform because it had the most stretch.

Faye glimpsed herself in the mirror before reaching for the shimmering empire-waisted gown that hung on a hanger off the door to her closet. The dress was blush pink, with a plunging neckline. She slipped it over her voluptuous body and then looked up to see Gregor standing behind her in the mirror.

"You look gorgeous," he said, kissing her neck. Even hugely pregnant, her libido had not died down. And Gregor couldn't get enough of her extra-curvy body. In fact, they were having sex at every opportunity, especially since the doctor said it was still alright.

"You ready?" Gregor asked, running his hands over her breasts. Faye watched in the mirror as he kissed his way down her neck and then moved the fabric of her dress off her breasts, exposing her swollen nipples. If she had been freaked out by the changes in her body, Gregor was only too eager to ease her worries by embracing them. Putting his mouth on her breasts, he kissed and licked them, making her feel so sexy and feminine. Faye turned and kissed Gregor on the mouth. He looked so handsome, now wearing a gray vest over his white shirt, with the sleeves rolled up, and his favorite trousers. Faye shivered as he ran his hands all over her body while they kissed. Part of her wished they were alone so they could continue what they were doing. But there would be plenty of time for that during the honeymoon/babymoon.

She wasn't sure if they would be able to go right away, but she was looking forward to going back to

Côte d'Azur and spending some alone time there with Gregor and seeing all of the special places he had yet to show her. She thought about making love to him on the beach and imagined them walking hand in hand through the seaside villages, stopping to taste the food and just enjoy being with one another. Travel was something they had in common and it was invigorating to do it with someone that you loved. Even if they went after the baby came, it would be amazing to see those sights together, as a family.

"Mmm," Faye said, smiling at him in the mirror. Her top was completely down and she knew that if they continued, Gregor would soon have her up on all fours on their bed, their preferred position these days out of both desire and necessity. She thought about the last time they had done it, just the previous morning, and how good it felt to have Gregor take her that way, to fill her up and enjoy her body as much as she enjoyed his. It was crazy how extra horny she had been these past few months, getting even wetter than usual when Gregor would touch her with his fingers, or rub his cock against the back of her pussy. Even he noticed how high her libido was.

You're insatiable! he had said to her in bed yesterday and she had to laugh, knowing it was true. Thankfully, she had a man who was so virile and sexual for a partner, there was no need he couldn't meet, no itch he couldn't scratch.

And although she knew there was more to a good marriage than a healthy sex life, she figured that at the very least this was something they definitely had going for them!

Even though she wanted nothing more than a repeat performance of the previous day's activities, she knew they shouldn't keep their guests waiting. Knowing her family, they would probably barge in and demand to be told what was going on. And anyway, being caught midcoitus by Erik and Janine was embarrassing enough to remind Faye to use a little discretion.

"We should probably get out there before my mom starts interrogating yours."

"Good idea," said Gregor, suddenly sobered by the thought of Helen and Gladys having a tête-à-tête. The two women were like day and night, they were such total opposites. Of course they both had their hearts in the right place. Faye just knew that sometimes not everyone found her family's humor and bluntness to be acceptable.

Faye gave her groom a quick kiss. Gregor led the way to the door that opened out to the backyard. So what if they were seeing each other before the wedding, and even making out moments before taking their vows? It wasn't a traditional way of doing things, but when it came to her and Gregor, there was nothing traditional about them anyway. If they were to be a successful couple, it would be because they did things their way and paid no attention to what other people thought they were supposed to be doing.

All of the friends and family that mattered to them

were gathered in the garden that afternoon and it was incredible to see all of their faces in one place. The guests all thought they were there for an afternoon visit. But when Faye made her entrance into the garden holding the small bouquet of roses Gregor had picked for her, and wearing a garland of flowers in her blond hair that she herself had fashioned, they all gasped and started to applaud.

Faye herself wasn't big on surprises, but Gregor had so much loved the idea of a surprise wedding that she didn't have the heart to stomp on his enthusiasm. To her, it didn't matter how they got there, what mattered was that they were going to spend the rest of their lives together. But, seeing the shocked looks on everyone's faces, Faye understood why Gregor had thought this would be fun. In fact all of it was surprising—that she was here, and doing this. All that time of mourning and sadness seemed so far away now, it felt like it had happened to another person. She would always carry the scars, but she now knew that it was possible to heal and thrive.

Taking Gregor's hand, they walked down a makeshift aisle. They had borrowed some chairs from the restaurant, and their top servers had volunteered to work for the afternoon. After the ceremony, they would be pouring champagne freely, and serving up the food Gregor and Erik had prepared for the occasion. It was the most perfect, intimate and personal party that Faye could imagine. Everything that they used and served was intentional, just as Gregor wanted it to be.

As they took their walk slowly together toward a friend who would marry them, Faye saw all of the familiar faces that mattered to her—her sister, Janine and Erik, who would serve as best man.

While most of the other guests gasped, Eden couldn't contain her excitement.

"A wedding?" she shouted, stopping her sister midmarch. "You're getting married!" she squealed gleefully, throwing her arms around Faye.

Somehow this moved Faye more than she had expected and tears started to well up in her eyes.

"Don't cry, you'll ruin your makeup!" Eden scolded her, even though there were tears pooling in her own eyes.

"I'm not crying, you're crying," Faye said through happy tears. She didn't care if her makeup was ruined, because nothing about the day could be ruined. It was perfect, exactly the way it was.

When Eden finally released her, Faye continued walking and spotted her boss. She wasn't sure if Bev was going to make it, but there she was, looking radiant and relaxed in a long floral dress, her new boyfriend, a handsome man who looked to be about sixty and was the spitting image of Kevin Kline, standing by her side. He was the rare online dating guy who turned out to actually be even better in person than his profile. Faye was so happy for her boss that after all her matchmaking, she had found someone to enjoy her life with. Faye smiled at Bev as she passed her, and Bev blew Faye a kiss, mouthing the words *Good luck* to her favorite employee.

When they reached the archway at the back of the garden, which Gregor and Erik had spent all of their spare time constructing, Faye gasped. It was the first time she had seen it, as they had done their construction in secrecy, not allowing her into the yard under any circumstances. The arch was completely covered in roses, and the most beautiful thing she had ever seen, the perfect embodiment of their love. She turned to face Gregor and whispered, "Thank you." Gregor looked extremely proud. Faye then turned to Erik, who was standing just behind Gregor. He was there in support of his friend and things were just as they should be. She whispered a thank-you to him and he gave her a thumbs-up in response.

As the ceremony began, Gregor locked eyes with Faye and they smiled at one another as they listened to the words of that would begin their next phase, not just as a married couple, but as a family.

"Dearly beloved, we are gathered here today…"

With one hand in Gregor's and the other on her belly, Faye smiled to herself, knowing that this was where she truly belonged.

* * * * *

MILLS & BOON

THE HEART OF ROMANCE

A ROMANCE FOR EVERY KIND OF READER

MODERN

Prepare to be swept off your feet by sophisticated, sexy and seductive heroes, in some of the world's most glamourous an romantic locations, where power and passion collide.
8 stories per month.

HISTORICAL

Escape with historical heroes from time gone by. Whether you passion is for wicked Regency Rakes, muscled Vikings or rugg Highlanders, awaken the romance of the past.
6 stories per month.

MEDICAL

Set your pulse racing with dedicated, delectable doctors in th high-pressure world of medicine, where emotions run high a passion, comfort and love are the best medicine.
6 stories per month.

True Love

Celebrate true love with tender stories of heartfelt romance, the rush of falling in love to the joy a new baby can bring, an focus on the emotional heart of a relationship.
8 stories per month.

Desire

Indulge in secrets and scandal, intense drama and plenty of s hot action with powerful and passionate heroes who have it a wealth, status, good looks…everything but the right woman.
6 stories per month.

HEROES

Experience all the excitement of a gripping thriller, with an i romance at its heart. Resourceful, true-to-life women and stro fearless men face danger and desire - a killer combination!
8 stories per month.

DARE

Sensual love stories featuring smart, sassy heroines you'd wan best friend, and compelling intense heroes who are worthy of
4 stories per month.

To see which titles are coming soon, please visit

millsandboon.co.uk/nextmonth